D0451254

E...

FORBIDDEN PLEASURE

LORA LEIGH

St. Martin's Paperbacks

This is a work of fiction. All of the characters, organizations, and events portrayed in this novel are either products of the author's imagination or are used fictitiously.

FORBIDDEN PLEASURE

Copyright © 2007 by Lora Leigh.
Excerpt from *Live Wire* copyright © 2010 by Lora Leigh.

Cover photograph © Vincent Besnault/Zefa/Corbis

All rights reserved.

For information address St. Martin's Press, 175 Fifth Avenue, New York, NY 10010.

Library of Congress Catalog Card Number: 2007004302

ISBN: 978-0-312-53537-7

Printed in the United States of America

St. Martin's Paperbacks edition / January 2011

St. Martin's Paperbacks are published by St. Martin's Press, 175 Fifth Avenue, New York, NY 10010.

10 9 8 7 6 5 4 3 2 1

For Lady Susan, for sitting up long into the night as I hashed out this plot, and for all your invaluable advice and hours of reading. Your insight, patience, and willingness to listen to and read more than a dozen different versions has made all the difference.

And to all my advance readers, thank you for your advice and for your patience. You make a difference that goes above and beyond the call of friendship.

AUTHOR'S NOTE

The Bound Hearts series is in no way connected to the book titled *The Club* by Lora Leigh. That is a different Lora Leigh. At the time I chose my pen name and began the first Bound Hearts book featuring the heroes who gather together in a place simply called The Club, the company I was with published only in electronic format and not in print. I didn't check for other authors using the same pen name, because I didn't foresee being in print. That was my mistake, and I apologize.

There is no book in the Bound Hearts series titled *The Club,* and there are no plans for one. I'm sorry for any confusion.

I hope you enjoy *Forbidden Pleasure,* and I hope my world grabs you as it has grabbed me. Thank you, the readers of the Bound Hearts, for all your support and your dedication to the series. I hope it continues.

PROLOGUE

"I resigned." John "Mac" McCoy picked up his drink, sipped, and let the calming heat of the whiskey seep into his system.

"So I heard." His best friend and now former partner, Jethro Riggs, took the seat across from him, set the whiskey bottle and glass carefully on the table, and leaned back to stare at his friend as he poured his own drink. "Honeymoon isn't even over yet and your resignation landed on the desk. Wish you had told me. I could have won the office bet on how long you'd make it."

Jethro's rakish smile went well with his overly long black hair and wicked blue eyes. The short, scruffy black beard and mustache drew feminine eyes, but the cold, bleak shadows in his gaze held them back.

Mac worried about Jethro. When he left, he knew the other man would go from case to case without stopping to enjoy life. And life was there to be enjoyed.

"I could have used the cash, man." Jethro's smile was laced with regret.

Mac snorted at the thought. "Cheaters never win, Jethro."

"Yeah, yeah. So I hear. So, what are you going to do? Security?"

Mac grinned. There weren't a lot of jobs out there that

appealed to a former undercover FBI agent, but Mac had always made certain he had a fallback position.

"Farming."

"Farming?" Jethro's eyes narrowed. "Hell, no."

"I still have that farm in North Carolina. I've saved enough to try to make a go at it. With Keiley's computer work and a little side work myself working Internet investigations, we should do well. It beats getting shot at on a regular basis."

Jethro only shook his head, a knowing light filling his shadowed blue eyes.

"And your membership here?"

That part sucked. Mac stared around the dark wood walls, the open space, the bar at one end of what had once been a grand ballroom, the fireplace crackling at the other end.

In between were two pool tables and several seating arrangements with large comfortable chairs, televisions, newspapers, and tables a man could put his feet on. But it wasn't the ambience that drew the members to the club. It was the chance to socialize with men who understood their ways, accepted them, understood them.

"I gave Ian notice earlier," he said quietly.

He was aware of the bomb he had just dropped, aware that Jethro had been waiting, even more than the others in the club, for the day Mac would choose a third.

The club catered to men with a particular sexual taste. Men who had seen the darkness in the world for whatever reason, and searched for peace in the extremity of sharing their lovers with other men.

Men who worshipped the female body. Who believed sex was an adventure and adventures were always more exciting when shared. Especially with someone who understood the particular pleasures to be found in pushing a woman to her sexual limits. In giving her more pleasure than she could have conceived possible.

Mac loved it. He thrived on it. He came here to unwind, to drink, to discuss world affairs, and to either choose a third for his latest lover or to become a third to another man's lover.

At least, he used to come here for that.

Six months of marriage, and the pressure was beginning to tell on him. The knowledge that the club members were just waiting to see whom he would choose to break his wife into the ménage lifestyle he practiced was beginning to fray his control. Knowing Jethro was growing more distant, more certain that the woman he had given to Mac would never know his touch, was starting to eat at him.

He knew Jethro's feelings for Keiley. Just as he knew that the other man would have never given into them.

"You haven't told her yet, have you?" Jethro said then. "I thought you were going to."

He had met Jethro during his first year in Quantico, where they had been paired together for a training exercise. Mac's easier, more relaxed demeanor had slowly rubbed off on the too rigid, too somber Jethro Riggs. And once each learned that ménage was the other's preferred sexual activity, they had become fast friends.

Not that the friendship hadn't been without its problems. They were both dominant men; both tended to want to control the sexual situations that involved their women.

But they learned they each had their own distinctive areas that interlaced perfectly in those relationships. Mac tended to indulge his lovers emotionally, while Jethro indulged them in more physical areas.

For years he and Jethro had trained together, worked together, and shared their women together.

Until Mac met Keiley.

"She's heard the rumors." Mac sipped at his drink, wishing he could just toss it back and let the fiery burn blaze through the regret in his gut.

"And?"

"And I told her it was in the past." He looked around the room again before meeting Jethro's gaze. "It's going to stay in the past. For now."

Keiley had come to his bed a virgin. Trusting. Innocent. She would never understand her husband's need to see another man cover her, pumping inside her, nor, he believed, would she be able to handle a ménage that would include a man she didn't love.

Keiley would have to love any man she took into her bed, even as a third. But he knew the curiosity was there. He had seen it in the flash of heat in her eyes as she questioned him. But Mac knew that right now, introducing her into the idea of a ménage or the ménage relationship he envisioned wasn't something Keiley could accept.

Perhaps later. He was counting on later. His new wife was adventurous, fiery, and curious as hell. But her youth held her back, whereas with other women it lent freedom. Keiley's past experience with gossip, and the destruction that came with it, wouldn't allow for the sexual games and the eventual bond Mac intended to see her forge with himself and Jethro.

Until his wife was more settled, until maturity gained her the edge she would need to overcome her fears, that wasn't going to happen. It didn't mean Mac was going to forget about it. It just meant that for the time being his plans would have to wait.

Moving her back to his hometown would help. The ways of navigating small towns and gossip was something Keiley needed to understand. A ménage wasn't tantamount to the hell she had endured as a child. But until she learned how to handle the gossip, his hungers and Jethro's would have to wait.

"Doesn't work that way, Mac," Jethro sighed then.

"I can make it work." He was confident of that. "I made this damned job work, I can make anything work."

Jethro's jaw clenched, and for a moment, bleak, furious pain and impatience sparkled in the blue depths before it was gone, iced over, and the agent he had become returned.

"Speaking of the job, were you any closer to tracking down that Internet stalker's whereabouts? The director was going nuts over that when I left the office."

Mac shook his head allowing the change of subject. "I turned the case over to Dell Roberts. He knows computers better than I do, and he's just finished up a major case. He has the time to deal with it. I'll help him online if he needs it."

The case was drawing a lot of fire. The stalker found his victims online, researched them, acquired their personal information, and spent months terrorizing them. In the latest case, he had finally attacked and nearly killed his victim. He was escalating dangerously.

"I'm going to miss you, my friend." Jethro lifted his drink in a toast. "To the good ol' days."

"To the future," Mac amended, tipping his glass to Jethro's, then bringing it to his lips before staring around the room once again.

He had drunk here, laughed here, found friends here. Hell, he had even fucked on most of the tables in the room here. Occasionally a married member had petitioned to allow his wife in long enough to get to know the members he had short-listed to act as a third. Many of those instances had ended up with the ménage playing out before the couple left the club.

There had been two female members at one time. One had married and dropped out of membership, though her husband still occasionally brought home a friend.

That relationship was working out much better than Mac had ever thought it would. Most of the married men in the club had found a way to balance those dark hungers with the women they loved.

Just as most of them had learned their hungers through the darkness of pasts they rarely spoke of, or lives lived within the shadowed corners of deceit and lies.

They all had their reasons for the hungers that tormented them, just as Mac did. But for him, the thought of his wife's happiness meant more to him than satisfying the shadowed specter that lurked beneath his surface.

"Keep in touch, buddy," Jethro said as he rose to his feet. "It won't be the same around here without you."

"I'm just a phone call away." Mac grinned. "Call anytime."

But don't visit. Not for a while. Not until his wife could handle the thought of another man in her life.

Jethro nodded, but his gaze was knowing, haunted. He knew what Mac meant.

As his friend walked away, Mac sat back in his chair, gazed around again, and tried to let the atmosphere seep inside him.

A frown tugged at his brow, though. He'd have to remember to remind Dell to requestion the latest victim and her husband. There was something that kept nagging at him about her statement. Something she had left out. Something he knew he should have asked her, but he couldn't think of what.

He would call Dell from the house tonight, and then put it behind him. Within the next four weeks he would be out of Virginia and back in Scotland Neck. North Carolina was far enough away from his old friends and his hungers to allow him to contain them for a while.

Keiley was worth the sacrifice. There had never been another woman who could make him feel as she did. She completed him, and he hadn't expected that. But from the moment he met her, he had realized there was something about her that warmed the cold reaches of his soul and eased the dark loneliness that had always been so much a part of him.

A man didn't walk away from that, no matter the obstacles. Once he saw his future in a feminine gaze, he found a way to make all parts of that relationship work. And that was what he was doing. Finding a way to make it work for all of them.

Especially Keiley. Her natural desires and adventurous personality had been restrained. The gossip concerning her father's embezzling from the company he worked for had destroyed her. At seventeen she had lost her home, her father had been imprisoned, and her mother had committed suicide.

There had been no one left for their community to punish except Keiley. They had watched her, gossiped about her lack of morals, predicted her downfall. If he dared let her know how desperately he needed to see her beneath Jethro now, it would terrify her. The rejection of it would be instant, and it would never falter.

He would have to steer her gently toward it. And once she grew to accept a need for those darker hungers that he saw in her eyes, then he would have to steer the relationship gently as well.

Jethro craved Keiley. He had seen her first and pushed her at Mac, despite his hunger for her. Mac knew the way to a woman's heart, but he also knew his friend. Keiley had already stolen Jethro's heart.

Not that Jethro would ever admit it or do anything about it. Mac knew that. A committed relationship was something that Jethro shied from as fiercely as Keiley shied from gossip.

His lips quirked at the thought. The woman he loved and the friend that was more than a brother to him. The three of them together would make a hell of a relationship. Once Mac managed to get the three of them together.

Getting there would be the hard part. Waiting would strain his patience to its limits. And if it never happened?

He would live with it. Ultimately it came down to Keiley. If she could accept it, if she could love Jethro with the same intensity that she loved Mac, then it would work.

If it didn't? If he lost them both, it would destroy him.

Obstacles stood in his path. It wouldn't be easy. But if his hunch was right, then the future that could stretch out before all three of them was one worth fighting for. It was worth risking.

Sharing his wife was considered a forbidden pleasure. It wasn't called that without reason. It was breaking rules, stepping past boundaries, and facing his own fears. His fear of losing. His fear of becoming too controlling.

In the end, either they would all win or they would all lose. Mac was betting, he was praying, on the win.

CHAPTER ONE

SCOTLAND NECK, NORTH CAROLINA
THREE YEARS LATER

"Mac, did you see my comb?" Keiley called from the bathroom, her voice a little sharp with irritation and simmering with impatience.

"I have my own, Kei," he reminded her in the same tone.

She moved from the bathroom, naked as the day she was born, water still beading on her shoulders, her cap of dark hair mussed around her face as she began searching the tops of the dresser, the vanity, the bedside tables.

Delicate and fragile. That was his wife. At twenty-six she still captivated him, made him harder than hell, and made him think of fairies on a fantasy night. A sensual, sexy fairy sandwiched between two male bodies and gleaming with moisture.

He shook the image away, frustration surging through him as his control weakened further.

"It was just in there yesterday," she muttered as Mac cinched his belt and considered uncinching it just as quickly.

If he moved fast enough, he could be undressed, have her flat on her back and his cock sinking into the fist-tight heat between her thighs.

He was loosening his belt when her gaze sliced to him.

"Don't even think about it." Hazel eyes were still dark with lingering anger.

"I'm still in the doghouse, then?" Mac grinned as he fastened the belt before sitting down on the end of the bed to pull on the scarred work boots he wore on the farm.

He tended to indulge Keiley whenever he could, but he had to admit, there were times he was tempted to indulge more than just her feminine wiles. That glimmer of confrontation and defiance in her eyes often tempted him to indulge a dominance he had so far managed to keep strictly under control.

"However you want to consider it." She bent down, her delightful little tush sticking up in the air as she looked beneath the bed.

"Keep flashing that ass at me and I'll show you how short that stay in the doghouse is going to be."

He felt he owed her at least a warning. She had good reason to be a shade upset with him, after all. Standing a woman up for an intimate dinner at home, complete with candlelight, because he had become distracted at a horse sale wasn't a good idea. Especially when he had been warned to be home on time. He hadn't forgotten a damned thing. His control was just that shaky. He hadn't dared show up on time.

She had waited up on him, too. Dressed in scarlet red silk, thigh-high stockings, and heels. She met him at the door, told him good night sweet as sugar, then went to bed.

His dinner had been in the oven. The candles had burned to nubs. She had obviously eaten. And he had managed, for one more night, not to mention the hungers tearing him apart.

"Touch my ass and you'll lose your hand," she informed him as she straightened and looked around the room with an expression of confusion. "That was my favorite comb, Mac."

"Did you look under the cabinet?"

She had so much fussy female stuff in there that he sometimes wondered how she found anything.

"Of course I did." She shot him a frown that warned him he should have already known that.

He flashed her a grin that had better warn her that he was getting damned horny watching her run around naked. He wasn't above seducing her. She could protest until hell froze over, but they both knew that after the first kiss she was going to cave. It was a given. He knew it, she knew it, and his cock knew it.

She did beat a hasty retreat back to the bathroom as Mac drew in a silent breath of relief.

"You know, you need to get a handle on yourself," she told him, causing him to catch his breath again minutes later as she left the bathroom.

"That waistband is too damned low." He glared at the sight of her lovely hip bones above the elastic band of the shorts. And the so-called t-shirt wasn't much better. It flashed too much belly, and showed her navel ring. A navel ring that had been driving him crazy the past few months.

"Get used to it, Daddy," she pouted sarcastically. "Do I bitch over your t-shirts that stretch over your chest, or your ass in your jeans?"

"My jeans aren't low enough to flash my dick, either. There's not enough material to those shorts to keep yourself decent, Keiley."

Let alone him. He was almost panting now. His balls were tight. He was ready to fuck and he was ready to go for it now. She was tempting a hungry man. And she knew it. Over the past year his fiery wife had become a sexual force to be reckoned with.

"That's too bad. I'm sure you would get a lot of notice if they were." She eyed the bulging crotch before glancing back at him with sparkling amusement. "Arrested, too, most likely, but it would definitely be interesting."

"Change clothes."

"Not on your life."

She slid her feet into a pair of sandals and walked sedately out of the bedroom, her ass twitching in those damned too-tight shorts, flashing it at him like a matador flashes a red cape at an enraged bull.

She'd been doing that a lot lately. Tempting him. Defying him. Pushing the boundaries he had allowed her to set when they first married.

A part of him had watched the progression with anticipation. He knew what was coming. She was tired of waiting on him to push her sexuality. She was pushing it herself now.

Her boundaries and his.

Did she intend to go out in public like that?

Mac jerked his shirt on, working the buttons as he stomped through the hallway and downstairs to the kitchen.

"Where are you going today?" He asked as he came to a stop in the doorway, watching as she put coffee on.

"Noplace, unless you start demanding I change clothes first. Then, I don't know. Main Street shopping, or if you prefer, hooking the street corners." She blinked back at him innocently.

"Smartass."

"Don't start, Mac." Her frown said it all.

"You might as well go ahead and forgive me, Keiley," he warned her.

"Why should I do something that stupid?" she asked incredulously. "This is three days in a row that you've come home late from some sale or meeting. Normally I'm in the bed asleep before you ever walk in the front door. If I did that to you, you would have a fit."

"I'd paddle your ass," he muttered.

"Don't tempt me, McCoy. I still have the baseball bat." Tense, narrow-eyed, and now spitting mad, she faced him like an enraged little fairy. All she lacked was the little gossamer wings fluttering for effect.

"Did you find your comb?" He changed the subject quickly.

She wasn't fooled, but at least she let it slide.

"No." Ruffling her fingers through her hair, that little confused look filled her face again before she turned back to the coffeepot and flipped it on. "I must have moved it without thinking."

Which wasn't like Keiley. Then again, the atmosphere between them had been more than a little strained lately. He shouldn't have stayed out late, no matter how hard he was trying to avoid looking at himself in the mirror. He just had to do it again the next morning anyway. And it wasn't as though he could forget the hungers that raged through his mind.

The missing comb bothered him, though. His mind refused to let it go.

"Have you lost anything else?"

"You're not an FBI agent anymore, Mac," she reminded him as she took cups out of the cabinet. "You are now a farmer and horse and cattle breeder. Remember?"

"You know what they say, Kei, you can take the boy out of the agency—" He shrugged.

"Well, un-agent." She pulled the refrigerator door open and collected eggs, butter, and bacon. "I've just misplaced the comb without thinking. That's all. I'll find it before long."

Maybe he was going a little overboard, Mac thought, but it felt funny. Keiley didn't just lose things. For all her fussy feminine girly stuff, she was so organized she made his back teeth clench at times.

"I've been distracted lately," she finally admitted. "It's been a long month."

He heard the note of censure in her voice and felt an edge of guilt. Guilt wasn't something he liked feeling in his marriage. It meant he was failing her. That he had hurt her, and the last thing he wanted to do was hurt Keiley.

Hell, he had said one could take the boy out of the agency, but this had nothing to do with his work as an agent. It had to do with his sexual past. One could take the man out of the club, but the club still lingered in him. The needs were beginning to eat him alive. But if he wasn't wrong, Keiley's were now eating at her, as well.

Restraining the dominance knotting his gut was becoming harder by the day. Restraining his sexual hungers was becoming impossible. And it was giving his delectable little wife the impression that his back was made for her delicately shod feet to walk right over.

"I'll try not to be late again," he promised, watching her back tense as she laid bacon in a pan.

"Doesn't matter. I'll just make certain I don't make any more plans to surprise you."

Damn, that one hurt. Mac winced. He liked her surprises. When she met him in silk, stockings, and heels and smelling of a faintly musk and floral fragrance that made his dick pound and his hands ache to touch her.

No more surprises meant no more wild sex on the coffee table, the couch, or the chair. That didn't suit him at all.

"I could always surprise you instead," he suggested.

"You could." She nodded. "You could start by telling me what has you wound up tighter than one of your studs during breeding season?"

She glanced back at him too fast for him to contain his reaction. Hell, he had been out of the agency too long. He knew she caught the flash of guilt in his eyes, the telltale wince of his expression. The tightening of his lips.

"It's been a busy month, Kei." That was his story and he was sticking to it. For now. Until he knew for certain where she was headed with it. In the past three years he had watched her grow in sexuality and confidence. He'd pushed the boundaries needed to help her deal with the gossip and the people of a quickly growing community and helped guide her toward the friends he knew would aid in that. Now, Keiley was making her own steps. For the past year, she had been pushing herself and him.

And it appeared she was beginning to reach for an even higher goal.

His dick tightened painfully at the thought, every muscle in his body tensing in preparation for it.

"As I said, it would surprise me." She turned back to the bacon, but her shoulders were straighter, her back still tense.

That damned sleeveless t-shirt was riding up her back, too, flashing skin. Skin he could be kissing right now if he weren't such a jackass. If nightmares and desires weren't haunting his dreams and pushing his own tension higher. A tension Keiley was obviously reading well. And reacting to as their marriage progressed.

In the past three years she had found a place within the social structure that existed in Scotland Neck. As an independent computer analysis and programming expert, she had joined the Business Council in town. She was a part of several charities and worked several hours a week as a volunteer at the local women's shelter. She was thriving here. The years she had spent under suspicion because of her father's embezzlement at a high-level D.C. accounting firm, and his subsequent imprisonment and death, were slowly being forgotten.

On the surface, their marriage seemed perfect. In a lot of ways, it was perfect. If it weren't for the darker sexual hungers that filled him, then the unnatural stress beginning to grow between them would never have been there.

"Coffee." There was a note of thankfulness in her voice as the machine beeped to indicate it had completed the brewing cycle. "Sit down, Mac, you make me nervous hovering over me like that."

He wasn't exactly hovering over her. Just trying to get a little closer as he considered another attempt to get into those indecent shorts.

Instead, he did as she suggested and sat down at the kitchen table while she cooked. It occurred to him that while she was frying bacon might be the wrong time to risk making her any madder. She only fried bacon in black iron, and if she ever decided to use it as a weapon, he was in some serious trouble.

But he couldn't help the hunger gnawing at his insides, either. Over the past three years he had become something, someone, he wasn't. And it was beginning to leave a funny taste in his mouth.

He had always been an extreme lover. The dark sexuality that drove him had always been a part of his character. It was one of the things that made him a good investigative agent. He understood the darkness, the shadows that could drive a man to extreme acts.

It was a part of himself he hid from Keiley. And in hiding it from her, he was beginning to become wary of the press of darkness in his mind.

"I think you miss your friends in Virginia," Keiley announced as she set breakfast on the table, causing Mac to stare back at her warily.

Mac arched his brow, allowing his expression to shift momentarily with the hunger eating away at him.

It was beginning. He could feel it now; it was in the air as thick as the scent of bacon frying and coffee wafting beneath his nose.

The challenge was being laid on the table. Finally.

For years he watched her navigate the gossip that begun with their appearance in his hometown. Old would-be flames prodding at her. Innuendo, smug smiles, and outright lies concerning his activities away from her had gone from worrying her to amusing her.

Now, she was stepping into territory she had left unexplored when she escaped Virginia, and confronting the fear of his past sexuality. The fear was no curiosity. The gleam of it in her gaze had fire ripping through his body and for the first time since he realized what she meant to him, he let it free in his expression.

Keiley's lips parted almost in surprise, as though the arrogance and sexuality of the look had come as a shock to her. And it would have. Mac rarely allowed enough of a chink in his façade to let her see the shadows that tormented him.

She cleared her throat delicately. "You know, all your male-bonding guy things at Sinclair's Club."

She stared back at him with supreme innocence. Her hazel eyes were bright and compassionate, her expression sympathetic. As though she were talking about a baseball buddy or guys' night out at the local bar. But he saw the heat shadowing it, burning behind the blander emotions.

"There were no bonding guy things there, Kei."

"Do you miss it?" She tilted her head to the side, watching him curiously.

"You know what the club was," he reminded her. "I don't miss fucking other women, if that's what you're asking me."

Keiley kept him more than satisfied sexually. She knew how to tease him, how to make him crazy, and she was as adventurous as hell. More adventurous than she realized.

"That wasn't what I was asking you, Mac." She rolled her

eyes before lowering them to her breakfast. "Just forget I mentioned it."

That wasn't going to happen.

"Why *did* you mention it?"

She stared back at him once again, her gaze reflective. "Because you're too tense. You have very few friends, and despite the invitations we receive, you never want to socialize. You weren't like this in Virginia."

"I'm busy, Kei."

"You're hiding," she told him. "And hiding never works. It's definitely not going to work with me. Are you missing your sex games in Virginia, Mac? Is that the problem?"

He wished he could have snapped at her. He wished he could have stood up and stomped out. He wished he could have avoided her.

But she was staring at him with that faintly frightened expression she had used the first time she asked him about the club. Wariness filled her eyes, and he felt like a jerk. Like a bastard. Like he was failing her. Pushing her. Stealing himself against it, he let her see the lie coming.

"I'm not missing any sex games." The lie didn't come easily to his lips. "Now eat your breakfast."

The curiosity blazed in her eyes then. He was daring her, whether she realized it or not.

"What was it like?" she asked, as he dug his fork into the scrambled eggs on his plate and fought the anticipation building inside him.

"What was what like?" The words nearly choked him.

"Sharing a woman with Jethro Riggs? Didn't you ever get jealous, Mac?"

Son of a bitch. He was going to come in his jeans!

If she hadn't been watching for his reaction, she might have missed the expression that flickered over his face. It was dark, carnal, arousing. His eyes lifted slowly from his plate a second later, his features smoothing out, but his eyes, his eyes were like storm clouds now, brewing with dangerous undercurrents.

She could see his response and feel it inside herself. See the sudden shift of hunger in his gaze as he stared at her, the tension in his body, the way it whipped through the air and licked over her flesh. In three years of marriage she had rarely seen that look on Mac's face, and it almost, just almost, frightened her. It would have frightened her if her own arousal hadn't tempered the fear. She had to force herself to control her breathing, to control her response to him. To the thought of that forbidden act.

She had suspected he missed the Club and the sexual acts he engaged in there with Jethro Riggs. Rough, edging on dangerous, Jethro's sexuality drew every woman she knew. Even herself at one time. Until she met Mac.

The thought of those acts had terrified her when she first met Mac, but something stronger, something darker had drawn her to him, made her love him.

She had thought she had pushed back her reckless impulses years before she met Mac. But in the past year or more, Keiley had found curiosity eating her alive. Mac never mentioned his sexual past with Jethro or the Club. He never referred to it, never suggested revisiting Virginia.

But that sexual darkness that had at first drawn her to him had been growing inside him, spurring her own. She needed to know what had drawn him to it. Why he had done it. For reasons that didn't make sense even to herself, that past was now tormenting her dreams and her fantasies.

"Why do you want to know, Kei?" His tone was a velvet rasp, rough, with the promise of a dark caress beneath it. It stroked over her flesh, reminded her that she had been days without feeling his possession.

Why did she want to know? Because it was killing her. Because in the past three years it had grown within her mind as her confidence within her own sexuality had grown. At first, it had been tainted with fear. The knowledge of the gossip that could arise, the whispers and destructive rumors that could build. But as she had found her place in Mac's hometown, watched it grow within the past three years even as she had grown, she had begun to wonder.

Why did he do it? And did he miss it? Was that the reason why the tension within him, the darkness that glittered in his gaze, had grown as well?

She shrugged uneasily. "We've never discussed it. We've talked about everything else in our lives except that."

And it was the truth. She had discussed things with Mac that she had never talked to anyone else about. The horror of facing the realization that her father had embezzled money from the company he worked for. The fear when she had lost her home, when her father had been imprisoned and her mother had committed suicide. Mac knew every part of her, but there was still so much she didn't know about him.

"It's not worth talking about." He turned his attention back to his breakfast as Keiley watched him closely. He was hiding from her, and that only dared her curiosity.

"That doesn't tell me why you did it, Mac." She continued to press the point even though the tone of his voice warned her that it was a subject he didn't want to discuss.

He was avoiding this subject just as he avoided other subjects when it came to explanations concerning the dark, shadowed parts of his soul.

Marrying Mac hadn't come without a little baggage. He was an alpha with a capital A, irritating, proud, arrogant, and bold. Mac didn't do anything by half measures and he sure as hell didn't offer a lot of explanations.

He avoided issues he didn't want to discuss, and when she pushed it they most likely ended up in bed where she couldn't remember the subject they were arguing over anymore than she could remember her own name once he started touching her.

He challenged her independence with his arrogance, and compromise hadn't come easily to him. She had the feeling that once she opened the door he was warning her to keep closed there would be no closing it again. There were parts of Mac so shadowed inside that she wondered if he wasn't just as wary of them as she knew she should be.

She was tired of the wariness. She was tired of feeling

that a part of her husband was hidden from her. That a part of her own life was missing when he grew quiet and dark.

She was tired of being more frightened of losing him than she was of getting to know him. That was the mistake she had made when they married. She had known it was too soon to make their relationship permanent. Known there was too much about Mac that she didn't know, and now it was time to figure it. It was time to get to know the man she had married, whether he wanted her to know him or not.

His fork clattered to his plate as he laid his arms carefully on the table and stared back at her, his gray eyes brewing like thunderclouds.

"Because I was horny," he answered.

"You were horny, so you shared your women with other men?" She lifted her coffee cup and drank from it as though her pulse wasn't racing, as though she wasn't suddenly nervous as hell and so aroused she could feel her juices heating the folds of her pussy.

"That about sums it up," he growled.

"So, the women you shared, they weren't your lovers in particular? Just someone else's?"

His eyes darkened. In the three and a half years they had been married, she had never seen such contradictory emotions roiling through his gaze. Anger, irritation, longing, and arousal. It was a little scary and a lot harder to accept the suspicions that had been brewing inside her for months.

Or maybe she had just finally seen it in the past few months. She knew she could feel it. As the past three years had seen the growth in their marriage, it had also seen a vague restlessness. One she hadn't recognized just in herself, but within Mac as well.

What was happening to her? Pushing Mac like this was never a very good idea. He was indulgent for the most part, but once his dominance was roused it seemed only to push a part of her that craved more and more within their sexual relationship.

"Sometimes they were my lovers," he admitted, his voice lowering, becoming rough around the edges. "Sometimes I even cared about them, Keiley. Sometimes I cared about them a lot. The more I cared about them, the more I enjoyed it."

He was pushing her now, daring her. In that second Keiley realized she had made a dangerous error of judgment when it came to her husband. She had suspected he was missing his friends, his sexual games, that a part of him wished he were back in Virginia. But now she knew he had been waiting knowing this was coming.

Now she had brought the subject out in the open. She had broken the boundary she herself had set, and she knew her husband, for whatever reason he had had for holding back, it would be gone now.

He could be amazingly ruthless. Mac lived by his own set of rules, and over the past three and a half years they had learned how to adjust, how to compromise with each other, and keep their marriage alive and growing. But she had always known he was holding something back. Had known and feared it.

"But you didn't love them," she said hopefully. "Not like you love me."

His lips quirked. "I've never loved anyone or anything like I love you, Keiley," he admitted. "You know that."

"Then you're not missing your friends? You're not missing the club?"

His gaze flickered with arousal and anticipation. "That wasn't what I said. That's what *you* said. And a word of warning, sweetheart. If you don't want to wake the monster, then don't poke at him. And right now, you're definitely poking."

Keiley felt her lips part, felt her mouth go dry, felt the tension shimmering in the air suddenly thicken, nearly choking her with the heavy undercurrents suddenly whipping through it.

She could see it in his face now, in his eyes, a desire that he kept leashed, a fantasy, a hunger, perhaps a need, she couldn't have fully anticipated. Then, just as quickly, it was gone. He picked up his fork, resumed eating, and let the subject drop while Keiley began wrestling with the implications he left in his silence.

"Stop worrying, Keiley," he stated, his voice still too dark, still too rough, moments later. "My membership in the club in Virginia isn't going to follow us here. No one knew for certain what Sinclair's Club was for."

"I don't care about the damned talk or how it follows us, Mac. I care about the fact that you're refusing to talk about it when I know damned good and well it's what you're thinking about."

She didn't give a damn what people thought about it. She had grown out of caring about gossip about six months after their move here and her realization that Delia Staten, one of the county's leading figures, intended to make her life hell. Because Keiley had Mac and she didn't. Delia had never forgotten that Mac had rejected her.

It was childish and stupid. Keiley had learned from the best exactly how to weather gossip. Whether or not anyone thought she was involved in one of the many ménage relationships in this damned county didn't really faze her.

The fact that Mac's lips had thinned warningly did faze her. It pissed her off that he was continuing to ignore the subject.

"It wasn't a whorehouse, Kei. It was simply a men's club. A place to relax, share a drink, and unwind."

"And find a friend to share your women with," she inserted.

"That was an added benefit." The tight, controlled curve of his lips held back the lush sensuality that could fill them. "Now, I have to get to work. I have to make a trip into town later, though. Do you need anything?"

"Just answers," she sighed. "We need to talk about this some more, Mac."

"Talking about this is the worst thing we can do at this point," he told her. "What you need to do is drop it. Let it go away, Keiley, just as you did before we moved here. It doesn't apply to our life or what we have here. That's all that matters."

Oh yeah, she was just going to obey him like a good little girl.

With that, he finished his coffee and rose from the table before bending to brush a kiss over her cheek and move to the back door.

"I love you, Kei," he said behind her.

"I love you, Mac." She returned the words and the emotion.

"I'll be up for lunch if you take a break, then," he told her. "I'll talk to you later."

About anything but what she could feel pulsing in the air now. As he left, Keiley grit her teeth in frustration.

When she had first heard the rumors of Mac's sexual history, she admitted a fear that had nearly ended their relationship. She had been terrified of the darkness of such a sexual act, and the darkness in the man she was falling in love with.

She had been a virgin. Uncertain. Still wary of gossip and still wary of the strength of her desire for Mac. And the strength of her interest in his best friend and known third in his sexual relationships. She had first met Jethro at an office party. A few weeks after that he had introduced Mac to her. Mac had stolen her heart within days.

She didn't know how to handle Mac, let alone another man. Especially a man as hard and as shadowed as Jethro.

She wasn't that frightened little girl anymore. But she wasn't certain she wanted fantasy to become reality, either. What she wanted, what she needed, were answers. And the only person she could get those answers from didn't seem willing to talk.

She stared at the backdoor and felt her resolve harden. That was just too damned bad. That was her husband. Her life. He could talk or he could deal with the consequences. Namely, she damned well wouldn't leave him alone until he did.

CHAPTER TWO

Mac didn't show up for lunch.

When Keiley realized the time, she closed out the program she was working on before standing from her desk and pacing to the wide patio doors that looked out on the barnyard in the back.

He was there, doing exactly what she had suspected he was doing, tinkering with the old tractor his grandfather had owned before his death. Bare-shouldered, sweat-dampened, his jeans hanging low on his hips as he worked.

Hard muscles flexed beneath the golden flesh, rippled and made her hands itch with the need to touch them, to feel them working beneath her fingers, tensing and flexing in pleasure from her touch rather than in tension from whatever was now brewing in his mind.

He was thinking. Deliberating. Working something in his mind. That was what he did when he worked on the old piece of farm machinery.

His thick black hair hung low on his neck, a bit shaggier than he usually kept it, but giving him a sexy, dangerous look. The look of an unconquered male. Exactly what he was. A man who would be very hard to fool and even harder to get to reveal his secrets, if he didn't want to reveal them.

Keiley had no intention of forgetting the fact that her husband had been an undercover FBI agent before his resignation. How could she forget it? It was one of the reasons so much of the man she had married was a mystery to her. He knew how to keep his innermost secrets while still loving her with a depth that amazed her.

She had tried to tell herself that she knew everything she needed to about the man she had married. That of course there were, would be dark places inside him, that he had seen the worse of humanity in many cases, that it would always mark his soul.

But over the past three years, Keiley was beginning to wonder if Mac hadn't gone into a career where he was dealing with something he had already understood. Something that had given him a chance to fight back against the demons of the past. A past he could never bring back or change.

And this was what had drawn her to Mac so strongly. This was the reason why she hadn't drawn back from him despite the gossip that surrounded him and Jethro.

Like her, Mac knew what it was to hurt, but he hadn't closed himself off from the possibility of love. Unlike his friend, Mac embraced life and he embraced emotion. Like Keiley, he had just been waiting for the right person to embrace it fully.

A soft smile tugged at her lips at the thought of those first weeks. How wary she had been, so uncertain, trying to figure out why he wanted her when he could have dozens of women who would have eagerly allowed Jethro into their relationship.

Those women hadn't known him, though. Before the end of that first dinner date with him, Keiley had known parts of him that she knew other women never would. She knew that dominant sexuality of his wasn't a game, it was a part of him. She had sensed that from the first.

As their relationship had developed, she had worried that he couldn't let go of the ménages, though he had promised her, assured her, that it wasn't something he couldn't live without.

She knew now. He could live without it. He could love without it. What he had neglected to mention was that eventually, he would be denying not just a desire but a part of himself in letting it go.

That was the undefined something about Mac that had nearly frightened her off then. And during those first months of their marriage, she had wondered why he had been so insistent on moving back to his hometown so soon. It was to take himself out of the area of temptation. Away from the Club, his friends, and Jethro.

Had he been hoping he wouldn't miss what he never saw? Had she known this was coming?

That question had tormented her more often in the past year or two. Had she been drawn to Mac because he personified everything she had been too frightened to reach out for? A sexual and personal freedom that had been so restrained within her? Had she let Mac steal her heart because she knew he would challenge more than just her intellect?

She snorted in disgust. This was insane. She didn't want a ménage. She liked fantasizing about it. She enjoyed daydreaming about it. But the reality of it raised problems within her mind that she couldn't solve.

Not the gossip, but emotions and feelings she had no business contemplating. If Jethro ever came back into their lives, she knew she would be torn. Knew that the past infatuation she had felt for him would raise its ugly head and risk everything she had with the man who owned her soul.

She couldn't allow that.

But that didn't mean Mac could get away with not discussing this forever. The longer it remained between them like this, the worse it was going to get.

Sitting in her office, Keiley had a clear view of the back farmyard. The tall red barn with its white trim surrounded by white fences and greener-than-green grass. And moving outside the wide double doors of the barn was her husband. Working once again on a tractor that was older than dirt and a hell of a lot less useful.

He had new tractors, but he continually worked on that old one, tinkering with it when he was worried or thinking. He had been tinkering with it a lot lately. Much more than often.

She leaned against the window, narrowing her eyes against

the sunlight spearing into the room, realizing that her husband was tinkering with that tractor rather than talking to her.

He used to talk to her.

He wasn't talking anymore, and she was getting tired of it.

Crossing her arms over her breasts, she tapped her fingers against her arm and glared at her husband. Three nights he had come in late, long after she had gone to sleep. And before that? Before that, sex had been hurried. Quickies. In the shower or afterward. While he was in control. That was something she had markedly noticed. He had only touched her when he was in complete control of himself and his sexuality.

She wanted all of her husband. She especially wanted the parts of him that he thought he should hide from her.

His sexuality. Because his sexuality was tied into so much of who and what he was.

From the information she had about his investigative work, she knew that many of the cases he had worked had involved sexual crimes.

Sexual deviants were his specialty. Had that talent grown from an understanding of them before he came into the agency? Had his own sexuality been influenced by something more than an excessive sex drive?

The questions were driving her crazy. As were the suspicions and her fears that this would end up affecting her marriage in ways that it couldn't be repaired.

Inhaling deeply, Keiley straightened from the edge of the patio door and moved into the warmth of the summer afternoon, heading for the barn and her husband.

The workhands had the day off; Mac normally didn't work all day Sunday. By all appearances, he intended to work today on that old tractor, though.

The tractor was his psychiatrist, she often mused. It had been his grandfather's. It hadn't actually worked since his grandfather's death twenty years before. But Mac still tinkered with it when he needed to think. She wondered if he would work out the problems that had that frown brewing between his eyes by the time he managed to fix the tractor.

She knew he was aware of her approach as she followed the graveled path to the barn. His bare shoulders were tense now, the sweat gleaming off them in the summer sun. He was a powerful male animal, and that was what she saw as she stopped at the front of the tractor and watched him silently.

"Lunch ready?" His voice was dark, brooding.

"Not yet. I wanted to see if you wanted to come up and talk to me while I fixed it."

He tensed further as he bent behind a large wheel and fiddled with something there.

"Why don't you just yell at me when it's ready?" he suggested. "I'm pretty busy here."

Oh yeah, she could see that. He was really busy getting his hands greasy as he picked and probed behind the tire.

"It's just sandwiches," she told him then. "Maybe a salad. A few minutes at the most."

He nodded. "Just yell when it's done."

"I don't think so."

He tensed further, stilling beneath her gaze before his head turned slowly and his gaze latched onto her with almost predatory awareness.

"Excuse me?" The inordinate politeness of his tone caused her heart rate to increase, the blood to surge stronger and hotter through her veins.

"You heard me, Mac. You can come up to the house with me while I fix lunch or you can do without it. I wanted to spend some time with you. It's something you make certain we don't do lately. I'm tired of it."

Mac shifted, straightening with a graceful, dangerous flex of muscles that had her taking a step back. Suddenly her husband reminded her more of a wild animal preparing to jump. And he noticed her reaction. His lashes narrowed over his eyes as he pulled a discarded rag from the tractor seat and began to wipe his greasy hands.

Not that it helped a lot. And grease should never, at any time, be sexy, but the streaks of oil on his hands and up his arms and the few slashes across his chest were highly arousing.

Sexual tension was like a smothering blanket between them now. As though they had never touched, never been intimate, as though the power of the anticipation for it was suddenly as strong as it had been the day she met him.

"You're tired of it," he repeated softly. "Tired of what exactly, Keiley?"

Her lips dried with nervousness. Stroking her tongue over them, Keiley nearly caught her breath as Mac's gaze flicked to the action.

"You know what I'm talking about, Mac." Suddenly she could feel the amount of skin her clothing revealed. The fact that she wasn't wearing a bra. That she wasn't wearing panties.

"Poor Keiley." He tossed the rag back to the tractor seat and began advancing on her. "Maybe you shouldn't have run away from me in the bedroom this morning."

"Don't turn this into sex, Mac," she ordered weakly.

Weak, because it was about sex. It was about the hunger that seemed to grow between them daily. About the need for his touch, his kiss, his very presence. And the need for the reality and the fantasy of his hunger.

"But it is about sex, Keiley," he murmured as he caught her hips, uncaring of the oil she was certain now marked the bare flesh.

He trapped her against the front of the tractor, the bulging erection beneath his jeans pressing against her stomach as her head fell back to stare up at him.

He was so tall, nearly a foot taller. At almost six four, Mac seemed to overwhelm everyone else. Especially her. She was only five-four, short, and fine-boned. She always felt alternately protected and undefended against his height and strength.

"It's not about sex." She tried to shake her head as his lips lowered to her neck. "I just wanted to talk."

"About sex." His lips grazed her neck, then his teeth scraped over it, causing her lashes to flutter as she fought to hold back a moan.

It had been like this from the first. He could seduce her

with nothing but the threat of a kiss, the anticipation and thrill of just knowing his touch was coming.

And he was doing it now. She shuddered in his hold, feeling his hands against her hips, his fingers subtly massaging as his lips and tongue tasted her flesh.

They were outside, nothing but the tractor to shield their bodies as she felt one hand move, felt it began to slide beneath her shirt.

"We should go to the house," she gasped, her head tilting to the side as her eyes closed.

The nipping kisses to her neck were destructive. She was highly sensitive there. Whenever Mac's lips moved over the tender flesh it weakened her, stole the strength from her legs, and left her fighting to just stand upright.

"Why?" His question shocked her.

"Anyone could see what you're doing."

"Just us here." His broad hand cupped her breast, his thumb stroked over her hard nipple.

"But we're outside."

"All alone. Take your shirt off for me, Kei." He leaned back, staring down at her with stormy eyes, with a hungry gaze.

Keiley stared back at him in surprise. Not that they hadn't had sex outside before. They had. By the pool. In the hot tub. But never like this. In the wide open, where her nakedness could be seen if by chance one of the workhands decided to show up.

"We have a bed." Her laughter was nervous.

The forbidden was always a draw for her. It always had been. It excited her, titillated her, made her feel alive when Mac drew it out of her. Undressing here, in broad daylight, was forbidden. Taking the chance of being seen, watched, as her husband caressed her body, was forbidden. And all the more arousing.

"Who needs a bed?" His head lowered, his gaze holding hers as he let his tongue stroke over her suddenly swollen lips. "Come on, Kei, be brave with me."

There was something different about him. She couldn't put her finger on it, couldn't make sense of it as his hands began to draw her t-shirt up her body.

"Come on, let me touch those pretty nipples with my lips while the sun heats your breasts. Wouldn't you like that, Kei?"

His voice was a velvet rasp. It was goading. Challenging. Primitive. That was the difference. He had never shown this side of himself to her in this way before. As though her invasion earlier into that dark, silent core of him had tempted the monster he had warned her not to awaken.

It exhilarated her.

Keiley pulled back, gripped the hem of her t-shirt, and pulled it slowly over her head before dropping it to the ground.

Mac's response was surprising. For a moment, blank surprise filled his expression; then it darkened once again, turned savagely carnal. His lips appeared fuller, his eyes darker, his cheekbones more pronounced. He looked dominant. Forceful.

"Beautiful." Calloused, heated palms cupped her breasts, lifting them to his lips as his head lowered.

Excitement surged through her like a tidal wave, ripping her from the moorings of self-control and thrusting her forcefully into the shadowed lusts she felt whipping around her.

Mac was always tender with her when he made love to her. But this wasn't lovemaking. It was a possession. She could feel it as his teeth scraped over her nipple. Then his lips covered it, drawing it into his mouth as he began to suck it with a heated, forceful suction.

Her shorts were loosening as her hands speared into his hair to hold him closer. Mac cupped her breast with one hand and disposed of her shorts with the other, leaving her naked beneath the heat of the sun. Leaving her open to the sudden powerful surge of hunger that tore through her.

She had never been so brave. Had never felt the need and

the hunger as she felt them tearing through her now. There was too much pleasure, too much passion. It was whipping through her mind, sinking into her pores, and tearing her loose from the moorings of control that she thought she possessed.

Pleasure was her reward, though. A pleasure that Mac was only now showing her. A pleasure that came from freeing the wildness inside her rather than controlling it.

There was no control here.

She jerked, shuddered, as his head lifted from her nipple only to have his lips cover hers as he lifted her against his chest. The hair-roughened contours rasped over her tender nipples, sending a cry into the kiss as his tongue tempted hers to spar with him.

Lightning. Electricity. Surging, destructive pinpoints of explosions detonated along her nerve endings as her flesh became hypersensitive. As the need suddenly began to grow and nothing he did seemed to be enough.

Keiley knew her husband's hands were rougher than normal as he lifted her against her. Knew that his kiss would leave her lips swollen long after he finished, but she didn't care. She needed it. Needed the rough nips, the hard clench of his hands at her rear. She needed this part of him and hadn't even realized it until she felt it. Until he unleashed it on her.

"Are you wet, Kei?" He suddenly tore his lips from hers, moving them over her jaw, her cheek, until he was nipping at her ear. "Are you ready for me?"

Ready? She could feel the juices flowing, dampening her, preparing her for so much more.

"Let's see how wet you are, darlin'."

She expected his fingers to skim between her legs. Expected his fingers to probe into the hidden folds. She didn't expect his lips to begin burning a path down her neck, over her breast, where he paused to lick, to suck, to nip at the hardened peak with a force that had her arching into his arms, her cries filling the summer afternoon as she tightened her thighs to still the ache beginning to burn there.

Sensation was lashing through her. The tug of his lips at her breasts speared to her clit, to her vagina. Spasms were flexing inside her, forcefully reminding her of the pleasure to be had when he took her.

He didn't stay at her breasts long enough. Even as her fingers clenched in his hair to pull him back, he was moving lower, his tongue skimming over her upper stomach, then her abdomen, as he knelt before her.

"Mac—someone could see us," she panted.

She stared down at him, shaking as he gripped her thighs.

"Part your legs for me, Kei. Now." His tone brooked no refusal. The forceful rasp of hunger in his voice had her whimpering even as her thighs parted.

The eroticism of the moment was searing her. She was suddenly seeing a part of Mac that she had only glimpsed in the past three years. The dark, dominant hungers that he kept carefully banked. And she loved it. Loved it so much that she could feel the sudden flow of her juices spilling from her body.

"Sweet and wet," he growled as his gaze dropped to the curl-shrouded flesh between her thighs. "You know, Kei, if this sweet pussy were waxed, you could feel even the breeze whispering over your clit, caressing your flesh. Wouldn't that feel good?"

He blew across her clit, the sensation of even that small caress drawing her to her toes as she fought for something to hold onto. A way to strengthen her legs.

One hand grasped hold of the fender of the tractor, the other reaching up and gripping the small handhold that opened the casing to the motor.

"Beautiful," he whispered. "I think I'm ready for lunch now, Keiley. But we don't have to go to the house for me to eat it."

Her cry shattered through the barnyard as his hand lifted her leg and his head lowered to the saturated flesh between her thighs.

He consumed her. Lips, thrusting, licking tongue, his suckling mouth. He devoured her over and over again as she clung helplessly to the machinery behind her and angled her hips to give him better access.

It was good. So good. The heat of the sun bearing down on her, the heat of Mac's mouth consuming her. She was lost in the sensations. In the pleasure. Lost in the overriding carnal intensity that began to build inside her.

It didn't make sense. It wasn't as though Mac had never gone down on her before. But the difference was in how he did it. The situation, the location, the hunger he was unleashing on her. Within minutes she could feel the electricity pouring up her spine, the pleasure building in her womb.

His tongue flickered through the wet slit, licked and stroked, moving ever closer to the engorged button of her clit as he hummed his pleasure into the sensitive folds.

She was rising, rushing toward orgasm, and she couldn't fight it. When his tongue licked around her clit she screamed for release. Begged for it. Then his lips covered the tender bud, and his tongue began to flicker, to lick with rapid, destructive strokes until she shattered into fragments of blinding ecstasy.

It was like lash after lash of agonizing pleasure as she strained closer, the ache in her womb only building. The clitoral release was usually enough to sate the desperate need, but this time, it only spurred it. She was dying for more.

"It's not enough," she cried out desperately as he began to rise before her. "Please, Mac. I need more."

"There's always more, Kei," he growled. "How much more do you want, sweetheart?"

"Everything." Her head tossed against the tractor as her hands tightened on the handholds she had found. "Now. Please. Now."

His hands covered hers, drawing them away as he stared back at her remorselessly.

"I can give you everything you need, sweetness. All of it." One big hand covered the back of her head, pressing her lips to his chest. "Take me now, Kei. Show me how bad you need me."

She needed him. Needed him until she could barely breathe for the hunger tearing her apart. Needed him so badly that before she anticipated what she meant to do, her teeth sank into the heavy muscle just below a flat, hard nipple.

Mac jerked in surprise at the feel of Keiley's bite. It was unexpected. It was violently arousing. His cock jerked beneath his jeans, so hard, so engorged that he knew that holding back once her hot little mouth got down there would be next to impossible.

But he would hold back. Control. Controlling himself, controlling this first step he was allowing her into the darkness of his lusts, was too important. One wrong move and she could shy away, unconsciously sensing the predatory hunger lurking just beneath the surface. The hunger that would push and push for more of the sensual, deeply held carnality that he knew his wife possessed.

"Sweet," he groaned, palming her head as her tongue licked over the little mark he was certain she had made. A mark he would carry with pride. "More, sweetness. Give me just a little more."

The bite was harder, centered lower, as a shudder wracked her small frame and her wicked tongue licked at his sweat-dampened chest.

Her hands moved restlessly down his chest to his belt, struggling to loosen it as he tipped his head back and let the sun warm his face.

Keiley was burning his flesh, moving lower, nipping at his skin, licking at it as she loosened his jeans and drew the heavy length of his cock free.

He thought he would explode when she wrapped the fingers of both hands around the engorged shaft. Thought he would spill himself to her fingers in a release that would tear his soul free.

His control was tattered, fraying. Gritting his teeth, he forced back the need to come, his fingers tightening in Keiley's short hair to hold her lips back from the throbbing crest of his cock.

"Mac," she whimpered hungrily.

Damn, he loved her voice like that. Husky and needy, stroking over his senses like dark velvet.

Holding her back, Mac moved her hands to his thighs before gripping the base of his cock with one hand.

"Like this." He needed it like this. Needed to control it, to stroke her hunger for him higher. Just a little bit higher.

Her hands clenched in the jeans material still covering his thighs as his fingers held her head steady for the hard head of his cock pressing against her lips.

She opened instantly, her hot pink tongue swiping over it as her lashes fluttered closed. It was sexy as hell.

"Open your eyes. Watch me while you take my cock, Kei. Don't hide from me." His voice was rough. He knew it was and could do nothing to stop it.

Her lashes drifted open. Her tongue flickered over the tiny slit in his cock, licking at the pre-cum that beaded there as she hummed her pleasure.

"Good girl." He could see the wariness, the hunger rising inside her. "Now, slow and easy."

He pressed inside her heated mouth, feeling her lips enclose him as electric pleasure shot up his spine and sizzled in his brain.

Damn, it was good. So hot. So good. Her mouth suckling at the engorged head of his dick, trying to draw him deeper as her hot little tongue licked and stroked around it.

He drew back, ignoring her little mewls of need before pressing back, pressing deeper, feeling the muscles of his stomach contract violently as pleasure seared through taut sinew and bone. Hell. He wouldn't last long at this rate. Sinking inside her mouth so slow and easy, feeling her take him nearly to her throat, sucking at him, humming little cries vibrating on the flesh.

Her hands pushed his jeans lower with jerky movements, allowing her fingers to slip between his thighs to that tight sac beneath his cock.

"Stop." He pulled back, forcing her to release his cock. "Put your hands on my thighs, Keiley."

Surprise glittered in her hazel eyes.

"Hold on to my thighs, sweetheart."

Her hands returned slowly to his thighs, but her gaze flickered with indecision.

"Sometimes it's best to let sleeping animals lie," he whispered, almost regretting what he knew she was seeing in his face for the first time. "Can you take it, Kei?"

It was a challenge. Challenging was never a good idea, because more often than not she would take the dare and run with it.

Her expression flickered before a smile tugged at her lips.

"Do your worst," she dared him in return.

Sweet heaven, she had no idea what she was daring him to do. Did she think the dare would end here? In this barnyard?

He pressed against silken lips once again, feeling them enclosed around his flesh as he watched. Drawing back, thrusting in, his erection glistening from the moisture in her mouth. He could feel his muscles tightening from the effort to hold back. Felt the sweat running down his back as he fucked her mouth, slid in and out, feeling her tongue tighten on him, feeling her grow wilder as she realized he had no intention of giving her his release in this way.

He wanted her wild. He wanted her flying. So desperate she was tearing at him. Refusing to obey the simple command to keep her hands on thighs.

And within minutes she was there. The sweet sounds of her suckling mouth were driving him crazy as he felt her trembling fingers snake between his thighs.

He pulled back again, sliding free of her mouth before she followed. His hands tightened in her hair, pulling her back as the other hand caught her wrists and held them tight above her head.

Then he gave her more. Thrusting past her lips until he knew that one more stroke into the liquid heat there would shatter his control.

"Enough." His voice was a hard growl, despite his efforts to temper it.

Pulling her to her feet, he caught her as she stumbled, wrapped his arm around her hips, and lifted her to him.

Her legs wrapped around his waist instantly, and his cock found the shelter it was dying for. If he thought her mouth had been hot, then her pussy was pure lava. He couldn't stop the harsh cry that fell from his lips as the crest of his erection tucked into the honey-slick folds and pressed forward.

Damn, she was tight. Tight and sweet, the tender tissue inside her sex flexed and rippled around him as he began to work his flesh inside her. Stretching to accommodate him, growing hotter, wetter with each stroke until he was seated fully inside.

His balls drew up tight at the feel of her pussy rippling over his cock. The need to thrust heavily inside her was making him crazy. But this, this was so good.

"You're tight, Keiley." He tightened his hold on her as he turned until he could press her against the side of the tractor, holding her firm as his cock jerked inside her. "Tighter than ever."

Her head fell back as her eyes drifted open. Her eyes were wild. Nearly as wild as the desperate attempts to move against him as he held her still.

"Mac, please—" Her voice was raw and thick with excited arousal now.

He rarely held her release back. He had sensed the wildness in her from the beginning, the deep-seated core of a sensualist that would one day meet his darkest desires head-on.

This was what he had waited on for more than three years. The hunger he saw in her eyes now, felt in her pussy. The needs rising to the surface, challenged by his restraint, his refusal to satisfy them enough to keep them banked. This was the woman he had known she could be.

He moved, drawing back before sinking inside the fist-tight channel once more, glorying in her cry of pleasure and the flex of her pussy.

"This what you want, sweetness?" He moved again, harder,

pressing deeper as her head thrashed and perspiration ran down her face.

Oh yes, this was what she wanted. She was panting, throttled cries falling from her lips as she fought against his hold.

"Look at where you are, Kei," he told her then. "Out in the open. Anyone can see. Should we stop now?"

She shook her head, her hips flexing as her thighs tightened on him.

"Do you know what they would see?" He growled, leaning down to nip at her lips. "They would see perfection. The sweetest honey in the world coating my balls."

He could feel it, like a wash of creamy, liquid silk tightening his balls further.

"Mac." Erotic hesitation filled her voice even as her juices became thicker, silkier. As though the thought of being watched filled her with both trepidation and excitement.

He flexed inside her again, stroking the back of her pussy, feeling her clench around him as her nails bit into his shoulders, digging in with sensual pain as he felt his control slip.

He gripped the cheeks of her ass, holding her tight as he began to move, shafting inside her with hard, deep motions of his hips. The pleasure was so intense it was nearly pain. The grip of the sweetest muscles in the world tightened as he felt her pussy begin to convulse. Her cries filled his ears, his senses, and tore free his own release.

Pumping inside her, each spurt of semen was followed by a hard punch of ecstasy. Driving. Fulfilling. For the first time since he had begun sleeping with her, Mac felt that hard, dark knot of lust in his gut easing marginally as he filled her with his release.

She was like a forbidden fruit. Tempting. Sweet. Innocent. Uncorrupted. So sweetly uncorrupted that her innocence shone in her eyes like a beacon of purity. It was one of the things he loved about her. One of the things that the dark sensuality inside him blazed in response to.

In that moment, as he held her tight to him, hearing her

wild cries ease, Mac knew that corrupting her was rising higher, much higher, on his list of priorities.

Before it was over with, he would lose his wife. Or he would gain his soulmate. The question was, could he survive losing both?

CHAPTER THREE

The next night, Mac stood on the balcony outside his and Keiley's bedroom, smoking. He stared at the glow of the cigarette in his hand, a frown marking his brow before he drew the filter to his lips and inhaled.

The restlessness growing inside him wasn't abating, and he knew why. It was the same thing that had drawn him to the balcony rather than into sleep, despite the lateness of the hour.

Keiley.

He stared into the night sky as he inhaled, drawing the acrid burn of the smoke into his lungs even as he lashed at himself for resorting to a crutch. Not that it did more than ease the restlessness in his hands anymore. It did nothing to ease the hunger that rose in his gut and had his dick so damned hard he could probably hammer nails with it.

And dumbass that he was, rather than relieving that hunger in the giving heat of his wife's sexy body, he was out here smoking. Because he knew he couldn't take her without putting the wariness back in her eyes that he had put there the other day.

A hard grimace had him grinding his teeth as he thought of the way Keiley had watched him that evening. With equal parts confusion and wary arousal. As though she were no longer certain how to approach him, or how to deal with his sexuality.

Not that he could blame her. Hell, he had taken her in the

barnyard against a greasy tractor. When he finished with her she had been flushed and streaked with oil, and nervous.

That nervous uncertainty would be the death of him.

Maybe he should just lay it on the line. Tell her what he wanted and take his chances.

He vetoed that idea instantly. Keiley was a brave woman, but if he gave her a chance to think about it first, then he was a goner. His wife would deliberate actions for months before making decisions. She weighed angles the way a criminal attorney weighed evidence. Looking for every loophole, for every possible crack in the defense of her privacy.

Privacy was golden to her. A product of the hell her parents had put her through as a teenager. The social humiliation had been decimating to her when her father's crimes had been revealed. She had been ostracized, criticized, and left to bear the burden of her mother's suicide and creditors who had no mercy on an eighteen-year-old girl with no means of paying the astronomical debts her parents had accumulated.

And he was asking her to risk that private part of herself with another man. Because he craved it. Because the sexual intensity and excessive hungers that drove him demanded it.

She had learned how to handle gossip, how to handle desire. Could she now learn how to handle loving two men?

Like Keiley, Mac was a product of his parents' actions and reactions. Unlike Keiley, he hadn't faced a public crucifixion for them; rather, the results of those actions had left him darker, harder than most young men.

And like Keiley's father, Mac's father had begun his journey into hell. His strict fervor and railing against sex had driven Mac to acts that had only increased his father's wrath. That had driven the man to drive his son to the edge of madness.

Joseph McCoy had been a nutcase. Mac swore his father had caused his mother to lose the will to live with his idiotic railing. Screaming at her whenever he imagined another man looked her way. Denigrating her supposed dark lusts, and accusing her of sexual crimes that had so humiliated the timid little Debra McCoy that she had finally given up.

But Mac hadn't given up.

His father had first suspected him of having sex at the tender age of fourteen. And he was. With a much older girl who had begun teaching him the ways of pleasing a woman without stepping over the line into hard-core sex.

The beatings had begun then. Mac still carried the scars from that first beating. And the mental scars from the lectures that followed. Lectures that had only driven Mac to push more boundaries, to break more rules. By the time he had graduated from high school he had already learned the delicate act of giving a woman anal sex. His first year in college he had mastered it. Then came his first ménage.

Sweet heaven, it had been good. He had watched his lover's face as he shared her with an older, much more experienced man. A mentor who had seen the darkness in Mac when he first met him. Had seen it and understood the danger inherent in it if he didn't learn how to direct it.

Ian Sinclair hadn't been much older than Mac, but he had been much more experienced. A natural sensualist, a lover of all things female. He had taught Mac how to direct those hungers and how to still them. And Mac's love for sharing his women had been born.

It was forbidden fruit. It was the most sensual pleasure a man could give a woman. It was an affirmation that he would never, ever become anything resembling his father.

And now, more than a decade after sharing his first lover, Mac had accepted his shortcomings. It wasn't something most women could accept. He had married Keiley knowing she might not be able to accept it. And yet here he was, a cigarette in one hand, his cell phone in the other, contemplating pushing her that much closer to another man's arms.

He was going to risk the destruction of his marriage and

his life because he had been too certain she couldn't handle the truth before he married her.

It was addictive, he admitted. Like a drug, watching a woman lose herself in a sensation that could come only one way was almost impossible to resist. He loved his wife, loved her with all his being, loved her enough that he wanted her every sexual limit satisfied.

Was it reason enough, he asked himself. Of course it wasn't. He knew that if he were to ask any man he knew in his hometown if he would share his wife, then the response could become violent. But he knew men whose eyes would gleam in pleasure and anticipation. And other men who understood the pleasure of sharing a lover and did so with regularity and with strict privacy.

He knew one of those men was only a phone call away.

He stubbed out his cigarette, flipped open the cell phone, and hit the speed dial.

"Do you know how late it is?" Jethro answered instantly.

"Three in the morning and you're still awake, dumbass," Mac laughed, careful to keep his voice low.

"Yeah, well, it's been one of those weeks." Jethro sounded disgusted.

"I thought you were on vacation. Started yesterday, didn't it?"

"Vacation," his friend snorted. "That's a good word for suspension, I guess."

"Hey, take the blow, take the vacation. At least it's paid this time." Jethro wasn't known for his self-control when it came to ripping a rapist off his victim, as he had done the month before.

"Yeah. It's paid," Jethro sighed. "So what has you calling at three in the morning? Other than rubbing salt in the wound here."

Mac stared into the night, watching the shifting shadows in the forests around him before he spoke.

"Why not take a real vacation?" he finally asked. "Come to the farm for a while."

Silence filled the line.

"Why?" Jethro's voice was wary, but deeper. Interested.

"I need a third, Jethro. Keiley knows you. You're familiar. I want you to be her first." Her permanent third.

Jethro blinked at the blank wall across from him, not more than a little surprised. It had been more than three years since Mac had married Keiley Hardin. They had kept in touch by phone, but Jethro had never suspected what he heard in Mac's voice now.

His friend was riding the edge of his sensuality. The restlessness and hunger were in his tone, and Jethro knew the hunger would be reflected in his eyes.

He knew because he was the same way. He could handle it for a while, doing without sharing a lover, but eventually it caught up on him.

It was catching up on Mac now.

"Anytime, you know that." Jethro hoped the anticipation spilling through him now wasn't spilling through the phone line.

Mac chuckled. "Still lusting after my wife, Jethro?" His voice was knowing.

"Hell, you know it," Jethro breathed out roughly. "She's one of the sexiest women either of us has ever seen, Mac. Any man would be panting for her."

But only a few would be panting with the emotion to back it up as Jethro did. Not that he could ever reveal that to Mac.

"What does Keiley think about it?"

The silence came again.

"She doesn't know," Mac finally answered. "She suspects."

"How do you intend to play this?"

"Your favorite sport, Jethro," Mac drawled. "We're going to seduce my wife."

"And she's seduceable?"

"She's seduceable," Mac admitted. "Whether or not she's willing to forgive being seduced is another thing. We'll take it a step at a time."

A step at a time. His cock was so hard he could feel the

driving pain of arousal ricocheting up his spine. The thought of Keiley—sweet God, soft, sweet Keiley—the woman that had tormented him for over three years, sandwiched between him and Mac, would make him crazy before he ever made it to Mac's hometown.

"Agreed." Jethro stared around his apartment, instantly planning his trip from Virginia to North Carolina. "I'll arrive tomorrow evening. Does she even know I'm coming?"

"She'll know tomorrow."

"But will she suspect why?"

"She's a smart woman," Mac pointed out, something Jethro was already well aware of. "She'll suspect. I'll make my decision regarding how far it goes as I see her reaction."

Her reaction as the seduction progressed phase by phase, Jethro knew. It was an interesting conundrum, he admitted. Seducing a wife. Jethro had never done that, not within or outside a ménage.

The women he had shared with their husbands had known up front what was coming. They had looked forward to it, anticipated it. They were aware of what was going to happen every step of the way during the ritualistic dance of the knowing seduction.

"Maybe this vacation won't be as useless as I anticipated," Jethro sighed. "If we have the time, we can run some scenarios on that old case of yours."

"The stalker?"

"He disappeared for a while. Showed back up about six months ago. We've had two attacks so far. The last one was an attempted rape. He couldn't get dinky-doo to come to attention, though, so he just scared the hell out of his victim with threats to kill her husband, her kids, and her dog."

After three years of silence, it was confusing why the man named by the Bureau the Playboy Stalker had reappeared in the area.

"How many victims in the past six months?" Mac asked.

"Two," Jethro breathed out roughly. "One in Virginia, one

in West Virginia, and a potential in D.C. The Bureau has a task force on him, but I don't like what they're coming up with. Doesn't feel right. I believe he's going to kill soon, Mac. The task force thinks he's still playing."

"He beat the crap out of the last one I investigated," Mac said thoughtfully. "When did he go back to just threatening them?"

"He disappeared right after you left town, right off the radar. Showed back up six months ago and started fresh. He's not following a pattern and that scares the shit out of me, I'll tell you right now."

"Bring what you can with you," Mac said thoughtfully. "We'll find the time to go over it and see what we can find out. Are there any suspects?"

"*Nada*. We have a profile, but even that feels more like a shot in the dark than a real analysis."

He could almost feel Mac thinking through the phone.

"We'll discuss it when you arrive," he finally repeated. "I'll expect you tomorrow evening."

"I'll be there." Jethro smiled in anticipation. He wouldn't have missed it for the world.

As the call broke off, Jethro ran his fingers through his disheveled hair and glanced at the closed bedroom door. Behind the panel his sometimes lover lay sleeping peacefully while he had sat out in the living room in the dark, staring at the door, wondering what the hell he was doing.

Janet Billings wasn't a romantic interest, no more than he was for her. It was an itch to be scratched, and he was damned tired of just scratching an itch. Sex used to be fun. It used to be enough to still the memories ripping through his mind. Not anymore, and he had finally started facing it.

He was tired of cold, emotionless sex. He wanted more, and he wondered if visiting an old friend would provide that. He and Mac had always had the unfortunate pleasure of going after the same women. It was one of the reasons they had gravitated toward each other at Quantico and then Sinclair's Club.

It was one of the reasons they had worked so well together in the Bureau.

He tilted his head back against the chair and closed his eyes, pulling up Keiley Hardin McCoy's face. She looked like a pixie with her stubborn chin, angular face, and pert little nose. Golden hazel eyes, high arched brows, and a short cap of dark hair that framed her high forehead and cheekbones.

She was damned beautiful. Innocent as sunrise, as Mac used to say, and sexy as hell. He had jacked off to fantasies about sharing her with Mac for years.

Shaking his head, he straightened before rising from the chair and moved through the apartment to the bedroom. Janet was still asleep, and she slept deeply. Sliding back into his bed wasn't a problem, and if he was aware of the fact that he made certain he didn't touch her as he settled down to sleep, then he didn't give it much thought.

Things had been odd for him for a while now. He was tired of the Bureau, tired of chasing damned perverts, and tired of being aimless. Maybe after this vacation he would follow Mac's example and just turn in his resignation. His cousin had a nice little investigation company that he had been begging Jethro to join. He was thinking about it. Some nights, he was thinking too damned hard about it.

He could pick his own jobs. Pick the deranged individuals he wanted to deal with, and maybe take a decent vacation rather than a forced suspension. Usually without pay. And he could kick some ass without getting written up over it later. He'd stopped a rapist, for God's sake. It wasn't like he had pulled a piddling teenager off a giggling girlfriend and beaten the shit out of him. Not that the director saw it that way. Hell, now, Director Scarborough was madder than hell that he had to deal with the fallout instead.

And maybe it was him. He knew he had been riding a fine line lately. The cruelty and horror men could inflict upon women were starting to really piss him off. He loved women. Cherished them. Thought there was nothing finer than the female mind and softly scented feminine flesh. They were a wonder. Treasures. They should be worshipped by a male hand for the pleasure they gave, never beaten, raped, or terrorized by diseased minds.

Yeah. Maybe it was time to resign. Before he did the world a favor and killed a few of them.

But first, he would go to North Carolina. Hopefully some of the restlessness would ease there, some of the darkness would find a shimmer of light in Keiley's presence. At least, that was his hope.

He stared at the darkened ceiling, the image of her flitting through his mind with a smile hot enough to heat the sun a few degrees hotter, and warm enough to ease the ice in his soul whenever he was around her.

She scared the shit out him.

His lips kicked up at the corner at the thought.

Keiley was the one woman he had dared go after, because he knew he could love her. Hell, he did love her. So he had given her to Mac, because he knew Mac would do more than love her.

His past had struck again. The moment he had met Keiley he heard his own screams as his uncle dragged him away from his mother's dead body. His father lay beside her in his own blood, a suicide-murder that had ended in Jethro losing the only stability in his life. His beautiful, adoring mother.

A week later he had entered his first foster home. His uncle had wiped his hands of him, sneering at the thought of raising his brother and sister-in-law's child. A child that came with nothing but the ragged clothes on his back.

And then hell had begun. One foster home after another because the angry child he had become was too much for the harried families to handle.

As he grew older, he grew colder. He pushed back that pain and let the ice build. Until Mac.

Hell, it wasn't even Mac. It was the fact that Mac had dared him to care about the women they shared. He had pushed Jethro, chided him, made him see the joy in sharing a part of himself with those women.

Mac wasn't a man that ever went into anything half-heartedly. And he hadn't let Jethro do it, either.

And then Jethro had seen Keiley.

God, he remembered her smile that night. Remembered her eyes. Remembered feeling his heart ache as he gently steered her and Mac toward each other.

Because he knew Mac would love her. He had known beyond a shadow of a doubt that the wild child Keiley kept carefully restrained inside her would call to Mac. That he would cherish her, marry her, and one day, perhaps, allow Jethro to share a stolen moment or two within that warmth.

Because Mac knew all the things Jethro had never learned, despite the other man's attempts to show him how. Mac knew how to capture a woman's heart. Jethro made them wary.

Mac knew how to show the gentleness inside him, whereas Jethro had never been able to temper the darkness enough to soften his dominance. Mac knew how to soften his dominance, and Jethro only knew how to pull away to hide his.

Mac had learned how to release the gentler emotions that filled him, whereas Jethro feared ever letting them go. At least, alone. Not without something he had come to rely on way too much. He had come to rely on Mac's ability to soften the fierce adoration he felt for his women. It wasn't that Jethro didn't know how to care. He knew how to care. And he knew how to fear it. Just as he knew how to drive away the women he cared for if Mac didn't temper that ferocity inside him.

What a pair they had made. Mac indulged his lovers, sometimes to the point that Jethro's dominance had kept them from walking all over him. And through it all, Mac had watched it with humor and with knowledge.

They had complemented each other, but would they do so again? For a moment, Jethro felt his guts cramp with the hunger and need that tore inside him. A hunger that went deeper and hotter than any he had ever known.

Keiley was his weakness. And hiding that from Mac was going to be hell. If the other man ever learned how much

Jethro loved his wife, then there would never be a chance of Jethro touching her. Intimacy was one thing, but he was afraid that if it came to sharing his wife's emotions, then Mac just might become the selfish, possessive bastard he should have been to begin with.

CHAPTER FOUR

"You snuck out of bed last night," Keiley said as she set his breakfast and coffee in front of him, her voice questioning.

He should have known that she would wake up when he left the bed; she usually did. Just as he did when she was restless. Sometimes, Mac thought, they were too attuned to each other. Knew each other too well.

It was one of the reasons she was suddenly pushing him, asking questions, her curiosity blooming beneath the sexual needs beginning to rise inside him. Needs he could suppress but couldn't totally hide.

"I was restless."

"You were smoking again."

She sat down across from him, sipping at her coffee as Mac lifted his gaze and met her eyes. Damn, he could use a cigarette now.

"Is there a point to this line of questioning, Kei?"

She crossed her legs and leaned forward, another of those damned strappy too-snug shirts stretching across her breasts.

"I don't know, Mac, would I be asking if there weren't?" she asked dryly, her eyes widened with teasing laughter.

Mac inhaled quickly, drawing in the scent of her, the herbal shampoo, the light fragrance she wore. It was nearly too much for a hungry man to endure.

He leaned forward himself, his gaze narrowing on her.

"Keep it up, and you're going to get more than you're bargaining for," he told her softly. "Is that what you want?"

She settled back with a huff, a flicker of irritation crossing her expression as he lifted his coffee cup to his lips.

"How do you know what I'm bargaining for anyway?" she asked as he sipped the coffee, causing him to nearly burn blisters on his tongue as he took too much of the liquid.

"Because you're determined to torment the hell out of me," he growled, setting the coffee down as he glowered over at her. "I'm warning you to stop pushing me like this, Keiley."

"What am I doing?" Her voice was filled with offended pride, her gaze narrowing on him with a flare of irritation.

"Tempting me." And doing a damned good job of it.

"Tempting you? Me?" Innocent offense shaped her expression now. And it would have been believable if those hazel eyes weren't gleaming with satisfaction. "I'm your wife, Mac. It's not like you're some priest that I'm tempting with my wicked lusts, you know. How am I tempting you?"

"By being you, damn it," he growled. "I was restless last night. I got up, smoked a cigarette, and enjoyed the peace for a while. Why should I have to excuse it?"

"Did I ask you to excuse it?"

"That's exactly what you're doing."

"So why were you out there smoking when you could have been cuddling and having hot, sweaty sex with me? And why is sex in our bed suddenly so abhorrent to you, anyway?"

He knew it. He knew that was what she had in that sharp little mind of hers.

Mac sat back in his chair and regarded her silently for long moments, considering how far he wanted to let this conversation go right now.

"I don't consider having sex in our bed abhorrent," he finally answered her. "I thought you were upset over the incident in the barnyard the other day. I thought you needed time to get over it."

"To get over having sex with my husband in our barnyard?"

Okay, when put like that, it sounded ridiculous, but he knew what he had seen in her eyes after the passion had receded.

"Deny the fact that you were upset when you realized you were naked in the barnyard and had just finished screaming out your orgasm to the sky," he accused her. "Deny that you were suddenly terrified that we were seen. That someone would gossip about it."

Her eyes flickered with guilt. "It's not like we have neighbors." She tried to blow off the accusation. "No one could have seen us."

"And if they had?" He wasn't willing to let her off the hook now. She was pushing him, daring him too often.

She shrugged. "They didn't."

"No, Keiley, that wasn't what I asked you. I asked you, what if we had been seen? What if someone was watching?"

He had asked her that as he fucked her. He remembered the arousal that burned hotter inside her, the response that had nearly burned him alive as she climaxed in his arms.

"Well." She cleared her throat. "It's not like we were cheating or something."

"And if our neighbors had seen? What would Becky and Bruce Halloway do? Becky would call her sister, who would call her sister-in-law—"

"Oh, shut up." She glared back at him. "So what if they told?"

"Gossip," he pointed out.

Her lips flattened. "As I said, we're married."

Mac allowed his lips to quirk into a smile as he decided to let the subject shift. He had planted the idea, planted the consequences. She could consider it from there. "Yes, we're married. And speaking of gossip, I invited Jethro to come out and visit for a while. He's been suspended again. I think he needs the break. If anyone gets curious about our houseguest, then he's just a friend from Virginia. Don't mention the fact that he was with the Bureau. I get too many damned questions about being an agent as it is. I can't believe Dad actually told everyone what the hell I was doing."

The last thing he needed was that the small-town suspicions would soon turn a visit into some kind of rumored cover-up investigation that wasn't real. It had taken nearly a year for him to convince the damned sheriff that he had indeed resigned from the Bureau and wasn't working on a secret investigation.

He picked up his coffee and sipped as he watched her closely now. She knew Jethro, not well, perhaps. He had been Mac's best man at their wedding. He had also been part of the gossip about the club that she had heard before they had left Virginia.

He saw her tense as she made the connection.

"Where is he staying?"

"I offered him the guest room." Mac picked up his fork and dug into his scrambled eggs. "He should be here a week or so. Are you okay with that?"

He watched the question form on her lips before she bit it back, and he knew what was on her mind. Was Jethro visiting with sexual intent or only for friendship?

He gave her credit that she didn't actually ask the question. He hadn't expected her to have the self-control. Keiley was a curious little cat at times, so her restraint surprised him.

She picked at her food as he ate, glancing up at him often as he felt her thinking. Hell, it was damned disconcerting knowing how close they were at times. So close that he could feel that quick little mind of hers working.

"You still haven't told me why we didn't have sex last night," she retorted as they finished eating. "You turned over like all you wanted to do was sleep, then slipped out of our bed hours later. You're going to give me a complex."

"Sex in the bed tempts me too far," he told her calmly, watching her expression closely. "A quickie against the tractor is easier to control."

"Excuse me?"

Mac stood to his feet. "You heard me, Keiley. If I don't have sex with you in the bed, then I'm not nearly as tempted to turn you over and paddle that tight little ass of yours until it's blushing and you're screaming in arousal. And I'm sure as hell not as tempted to tie you to the bedposts and make you beg for acts you've never shown an interest in. Until I get a handle on that, then I suggest you stop challenging me to do it. Because as I said, you're going to get a hell of a lot more than you're bargaining for. Now, I have work to do." He leaned across the table and kissed her parted lips. "I love you, babe. But if I don't get the hell out of here, I might end up fucking your ass, literally, on the breakfast table and to hell with shocking your innocence. I'll see you at lunch."

Keiley could only stare in shock across the table at where Mac had been. He had made those statements calmly. As though he were discussing no more than the weather. As though those acts were commonplace within their marriage.

They weren't.

Mac had never dared spank her. And he had never, ever mentioned tying her to the bed. And anal sex? Anal sex?

She waved her hand over her flushed face as she stared at her half-eaten breakfast with wide eyes. Mac was definitely showing a side of himself she hadn't anticipated. A side that excited her. It made her nervous, but it excited her.

The information that Jethro Riggs was arriving for a week had done more than shock her, though. It had left her speechless. Jethro was Mac's partner and best friend in the Bureau; he was also Mac's third in the sexual games he had played before marrying her.

Mac and Jethro were the "Trojan Duo" of choice among the women who knew the men and their sexual preference for a ménage. Jethro was as dark-haired as Mac, with a bad-boy smile and a wicked twinkle in his eyes.

He had teased her steadily during the wedding reception. At one point, he had made the comment to Mac that if she got bored during the honeymoon he would be more than happy to fly out and help Mac keep her company.

Keiley had known what he was talking about at the time and had checked around quickly to make certain no one else had overheard him. She hadn't gotten up the nerve to actually question Mac about the rumors of his sexual games until nearly six months after their marriage, though.

A part of her, she admitted, hadn't really wanted to know

the truth. But some imp inside her had pushed and pushed until she questioned him about it.

It's in the past, Kei. That had been his only response, but the flicker of regret in his eyes had terrified her at the time.

She had dropped the subject just as quickly, and several weeks later, when he announced his intention to resign and return to his hometown and the farm, she had felt a sense of relief that had been nearly weakening.

The gossip concerning them had been heavy at the time. Those who seemed to know about Sinclair's Club had seemed certain that Mac would return to it. For something that was supposed to be quiet, private, there was enough gossip about the men's club to fill a full-length book.

A disgruntled wife had begun the tales several years before Keiley had met Mac, and over time, names associated with the membership began to filter through D.C. and Alexandria. No one had any true proof, but there was enough talk that at the time Keiley had wondered if proof mattered to any of them.

And that was what terrified her. The fact that proof wasn't needed, only supposition. The fact that Mac had retained his membership for several months after their marriage only fueled the talk. Sometimes he met there for business or for drinks with his friends. Each time he returned he had been quiet, brooding.

At the time, rumor was that bets were being placed on who Mac would eventually approach to bring to their bed as the third for her first ménage.

The gossip was the worst part. Whispers behind her back. Veiled comments that she could never fully confront. Smug smiles from the men and a glimmer of jealous snappishness in the women. Things she could have ignored if she hadn't suspected the truth behind them.

Standing up, Keiley cleared the kitchen table, loaded the dishwasher, and stood in the middle of the kitchen as she tried to figure out how to handle this.

The best bet was to confront Mac about it. Just ask him

about it. He wouldn't lie to her if she asked him straight out if he intended to invite Jethro into their bed.

Another part of her warned her to stay silent. If she didn't push the subject, then neither would he. If Jethro was visiting on the off chance of being the third in their bed, then Mac would hold back if she pretended ignorance.

If she could pretend ignorance.

She waved her hand before her face again, realizing that she was overheating, flushing from her thoughts and the images her mind was suddenly flashing before her.

Mac holding her, kissing her, but other touches as well. Touches from strange hands. Kisses from strange lips. Mortification blazed within her as she gave her head a quick shake and moved quickly from the kitchen to prepare the guest room for Jethro.

She wasn't going to think about this right now. She couldn't think about it right now. She was already aroused, already upset over the fact that Mac hadn't touched her since the afternoon before last. And too aroused by his statements before he left the house. She didn't need to add the forbidden to the mix.

And she could be wrong, she told herself as she moved up the stairs. She knew for a fact that her husband was incredibly jealous if other men came on to her, so it could simply be paranoia. Jethro Riggs's visit could be entirely innocent. A friend on vacation dropping by for a little male bonding or whatever men did. That simple.

Yeah. Right. The suspicious part of her brain was snickering smugly. Because it knew better.

Keiley knew her husband, and she knew something had been growing inside him for months now. A well of dark hunger that marathon bouts of sex hadn't sated had turned into a brooding predatory interest whenever he watched her that made her highly nervous. Excited, yes. Interested in that darkness, most definitely. But also extremely wary of it.

Aroused by it.

After finishing the preparation of the guest room and laying in clean towels, washrags, and essential items, Keiley moved back downstairs to the back of the house and her office.

She didn't sit at her desk, though; instead she walked to the patio doors and stared out at the barnyard where Mac had taken her so wildly not two days past.

Today, the farmhands he employed were working the horses in the attached corral. The Thoroughbreds Mac raised were gorgeous, high-spirited, and extremely intelligent. The foreman, Teddy Raymond, had been hired out of Virginia two years before, and he seemed to love the horses as much as Mac did. He was an odd little man who kept to himself when he was working, but Mac seemed to think he did his job well enough.

The trainer, Wes Bridges, was working with the yearlings outside the stables, and beyond that, cattle grazed the grass-rich fields and beyond. The farm sat in a wide, lush valley dotted with natural ponds and streams and thick, nutritious grass. Mac's cattle sold well, and the horses were becoming a very lucrative sideline with the bloodlines Mac had chosen.

The farm was idyllic, serene, but suddenly Keiley's life was anything but that. She felt as she had when she first met Mac. Jittery inside, excited, nervous, and so aroused she could barely sit still.

Tonight, he was going to have to take care of business, she thought, because she would be damned if she was going to toss and turn all night long again, burning for her husband's touch.

She pouted at the thought. Married women should not have to do without their daily allotment of sex, no matter their husband's brooding determination to drive them insane for it. He could be broody through the night. When he slipped into the bed beside her, then he should be ready to perform those husbandly duties that she had become so well accustomed to.

A smile flitted across her lips. Maybe he just needed a little push. She could provide the push. He could provide the orgasm.

With that thought she turned to her desk, sat down, and powered up her computer to get to work. She had clients waiting, and the paycheck was dependent on keeping them happy. She would take care of that; then she would take care of her husband.

Jethro took the exit to Scotland Neck, staring around at the rather large town curiously as he drove through it. With the top down on his Mustang, the fresh air blowing through his overly long hair, he got more than his fair share of feminine looks as he traversed the main thoroughfare and followed Mac's directions out of town toward the farm.

His lips quirked as the red light brought him to a stop into a turn lane. The young women in the car beside him waved flirtatiously, then giggled like teenagers as he shot them a wink.

Damn, he loved women. Blondes, brunettes, redheads, or dark as midnight. Women were his favorite subject, hobby, and sport.

As the light turned green, he threw his hand up in a farewell and, with his foot heavy on the gas, sped out of town and checked the clock on the dash.

He was a little late. It was edging into evening rather than afternoon, but the more leisurely pace he had taken on the drive had helped to clear his head. And his head sure as hell needed clearing.

Janet hadn't been happy when she awoke to him packing his bags for a trip out of town. Actually, she had been downright pissed.

How the hell was he was supposed to know she had planned to shack up with him during the suspension? The thought of it sent a shiver down his spine. It wasn't the good kind of shiver, either.

Mysterious and contradictory, he loved the female mind, but damned if it didn't throw him for a loop sometimes. Janet, it seemed, was dreaming of an engagement ring and wedding bands, wedding bells, and the long white dress. And where she got that idea, Jethro had no clue.

He wasn't the marrying kind. The bitterness in his soul still held the power to make him run hard and fast whenever he caught the gleam of forever in a woman's eyes.

Janet had that gleam when she woke up and caught him packing. She had tried to cover it. To hide it. But the moment he had caught that glimmer he had known the on-again, off-again relationship they had shared was now stone cold. No way. No how.

Shifting back in his seat, he made the turn onto the country road that led to Mac's farm and let a smile cross his face.

Hell, he needed this vacation. Even more, he needed the time spent with Mac and his wife. The chance to be a part of the relationship Mac had with Keiley was an irresistible lure.

It was the love, Jethro knew that. Keiley loved her husband, and if she accepted a third into their bed, then the passion and emotion that she shared with Mac would extend to that third.

It was a gift Mac's women had always given him. They loved him, some more than others, but those willing to step into the ménage had extended those softer feelings to Jethro.

How much better would it be on the periphery of true love? Would it still the restlessness building inside him, or would it only make it worse?

Breathing out at the thought, Jethro lifted his cell phone from the seat beside him, flipped it open, and punched in Mac's number.

"You're late." Mac answered on the third ring.

"I was being lazy today," Jethro drawled. "I'm about ten minutes from the farm. You watching for me?"

Mac straightened from the tractor he was attempting to repair. Tucking the cell phone between his shoulder and cheek, he wiped his hands on the discarded rag and glanced toward the road.

"Laziness doesn't become you, Jeth," he stated. "I'm heading to the house now to clean up. I'll meet you there."

"Looks like a nice little town I drove into. I can see why you like it here. It's larger than you described."

"Yeah, it's growing fast," Mac agreed as he stepped over the little picket fence Keiley had around the house yard. "Good people, though. Keiley has your room ready and she's fixing dinner. I'll let her know you're coming and jump in the shower. She'll let you in."

He could be making a mistake, he knew, in bringing Jethro into his home, but Keiley was finally becoming curious about his sexual past.

"I'll be there soon, then," Jethro assured. "See you in a bit."

Mac disconnected the call as he stepped into the house, inhaling the aroma of baked ham, rolls, and a myriad of other delicacies his wife had been working on. She might be a bit of a computer geek, but when she put her mind to it, she could turn out a meal to make a man's mouth water.

"Hey, babe." He caught her as she stepped out of the washroom, grinning devilishly as he managed to trap her against the wall, careful to keep his greasy hands off her and the pristine white walls.

"You're dirty, Mac." But she still lifted her face for his kiss and softened into his body.

He couldn't resist deepening the kiss. Parting her lips and allowing his tongue to taste the erotic flavor of her. Heated feminine warmth filled his senses as he felt her arms twine around his neck, her fingers sinking into the strands of hair at his neck.

"You taste like sunlight," she whispered when he pulled back, her gaze drowsy with passion as he dipped his knees and pressed the engorged length of his cock into the V of her thighs.

"You taste like sex." He grinned, kissing her quickly before easing back. "Jethro just called. He'll be here in a few minutes. I'm going to run upstairs and shower real quick."

"At least he has good timing." Pushing away from him, she headed to the stove to check the various pots and pans there. "Hurry and shower."

He followed, kissing the nape of her neck as she bent her neck back with a laugh and shooed him from the kitchen.

But he had achieved his object. She would have to greet

his friend, socialize with him, giving her time to accustom herself to him before he came down.

She would need that time. Her reaction to Jethro would decide any further course toward what he was going to ask from her. It could be a mistake. It could be the biggest mistake of his life. But he was hoping instead that it would ultimately be his greatest pleasure.

CHAPTER FIVE

Jethro Riggs was a bad boy. It was in his blue eyes, in his overly long black hair that he had pulled back into a low ponytail at that nape of his neck, and in the closely cropped beard and mustache he wore.

He winked the second she opened the door. "Keiley, you're too pretty for Mac. Come on. Run away with me now and I'll rescue you from him."

"And you are just as hell-bent as you always were," she informed him, stepping back from the door as he stepped inside the foyer of the large farmhouse. "Mac is still showering, but he should be done in a bit."

"I called him and warned him I was coming to steal you away. See how lacking in consideration he is? He's not even down here to protect you."

"Who needs his protection?" She arched her brow mockingly. "I have a black belt in tae kwon do, Jethro. I can almost kick his ass."

"Eh. A five-year-old could kick his ass." He set his duffel bag in the hall and stared around the open foyer curiously. "Still can't believe Mac's a farmer, Keiley. Tell me he doesn't pitch hay all day."

"He doesn't pitch hay all day. There's actually a few hours when he's cleaning out stalls."

Jethro grimaced. "He's pitching something else instead, then?"

Keiley chuckled as she closed the door. "Grab your bag.

I'll show you to your room and you can freshen up before dinner. I'm sure Mac won't take long."

She hoped he didn't take long. After the images that had played in her mind all day due to the suspicion that Mac had brought his friend here for reasons other than a friendly visit, she felt strangely vulnerable in Jethro's presence.

As he picked up his large duffel bag, Keiley headed for the stairs, heading for the second floor and the guest room she had chosen for him. The room furthest away from her and Mac's. He could make her rather loud when they were having sex. Too loud. She was going to need a gag; then she might have a chance that Jethro wouldn't hear them at the other end of the house.

"It's a damned nice place," Jethro said as he followed her up the stairs.

Why did she feel his eyes on her ass?

"We've done a lot of work on the house since we moved in." She cleared her throat uncomfortably, suddenly very much aware of the fact that her jeans molded to her butt. "Mac's very handy with a hammer."

"That and a gun is all a man needs," he joked.

She paused at the landing to stare back at him with narrow-eyed intent. "Mac no longer carries a gun, Jethro."

His lips quirked. "A screwdriver?"

She inclined her head in acceptance and began moving down the hallway.

"Here's your room." She opened the door that led into the spacious guest room. "There's a private bathroom." She opened the nearby door before moving across the room. "And this is the closet. The phone line has its own number, and there's wireless and wired Internet access from the port on the desk." She motioned to the wide cherrywood desk.

"The perfect hostess," he murmured as he set the duffel bag on the queen-size bed and watched her carefully. "All the comforts of home."

His voice was quieter now, deeper. His blue eyes watched her closely, the colors shifting and changing, much like Mac's did as emotions or passion filled them.

Keiley cleared her throat. "Dinner should be ready in about half an hour if you want to shower or anything. Just come downstairs and take the doorway to your right."

He tucked his hands in the back of his jeans, causing his dark blue t-shirt to stress across his broad shoulders.

He looked dangerous, too similar to Mac when she first met him. In the past three years the suspicion in Mac's eyes had begun to ease, the paranoia she associated with being an agent not as present as it had been before they left Virginia. Mac was more relaxed now, more prone to smile, while Jethro still carried the look of a man ready to kill if need be.

"I'll be done in plenty of time to eat," he assured her. "It's been a long time since I had a decent meal."

Keiley breathed in deeply, her gaze flickering around the room.

"Well, I'll talk to you later—"

"There he is." Mac's voice surprised her. She hadn't been aware he had entered the bedroom and had no idea he was behind her until his arms surrounded her, pulling her back against his chest. "Is he behaving himself, Keiley?"

Keiley tensed. It wasn't normal jovial good cheer in Mac's voice. She heard the dark undercurrent of desire and felt the proof of it pressing imperatively into the small of her back.

His voice clued her into much more than his arousal, though. It was different, unlike any tone she had heard in his voice before.

She knew it.

Jethro wasn't just there to visit. She stared back at the other man, watching his gaze flicker to Mac's before he stared back at her, his eyes darkening, a subtle cast of sensuality sharply defining his features.

Her lips flattened, and before she considered her actions or even thought, her elbow rammed into her husband's undefended abdomen, bringing a surprised grunt from him as he released her quickly.

"What the hell was that for?" He was rubbing his hand over his stomach as she turned and glared at him, a frown brewing on his face.

"For being an ass." She smiled tightly. "Dinner will be ready in thirty minutes. That is, if you're brave enough to come down and eat it."

She pushed past him. The blood was thundering through her veins, her emotions were rioting, and God help her, but she was aroused. She hated that. She hated being manipulated, hated being lied to, and she had never believed Mac would resort to such games with her.

He had. He had brought Jethro here with every intention of inviting him into their bed and she knew it. She knew it, and she hated the contradictory emotions that knowledge fed through her body.

Her flesh was sensitive, her breasts swollen, and she could feel the heat building between her thighs. Suddenly her beliefs in herself, her relationship with Mac and what she felt they shared, began to waver.

A fantasy was just that. She was aware he had fantasies, and over the past months she had guessed at the source of them. But fantasies were supposed to stay in the mind. They weren't meant to ever meet reality.

She had fantasized herself for years. Ever since the first rumor she had heard of Mac and Jethro sharing their women. Both men were darkly handsome, both were dangerous and broody. But it was a fantasy.

As she rushed into the kitchen she could feel her hands shaking, her stomach rioting with something that she refused to accept as excitement. It was repulsion, she assured herself. It had to be. No way, no how was she actually going to let this happen. She wouldn't.

She jerked a cabinet door open and pulled three plates free before slamming it closed with a surge of strength that had the panel cracking into the frame with such force that it sounded like a gunshot. Tears flooded her eyes, but she refused to let them fall. They weren't tears of pain, they were tears of confusion, of anger. Anger not just at Mac, but at herself.

He had brought another man into their home to touch her. She slapped the plates to the table.

He meant to allow another man into their bed.

Her palms flattened against the table as she glared at the doorway.

He meant to seduce her into it. She knew it. She had seen it in Jethro's eyes, felt it in Mac's aroused body. He had no intention of confronting her with it.

Damn him.

Damn her.

Because rather than puking in disgust, she was nearly panting in excitement. And that was even scarier than the knowledge of what Mac and Jethro intended.

By the time the two men entered the large country kitchen with its tall wide windows and view of the pastures, Keiley had herself under control and the table set.

The meal progressed with more ease than she had anticipated, considering her own fractured emotions. Jethro and Mac together were a potent combination. Mac alone could sear her senses no matter what the situation, but when these two men set out to charm, even she, knowing exactly what they were up to, wasn't immune.

With Jethro's presence, a part of Mac that she rarely saw showed itself. She could see the dominance glimmering heavily in his stormy gaze now. He watched her like a cat watched a bowl of cream. And Jethro. Jethro watched her like a man observing a favorite treat.

He seemed to draw from her and Mac somehow. To absorb the emotion between them, to make her more aware of it than she normally would be.

As the meal finished and Keiley and Mac stacked the dishes, she wasn't surprised to realize that the intensity of the atmosphere had heightened her awareness of Mac's body, and of his hunger.

The hunger was boiling in his gaze. Like thunderclouds, pitching and rolling, glittering with quicksilver bolts of wicked lust each time he glanced at her.

"I'll leave you two men to catch up," she announced as she loaded the last dish and turned to face them. "I have some laundry to take care of and a few things to catch up on the computer before I turn in."

Let Mac wait on her for a change. He was lucky she wasn't heading out of the house.

Turning, she headed along the back hall to the laundry room where the week's laundry waited. She had a meeting tomorrow with the charity committee that ran the annual summer festival and the outfit she had decided to wear needed cleaning first.

The Egyptian cotton dress was one of her favorites, but she had worn it to the monthly office meeting in D.C. the week before.

She was lucky that the programming firm she worked for and her specialties allowed her to work virtually independently, with only occasional trips into the office.

"Don't you think it's a little impolite to leave our company so soon?" Mac asked as she moved to the narrow rack where she had hung the dress after removing it.

It wasn't there. She flipped through the hangers quickly, then looked on the floor beneath the rack.

"Did you hear me?"

Keiley turned back to him slowly. It wasn't so much what he said as how he said it. It was the way his eyes narrowed with a just of hint of sensual determination, the way his shoulders seemed broader, his chest wider. The way the bulge in his jeans seemed more intimidating than ever before.

Keiley could feel her heart rate picking up as he advanced on her slowly.

"I can't find my dress." Her voice was weak, breathless, as she turned from him quickly. "I hung it in here last week to clean. You moved it."

"Fuck the dress, Kei."

His hands caught her shoulders. He turned her to him relentlessly, holding her still as she tried to move away from him.

She tried to swallow. Tried to catch her breath at the strength of the desire she saw in his face.

"You're scaring me," she whispered.

His brows lowered further. "Do you think I'd hurt you?"

She could see the conflict in his expression. His desire warring with his love for her. If there was one thing she knew about Mac, she knew he loved her.

"Where would this leave us, Mac?" Keiley tried to still the trembling of her lips, the sensual fear weaving through her mind.

She felt more confused now than she had felt the first time Mac kissed her. The first time he had touched her.

A sibilant whimper left her lips as his hand framed her face.

"Do you think I'd force you?" He leaned forward, touched his lips to hers, electrifying her with the velvet rasp of his lips over her own.

"We need to talk about this."

"What's there to talk about?" His arm moved around her hips, pulling her to him, lifting her to the cradle of his thighs as he nipped at her lips. "You've known it was there, just beneath the surface. You wouldn't have questioned me otherwise, Kei."

"No." She shook her head, shuddering as she felt his erection wedge between her thighs, the heat of it barely contained by the denim between them.

"You saw it, didn't you?" he asked her then, one hand threading through the hair at the side of her temple while his lips drifted to her jaw. "You saw the restlessness, and you had to start pushing. Such a curious little cat." He raked his teeth down the side of her neck.

Keiley tightened her hold on his shoulders as her head fell back and the familiar weakness Mac caused inside her body began to build. She could just drift here, in this pleasure. Let him take control. Let him—

"Enough." She was out of his arms before he could stop her.

Pushing her hands through her hair, she stared back at him in shock, seeing the glittering purpose in his eyes, the amused, indulgent certainty in his expression.

"You weren't honest with me, Mac." Surprise glittered in his eyes as she made the accusation.

"Did I have to put it in words, Keiley?" He leaned against the wall as he crossed his arms over his chest and watched her with that half quirk to his lips that always made her crazy with lust.

"It would have been nice," she pointed out a shade sarcastically. "Excuse me here, Mac, but I don't think it's exactly common practice for most friends to show up on the doorstep expecting to share a couple's bed. I believe that is highly unusual. Not in the least standard matrimonial fare there."

His eyes gleamed with laughter, and she didn't appreciate it in the least. But they were also filled with banked hunger. Moving over her face, her breasts, her thighs, with carnal intent.

"Go entertain your company," she snapped. "I have work to do."

She turned to look for the dress, only to screech in surprise when she found herself sitting atop the washing machine instead and her husband wedged firmly between her thighs.

He didn't give her a chance to protest. His lips were on hers, his hands were beneath the shirt, palms cupping her breasts, fingers rasping over her nipples as she cried out in pleasure.

It was depraved. Jethro was most likely still in the kitchen. One hard moan and he would know what the hell was going on. And Keiley wasn't exactly a quiet lover. She never had been. Keeping quiet while in Mac's arms was impossible.

"You knew what was coming," he growled as his lips left hers to follow a broken path down her neck. "You've sensed it since the beginning, Keiley. Admit it."

She shook her head rashly. "No—"

"Don't lie to me." Then he did something she couldn't have expected to enjoy. Something he had never done before. His teeth caught her nipple, nipped the tender peak, sending pleasure exploding in her womb with enough force to steal her breath.

It was a sharp little nip. Bordering on painful. An agonizing pleasure that had her yelping in surprise.

"I've tried to hold back." He licked the tender peak. "I've tried to be the husband I thought you wanted." His head lifted, his eyes nearly black with hunger. "I've tried, Keiley. And it hasn't worked. Now you have the man I am. It's up to you to decide if you can live with him."

"Do you think you can frighten me into giving you what you want?" She pushed against his shoulders. Not that he moved, but his eyes narrowed and his gaze became sharper. "Not likely, Mac. Don't try threatening me—"

"You think that's what I'm doing?" he growled in return. "I don't have to threaten, Keiley. I'm giving you fair warning. Because I know you. I know you. And by God, I know the needs I have aren't too damned far off the mark from yours. Deny it. Deny the fact that if Jethro were in here watching right now you wouldn't be hotter than hell. Go ahead. Lie to me."

Lie to him. She had never lied to him.

"Some things should remain fantasy," she whispered desperately. "I don't want to lose you, Mac. I don't want to lose what we have."

He pulled her t-shirt down slowly.

"You'll never lose me. But think about this, Keiley. You've never had all of me, either."

"Because I haven't let another man fuck me?" she exclaimed, confusion and wariness blooming into fear. "Let me jump right out and take care of that. Why should I wait for you to pick someone for me? I'm highly capable of doing it for myself."

Confidence. Dominance. Self-awareness. They glittered in his eyes and tightened his expression.

"This has nothing to do with fucking another man. It has to do with accepting the pleasure I have to give you. I'm not hiding it anymore. Accept or reject it, however you want to. But don't start lying to yourself because you're scared. That I won't accept. And don't think you're going to spend the night on that damned computer working. You wanted to be fucked in the bed. Tonight that bed is going to see some action, sweetheart."

Her eyes widened. "Excuse me? You think I'm going to let him—"

"Me," he snapped. "Me. You. All night, Keiley. Every night. You know the truth now; there's nothing left to hide. Now you get to see the man you married. Not the man I've been giving you. And I sure as hell don't need any help with that."

And he didn't need any help silencing the protest forming on her lips. Before she could stop him, his lips covered hers. Not roughly, but firmly. His tongue parted them, licked, stroked, forged into her mouth and warred with her own as she felt the hunger surge through her brain.

This kiss. It was a demand. It wasn't a request.

She met it. Her tongue pressed against his, licked at his lips as he drew back; her teeth nipped, and a cry of pure pleasure left her throat as he took control once more.

He devoured her lips. This was no regular kiss. He was feeding from her hunger, his own growing, whipping around her, burning through her, until he reclaimed it from her lips, her tongue, and allowed it to burn into her once again.

She was in flames. She couldn't touch him enough. She had to get closer.

The sound of fabric tearing barely penetrated the haze of lust that seemed to enfold her. Mac's muttered groan only increased her need.

But she could touch his chest now. Her nails scoured down the muscular contours, sifting through the light sprinkling of hair before encountering the band of his jeans and the wide leather belt he wore.

"There you go, sweetheart," he muttered, tearing his lips from hers as she tugged desperately at his belt. "Take what you want."

What she needed. As though the dark hungers that were a part of Mac were suddenly filtering through her own head.

She couldn't touch him enough. She tore at his belt, releasing it, only to tug open the metal snaps of his jeans to reach inside and draw the thick, hard length of his cock from beneath the snug briefs he wore.

"Damn." His fractured groan only spurred her on.

He filled her hands. The hard length with its thick veins and silky flesh over iron hardness had her stomach clenching, her womb spasming with the need for release.

"Come here." Before she could protest, he lifted her from the washing machine only to set her to her feet before pressing her to her knees.

There was no request. He was always considerate when he asked her to go down on him. But this time, consideration had gone to hell. One hand was buried in her hair, the other gripped his cock, and within seconds Keiley found her mouth filled with the wide, damp head of his erection.

He tasted earthy, like a storm coming over the mountains. Wild and irresistible, strong and determined.

"Suck it, Kei," he ordered hoarsely. "Let me watch you take me, sugar."

Her eyes drifted open, widening fractionally at the hard, savage cast of his expression.

In the back of her mind she knew that Jethro could hear it all. There wasn't a sound coming from the kitchen. The only sounds in the house were those of her cries, muffled only by the slow, heavy thrust of Mac's cock into her mouth.

And she didn't care. She knew he could hear. Knew he was listening. Lusting. She was driven by the knowledge glittering in Mac's eyes and the hunger burning through her body.

The hand at the back of her head tightened, causing a slight, stinging burn to fill her scalp.

She loved it.

His hard flesh stretched her lips, filling her with a power and a hunger she couldn't control.

She exhilarated in it.

"Your mouth is so damned hot. So sweet and tight," he groaned, staring down at her as the gray shades of his eyes shifted and clashed together.

Her tongue flickered over the throbbing crest as he drew back, grimacing as she tightened her mouth on him.

Her hands slid over his tight abdomen as she began to suckle the broad head, moaning, fighting the dazed lust welling inside her as she tasted the pre-cum that greeted her efforts.

"That's it, baby. Suck my dick. Show me how much you need me, Kei."

Needed him? She was dying for him. Aching. She could feel her swollen clit pounding for attention, the juices gushing from her vagina in such exquisite need that it was agony.

She needed to be touched. Just one touch.

"I can't touch you like this, can I, sugar?" He stared down at her with savage frustration. "How good would it be to have those pretty nipples caressed? Lips at your neck, your back? Hands between those pretty thighs?"

His hand tightened in her hair to hold her in place as she tried to draw back, tried to escape the promise in his voice.

But she couldn't stop the moan that fell from her lips. She could almost feel it. A phantom's touch over her breasts, between her thighs, the sharp aching need for those fingers between her thighs.

"I could give you that." His gaze darkened further. His fingers tightened in her hair, tugging further.

And it shouldn't have felt good. It shouldn't have sent flames shooting from her scalp to her clit with devastating results.

"I will give that to you, Keiley." His voice hardened, with determination, with approaching release. "All of it—all of it."

He was thrusting past her lips, short, fierce thrusts that stroked his cock over her lips as her tongue licked, stroked, spurring him on until with a shattered groan he exploded.

Keiley's hands clenched in the material of his jeans as his semen spurted into her mouth. Fierce jets of heated male warmth that only made her hungrier, only made her need more until he stilled, holding her still as he eased past her lips and stared down at her with blatant satisfaction.

She could barely breathe, her eyes clouded with her own arousal now as weakening sensuality burned through her veins.

"We're not finished," he informed her roughly, drawing her to her feet before fixing his jeans. "I think it's time we both went to bed. Now."

CHAPTER SIX

Keiley kept telling herself that she couldn't do this. Not that she could force the words past her lips. Each time she tried, her throat tightened and the heated moisture between her thighs reminded her that she wanted this more than anything.

It was when Mac drew her through the kitchen, beneath the watchful eyes of Jethro Riggs, that Keiley began to tremble.

His eyes were glittering with lust as he lounged back in the kitchen chair. His obviously aroused body tensed, his expression as savagely hungry as Mac's.

Then Mac stopped at the doorway, secured Keiley in his arms, and turned back to his friend.

"Do you have any plans for tomorrow?" Mac asked the other man as his hand slid beneath her shirt, his calloused fingers caressing her stomach.

The touch was devastating, especially beneath Jethro's gaze as he rose slowly from the table.

"Nothing planned." Jethro's voice was strained.

"We have the boat out at the lake," Mac informed him. "I'll take the day off tomorrow and we'll go out for a while."

Jethro stepped closer as Mac's fingers stilled, and she felt the tension thickening in the room.

"Mac," Keiley whispered, feeling Jethro's body heat from the distance that separated them.

She couldn't do this. Oh God, she needed to tell them she

couldn't do this. But all she could do was watch as Jethro neared them, his eyes suddenly on hers, the brilliancy of the blue color sinking into her.

"She's scared, Mac," he said gently as he stepped to her, his hand reaching out, his fingers touching her cheek in a brief caress.

It felt like flames sinking into her flesh, burning her alive.

"I can't—" She jerked as Mac's hand moved, his fingers skimming over her flesh, lifting the t-shirt along her midriff as Jethro continued to stare down at her.

"Say no," Jethro whispered then. "Just say no, and it all goes away, Keiley."

She shook her head roughly, feeling Mac's free hand caressing up her arm, her shoulder, until it wrapped over her collarbone and his palm cupped her cheek.

"Do you want it to go away, Kei?" He nipped at her earlobe as she shuddered in his grasp.

"It can go away very easily, sweetheart," Jethro whispered then. "It can go away, or it can turn to this."

She whimpered as his head lowered. He was going to kiss her. Sweet God, she was standing in her husband's grip. He was watching. Watching as another man bent to her, his lips parting, his lashes lowering sensually.

Mac's hand drifted lower to the button of her jeans, flicking it open as Jethro's lips touched hers. She stood still, panting for air, staring into his eyes as the kiss sent quaking shudders racing through her.

Jethro wasn't taking her kiss. His lips were asking for her kiss, but his gaze was demanding it.

The band of her jeans loosened.

"What did I say about touching?" Mac whispered at her ear then. "Every part of your body caressed at once?"

His hands slid from the loosened band up beneath her t-shirt to her swollen, sensitive breasts. But Jethro's hands were at her hips then, his fingers lowering the zipper of the low-rise jeans.

The band was too low, she thought inanely. Once the zipper had completely lowered—

Keiley whimpered as Jethro's tongue licked at her lips and his hands peeled back the edges of her jeans.

"No!"

Where she found the strength to tear away, she wasn't certain. The impulse slammed inside her as a wave of pleasure nearly took her to her knees and a millisecond later she was backing away from them, shaking her head, fighting to breathe.

"No," she snapped again, staring at Mac and seeing a stranger.

A stranger who stared at her with her husband's eyes. Eyes heavy with arousal, love, and regret.

"Good night, Jethro," Mac said as he began to walk toward her. "We'll see you in the morning."

The intent was there in his face. He was a conqueror. He was the ravisher. His expression assured her that it didn't matter whether Jethro joined them or not—tonight he would have his wife.

"You think you just can just give another man leave to touch me and then drag me to bed?" Keiley stared back at him in outrage. "Have you taken leave of your senses, Mac?"

Had she taken leave of hers? Because this new side of Mac was making her hotter than hell.

"Pretty much," he announced a second before he stepped to her, picked her up, and tossed her over his shoulder before leaving the room.

Her last glimpse of Jethro was the wicked amusement glittering in his eyes a second before Mac headed up the stairs.

"You are so going to get your ass kicked," she snarled as she hung over his shoulder.

"Probably."

"I mean it, Mac. This is not happening."

"Of course it is," he grunted. "Stop deluding yourself. And stop pretending you're not hotter than hell. I'm amazed your jeans aren't damp from the juices spilling from your pussy."

"Asshole," she snarled.

Unfortunately, he was right in one respect. She was hotter

than hell. But wrong in the other. She believed her jeans just might be damp after all.

Once he stepped into the bedroom, he didn't bother just setting her on the floor. The next thing she knew she was on her back and Mac was jerking her sandals off before pulling her jeans down her legs and discarding them.

Just that quick. That fast. Her jeans and panties were on the floor and her husband was kneeling at the side of the bed, his tongue swiping through the saturated folds between her thighs.

"Oh God! Mac!" She screamed his name as his tongue thrust inside her, licking over tissue so sensitive that he caused an avalanche of sensations to pile upon her.

Wicked heat. Electric pleasure. Fiery, intense, brutal desire.

Her hips jerked up, grinding her clit against his lips as she gasped for breath. Her hands locked in his hair, holding him to her as her legs twined around his shoulders.

It was so damned good. Better than ever. It was like the first time. The last time and all the times in between combined in one caress. All the pleasure she had ever known in her life and more was coming.

Because his fingers gripped her rear while one wicked thumb began to press and massage the forbidden entrance below.

It was wicked and wild, and when she felt her juices being smoothed onto the area, his thumb pressing in each time to lubricate the area, she lost her mind.

It was the only excuse for allowing it. It was forbidden, a touch she had never known before, and she wasn't protesting. She had lost her mind, that was the only excuse.

A second later the lubrication was cooler, thicker. How had he done that? Managed to secure the lubricating jelly he kept in his bedside drawer without her knowing it?

And who cared, but suddenly his thumb was stretching her anal entrance, burning her, filling her where no one had ever touched before and sending her senses exploding in an orgasm that ripped her head off and still left her begging for more.

"Are you scared now, Kei?" he growled against her clit, his tongue licking around it, building the pressure once again as two fingers worked inside her vagina.

She couldn't stand this. She couldn't survive it.

"Do you know what I'm going to do?" His voice was black velvet, rough, wicked, carnal. "I'm going to stretch you here." His thumb moved inside her anus. "Then I'm going to fill it with a little toy I bought just for it. Make it burn and ache before I fill your pussy."

"Oh God. Mac." Her head thrashed on the bed.

"You're going to be so tight, Kei. Your pussy is going to burn when I fuck you. The pressure will make you crazy for more."

"I'm crazy now," she panted. "Don't tease."

"No teasing, baby." His thumb slid free of her anus.

"No. No. Don't stop."

"Never."

"Put it back."

His tongue licked down the soaked slit of her sex, licked and stroked as he shifted between her thighs, his shoulders bunching before she felt the cooling application of more of the lubricant against her rear.

"Mac, what are you doing to me?" she cried, feeling the entrance open as a finger slid inside her. "You're killing me." It retreated, worked inside her again, then another joined the first. "Please, Mac."

A second later her hands slapped to the mattress, her fingers curling into the comforter as she felt the heavy pressure of whatever toy he had promised to use on her. He was working it inside her slow and easy, stretching her, creating a burning pleasure/pain she couldn't process in her fractured mind.

"There you go, sweetheart," he crooned as the tender opening continued to stretch, the pressure building. "All of it, Kei. So sweet and tight. Just let go for me. Close your eyes, baby, and just let go for me."

She screamed as she felt the pressure increasing, only to feel a slight easing as the toy became lodged inside her. She knew what it was. She had seen the exotic toy, tapered at the tip, widening to the bottom before it indented to create a natural lock inside the anus. The butt plug was supple and smooth rather than hard and cold as she imagined when she had seen the pictures, but there was no doubt what he had used on her.

"Perfect." His voice was harder now, deeper as he moved away from her. "Let's get that shirt off. I want to see your pretty nipples, Kei."

The shirt was pulled from her body and then she realized that sometime in the laundry room she had ripped the buttons from his shirt. It was only hanging on him as he stood to his feet and shrugged it off.

He undressed quickly, tossing his clothes aside before he stood staring down at where he had placed her across the bed.

"Fucking you is going to be like taking you the first time all over again." His expression was darkly sensual. "You're going to be so tight. So hot."

She was so insane, because that carnal intensity in his voice was making her womb clench in heavy hunger as he came over her.

"Why now?" she whimpered. "Why are you doing this now?"

"Because you're ready for it." His lips touched hers. "You weren't ready before, were you, sweetheart? You're ready now."

"No." She shook her head. "I'm not ready—"

"So ready," he whispered, his tongue licking over her lips, making her taste herself, taste the wildness of her own response to him.

"Mac, I'm scared," she begged.

"You're not scared, Kei," he argued with a sexy quirk to his lips as he drew back. "Wary. Restless. Uncertain. Admit it. You know I won't hurt you. You know that anything that happens between us I'll only love you for. No matter what it is, Kei. No matter how it is."

She jerked as he tucked the head of his cock between the folds of her sex. Jerked and shuddered at the sensation of largeness pressing into her.

"This is what it's like," he whispered devilishly, bracing his knees against the bed as his powerful arms held his weight above her. "Just like this, Kei."

"Like this" was killing her. Her eyes widened as he began to work his cock inside her, stretching her in ways she had never known before, making her more and more aware of the toy in her rear.

"You feel it, don't you, sweetheart?" The dark croon fed the eroticism driving her now. "How much tighter, how much hotter it makes that sweet pussy. Pleasure bordering pain."

Her hands braced on his chest, her nails raking against his flesh as he worked deeper inside her. She couldn't stand it. Pleasure and pain were blooming inside her with equal force as her cries tore from her throat.

She wanted it to stop. She wanted it to go on forever.

"Take me, Kei," he groaned, his hips flexing. "Take all of me now."

She screamed out his name as he plunged inside the last inches.

Keiley stared up at him, dazed with an extremity of sensation, fighting to adjust to the width of his cock inside the tightened confines of her vagina. In her rear, her tissue spasmed around the toy as she felt Mac's erection throbbing inside her.

"God. You're so fucking tight." He grimaced as he flexed within her, his hips shifting, causing his cock to stretch her further. "Put your legs around me. Come on." He lifted one leg, guiding it to his hips before he lowered himself to his elbows. "Now. Now scream for me."

She screamed. She begged. As he began thrusting inside her, his strokes hard and relentless, driving her through sensations and a pleasure that bordered on insanity, Keiley screamed his name. She pleaded for release. She could feel it just a breath away as he drove her from one peak to the next, steadily building an ecstasy that when it exploded inside her left her writhing beneath him as he poured himself inside her.

And it still wasn't enough. She needed more, needed something she couldn't describe, couldn't understand. And Mac wasn't nearly finished, either. He turned to his back without releasing her, encouraging her to ride him to take her pleasure as one arm wrapped around her, the other gripping the toy in her rear and sending her into cataclysms of rapture.

The slight thrusting of the plug inside her in time to Mac's heavy thrusts between her thighs was too much. Weak, soaked with perspiration, and confused by the brutality of the pleasure driving her, she could only lay against his chest and let the orgasms tear through her. They were violent. Shaking through her, shuddering inside her until finally, with a muffled male cry, Mac was pumping his seed furiously into her swollen flesh as his arms held her tight to his chest.

Satiation was all-consuming, just as the hunger had been. She lay against him, quiet, feeling her heartbeat ease to a more normal rate as Mac finally lifted her from his chest to the bed.

"Okay?" He leaned over her, smoothing her hair from her forehead as he stared down at her in concern.

The sex warrior had eased from his expression, leaving the husband she knew in its place.

"No. I'm dead," she muttered. "Go away until I can think again."

He chuckled at that, moving to her hips as he turned her slowly to her side.

"What are you do—," she gasped as he eased the toy from her, shuddering with a whiplash of pleasure she shouldn't have had the energy to feel.

Then he was leaving the bed and padding into the bathroom. Seconds later she heard water running and sighed at the wishful thought of a shower. She was sweaty and weak, and the thought of dragging herself from the bed was only a distant wish.

"Come on, wildcat." The next thing she knew, Mac was picking her up and carrying her to the bathroom.

"I'm drained." She cuddled against his chest. "Just let me sleep."

"In a bit. Let's get you showered up first, then you can sleep all night."

She pouted as he set her on her feet beneath the warm spray, but the feel of the water sluicing over her exhausted flesh was just too damned good to bitch over it.

"Let me take care of you now, Kei." He pulled her against him once more before soaping a washrag and beginning to wash her gently. "I'll take care of everything."

It was beginning to occur to her that perhaps he was a bit more of a control freak than she had ever imagined.

"We're going to have to talk about this," she warned him.

"In the morning," he promised. "Tonight, just rest. Just let me hold you tonight."

There was no request in his voice. It was a demand, and her lips twitched.

She sighed. "I was right about you."

"How's that?"

"When I first met you, I told one of my coworkers you were like one of those storms that come up at sea all of a sudden. Powerful and wild. I don't know if I can keep up, Mac."

He turned her, staring down at her with dark, wary eyes.

"I'm not asking you to keep up," he finally said softly. "Just let me hold you through it. Unlike the storm, Keiley, I know what's precious to me. I promise not to let you drown."

"What if I can't give you what you want?"

A small smile tipped his lips. "I have no doubt you can give me exactly what I want and more. But if you need space, if you need time, we can discuss that."

They could discuss it? She tried to frown, but she was just too damned tired.

"And we will discuss it," she told him. "As soon as I find my mind again. I think you just blew it away."

"I'll help you find it." He kissed her head gently. "That and so much more, sweetheart. More than you could ever imagine."

CHAPTER SEVEN

She still couldn't find the dress and she didn't have time to search the rest of the house for it. Not that she would have had time to wash it before the meeting anyway.

When Keiley awoke the next morning it was much later than she had intended, leaving her only a few hours to dress for the meeting with the charity committee and head out the door.

Mac was already out of bed and obviously working, and as Keiley pulled on the charcoal sundress she chose to wear in place of the Egyptian cotton, she hoped Jethro was with him.

How was she going to manage to face either one of them today? The events of the night before felt more like a dream than reality, but she couldn't manage to convince herself that they had just been a strange little illusion.

Mac had held her, his hard body cushioning her back as another man kissed her. Not just another man, but his best friend. The man he was rumored to almost exclusively share his women with before his marriage.

The memory of it had her knees weakening as she buttoned the small pearl buttons that ran from the neckline to the hem of the summer dress.

The cotton blend was incredibly light and cool, the sleeveless straps crisscrossed at her back, and the skirt flowed to the midpoint above her knees. The bodice skimmed her breasts, but the material and cut of the design were flattering to her figure without being provocative.

She looked informally businesslike, she assured herself before heading from the bedroom.

She couldn't hear any movement in the house, which she hoped meant it was deserted. Rushing to her office, she grabbed her purse and leather briefcase. Opening the butter-soft leather satchel, she checked to make certain the check she had written out the night before for the booth for the charity committee was inside, as well as a copy of the map of the booths. She closed it and moved quickly from her office.

Rushing through the doorway, her head down to find the keys in her purse, she ran headlong into an immovable object.

The purse went flying. The briefcase fell to the floor, and Keiley looked up in shock to meet the wickedly amused gaze of her houseguest.

"This beats a 'good morning' any day of the week," he murmured, his fingers caressing her shoulders where he had caught her to steady her, his body pressed closely against her own.

Keiley felt frozen in place, staring up at him as contradictory emotions tore through her. She should run. She should stay. She shouldn't be frozen with arousal, confusion, and fear. And she sure as hell shouldn't be remembering that kiss the night before as his fingers had worked the snap of her jeans loose.

"I—" She swallowed tightly. "I have to leave."

His hands smoothed down her back, warm and calloused through the thin material of her dress. Heated flares of sensation snapped to life beneath her flesh as she felt a tremor ripple through her body.

Seduction. It scented the air, filled her senses, and slapped her with the knowledge that her body was responding.

Finally, she found the strength to push away from him, bending to grab her purse from the floor and tried to shove the items that had fallen back inside.

"Let me help you." He knelt in front of her, reaching for each item that she tried to capture, his fingers tangling with hers more than once before she managed to gather up the fallen items.

Men. God, they were like a plague of testosterone, and she felt like she was on overload after the night before.

"I could have done it myself," she muttered.

"But it wouldn't have been nearly as much fun," he assured her, smiling as he helped her to her feet, his hands gripping her shoulders firmly.

The memory of the night before glittered in his eyes, tightened his expression.

"I have to go." She gripped her purse and case as she moved to go around him.

"There's nothing to be embarrassed about, Keiley," he said then, his voice gentle as her gaze jerked back to his. "You're an incredibly passionate woman. There's no shame in sharing that passion."

"Don't start this with me, Jethro," she snapped, her eyes narrowing on the sensuality that seemed to bleed into his expression. "I don't have time for it."

Surprise gleamed in his eyes as a smile tugged at his lips. "You're a confrontational little thing, aren't you?"

"Only when confronted." She smiled tightly, moving quickly around him. "I'll see you and Mac later. I have to run."

And she was almost doing just that. Keiley breathed a sigh of relief minutes later as she drove the car down the narrow lane that led to the main road.

It was a welcome relief to leave the house today, to get away from Mac and Jethro, to find time to think. She needed the time to put this crazy situation into some kind of perspective within herself.

Keiley wasn't the type to lie to herself. She had done that once, lied to herself, buried her head in the sand and tried to pretend there was nothing wrong. That the nightmare her parents had created for her would just go away. It hadn't worked, and it had taught her a valuable lesson. Ignoring the little curves thrown her way wasn't going to work. One had to deal with them from the onset or pay the price later.

She was going to deal with this. First and foremost, she

was going to accept the fact that she had known all along that it was coming.

She had ignored the rumors about her husband. She had accepted his declaration that it was all in the past and hid from the burning curiosity as long as she could. Perhaps if she hadn't sensed the reason behind Mac's broodiness lately, then it wouldn't have come to this. Or if she had let him know from the first moment that it wasn't something she didn't want, then she could have avoided it.

Unconsciously, Keiley wondered if she hadn't pushed him because she was too curious about it. Because she had sensed the need rising inside him, and it had only made her more curious about the whole thing.

It was going to happen. She had known last night as Jethro's lips had touched hers that it would happen. She was going to allow her husband's best friend to become a third in their bed.

She was insane. Mac was insane.

Unfortunately, insanity wasn't contagious, so she couldn't blame Mac entirely for this. She was a grown woman, capable of putting her foot down and saying no. And Mac would accept it. He might get broody sometimes, he might fantasize about it, but he would have accepted it.

So why wasn't she doing it?

Because she wanted all of her husband. Because she was curious herself. Because she was honest enough with herself to admit that she had fantasized about it much too often herself in the past three years.

Fantasy and reality weren't meant to be mixed, though. What would happen to her marriage, to her dreams, if she allowed this to happen?

That was her fear. That somehow, some way, this would destroy the marriage that meant more to her than her own life.

Keiley gripped the steering wheel tighter as she made the turn onto the county road and headed to town. She had too much to do today to let this mess with her mind right now. If she didn't get her head on straight, then everyone at the meeting would be aware that something had her nerves on edge.

The last thing she needed right now was to allow that bunch of gossiping women to find out there was some kind of stress in her life other than them. From the day she had moved to Halifax County with Mac, she had sensed the keen interest of the community that had taken notice of her. Especially Delia Staten. That woman was dying to learn something that would hurt her and Mac.

Keiley wasn't the type to hide from society. She had immediately joined the business community as well as the charity organization that seemed to oversee all the various charity needs in the county.

Every preacher's wife and deacon's daughter seemed to be on the committee, though not all had joined the summer festival committee. The meeting Keiley was heading to was comprised of a little over a dozen women and headed by Victoria Leia Staten, one of the matriarchs of the county.

The committee board was headed by Mrs. Staten and included five other influential women. There wasn't a woman under fifty on the committee board except for Victoria's daughter-in-law, Delia, and their combined censure had the power to ostracize anyone from within their ranks and those of the community.

That was one of the things Keiley had had a hard time accepting when she first joined the charity committee. Those six women had an incredible amount of influence on both the social as well as the business community.

Morally upright, censorious, and sometimes judgmental, they could nevertheless make it extremely difficult for anyone whose business interests were based solely within Halifax County.

Not for the first time, Keiley was thankful that her and Mac's financial solvency wasn't dependent on the county. She was on the outside of that little group the way it was. The interloper, so to speak. The last thing she needed was to have those women decide they had any power over her.

This meeting was being held in the Staten mansion just outside Scotland Neck. The three-story plantation-style home had been restored to its former glory decades before and stood on a hill overlooking the town like a silent sentinel.

Keiley parked her car behind the dark blue Mercedes driven by one of the few women Keiley had become friends with. She stepped from her car and moved along the stone sidewalk alongside the driveway that led to the side of the mansion and the gardens where the members gathered before the meeting.

"Keiley, you're early for a change." Maxine Bright detached herself from the small group of women who threw Keiley friendly waves before going back to their conversation.

Maxine was a powerhouse of energy. Five feet six inches tall with flaming red hair and bright green eyes. The wife of the most influential banker in town, Joseph Bright. He was also quiet, thoughtful, and seemed to adore the cheerful, effervescent women he had married.

"Max, you look gorgeous." Keiley smiled as her gaze went over the chocolate-colored linen dress her friend wore.

Max's vivid red hair was pulled back into a low ponytail, the corkscrew curls trailing halfway down her back from the large matching bow.

"Joey liked it, too." Max waggled her brows as she caught Keiley's arm and practically dragged her into the gardens. "I had to take it back off and iron it before I ever made it out of the house."

Keiley barely restrained her surprised laughter. Unrestrained sex and Joseph Bright didn't seem to go hand in hand.

"Lucky woman," Kei murmured. "Mac was already out of the house working before I even woke up."

"And his friend who's visiting?" Max whispered. "Was he working, too?"

"Damn, news travels fast in this county," Keiley laughed. "He just showed up yesterday."

"I hear he drives a flashy bright red Mustang and wears mirrored sunglasses. He has a bad-boy grin and muscles a woman would drool over."

Keiley arched her brow as she accepted a glass of sweet iced tea from one of the housemaids.

"What did he do? Stop and pose for the masses on his way in?" She chuckled.

Max snickered at the image as well. "I heard all about him the minute I stepped into the garden this afternoon. Everyone was certain I'd know all the best gossip where you're concerned. You didn't tell me about him. Why?" Max pouted good-naturedly.

"Even I didn't know he was showing up until the day before yesterday." She shook her head at how quickly news had reach the group that she and Mac had company. "He's a friend of Mac's from Virginia. We haven't seen him since the wedding."

"And the rumors that he and Mac used to enjoy sharing girlfriends? Laura Tolbert is all agog over that little piece of information. Being the resident slut, you know how bad this is going to make her look." Beneath that laughing amusement was an edge of concern in Max's gaze.

Keiley blinked back at her in shock. "Are you kidding me?"

She could feel her heartbeat accelerating, a sick feeling of panic filling her stomach before she straightened her shoulders and fought it back.

Damn, how had something like that gotten out?

"I haven't found out where that little gem of information came from yet." Max lowered her voice as they moved further away from the other women and their curious looks. "It was an amusing little on-dit they were giggling over. Thankfully, no one seems to be taking it seriously. But you know how Delia Staten can be. So watch your back."

Delia Staten was Victoria's daughter-in-law. A pious, moralistic pain in the ass.

"Good God," Keiley muttered. "I wonder what would happen if I ever invited one of my friends up for a visit."

"You would instantly become a lesbian with plans to divorce Mac for your girlfriend rather than just becoming the tasty filling for a male sandwich," Max snickered.

Keiley couldn't contain the blush that rose in her cheeks.

"Now don't get upset." Max smiled as she laid her hand on Keiley's arm. "You know how the chickies are in this bunch, sweetheart. Though I have to admit, someone outdid themselves this time. Normally the gossip isn't nearly as interesting. Maybe they're getting bored with the whole cheating-with-the-husband's-best-friend angle. The three-some sounds much more fun."

"Not to mention much more tiring." Keiley rolled her eyes, forcing herself to treat the information as a rabid joke rather than the truth it was.

As Max had said, normally she wouldn't have had to worry about anything more than a little gossip that she was getting some on the side.

"I wouldn't worry about it." Max waved it away. "Everyone here mourned the day Mac married outside the county and cut off the potentially juicy sex details they could have gotten. It's a compliment. They at least believe you're too refined to cheat."

"Oh joy."

"But be on guard," Max warned her. "Delia is heading this way and she looks like a woman on a mission."

Keiley was ready to walk out. She had sworn she would never subject herself to the petty viciousness of people like Delia Staten again. The same type of woman who had helped destroy her life years ago. And yet here she was, turning as Delia approached and pasting a welcoming smile on her face.

Delia had once been a pretty woman, and she could be again if she would take the pinched look of judge and jury off her long, slender face. Thick brown hair with russet tones was pulled sharply back from her face into a tight French braid. Minimal makeup showed the lines at the sides of her eyes and lips, and her brown eyes glittered with bitter anger.

She was thirty-five years old, but she looked ten years older.

"Keiley, dear, how are you doing?" The older woman's smile was all teeth as she approached. "You're early today, too."

It wasn't as though she was ever late, damn it.

"Mac was otherwise occupied on the farm this morning when I woke up." Keiley smiled calmly. "He didn't distract me."

Delia's lips tightened. It was no secret that the other woman had seen Mac as a potential husband years before. Instead he had left town and headed to Virginia after his high school graduation. Evidently, no woman married to Mac would ever be safe from her hatred after that. She had definitely spent the last three years looking for ways to spite Keiley.

"I hear you have company." Her brown eyes were alight with cruel interest. "Very handsome company."

"News travels fast. One of Mac's friends from Virginia. He stopped by for a visit while he was on vacation."

"And how long will he be staying?"

"Why, I don't know, Delia. He and Mac didn't say. But you raise a point. I really should ask. I was busy working and didn't even think to question them." She widened her eyes innocently as she stared back at Delia. "Sometimes Mac doesn't think to tell me his plans."

Delia's eyes narrowed, though a tight smile curled her lips. "Yes. He does have that habit."

Keiley almost winced. She hadn't meant to prick at the past, but obviously she had. Mac hadn't informed Delia when he left town all those years ago. He had just packed up and left, and Delia Staten had never forgiven him.

Keiley reminded herself mockingly to have a talk with him about not informing the *world* next time he decided to make a personal decision.

At that point, Max broke in. "Keiley, I saw the updates you did to the charity Web site. They're gorgeous," she stated. "Didn't she do a wonderful job, Delia?"

"I haven't checked." Delia's lips were pinched with distaste at this point. "If you'll excuse me now, it's nearly time to call the meeting to session. Good day, ladies."

Delia turned and swept across the stone-lined patio in a cloud of flowery perfume and acrid disapproval.

"That is one mean old bitch," Max muttered. "What the hell is going on, Kei? I'm almost afraid to let Joey's brother come stay the summer now. He's divorced, ya know?"

Keiley breathed out roughly. "Maybe it's that 'outsider' thing again?" She turned to Max and rolled her eyes. "Maybe I'll get lucky and they'll toss me off the charity committee. You could run my booth *and* yours."

Max narrowed her eyes in promised retaliation. "Don't even consider it, girlfriend. I'd hate to have to hurt you bad."

Keiley snickered. "I could always tell Delia about your toy chest."

Max's eyes widened as mock horror swept over her face. "She would have a stroke. And Joey would certainly have a meltdown. He can barely say the word *vibrator*."

"Knows how to use it, though, doesn't he?" Kei snickered as she linked her arm with her friend's and headed to the house. "That's all that matters. Right?"

"Oh hell, yeah," Max sighed in remembered bliss. "Who cares if he can say the word as long as that bad boy can do the deed?"

They were laughing as they entered the sunroom, but inside Keiley could feel the worry beginning to build. She didn't believe in coincidence. Coincidence didn't account for the rumor that Mac and his friend were now sharing her bed. Somehow, someone knew something.

Perhaps one of the farmhands? Keiley wondered. Had someone overheard something?

They couldn't have. The farmhands lived off the farm, they came in the morning and left in the evening. They couldn't have seen or overheard anything.

But what else?

She was aware of the interested looks she received through the meeting as well as a general air of speculation. She hated it. But even as she hated it, feared it, it began to piss her off. She wasn't a child anymore. And by God, these people had no control over her life now.

Jethro had been at the house one night. One damned

night. They had no right to begin gossiping so soon. To want to see her ostracized so easily.

These women whom she had laughed with for the past three years, whom she had helped at various times. She had babysat for several of them. She had helped out in Lissa Ryker's store when she had been sick last year. She had helped Beulah Paddington the month before in her florist shop. At one time or the other, Keiley had lent a hand to each of these women, and yet they were whispering about her.

Max was one of the few whom Keiley doubted was joining in the gossipfest. Max generally waved gossip to the side and treated it like an amusing little joke.

By the time the meeting came to an end and Keiley had received her receipt for the booth she had rented in the charity's name, she was more than ready to head home. Paranoia was beginning to get the best of her. She was feeling so paranoid that as she headed for the doors she came to an abrupt stop, certain she had heard something she couldn't have heard.

Ménages. The insidiously muttered word had her freezing before she whirled around, searching the small group of women behind her.

They appeared innocent, chatting among themselves, though she couldn't hear what they were saying.

Shaking her head, Keiley moved quickly from the house and to her car, certain that her own imagination at this point was making her hear things that hadn't been said.

Grimacing at her own overactive imagination, she strode quickly to her car, unlocked the door, and moved into the stifling interior before turning the key and lowering the windows.

As she drove from the Staten mansion, she was pensive. The ringing of the cell phone at her side dragged her out of her thoughts as she flipped it open and brought it to her ear.

"Hello?"

"Kei, let's take lunch in town." Max's cheerful voice came over the connection. "Joey's mother has the kids and I can bum around all day if I want to."

Keiley grinned. "I'm game. Where do you want to meet?"

"I'm sick of the Goody Two-shoes," Max snorted. "Let's hit Casey's outside of town. We can enjoy a beer in peace rather than having to pretend enjoy that sucky wine we'll have to stick to in town."

"Your roots are showing, Max," Keiley teased her. "Better be careful or Delia will learn your daddy worked the dock-yards before he came to Scotland Neck with all that money."

"I could only get so lucky," Max retorted dryly. "Just think of all the bullshit I could get out of that way. Old Victoria Staten wouldn't harass my husband whenever I didn't sign up for her little pet orgs anymore."

The charity "orgs," or organizations. Keiley laughed in genuine amusement.

"I'll meet you there," she promised her. "If you get there first, order my beer. I'm going to need it."

"No kidding," Max agreed with her. "The place was like a school of sharks moving in for the kill. Maybe I need two beers. I'll see you in a few."

"In a few." Keiley hung up, frowning at the edge in Max's voice. Just what the hell had gotten into those damned women on the charity committee? At this rate, she wouldn't have to worry about working a booth at the festival because she would be blacklisted before she bought the supplies.

She sighed wearily. Maybe the planets or something were just out of phase. What else could explain it?

CHAPTER EIGHT

"Okay, what do you have?" Mac sat down at his desk and powered up his laptop as Jethro opened his own at the side of the desk.

"Dell hasn't been able to track down anything on our play-boy," Jethro said. "That boy just doesn't have what it takes to investigate sex crimes. He doesn't have a clue."

"Neither did I," Mac grunted.

"Only because you left too soon," Jethro grunted as Mac opened the P2P port between the two computers to access the information Jethro had brought with him.

"You think it's a sex crime, then?" Mac asked. That had been Mac's specialty.

"Our boy is working himself up to it."

"What makes you think I left too soon, then?" Mac asked.

"This." Jethro pulled up the information on his laptop. "What we have is a stalker that likes to play games. His female victims are the pawns, but what he's after are the knights."

"You're screwing your chess up, Jeth," Mac growled. "Women are queens, the men are the kings. Stalkers are always after the queens."

"Not in this case," Jethro said. "Were you aware that the first victim's husband was in law enforcement?"

Mac nodded. "That's how I got the case."

"Did you also know that each of the victims' husbands were or had been involved in investigations involving stalkers or sexual predator cases with a high rate of success?"

Mac leaned back in his chair and stared back at Jethro with narrowed eyes.

"I questioned her husband rather than her first. The stalking began during the period of time that her husband was involved in a similar case. She was active online. A well-respected accountant with several influential clients. We think she was targeted here." An open chat forum popped up on the computer screen. "This is the Advanced Electronics open business forum. They hire various professionals to come in to give advice to whoever pops in. Registration is minimal. Our other two victims were hit here." Another forum popped up, similar in design and intent. "And here." Yet another forum window pulled up. "From what I've been able to figure out, the three victims were the only ones who reported the stalking at the time. We had four others who didn't report it because it eventually went away."

"Were the four victims' husbands involved in similar cases?" Mac asked.

"Two of them were married. One was divorced; one was single. All with spouses, exes, or lovers in investigative fields. He played with those, though not to the same extent. Missing or moved personal articles during a span of two to four months on the unreported four as well as those reported. Then a farewell e-mail that clued them in to the fact that they were being played with. Scared the hell out of them, but when it never occurred again, they went on with their lives."

"He went further with the three who reported the stalking," Mac mused.

"Began the same, though," Jethro pointed out. "Missing and moved items. These are organized professional women. They don't just move or lose items. But suddenly they can't find a tube of lipstick, a favorite shirt, or car keys. He's found easy access into their homes, despite the fact that they were married. He finds a way to watch them or listen in. These women, three pictures popped up, were also in the process of becoming involved in relationships with investigators. These three he began e-mailing, harassing online, and embarrassing them during their online forums."

Mac shook his head. "Embarrassing them how?"

"Personal or Professional Secrets. Intimate details of their lives and so on," Jethro reported.

Narrowing his eyes, Mac stared at the screens on the computer, flipping between the statements, pictures, and vitals of the victims and their spouses. "Each husband or boyfriend was involved in the security field. A private investigator, two cops, a security analyst, two bodyguards, and a former investigator."

"He fixated on the men's career fields," Jethro pointed out.

Mac stared at the screen thoughtfully. "The three women he fixated on strongest were the private investigator's and the two cops' wives. Men he would consider better able to protect their women. Is it a sex crime? Or is he trying to prove to himself and to these men that he's the better man? It's a power trip that goes beyond sex. He's striking at the men and punishing the women for what he considers their incompetence." Mac leaned forward as he typed in the commands that would pull up more information on the seven women. "The three who had no spouses had boyfriends, and they were the earliest occurrences. He was just stepping in here."

Mac wished he had had this information when he first started on the case three years ago. He had only started the investigation with the first victim who had been violently attacked.

"The last, fourth one he attacked just before I resigned. Her husband was a private investigator. It went on longer than the others, escalated in stages. First the missing items, then online attacks. Then the physical attack. Then he just drops out until the past six months. That's two and a half years of silence. Why?"

"Where the hell did you get this program?" Jethro was leaning over his shoulder as Mac typed in commands. "This isn't the standard one we're using at the Bureau."

Mac's smile was smug. "Keiley fiddled with it a time or two. I normally use it for the farm, but it's applicable in damned near any field. All I have to do is give it the commands and search criteria and it pulls from the files I command. Or—" He hit another key. "We search the Internet with the same criteria that's already been loaded in. That takes awhile, though."

Mac leaned back in his chair, frowning as Jethro moved back to the side of the desk and pulled a chair close. He could feel something niggling at the back of his mind, but couldn't bring it into focus.

His gaze went over the files pulled up at present as he minimized the program to work in the background.

"Why haven't there been any attacks from when I gave the case to Dell up until the last six months?" he questioned absently. "It's been three years."

"Maybe he moved. The attacks could have gone on elsewhere without our being aware of it."

"Possibly," he murmured. But it didn't feel right. That was the problem with this investigation to begin with. Too many things just didn't feel right once he began the investigation.

"Have you had another profile worked up on him?"

Jethro shook his head. "We only had the three instances to work on until I found the other four recently. The director wanted more information before we went back to the profiler."

"This isn't a sex crime, Jethro." Mac could feel it. It was something else, something more dangerous. "And he wouldn't just stop. He would go on, and the attacks would get worse. He wants to prove something."

"So we're looking at someone who couldn't get into the investigative field for whatever reason?"

Mac nodded. "Someone who managed to get in close to the victims. Close enough to gain access into their homes. Call Dell, have him interview these victims again. Get a list of close friends and family who could have had that access. Let's see what we get when we run the names."

"That will take awhile, too," Jethro pointed out.

There was a warning flaring in his gut that didn't make sense.

"Have him get started on it. We could get a strike early."

"I only have a few days' enforced vacation left." Jethro leaned back in his chair. "I've been considering a real vacation. I'll put in for a few weeks' leave if you can work this with me. It might give us an advantage if Dell's working the information and we follow it from here."

Mac tapped his fingers against the arm of the chair. "Do it." He finally nodded, not certain why the tingling in the back of his neck was becoming an itch. "It's going to take a couple of days for Kei's program to finish running the Internet and then we'll need a few days to clear out the extraneous junk it pulls in. When it's finished, we'll see what we have."

Mac stared at his computer, his eyes still narrowed, working through the information that had come up so far.

"I'll work up a list of questions for Dell to take with him," he told Jethro. "He's a good field agent, but he's not the best when it comes to questioning victims."

"No shit," Jethro murmured. "I hadn't had time to fully investigate all seven victims and their associations."

"You would have soon." Mac breathed out heavily. "What concerns me is the silence between my last case and six months ago. The four cases took place in the Alexandria-D.C. area within a period of four years. Then nothing after that until the last three. I wonder where he went?"

"With any luck, Keiley's genius will pull that one out." Jethro nodded at Mac's computer. "Too bad we can't hook into the law enforcement databases with that baby."

"It would take years," Mac sighed. "Keiley keeps threatening to fine-tune it, but she hasn't figured out how to make it work through millions of cases amid dozens of agencies. We'll be waiting days just on Web and newspaper hits in the Virginia-Maryland area. Reach out further and you're waiting weeks and months."

"The more you narrow the criteria, the quicker it gets?" Jethro asked.

Mac nodded. "But at this point, there's not enough information to find a single common denominator other than the spouses who are in the investigative field. The amount of key words I've had to use will fill the program with junk as well. But it could give us a clue. Something else to move on."

"At this point, anything would help." Jethro shrugged. "I'll contact Dell and get him to work on the additional information. And pray he doesn't go to the director."

Mac grinned. "Dell won't go to the director. He'll just demand credit."

"He can have the credit."

Mac glanced at Jethro sharply. The edge of frustration in Jethro's voice was telling.

"You've about had it, haven't you?" he asked his friend, seeing the signs clearly.

"I stay suspended more often than I'm at my desk. It's becoming a pain in the ass."

"So stop beating the shit out of the perps," Mac suggested.

"Might as well tell me to stop breathing. Sons of bitches. We spend months, years, working to catch them and the next thing you know some wing-tipped fancy-pants lawyer has them out on a technicality. That or a witness disappears and turns up dead or suddenly information is corrupted and the bastards are back on the streets destroying lives again. It pisses me off, Mac."

Yeah, it pissed Mac off, too. It was one of the reasons he had resigned and come back to the farm. Keiley and the temptation Sinclair's Club afforded hadn't been the only reasons. They had been prevailing reasons, but there had been others.

"Cameron's firm is doing well," Mac pointed out, referring to Jethro's cousin, the investigator for Sinclair. "He's been after you for years to join him."

"I'm thinking about it." Jethro propped his feet on the desktop as he leaned back further into the chair. "The new director doesn't appreciate my unique abilities," he grunted sarcastically. "Resigning beats being fired any day of the week."

Mac shook his head. Jethro was the bad boy of the Bureau, there had never been any doubt about that.

"I saw Keiley this afternoon before she left." Jethro said, changing the subject yet again. "She was nervous as hell."

Mac felt his body clench in sudden arousal.

"Did she mention last night?"

"She didn't mention it, but she was remembering it. That was a hell of a chance you took last night."

Mac was well aware of the chances he was taking with his marriage. He didn't need Jethro to point it out to him.

"I'll take care of my marriage, Jethro," Mac sighed as he slid his chair back and rose to his feet. "See what else you can pull out of Dell. I have work to do outside."

"Need any help?" Jethro asked instead. "I'll get more out of Dell tonight after he goes home. That leaves the day pretty free."

Mac glanced at the clock. Keiley was due home anytime, unless she decided to take lunch with any of the women on the charity committee, which she sometimes she did. Her friendship with Maxine Bright seemed to be growing, and with it, Keiley had begun settling into country life much easier than he had anticipated.

Maxine was a good woman. She and her husband, Joseph, were two of the few friends from high school Mac had kept up with over the years. Joseph had kept him up with local gossip and helped with investments enough to make certain that when he made the move home, he would have the cushion he needed to make the farm thrive.

Of course, Mac hadn't anticipated at the time that he would marry a woman whose hobby was as lucrative as Keiley's career. The woman thought it was fun to play with computer programs, where Mac tended to pull hair when he had to mess with them overmuch.

"Come on, then," he finally answered Jethro's suggestion to help with the farm work. "I have to move some cattle and check on my favorite mare. The foal she's getting ready to throw is a potential moneymaker. I like to baby her."

"You baby all the females," Jethro grunted as he rose to his feet. "That's why they all love you."

"And you just wash over them like a tidal wave," Mac shot back. "Scares the hell out of them, Jethro. That bad-boy persona needs a little adjustment here and there."

"My adjustments are fine."

"I can tell. You're currently without a steady lover. Not like you, my man."

"It's just a slump."

"Be careful, it might become a way of life."

Keiley slammed the front door, kicked her sandals to the side of the entryway, and threw her purse and briefcase on the small chair that sat to the side.

Maxine had been a fountain of information once they were well away from the women of the charity committee. And that fount was filled with small-town politics and petty jealousies. She had tried to ignore Delia's pettiness for three years, but it was now getting out of control.

Watch your back, Kei. Delia never forgave Mac for leaving town and not marrying her. She hates you. And she's determined to hurt you. I don't know what she's up to, but she's gloating and so are her little chickies that she runs with.

Insanity. Delia had married one of the richest and most influential men in the state of North Carolina, and she was still pissed off about the one who got away.

How had Delia known about the sharing Jethro and Mac had done in Virginia? Who did she know?

"Keiley?" Mac stepped from the hallway that led to the washroom and kitchen from the back of the house. "What's wrong?"

"Did you fuck her before you left all those years ago?" She suddenly snapped. "Is that why she decided to make my life hell? Because she never forgot her first fuck?"

His eyes widened as he moved closer. "Did I fuck who?"

"Delia Staten." Her hands went on her hips as she confronted him. "And who in this little neck of the woods, Mac, knew about your and Jethro's little high jinks in Virginia?"

Surprise glittered in his eyes then. "No one here knows, Kei."

"Someone knows Mac, or they're psychic, because the latest little piece of gossip to reach Delia Staten is that you and Jethro are now sharing me."

She watched as he tensed, his broad shoulders appearing wider, his chest beneath the gray t-shirt he wore appearing wider.

"They're guessing."

"Oh, you suddenly believe in coincidence now, Mac?" she asked him tightly. "Weren't you the one who told me more than once that there was no such thing as coincidence?"

"The rules are different in small towns, Kei." He grimaced roughly. "Here, rumor and supposition are a game all their own, sweetheart, you know that."

"They're gossiping about me, Mac," she whispered. "Hell, I haven't even done anything yet and they're gossiping about me."

She raised her hand as he started toward her, his expression suddenly quiet, thoughtful.

"I need to change clothes. Shower. Think." She shook her head as she headed for the stairs. "I'll be down later to fix dinner."

"Keiley." He caught her arm as she headed to the stairs.

Keiley stared at his fingers wrapped around her wrist before lifting her gaze slowly to Mac.

"I said I need to think," she told him icily. "I will not step into this little game you and Jethro want to play without considering where it will go and how it will end. Don't make the mistake of thinking you can alpha me into this, Mac."

"Alpha you?" His brow arched. "Is this another word for force?"

"It's another word for all this supersexy dominance you think you can suddenly control me with. The dominance doesn't control me, Mac. You don't control that. And you won't use it to get what you want until I decide it's what I want. Do you understand me?"

His other hand moved, lightning fast, cupping the back of her head as his fingers speared into her hair.

"Understand me," he said then with heavy sensuality as he pulled her closer, his lips a hairsbreadth from hers, stroking them, reminding her of his kiss last night, of the fiery storm that had overtaken her. "Our sex life is just that. Ours. I'll take care of Delia. I'll take care of anyone, anywhere, who decides my business is theirs."

Keiley gasped as he pulled her to him then, one arm going around her back as the other hand held her head in place and his lips covered hers.

Like the night before. Like every kiss they had ever shared combined into one. The heat that blazed from it was searing. The feel of his tongue controlling hers, his lips holding hers, his powerful chest beneath her palms.

She couldn't touch him enough. He couldn't kiss her enough.

Her hands pushed up his chest, twined in his hair, pulled him closer to her. Dragged him closer into the kiss, tried to climb into him.

Damn him. Damn her. A whimper left her throat as her back met the wall and Mac lifted her to him.

Rage and fear flowed through her. Rage at Delia Staten for daring to strike at where she was most vulnerable. Fear because she had been struck. And hunger. Oh, God, the hunger he inspired in her was too much to bear. It burned through the anger and the fear. It wrapped her in white-hot wonder, filled her with blistering pleasure.

"I tried to be what I thought a good husband should be," he snarled as he drew back from her, one hand covering her neck before moving to the buttons at the bodice of her dress. "I tried to give you what I thought you deserved."

Buttons were falling away beneath his fingers as a storm raged in his eyes.

"What do I deserve?" She arched against him, one leg rising to hook at his hip, to draw closer to the steel-hard bulge beneath his jeans.

"Everything." The material fell back to reveal the black lace pushup bra she wore beneath the dress. "You deserve everything I can give you. Every touch. Every cry of pleasure, every whisper of sensuality that I can give you."

"And you know how to give it all?" she panted, her head falling back against the wall as his lips trailed down her neck.

His head lifted slowly. "I know how to make certain you get it all," he amended.

Keiley licked at her lips, feeling the blood pounding through her body, pleasure ripping over her nerve endings. She was so aroused, so wet now, so desperate for everything his eyes promised that it terrified her.

"No matter how it destroys us?"

He shook his head slowly. "I would never let anything destroy you, Keiley. Ever. I'll always shelter you."

His love sheltered her. She had known that from the beginning, from the first night when he had looked into her eyes and told her he was hers forever.

"You're my forever," she reminded him then.

"Always," he promised, his lips touching hers once more.

"I need to think." She closed her eyes against the promise in his eyes. "I can't just—do this."

"There's nothing to do, sweetheart." He caught her bottom lip, licked at it, nipped it before slowly releasing her and stepping back.

"Nothing to do?"

He shook his head slowly, the overly long black strands caressing his neck as she wanted to caress it with her lips.

"Just be you, Kei," he said gently. "All you. It's about your pleasure, honey. It's about what makes you burn, makes you scream for more. It's about your fantasies and desires. I'm just your guide."

"My guide," she breathed out roughly as she clutched the edges of her dress together and stepped toward the stairs. "You're not guiding me, Mac. I feel more like a very small boat riding a tidal wave."

"Become the wave, baby." He grinned. "It's real easy."

"So is drowning, I'm told." Shaking her head, she started up the stairs, praying her legs would hold her. "I'm taking a shower. I'll see you later."

"Keiley." His voice stopped her as she started up the stairs.

Turning, she stared back at him, almost shivering at the power in his expression, the sensuality and pure unadulterated lust.

"Don't think this to death. Thinking about it will only make it seem frightening, and more than what it is. And no matter what gossip Delia Staten wants to start, no one will know but the three of us. No one, Kei."

She nodded slowly. "As I said, I'll think about it."

"You do that," he murmured. "And I'll keep seducing."

She waved her hand back at him as she moved up the stairs. "Go harass Jethro. I'm too tired and aggravated to deal with you."

Mac watched her go with a smile. The short little skirt of her dress skimmed over her perky little butt and swished above her knees. It wasn't the cutest little summer dress she had, but it did wonders for her lightly tanned legs and bare feet.

She was the most honestly sensual woman he had ever met in his life. Nothing like Delia Madden Staten. Even at twenty, Delia had been a calculating witch. She had been determined to possess him, and Mac had been just as determined to foil her plans.

Hell, that had been more than fifteen years ago. He hadn't returned to Scotland Neck until he came back with his wife. And it seemed Delia was still holding a grudge.

"I remember telling you that small-town life would make you nuts, Mac," Jethro drawled from the end of the hallway.

Mac ran his hand over his jaw. "I'll deal with Delia if I have to. If that doesn't work I'll talk to her mother-in-law. Victoria used to be reasonable."

"You're going to talk to mommy-in-law?" Jethro snickered.

"Mommy-in-law could chew you up and spit you out for breakfast," Mac informed him as he restrained a shudder. "But she can be reasonable."

"And if she's not?"

Mac's smile became feral then. "Then I pull out the badge and put the fear of the Bureau in their asses. If that doesn't work, then you can bring the Bureau down on them. With Delia, subtlety doesn't work so well."

He should know. He had tried subtle from the age of sixteen to eighteen with the manipulating little witch. What Delia couldn't possess, she tried to destroy. He had learned that lesson well during their youths.

Mac had recognized the trait in her easily enough. She reminded him much too much of his father. The rabid determination to win at all costs and to possess rather than to love.

"Maybe I should slip into town tonight and see what I can see. Hear what I can hear." Jethro moved through the foyer toward the stairs. "Loan me the Harley. Dollars to donuts I come back with info."

"But will you come back with the Harley?" Mac grimaced.

"We'll both return unharmed," Jethro promised with that damned smug smile of his.

"It's not you I'm worried about, bro," Mac growled as he pulled the key from the key ring he dug out of his pocket. "That Harley is second only to Keiley. Take care of her or you die."

Jethro flipped him the finger as Mac flipped him the key.

"Keep the bird in hand, Jeth, and the Harley on her wheels."

"She'll fly like a bird and land like a cloud," Jethro promised on his way out the door. "Like a cloud."

Mac winced. Jethro and motorcycles, they were chancy things. He just prayed his friend took better care of his Harley than he did of his own.

CHAPTER NINE

Keiley stood beneath the shower's spray, allowing the warm water to wash over her as she leaned her head back, allowing the water to soak her hair.

Her body was incredibly sensitive, her rear still tender from the night before, her flesh tingling with the memory of the dominance he had displayed. He knew his own hungers, and it seemed he had guessed hers far better than she could have imagined.

Because she had fantasized. From the day she had heard the first rumors about his supposed membership in the very exclusive men's club in Virginia, and had met his friend Jethro, she had fantasized.

She had imagined Mac's lips and hands caressing her. Holding her. Restraining her as Jethro moved between her thighs. Or the other way around. The two men controlling her passion and her responses until she was screaming, begging for release.

She closed her eyes, gritting her teeth as she felt the ache in her clit and her vagina build. Mac had fueled the latent arousal simmering inside her all day. The strength of his body and his lust as he trapped her against the wall downstairs had her creaming furiously. And yet it had her pulling back.

She had seen the deliberate restraint in Mac's face then, and realized he had been employing that restraint for more than three years. She had sensed it, and for a long time she had refused to tempt it. But for the past year she had been dealing with her own restlessness. With the need to push that careful control she knew Mac was employing.

Had she known what it would come to?

Shaking her head, Keiley quickly washed her hair before soaping a sponge and washing her body. She felt too restless, her flesh too sensitive.

Her marriage was changing, and she could feel it. The implications of it kept her on edge. She wished she could say Mac was changing, but she had a feeling that all he was really doing was removing the kid gloves he had touched her with all these years. It was up to her to decide now if she could love and still live with the man he really was, rather than the man he had let her see.

If she could handle his hungers.

The ménage wasn't an either/or. She had no doubts that if she said no, he would respect it. He wouldn't force her. He would try to seduce her. But if he sensed for even a second that she didn't truly want it, then he would draw back. The sex would still be harder. Mac would still let the darker part of himself free.

Unfortunately, she couldn't convince herself that she didn't want this. And her fantasies over the years assured her that she did want it. With Mac. She wanted every sensual, forbidden promise she had seen in his eyes in the past three days.

Rinsing quickly, she shut the water off before wrapping a large towel around her body and stepping from the shower. A quick blow-dry of her hair before she brushed it in place quickly and dried off with swift, economical movements.

Opening the medicine cabinet door, she reached inside for the small bottle of scent she used, only to come up empty-handed. Bending, she looked inside on the shelf before pulling out the drawer beneath it.

There it was, along with her missing comb.

Shaking her head, she pulled the perfume free, spritzed it over her body, then placed it back on the shelf before pulling the comb free and placing it back on the small silver shelf on the sink. She knew she had searched that drawer the other day for the comb.

Which reminded her, after dinner she was going to have to find her dress. It had to be in the washroom somewhere. How she had managed to misplace it she couldn't figure out.

After pulling on a white lacy thong and a matching bra, Keiley dressed in a pair of light cotton summer pants that went over her hip bones and a loose-knit top with a dozen small wooden buttons holding the edges together. It was sleeveless but loose and comfortable.

She didn't have the nerve to wear the low-riding snug cut-offs and short t-shirts she normally wore around the house in the summer. She had learned the day Mac took her against the tractor exactly what those clothes could do to his libido. Not that she hadn't wanted to tease him, torture him a little for missing the surprise dinner she had planned. But she had a feeling that tonight wasn't the night to push his hunger. Or Jethro's.

With her feet encased in light socks, and a bit more relaxed than she had been earlier, Keiley moved from the bedroom and headed back downstairs. No doubt Mac was back outside working somewhere, which would give her a few hours of peace to get dinner on and finish a few things around the house.

Maybe it would even give her time to repair the break in her own defenses that Delia Staten had caused. She couldn't excuse the rumors to coincidence. Delia had been too gloating, too certain.

But she wasn't a child anymore, she told herself. And she wasn't breaking the law or bringing humiliation down on an innocent family. This was her marriage, and it was her business.

As she straightened the house and ran the sweeper she let the pros and cons of this changing relationship whip through her mind. At the end of the day it came to one thing, though: Mac had made her curious. His and Jethro's touches had made her more aroused than she had ever thought possible. When it was all said and done, she knew that in the end, it was going to happen. And what happened from there she had no idea.

One thing she was starting to believe to the bottom of her soul was that Mac was definitely going to make it an adventure.

"Wes," Mac called out to the trainer as he entered the shadowed interior of the stables and looked around with narrowed eyes. He knew he had seen the other man step in here moments ago.

Wes Bridges, the trainer, he had hired for the Thoroughbreds he raised on the farm, was a solitary person, but he was a damned good horse trainer.

"Wes!" The snicker of the horses was his only greeting for long moments.

"Mr. McCoy?" The stout little man stepped from the tack room, a frown creasing his face as he wiped his hands on a damp rag and stepped into the wide center aisle of the stables. "Can I help you, sir?"

Dark brown hair fell over his creased brow, nearly hiding his matching eyes. Everything about Wes was dark, from his hair to his sun-baked leathery skin.

"I have a buyer coming in from Kentucky in the next few days to look at Storm Wind. He'll want you to be available in case he has any questions." Wes had a bad habit of disappearing whenever buyers arrived.

"I'll have her ready." Wes shifted nervously as he usually did whenever he talked to anyone other than the horses.

"Make sure you're here with her, Wes," he ordered. "Disappear on me again and we're going to have words."

Wes blinked back at him. "I'll be here, sir."

"Good." He nodded as he stared around the neat stalls and the glossy, well-cared-for animals.

Wes was a stickler for keeping the stables in perfect condition. He frowned on anyone messing around in them, even Mac.

"Is that all, sir?" Wes asked. "I was cleaning tack in the back room, if you don't need anything else."

"That should be all." Mac nodded shortly as he stepped

over to the stall that held his favorite mare and rubbed her neck gently.

Grace had been his first buy, and her first foal had made him a mint. She was fast as the wind, and as graceful as her name implied.

"Mr. McCoy, have you noticed any strange goin'-ons around here?" Wes asked nervously as he started to turn back to the tack room.

Mac paused, his palm pressing against Grace's neck as he frowned back at the trainer.

"Such as?"

Wes scratched at his grizzled cheek. "Well, that dog of yours, Pappy?"

Mac frowned. Pappy was the farm dog, a mutt of undetermined heritage who had made the farm his home just after he and Keiley had taken up residence. Mac suspected there was some shepherd in the rangy animal, but he couldn't be certain.

He glanced out the door of the stables to where he had seen the dog earlier. Pappy was still laying in his usual spot in the spot just outside the backyard.

Mac turned back to the trainer. "What about him?"

"Well, last coupla weeks, I've come in to find him cowerin' here in the stables. Pappy's always slept on the porch till daybreak, ain't he?"

That had to be the most Wes had ever spoken to him. But he was right; Pappy had always slept on the porch.

"An' I noticed, too, he don't like being petted like he used to. Used to let me rough him up whenever I had time. Now he shies away from me."

"I'll check him out." Mac nodded in concern. "Thanks for letting me know."

Wes shrugged. "Just missed having him trail after me sometimes."

"Have you noticed anything else out of the ordinary?" Mac asked him then, feeling a warning tension growing within him.

Wes paused again. "Well, Grace's stall bein' opened a time or two when I come in of the morning. Just little things that could be nothin' other than that."

Little things. Coincidences. Mac felt the hair on the back of his neck tingle.

"Is there anything missing?" he asked.

He had wondered where the stalker was now. He could be closer than Mac imagined.

Wes shook his head. "No. Nothin' missin'. Just the animals actin' a little funny and Grace's stall being unlocked. Just thought I'd ask about it."

Wes ducked his head and shuffled his feet again.

"I'll check Grace's stall in the evenings before I go in." Mac nodded. "Let me know if you notice anything else."

"I'll do that." Wes nodded. "Gonna go clean the tack now."

Mac frowned as he stared around the stables. Turning back to Grace, he let his gaze go over her carefully, looking for any signs of injury or distress.

She snuffled and nudged his arm for attention, but nothing seemed out of the way. Patting the horse's neck in farewell, Mac checked the lock on the stall before heading outside to the dog basking in the sun. But too many coincidences were suddenly beginning to add up.

Pappy seemed well, eager for attention and as playful as always. Mac stared back at the stables, though, as he petted the animal, wondering if they were being watched now.

Wes was a strange little person on a good day, but he had never seemed paranoid or forgetful in making certain the latches on the stall doors were secured.

With Keiley's lost comb earlier in the week, the rumors of a ménage no one should know about, and now this, he was starting to slip back into agent mode. And he didn't like that. It had taken nearly two years for him to shake free of the almost paranoid suspicions that came with his job at the Bureau. But was it paranoia, or were he and Keiley being targeted?

"Come on, boy, we'll find you a treat." Mac patted the dog one last time before he moved through the gate and headed to the house, the dog trotting happily at his heels.

Stepping through the backdoor, Mac pulled one of the store-bought dog bones Keiley kept on hand for the dog from a shelf and tossed it out to Pappy. He loped happily away, the smoked meat bone clutched possessively in his mouth.

As he closed the door, he could hear the drone of the Harley in the front drive and grunted at the time. Jethro was back well before midnight. Mac was surprised. He had expected to have to collect Jethro, not to mention a mangled Harley. It wouldn't be the first time he had done so. Jethro had totaled his own ride four years ago, and Mac had sworn he would never allow his friend on his own Harley.

Moving through the house, he met Jethro as he entered the front door.

"Your key, my friend." Jethro tossed him the key and a rakish smile. "That's quite a little town you have. Lots and lots of scenery, if you don't mind my saying so."

"I don't mind in the least." Mac pocketed the key as he motioned Jethro back to his office.

He could hear Keiley back upstairs, the sound of the vacuum cleaner droning down the stairs.

"Were you able to find out anything?"

"Only that Delia Staten hates Keiley with a passion that most women reserve for loving men," Jethro grunted. "She has a hard-on for your marriage, Mac. That's a dangerous thing."

"I already figured that one out, Jethro."

"Well, figure this one out. What little bit I was able to charm from a few of the ladies I talked to in town, it seems Delia Staten is the one spreading the rumor that we're sharing your pretty wife. But no one knows how she found out I was here so quickly."

"One of the farmhands, no doubt." Mac grimaced, trying to push suspicion aside. "There's not a whole hell of a lot that you can keep secret here. For Keiley's sake, I had hoped to keep this a secret, though."

Mac raked his fingers through his hair as he paced to the wide window and stared out at the stables. Wes was still down there, closing up the stables for the night, making certain the horses were comfortable before he left. Suspicion hell.

"How did she hit upon the truth, though?" Mac murmured. "I told Keiley it was coincidence, but that doesn't sit well in my gut, Jethro. She knows something she shouldn't know."

Jethro shrugged easily. "She could have friends in Virginia. It's a small world now, Mac."

"Then the rumors would have begun sooner. As you said, Delia has a hard-on for my marriage."

"What do you want to do? I could take a room in town—"

Mac was shaking his head even as the words were coming out of his friend's mouth.

"This is my home and my life," he growled, restraining the anger beginning to build inside him. "I don't mess with their sex lives and they will stay out of mine. Period. I'll make certain of it."

Jethro winced. "Cowboy tactics aren't going to work here, Mac."

"I was raised in this town, Jethro," Mac pointed out savagely. "Born and bred here. I know how to handle them. You don't."

Some people understood only one thing. Fear. He might not have been back to Scotland Neck in the fifteen years before his marriage, but he had made a point to learn everything he could before he returned.

He had to admit, he hadn't expected Delia to throw a wrench in the works. But he would take care of her through her husband and her mother-in-law. He knew where to strike that viper for the most effect.

"That doesn't solve where the information came from," Jethro pointed out.

"I'll find that one out as well."

His head lifted as a knock sounded on the door. A second later Keiley stepped into the office.

Mac almost grinned at the way she was dressed. He hadn't seen her covered so well in their home since he had married her. Not that the summer soft cotton pants and loose shirt detracted from the lush curves beneath them. The buttoned top draped over her breasts with a soft touch, inviting a man to find out what lay beneath it. The pants were just loose enough to hide her rounded thighs and hint at the soft cleft between them.

"I'm putting dinner on," she announced. "Is there anything in particular that you have a taste for?"

From the corner of his eye he caught the sudden flare of lust in Jethro's expression and the unusual tightening of his lips as his friend held back what Mac was certain would be a less-than-decent suggestion. The sight of the heated blush rushing beneath her cheeks assured him that Keiley hadn't missed it, either.

"Pervert," she muttered under her breath.

Wicked amusement lit Jethro's eyes as he turned to her more fully. "I resemble that remark."

She rolled her eyes before turning back to Mac. "Restrain him."

Mac arched a brow. "I'd much rather restrain you, but only after dinner."

"Fine, you can eat whatever I fix."

"Keiley." His voice was harder, darker, as she turned to leave, and he knew it. He heard it in his own voice, but her reaction was much more telling.

She froze, an almost imperceptible shudder working up her spine before she turned back to him.

Her expression had his balls drawing tight in his jeans. Her lashes had drifted lower, her lips appeared fuller, and a flush that had nothing to do with embarrassment darkened her cheeks.

"What?" A little frown also creased her brow as he stared back at her.

"Come here." It wasn't a request.

Her eyes narrowed as she glanced between him and Jethro. She gave him a ladylike snort and said, "In your dreams."

With that she turned and closed the door firmly behind her nicely rounded little rear.

Mac almost jerked from the sudden tension that tore through his body at her deliberate challenge. His teeth clenched with an arousal so hot, spiking so hard, that he swore he was on the verge of release.

He stood slowly from the chair, staring at the door with a sense of anticipation.

"I want all the blinds closed through the house," he told Jethro softly. "Then join us in the kitchen."

His entire body was tight now, his control fraying by the second. All he could think about was holding her, restraining her, controlling that sweet, hot little body while he and Jethro worked her toward a pleasure she couldn't imagine. Keiley wasn't going to cook dinner tonight. They could order out later. Much later.

CHAPTER TEN

Keiley sensed she had just offered a dare that there wasn't a chance in hell Mac would refuse. She had seen it in his face that second as she glanced back before closing the door. In an instant the taut, savage angles of an expression tight with lust was clearly revealed.

He had warned her not to awaken the animal inside him, but she had done it anyway. Deliberately? She couldn't say. She knew her nerves were stretched to the limit, and her awareness of the two men in the same room had heightened the nervous arousal building within her all day.

She breathed in roughly as she heard Mac's office door close. Steeling herself, she turned to the kitchen entrance, watching as he stalked into the room.

"Come here." He crooked his finger, beckoning her toward him.

"Why?" Keiley retreated further into the kitchen, her breathing escalating as she stared at the conquering lover she knew he was.

The gray shirt he wore stretched across his chest and shoulders, skimmed his tight, hard abs before it disappeared into the leather-cinched snug jeans he wore.

The leather was coming off. His hands worked the belt buckle, loosening it slowly as she backed away from him slowly.

"I don't think so, Mac." She smiled sweetly. "I have too much to do tonight to play games with you."

She was pushing it and she knew it. Pushing his arousal, pushing her own boundaries. She was tired of the restlessness, tired of the tension growing within them both, the knowledge that there was more left to explore, that there was more pleasure, more adventure in his arms than he had ever let her see so far.

"But I want to play games, Kei," he informed her with dark amusement as the ends of his belt released.

God, that was sexy. Just the belt open, the heavy bulge of his cock straining beneath the denim.

"We don't always get what we want." She pursed her lips in mock sympathy. "You should know that by now."

His chuckle was deep, shadowed with a hidden power that she knew she had yet to glimpse. Who was this man she had married? She thought she knew him so well, but she was beginning to realize that perhaps she only knew a shadow of his sexuality. The hunger lurking beneath the controlled exterior had excitement racing through her veins. She could see it now. His eyes weren't stormy; they weren't dark with shadows of a hunger he wasn't revealing. They were clear, bright, heated by an inner flame that reached out to burn her as well.

She could feel her breathing growing rougher, heavier. Her breasts became swollen, the nipples so sensitive that their rasp against the lace of her bra was incredibly arousing. And between her thighs, her clit was swelling, her sex spilling its slick moisture, preparing her for him.

"I'm going to get what I want in this case," he promised, moving too quickly for her to evade, catching her wrists and drawing them behind her back as he jerked her against him.

His erection dug into her stomach, pressing hot and hard against her as he held her wrists at the small of her back and arched her into his hold.

"Now what?" she challenged him, struggling against him, feeling her pulse racing at the knowledge that he wasn't letting her escape.

She loved this. It sent a spike of heat tearing through her, clenching her womb and spasming through her vagina as he lifted her from her feet.

"Now we play my way." His tone warned her that what was coming could be more than she had ever anticipated. "We show you exactly what the meaning of true pleasure can be, sweetheart."

"We." Him and Jethro.

Keiley breathed in roughly as he lifted her from her feet, still holding her wrists while the other arm wrapped around her hips to move her from the kitchen, through the foyer into the open, dimly lit living room.

"Dinner," she whispered, suddenly uncertain, nervous as Jethro moved from the shaded window, doing as Mac had done and loosening his belt first.

"Scared, baby?" Mac cupped her face with his hand, turning her head until he was staring into her eyes, the heavy dominance in his expression stealing her breath.

She could feel her lips trembling, fear and hunger and uncertainty clouding her mind.

"I—" She whimpered as his lips lowered to hers, tears dampening her eyes as the ramifications of what they were about to do began to pound into her brain. "I love only you," she whispered against his lips. "I love only you, Mac."

His head lifted, his expression at once gentle and filled with lust. She could see the love in his eyes, the hunger and the promise. But fear began to edge into her mind. No other man had ever touched her, had ever taken her.

"And I love only you, Keiley," he promised her. She heard the promise in his voice, the emotion, the need.

"We need to talk about this," she protested again as his lips lowered to hers once again.

"The time to talk is over," he told her firmly. "Unless you say no, then all I want to hear are your cries of pleasure."

"If I say no?" But did she want to say no?

"No means no," he agreed, his lashes lowering over his eyes as his thumb smoothed over her lips. "But is that what you really want to do?"

Was it what she wanted to do?

Mac's hand slid down her neck then, over her chest, to the buttons that secured the knit shirt. Keiley fought to keep her eyes open, to hold onto her senses as she felt Jethro moving behind her.

"Mac—"

"It's okay, sugar," Jethro whispered then. "Nothing too heavy this time. We're just going to play a little bit."

His voice was a breath of sound at her ear, the warmth of his body heating her from behind as Mac held her steady against his body.

"Feel how hot it can get, Keiley," Mac told her then. "That's all. Do you think I would force you?"

She shook her head jerkily.

"Good girl." His smile was tight, hungry. "Now, let me show you part of what you could be saying no to."

She expected his kiss. She expected the flaming, destructive hunger she had seen in the past few days. She didn't expect his control. She didn't expect Jethro to suddenly have possession of her wrists as Mac had both hands free to unbutton her shirt.

"I love these little buttons," he growled. "Opening them up is like Christmas. Because I know the sweetest, plumpest nipples are waiting just below it."

The edges of the shirt slid open, revealing the lace bra.

Mac's look was frankly sensual and filled with a wry humor.

"Armor, sweetheart?"

She shuddered in Jethro's grip as she stared up at her husband. Of course, she might have been able to maintain a semblance of strength if Jethro's lips hadn't lowered to her neck.

Mac's gaze was caught by his friend's movement, his eyes darkening, deepening, as his jaw flexed with the effort it was obviously taking to maintain his control.

The feel of the soft kisses at the tender cord of her neck as Mac watched, the scrape of teeth as her husband drew the shirt from her shoulders and allowed it to drape over her bound arms, had sensation clawing through her womb.

"I'm going to have to punish you for this."

Keiley's gaze widened as he tugged at the little clasp of the bra between her breasts.

"P-punish me?" she stammered. Why did the threat sound so damned erotic.

"I've never spanked you, have I, Kei?" He almost crooned the question.

"No." Keiley swallowed tightly. "Never."

Did she want him to? Why was her rear tingling as though in anticipation?

"I've been dying to watch your pretty ass blush."

The clasp released with a flick of his fingers, the lace cups shielding her breasts and their tight tips despite the release.

But they couldn't hold out against Mac's fingers. Fingers that peeled the lace back as though he were unwrapping a particularly delicate present.

"Damn. That's pretty," Jethro suddenly growled behind her, his hands releasing her wrists slowly before he drew the shirt and bra from her.

"Too damned pretty." Mac's voice was tight now, throbbing with lust. "Pretty enough that it's a damned shame to cover them."

His head lowered as his arms went around her, his tongue licking over a tight peak as she jerked and cried out. Pleasure whipped through her body. Nerve endings that normally required dedicated foreplay to flare to life were suddenly throbbing in welcome.

She was barely aware of Jethro stepping away from her. She realized his body was no longer there, but she didn't care that it was gone. Mac was holding her, lifting her against him as his lips covered the tight peak of her breast and began drawing on it with tight, deep draws of his mouth.

"Mac. Oh God. It's too good."

She was going to orgasm. Her nipples were so sensitive, so throbbingly aware of each brush of his tongue, each draw of his mouth, that she could feel the sensation tearing into her womb. Her arms wrapped around his neck, her fingers pushing into his hair. All she wanted to do was hold onto him. To hold this exquisite pleasure inside her forever. To hold Mac inside her forever.

It was different. So much different that she could barely

process the additional sensuality, the pure eroticism over-taking her.

She was different. She could feel the differences now. Something wild and uninhibited was rising inside her. Something she couldn't define, couldn't make sense of. Something that washed over her like a tidal wave of erotic heat and held her beneath its simmering waves.

"I love your nipples," Mac groaned seconds later as he lifted his head from one peak and went to the next. "How hard and tight they get. How they redden from my mouth. My tongue."

He licked over the other peak, drew it in, sucked at it strongly as she arched into his arms and held tight to his shoulders. The world was rocking around her. Spinning around her in heat and arousal, stealing her breath and her senses.

His head lifted, his lips damp from his ministrations to her nipple, his eyes nearly black with arousal.

"You've fantasized about it," he told her ruthlessly. "I saw it in your eyes at our wedding. I've seen it in your face each time you've asked about it. I've felt it more than once when you've gone wild beneath me."

She shook her head in denial, whimpering because she couldn't push the lie past her lips.

"And it made me hotter knowing. It made me want to devour every inch of your body. See you devoured. It made me want to give you everything you fantasized about."

Determination stamped his features as he glanced behind her.

A second later she jerked in shock, a surprised cry falling from her lips as the heated warmth of a naked male body pressed against her back.

"Easy," Mac crooned as she began to tremble, staring up at him as her brain processed the presence of a thick, heavy erection at her back. "Here. Let Jethro hold you a minute, baby. Just a minute."

His voice was gentle, but his expression was implacable, tight with arousal, firm with his demand as Jethro eased her from Mac's hold.

Mac gripped her wrists, pulling them from around his head as Jethro eased her away from him.

Her hands gripped Jethro's wrists, feeling the tough flesh, the sprinkling of hair on his arms beneath her palms, from his chest at her back.

She stared at Mac, watching as he began to pull his shirt off. Watched him until Jethro turned her in his arms and forced her to watch him instead.

Sapphire-blue eyes and hawkish features. Hunger tightened Jethro's expression, and his eyes narrowed with erotic intensity.

"How did you fantasize, Keiley?" His head lowered, his lips raking down her neck as he moved her to the low cushioned stool that sat in front of the wide, thickly padded chair across from the couch.

She looked over her shoulder, searching for Mac, her breath catching as he shrugged his shirt from his broad shoulders. Muscles rippled from his powerful chest down to his hard abs.

"Look at me, baby," Jethro growled, turning her head back to him, his lips caressing over hers. "Let me watch your eyes. Do you know they go from hazel to the prettiest green when you're turned on?"

"Jethro." She moaned his name as he nipped at her lips, the sharp little sting quickly licked away by the soothing warmth of his tongue.

His hands traveled over her back, her waist, then pushed beneath the loose pants to cup the cheeks of her rear. She could feel his calloused palms stroking her even as her lips opened to his kiss, just as she could feel Mac watching. His eyes on her, seeing her response to another man, the arching of her body, Jethro's fingers stroking along the silk that parted her buttocks and covered the aching flesh between her thighs.

"Your pussy's hot," he groaned roughly as he jerked his lips from hers. "So hot and wet, your panties are damp."

His fingers were massaging over the folds, making her hotter, wetter. Keiley couldn't keep herself from rubbing against him, from pressing her rear back to force his fingers more firmly against her. He rewarded her with a few brief caresses over her straining clit as his teeth raked down her neck.

"Come here, sweetheart."

Keiley uttered a broken cry as Mac's hands lifted her from Jethro's hold, easing her to the stool before pressing her back into the chair, the back cushion of the seat supporting her weight where he had set it at an incline. As he eased her back, Jethro whisked the pants from her hips, then over her thighs and legs, leaving her naked but for the white lace thong.

She was laid out before them like a banquet, staring up at two dark, naked, fully aroused males.

"I feel like a damn virgin sacrifice." Her voice trembled worse than it had the night Mac had taken her virginity.

"A tasty sacrifice," Jethro whispered as he eased her legs apart, pulling her to the edge of the stool as Mac knelt beside the chair.

There was no time to protest, if indeed she had meant to protest. Mac's lips covered hers as Jethro's pressed damply against the lace between her thighs, sending riotous, violent pleasure singing through her body.

Her hips jerked, twisted against the ravaging lips between her thighs. The feel of Jethro consuming her through the lace of her panties was destructive. Mac's lips on hers, his hands caressing her breasts, tweaking her nipples, was destroying her control. Sensation clashed into sensation as the pleasure became torturous. She was lost within the building, crashing waves of heat and erotic fervor as the world centered around the heated kisses flaming through her nerve endings.

"Mac." She whimpered his name as his head lifted, his gaze narrowed on her face as her hips arched to Jethro's mouth. "It's too much." Too much sensation. Too much pleasure.

"It's not enough, Kei." He lowered his head to her breasts, his lips surrounding a nipple as his fingers plucked at its mate, sending clawing, desperate shards of pleasure to tear across her flesh. "It's not nearly enough."

Lower, Jethro's lips were pulling at the lace, his hands

holding her thighs apart, his tongue moving beneath the material to stroke flesh saturated with hunger and need.

Keiley writhed beneath the caresses, beneath the heat beginning to flame through her body. Erotic, forbidden, hands and mouths caressing and cajoling until her cries became hoarse pleas.

Calloused hands stripped her panties from her. A wicked, hungry mouth devoured the passion-soaked flesh as she felt broad fingers filling her. Lips suckled at her breasts, and when her eyes opened, it was to see Mac watching her, pleasure and lust suffusing his expression.

As far as Mac was concerned, Keiley had never been more beautiful than she was now. Stretched out on the stool and the chair, her breasts arched to his lips and tongue, heat mounting her cheeks and dazed pleasure filling her eyes.

Her arms were arched over her head, fingers digging into the wide cushion that supported her back. Pulling back, he looked down her body, his eyes narrowed as he saw Jethro's tongue working her swollen, delicate clit. It was enflamed, engorged, throbbing from the erotic kisses bestowed upon it.

Jethro's cheeks were flushed with his lust, his gaze heavy-lidded as Mac allowed him a view of Keiley's expression.

"More," she gasped roughly as she tried to twist beneath Jethro's lips. "Oh God! Oh God!" Her eyes flared open, locking with his. "Mac! Help me!"

The green in her eyes glittered, flaming like emerald stars in a hazel background. Perspiration dampened her body and desperation twisted her features as she reached for him.

Mac caught her wrists, pushing them back to the cushion as he leaned closer. "Stop fighting it, Keiley," he commanded roughly. "Let it go, sweetheart."

Her head thrashed on the cushion, her body tightening as she fought the release Mac could feel building in her body.

"Mac, please—" Her fractured scream had his jaw tightening and his dick pounding.

Watching her like this, seeing the pleasure that transformed her, was almost as erotic as giving her all the pleasure she was receiving.

His lips lowered to a hard, cherry-red nipple to suck and nip at the tight peak. A growling vibration of ecstasy left her throat, the sound felinish and filled with desperation.

"She's close," Jethro suddenly snarled, his voice deepened, filled with his own arousal. "Her pussy is so tight around my fingers it's like being trapped in vise."

Mac lifted his head again, his hands caressing over her upper body, his lips lowering to hers for a brief, hard kiss before drawing back.

He wanted to watch her. God help him, he needed to watch her. The forbidden eroticism of the act always pushed a woman's pleasure higher. It was pushing Keiley's higher. She was staring back at him, her eyes dazed, her expression tightening as she fought the violence of the orgasm building inside her.

"Mac, we don't have a lot of time left here," Jethro warned him, his voice tight. "She's creaming so hard now she's flooding my fingers. If she doesn't come she's going to lose it."

"Move," Mac ordered harshly as he lifted her, pulling her into his arms as he took her place in the chair and forced her to straddle his lap.

She went wild. Mac stared into her eyes as she impaled herself on his dick and surrounded it with a fist-tight friction and a heat that had him snarling with the pleasure.

One hand clamped on her hip as he pinned her to his chest with the other arm, holding her to his shoulder as he stared up at her face. Frantic with sensations she couldn't contain, crazed with a lust she couldn't control. She was at her most defenseless now, her body stroked to a pinnacle of pleasure that required more than a soft caress.

She was riding a wave of violent need so intense, so heated that the edge of pain became a craving her body wouldn't deny her. She was there now. He had felt it when she slammed her body onto his cock, taking him in one deep stroke that normally took several to seat him entirely inside her.

Even now, her pussy was flexing, fighting to adjust to the impalement, and she was begging for more.

Mac knew the second Jethro's heavily lubricated fingers

began to caress her rear entrance. Her eyes widened, then closed, and a shudder tore through her body as Mac angled his body closer to the edge of the chair to allow Jethro the position he needed.

A second later the sound of a heavy caress landing on her rear had Mac grinding his teeth against the need to come as Keiley suddenly bucked. Writhed.

"She's blushing so pretty," Jethro muttered roughly as another hard caress landed. It vibrated through her flesh to Mac's cock, creating a wave of pleasure that broke over both of them.

He could feel the tightening of her pussy as Jethro's fingers impaled her rear. The vibration of the sharp caresses as he spanked her rounded ass, the feel of her coming apart in his arms. The sound of her screams. Screams of pleasure, of hunger, of need.

"She's opening." Jethro's voice was a rough, primal sound. "She's on edge, Mac."

On the edge of that precipice that allowed pain and pleasure to mingle. Another heavy caress, a heated spanking that moved over her rear and had her nails clawing at his shoulders.

"Two fingers, easy."

Mac clenched his teeth together tight as he felt her pussy flexing, tightening as her anus accepted Jethro's fingers.

Another erotic slap sounded as Mac stared at her face. Her dazed eyes, her lips parted and damp, swollen with passion and his kisses.

"I need—," she mewled.

"Three, Mac."

She was tighter now, whimpering, her fingers digging at his shoulders as her lips opened on a gasp of helpless pleasure/pain. Jethro's cool, thickly lubricated fingers eased inside her, stroking tender tissue and nerve endings until she was a mass of desperate hunger.

"Take her." Mac snarled the order.

"Fuck, she's going to be tight," Jethro groaned. "So damned tight."

Keiley heard the words drifting around her, but nothing processed except the incredible sensations tearing through her, the hunger ripping her apart from the inside out.

She knew what was coming. She had sensed it the minute Mac's cock had filled her and he suddenly clamped her to his chest. Helplessly pinned against him, she couldn't move, couldn't ride him as she needed, couldn't still the flames burning through her body, demanding release.

Then Jethro behind her.

"Oh God. Mac. Mac." She shuddered violently as Jethro's fingers filled her first, stretching her, burning through her senses with a pleasure so close to agony she felt tears seep from her eyes. "Mac, help me."

"Now, Jethro."

Her nails bit into his shoulders as she felt Jethro behind her, felt the head of his cock pressing against the tight anal entrance as Mac tore the cushion from behind them, allowing him to lay full length along the stool and the chair as Jethro began to press inside her.

She could feel the cooling lubrication easing the way, creating a counterpoint between the magnified heat of Jethro's cock and the hot depths of the channel he was invading. His hands, calloused like Mac's but not as broad, parted her buttocks. Warm. Clenching into the flesh with almost catlike strokes.

As she felt the broad head slip fully inside her, Keiley screamed out mindlessly. In acceptance or denial, she wasn't certain. But her body opened for him. She felt it. Felt the burning, searing acceptance as the iron hard length of his erection began to work inside the ultratight, ultrasensitive channel.

She stared back at Mac, weak, her body flooded with sensations that echoed and resounded, built and intensified by the second.

She could feel both of them now. Their differences, the alternate scents of each man weaving around her. Mac's stormy scent, laced with the scent of lightning. Jethro, wild and untamed, not quite like a storm, more like the scent of the earth just before the storm hits. Different, and yet familiar. It attacked her senses as the pleasure attacked her nerve endings.

"Mac." She tried to arch in his arms as another scream came out as a whimpering sound of demented pleasure. "He's—" She tried to swallow. "He's inside me."

"He's inside you, baby," he crooned gutturally. "Tight inside you."

"Mac. I don't know—," she whimpered as she felt both their cocks jerk inside her. "I don't know if I can survive—"

Her eyes drifted closed as a surge of lust tore through her. She needed them to move. To do something. To ease the burning, gnawing ache for release.

"Look at me, Keiley." His voice was strained, growling. "Open your eyes, damn it. Let me see them."

She forced her eyes open, tightening, writhing beneath the combined penetrations as she whimpered his name again.

"God, yes," he muttered savagely. "The pleasure in your face, Kei. It's gorgeous. So damned gorgeous."

She could feel his cock throbbing inside her as her rear stretched further, sending hard, agonizing bursts of sensation through her nerve endings.

"Help me," she gasped, aware that she was clawing his shoulders but unable to pull back. "Please. Please, Mac."

His eyes were nearly black, his corded muscles like steel beneath her. She suddenly jerked, shuddered, and felt every inch of Jethro's cock impaling her.

Keiley wasn't certain at that point if she could maintain consciousness. Keeping her eyes opened and locked on Mac's took superhuman effort. Nothing could control the frantic writhing of her body, the internal contractions around the thick intrusions filling her, or the kaleidoscope of sensations racing through her body.

"I love you," Mac whispered then, his hips flexing, drawing his cock back slowly, then filling her as Jethro retreated slightly from her anus.

Coordinated. Wickedly practiced. The gentle, slow strokes were more destructive for the very fact that they were so well timed, one with the other.

Keiley could do nothing but take the rapturous pleasure exploding through her body now. Each stroke, each thrust, each muttered male groan tore through her with the force of a hard, electrical jolt. She was pinned between them, held, caressed.

Jethro's lips smoothed over her neck, his teeth raked. Mac's lips nipped and possessed hers, his tongue licking and penetrating as he forced her to keep her eyes open.

"Don't close your eyes," he demanded as they began to drift shut. "Watch me, Keiley. I want to see your eyes. They're green now, baby. So green I could drown in them. Like the seas. Like emeralds that live and breathe."

They were moving harder now, taking her, fucking her with driving thrusts and powerful strokes as they strained beneath and behind her.

"Let go!" Mac suddenly snarled. "By God, you will let go!"

Let go? What was she holding besides her sanity?

But a second later, even that was gone. One hand moved from her hips, cupped her breast, his fingers and thumb gripping her nipple as his lips covered hers and his tongue plunged home.

The heated grip on her nipple speared to her womb. His kiss electrified her as Jethro's teeth bit into her shoulder, and she exploded. She died in their arms. She hurled through a vast, star-studded sky of racing colors and sensations that tore her free of her body as she felt the hard, fierce thrusts inside her body stroking her faster, flinging her higher into an orgasm she knew she would never recover from.

Her muscles tightened to breaking point, her pussy began to convulse as she tightened on the erection thrusting into her rear and felt the tension in her womb begin to melt with a shattering force.

"Fuck!" Mac's cry was savage. A second later he tensed beneath her, thrusting harder, the strokes tighter before she exploded again amid the heavy, fierce spurts of liquid fire he began pumping inside her.

Behind her, Jethro growled her name, then he, too, fueled the secondary explosions with his own release. She could feel his cock throbbing fiercely inside the tight channel of her anus, but unlike Mac's release, the fiery drenching was absent.

It didn't hamper the final explosion of pleasure that raced through her, or the satiation that began to weave through her. She collapsed in her husband's arms, boneless, drenched in their combined sweat, and quite happy to leave the effort of peeling her from where she rested in their hands.

Hands that were smoothing her body now, gentling the tremors that still ran through her. Hands that joined, gentle male lips that kissed her face, her shoulders, and her back. Hands that soothed and warmed and eased her into a dream-like state that Keiley realized she never wanted to leave.

CHAPTER ELEVEN

He was fucked. Jethro realized the curious melting sensation inside his chest for what it was as he lifted Keiley's boneless body into his arms and stepped back from the chair-stool combination they had used.

The rules were always clear. They always had been. He could share in the tender emotions Mac's women had for him, but he couldn't possess them. He couldn't claim a part of their hearts as his own.

Until Keiley, he hadn't wanted to.

Now, as Mac forced himself from the chair and set the cushions right, Jethro cradled the tender, nude body of another man's wife and felt the first stirrings of regret.

"I'll take her to the bathtub." Jethro didn't wait for Mac to take her out of his arms. Hell, he didn't know if he could bear for Mac to take her from him right now. Not until he immersed himself in this feeling, let it ease into his mind and implant itself forever in his memories. He didn't want to forget it.

"I'll be up in a few minutes," Mac stated impassively. "I put the bath salts under her cabinet."

There was a ritual to this. Caring for the women who allowed them to share their bodies in such a way. It was a ritual Mac had begun with the first woman he had ever taken with the assistance of another male. It was one Jethro had readily embraced himself once he and Jethro began sharing their lovers.

Or rather, after Mac began sharing his. Jethro had learned early in their friendship that Mac had a way of attracting the gentle, caring women, whereas Jethro always seemed to scare them off.

He moved through the house and headed up the stairs, feeling Keiley's small hand caress his chest. She thought he was Mac. She was still lost in the dazed aftermath of the powerful orgasms that had torn through her. She didn't know who held her. She couldn't know or she wouldn't be stroking him so gently.

As he stepped into the bedroom she shared with Mac, Jethro couldn't help but stare at the peaceful, warm atmosphere as he walked through it.

Traditional dark wood was softened with touches of her feminine presence. The flowered comforter over the bed, the vase of dried flowers on the bureau. There was a print of an aerial view of the farmhouse and surrounding pastures on one wall. A print of a fairy in flight on another.

A violet silk robe lay over the end of the bed; a teddy bear that he knew Mac had bought her sat on one end of the dresser.

In this room, the fact that she and Mac suited each other to a tee couldn't be more apparent. And the fact that he had no place in it had never struck as hard as it did now.

Tightening his jaw, he moved into the bathroom, shifting his precious burden in his arms as he sat on the rim of the large tub.

Son of a bitch. Mac had installed a tub big enough for five people. It was easily the size of the hot tub on the deck behind the house.

Adjusting the water, he kissed Keiley's head as she began to move about.

"Easy," he murmured. "You need a hot bath, then you can sleep."

"I'm hungry," she muttered.

Jethro grinned at the telling comment. She had burned off enough calories climaxing between him and Mac that she had every right to be hungry. Hell, he was damned hungry himself.

"We'll feed you after you soak for a while." He grimaced as he pressed his cheek to her hair, closing his eyes briefly before forcing back the regret.

He was the third. He couldn't let himself forget that. Mac and Keiley were the whole; he was just there to add to the fun for a while.

Where the hell had his mind been when he came here thinking it would be like it had been all the times before? Fun and games. Laughter and pleasure. He hadn't expected to be affected by Keiley's warmth and generous spirit, but in the past two days, he had found himself more than affected.

"Are you okay, Jethro?" she asked quietly, still resting against him as he poured the salts into the water and tested the temperature.

"Just making sure the water's not too hot." He closed his eyes again, only to open them again at the sound of movement at the bathroom door.

Mac stood there, dressed in jeans, his chest and feet bare, his gray eyes thoughtful.

His best friend. And Jethro was doing more than lusting after his best friend's wife.

"She said she's hungry." He copped a grin, flashing it quickly before turning away and lifting Keiley into the steaming water of the tub.

"I'm starving." She settled into the water with a blissful sigh.

"What's your pleasure, sweetheart?" Mac padded into the room, kneeling on the step of the tub to lean in and kiss her swollen lips.

His hand cupped her cheek as her slender fingers curled against the back of his neck. Jethro felt more like an interloper than he ever had in his life. And he had felt that way often.

"I want pizza," he heard her murmur as Mac leaned back, bracing his arms on the rim of the large tub as his fingertips caressed her cheek.

"You rest, I'll order your favorite," Mac promised her softly, his voice low, intimate as he leaned forward and kissed her forehead. "Jethro can wash your back for you," he finished teasingly.

"He should be offering a full back massage." Her laughter was low, teasing, rueful. "I don't think I can walk straight for a while."

"We'll carry you." Mac came to his feet and glanced back at Jethro. "I'll order the pizza. You okay to stay up here?"

Never leave a woman alone after shattering her previous impressions of pleasure. Cuddle her. Spoil her. Keep her comfortable. Mac knew how to do it, and over the years he had taught Jethro how to do it.

"I'll take care of her." His gaze flickered to her, watching as she relaxed back into the water and Mac stood.

"I'll leave her in your hands." Mac clapped him on the shoulder as he left the bathroom.

Jethro looked around the steamy intimacy of the bathroom. Here, Keiley's influence was more felt. It was softer than the bedroom, with slate-gray marble cabinets and sink and several narrow shelves that held an array of feminine products: soaps, lotions, and scents. He knew that beneath the cabinet was a built-in drawer system that held makeup. Hanging on an inner wall was a blow dryer and assorted curling irons.

A French door led to a balcony that ran the length of the bathroom and bedroom, the pale gray sheers covered with darker pearl-gray curtains that were presently pulled back.

"You're too interested in the bathroom walls," she said with an edge of uncertainty. "I'll be okay by myself."

Jethro whipped his head around, staring at the water lapping at her breasts before he let his gaze meet her wide hazel eyes.

He shook his head slowly as he knelt on the lower step that led up to the rim. "Not a chance." Snagging the bath sponge, he lifted a bottle of bath gel from the wide back rim and soaped it slowly. "Taking care of you will be my privilege."

"I should be totally embarrassed," she said as he caught her hand and drew her toward him so he could reach her back. "I've never made love with anyone but Mac until now."

He watched, entranced, as the bubbles gathered on her back, and then her words slammed into his chest. Made love. Had he ever made love until now?

"Did you enjoy it, though?" he murmured as he smoothed the sponge over her shoulders.

She sighed heavily. "Very much. Too much. I'm sure I should be feeling embarrassed or something by now."

"Don't have the energy for it?" His lips quirked into a smile.

"I don't know." Her voice was reflective as she stared back at him, the short strands of her hair clinging to her cheek and neck as she stared up at him. "Maybe I should be more frightened that I'm not."

Confusion filled her pretty eyes. They were hazel now, the blend of browns and light greens that he loved so well. But earlier, her eyes had sparkled with green fire. Like gems held suspended within a brown velvet background.

Jethro shook his head at his wary suggestion. "No reason to be frightened, sugar. Mac loves you. You know that. Nothing that happened tonight changed that. I'm just here to help him give you a little extra. That's all."

A frown flitted between her brows. "And what do you get out of it, Jethro?"

What did he get out of it? A chance to feel loved, at least the periphery of it. A chance to feel alive as he never had until he saw her.

"More pleasure than you can imagine, Keiley," he assured he softly.

More pleasure than he had ever believed possible. The darkness of his past and a lifetime of loneliness receded when she was near.

"Enough pleasure to stick around a while?" Mac's question had him jerking around, almost guiltily.

"You never know." Jethro grinned, injecting a humor he didn't feel. "Director's in no hurry to have me fill my desk right now."

"Jethro likes to pound on the criminals." Mac glanced at his wife, his gaze assured, confident of his place in her soul.

"I'm trying to convince him to take a vacation when his suspension is up at the end of the week."

Jethro watched the silent communication between husband and wife. That bond that allowed them to read each other. To see each other without words.

"You should," Keiley agreed softly, turning her head slowly to meet Jethro's gaze.

She didn't say anything more. Instead she took his wrist, the sponge still held loosely in his hand, and pulled it to her shoulder.

Jethro couldn't speak. There was no need to speak. Aware of Mac behind him, he did what he had done many times in the past: he bathed the woman they had shared. Unlike those other times, he didn't tease or joke. There was no teasing in him tonight. Nothing to joke about. This was more serious than he had ever imagined it could be.

She had given him a gift that shook him to his soul, and he couldn't even explain exactly what it was.

He washed her thoroughly, even going so far as to ignore the blush that seemed to blaze across her enter body when he nudged the sponge between her thighs.

As he cleaned her, Jethro watched the languorous pleasure that suffused her, the drowsy sensuality that began to bloom on her cheeks once again.

After rinsing her, he stepped back, glancing at Mac as he leaned against the doorframe, staring at her with a gentle quirk of a smile and an expression that Jethro had never seen him use with anyone but Keiley.

"Come on, princess." Mac grabbed the towel before Jethro could reach it and moved for the tub. "Let's get you dressed before that pizza arrives."

Jethro moved back, watching as Mac drew his wife from the tub and wrapped the towel around her body. He dried her slowly, peppering kisses over her shoulders as she leaned into him, clearly luxuriating in her husband's touch.

Her husband. She belonged to another man, and he couldn't forget that. He didn't want to change that, but he had to consciously force himself to remember it.

Her soft laughter as Mac lifted her into his arms and carried her out of the bathroom stroked over his senses. It melted something hard and tight inside his heart and chipped away at the shield that guarded his soul.

"Come on, Jethro, pizza will be here soon," Mac called out. "I'd prefer we be dressed and at least pretending to be decent when they arrive."

Hell. Small-town life. Mac should have kept his ass in Virginia. Now Jethro was going to have to get up close and personal with the demented and country-loving inhabitants of this small town to find out where the rumors against Keiley were originating. And he *would* find out.

Something dark and vengeful flared within him then. He'd be damned if he would let some petty, jealous witch strike out at her in this way. Delia Staten wanted Mac; he had learned that much earlier in the day. Even now, fifteen years later, lust and hatred drove her.

Mac had told him about her and various other members of this fine community. How they had stood aside and kept silent whenever old man McCoy had beat the shit out of his son and publicly humiliated his wife. How they had gossiped and made Mac's mother's life more of a hell than it already was.

How Mac had found it within him to return here, to be sociable and polite to these damned people, amazed him.

Shaking his head, he moved from the bathroom and through the bedroom. From the corner of his eye he could see Mac dressing Keiley. Drawing another pair of those loose pants over her legs, kissing her stomach as he pulled the elastic band just over her hip bones.

The intimacy that connected the two had his teeth gritting in a hunger that had nothing to do with lust and everything to do with a threat to his soul.

Naked, aroused, he moved through the hallway to his own room, coming to a hard, abrupt stop at a whisper of sound from below.

Jethro eased back into the shadows of the hall, staring down the stairs with narrowed eyes. There it was again, almost not there, like the slide of displaced air over a sinister whisper.

He eased back the way he had come, moving quickly back to the bedroom and giving Mac a hard, warning glance as his friend's gaze jerked suddenly to him.

Mac clamped his hand over Keiley's lips as she began to utter a surprised question. Jethro was jerking a pair of pants from Mac's closet, dragging them over his legs even as he gave Mac a quick hand motion for a weapon.

"Stay silent!" Mac mouthed to Keiley, pointing to the corner of the room that would hide her from the doorway.

She eased back, her eyes widening with fear as a tremor shook her frame. They had discussed this, how if trouble ever came, she would make certain Mac wasn't hindered by her inexperience.

Silently, he jerked a dresser drawer open as Jethro zipped up the jeans and pulled two Glocks free along with the extra clips. The third, a smaller version, he loaded quickly, and strode to where Keiley was hugging the wall. He pressed the weapon in her hand, pointed to the safety, then pointed to the floor. She flattened herself to the carpet.

Rounding back, Mac caught Jethro's attention and pointed to the door. They moved from the room quickly, weapons at their shoulders, bodies prepared.

It had been three years since he had been with the Bureau, but Mac hadn't forgotten the chill of danger that he felt racing up his spine.

Following Jethro's hand signals, they moved to the stairs, Mac covering him as he started down the stairs. He couldn't hear whatever Jethro had heard, but he could feel it. Someone had invaded his home.

Jethro held up a hand, a finger flicking to the living room where they had just given Keiley the pleasure he had dreamed of giving her.

Mac listened carefully, but all he heard was the ticking of the clock just inside the room and the silence of the dim house.

Jethro was tense, listening as he flattened himself against

the wall. His finger curled toward the room, indicating he would go in low and fast. Bracing himself, Mac moved into place on the opposite side of the steps and nodded at Jethro's quick glance.

Jethro moved fast, throwing himself into the living room before Mac ducked and rolled into the opposite side of the doorway. His weapon came up, his senses alive with the silence that filled the room.

There was nothing but silence. His gaze swept over the dimly lit room. At first, nothing seemed out of place until his gaze speared to the cushioned stool and chair where Keiley had lain.

It had been moved. Her clothes were inches from where they had been, and her panties were missing. White lace that had been wet with her sexy juices.

"Keiley," he hissed, turning and racing back up the stairs.

His chest tightened with sudden terror, fear pumping through his mind as adrenaline raced through his body. He tore into the bedroom, coming to a hard, furious stop as he glimpsed Keiley. She stood in the corner, her back flat against the wall as she stared at the French doors that led onto the balcony.

She was out of line of a shot, but her weapon was held in a two-handed grip and pointing at the door latch. Ominously, with sinister intent, the brass door latch shifted.

Mac didn't think first. He fired.

"Motherfucker!" he yelled, running to the shattered doors as Keiley screamed and Jethro threw himself through the glass.

Following, Mac came to a crouch, weapon raised as he heard Pappy's furious barking below.

"Pappy, down!" he yelled as he gripped the railing and threw himself over the banister.

He hit the ground in a roll, coming up behind the heavy cement fountain that sat feet away. He was aware of Jethro rolling to the opposite side, taking cover behind the aging dogwood that grew alongside the house and led to the balcony.

A motorcycle roared to life from the front of the house, and even as Mac dug in his heels and raced for the front drive he knew he was too late.

"Bastard! You fucking bastard!" he snarled as he caught the receding lights of the dirt bike in the distance.

Aiming, he emptied the clip into the distance, rage beating through his blood as he heard Jethro cursing behind him.

"Son of a bitch!" His fist slammed into the side of his pickup. "You bastard!"

"Mac." Jethro rushed to his side. "He's gone, man."

"Keiley." Mac turned and rushed for the house, ready to kick in the front door rather than pausing to unlock it when it suddenly opened.

His weapon came up, pointing straight into Keiley's horrified face as Jethro cursed violently behind him.

"God damn you! Damn you, I told you to stay put!" Mac yelled into her pale, tear-soaked face as he gripped her shoulders and pushed her into the house.

Fear was an entity possessing him. Rage beat at his brain as he pressed her against the wall, glaring into her wide, horrified eyes as he restrained himself from shaking her.

"What don't you understand about staying put, Kei?" he yelled. "I could have blown your fucking head off!"

"Let her go, Mac," Jethro said in a dangerous voice, his hands locking on Mac's wrists. "God damn it, you're hurting her. Let her go."

He was thrown back as Jethro moved between him and his wife.

"Get the fuck out of my way." He went to push past his friend, to get to his wife, to make certain she was alive even if he was madder than hell.

He had never been so furious in his life. Never so terrified as he was at the thought that that bastard had slipped upstairs and nearly caught her undefended.

"Not until you calm down!" Jethro yelled back at him. "She's fucking terrified. Don't make it worse."

"I nearly fucking killed her." He pushed Jethro back, then stared at Keiley's crumpled form.

"God. Kei. Baby."

She was sobbing silently against the wall, her face pressed into it her hands, her shoulders hunched against the force of the violence raging through her room.

Gripping her shoulders, he turned her to him gently. So gently. His hands touched her hair, her shoulders, his arms contracting around her as he closed his eyes against the moisture suddenly filling them.

"Kei, baby," he whispered at her ear. "I'm sorry. Ah, God. Sweetheart. I almost killed you, Kei. I would have died. Do you know that?" He pressed his lips to her brow as she shook in his arms, sobs tearing through her. "Keiley, I would have died. I couldn't live, baby. I couldn't live—" He couldn't live without her.

Her arms latched around his neck, holding tight as the sobs became louder, as the shaking became worse.

"I have you." He bent over her, sheltering her, aware of Jethro moving closer, his hands touching her back, pressing her closer to Mac as he sheltered her from behind. She was surrounded. No one could touch her now. Nothing could touch her.

But something, someone nearly had.

"I'm sorry!" she cried out. "I heard the motor racing away. Heard the shots. I was scared, Mac. So scared—"

"Never, ever again, Keiley," he ordered, his voice rough, shaking with fear and pain. "Swear to me. Never again. You hide. You don't face anything. Especially not me without warning. Never again, Keiley."

"Never." Her head shook, her body trembled. "Oh God, Mac. What's happening? What's going on?"

Lifting his head, he looked over her shoulder to Jethro. His friend lifted his hand, and between his fingers were the white lace panties that had been missing from the living room.

Beneath the balcony, Jethro mouthed.

"I don't know yet, honey," he answered Keiley, flicking Jethro a hard look as he tucked the material out of sight.

Easing her back, he stared into her pale face, his gaze going over her quickly, searching for injuries.

"Are you okay?"

"I'm fine." She sniffed, her hands going over his shoulders, his chest, and his abdomen, obviously ascertaining that he was just as fine. "Just terrified. Mac, who would be that stupid?"

"I don't know yet." He drew her back into his arms, watching as Jethro moved back into the living room and stood staring around. "I don't know, but I'm going to find out."

CHAPTER TWELVE

Her home was a damned crime scene. She wasn't allowed in past the living room door. She was to stay out of the way, but she was to stay close, and she was more terrified than she had ever been in her life.

Keiley sat on the stairs, the boxed pizza sitting untouched beside her, a half-empty glass of wine clutched in her hands as Jethro and Mac dusted the living room for fingerprints. They hadn't called the sheriff. They had called Jethro's boss, then began investigating.

She had no idea Mac had kept all the equipment he had from his time in the Bureau. But he had. Stored in a large duffel bag in the attic had been stuff she hadn't even recognized and hadn't understood as he tried to explain some of it. All she did understand was that it seemed to be connected to an old case of Mac's.

Finally, she had taken her wine and moved to the stairs, where Mac had sat the pizza after collecting it from the delivery boy. A boy who hadn't even gotten out of his truck. Mac had met him in the driveway with the money and sent him on his way before striding into the house, ordering her to eat, then joining Jethro back in the living room.

She could hear their voices and had managed to catch part of the conversation. Something about her panties under the balcony. Someone had stolen her panties.

She pushed her fingers through her hair, took another sip

of the wine and rose to her feet. She moved cautiously back to the doorway, aware of the wary looks Mac and Jethro were casting her as she watched them.

"Do you think he's the reason I've had so many things come up missing lately?" she finally asked, realizing she should have mentioned the other articles before now.

Both men froze, their gazed sharpening, expressions becoming savage.

"Like what?" Mac asked dangerously.

"Well, my comb. Remember?"

He nodded sharply. "All you mentioned was a comb."

"There was a bottle of my favorite perfume. The dress I wore last week to that meeting in Virginia. The engraved pen you bought me for Christmas. Just little things, Mac."

His jaw hardened dangerously. "What else?"

Keiley frowned. "That's all I've noticed."

"How long has this been going on?" Mac snapped. "And why the hell didn't you tell me about it?"

She hunched her shoulders defensively. "I've been busy. I thought I had misplaced them until I went looking for the dress last night. I was going to mention it, but—" She cleared her throat. "Things happened."

"Mac, anyone could have found out you were investigating that case before you left," Jethro muttered, barely loud enough for her to hear.

"What case?"

She caught the sharp look Mac gave him as she questioned the comment.

"Mac, don't you think it's just a little too late to shield me here?" she snapped in frustration. "I'm not a child, nor am I an imbecile. It's a stalker, isn't it?"

It was one of a woman's worst nightmares.

"Shit," Mac growled as he pushed his fingers through his disheveled hair. "Damn it to hell."

"You were working a stalker case before we moved, weren't you?" Her voice trembled on the question. "The one that led to the attack on the accountant in Alexandria."

He nodded shortly. "We called him the Playboy. Until that attack he had never hurt any of his victims. He played with them. Or more to the point, he played with their lovers and husbands."

She shook her head in confusion. "What do you mean?"

"He focused on women whose husbands or lovers were in the investigative fields. Cops, bodyguards, private investigators. As though he were testing himself against them. He would steal their personal items, then later begin returning them in places where they knew they wouldn't have left them. It was a dare. He put their men on alert, then began escalating, getting closer and taunting them with the knowledge that he could strike at any time."

"Then he attacked one of them?"

"Her husband was a private investigator. He slipped into the house, managed to knock him out, and then attacked her. Then he just disappeared."

"Until now." Her breath hitched violently as her stomach contracted.

"He must have found out who was investigating the case with the FBI," Mac snapped. "It wouldn't be that hard to do. I questioned three of the seven victims."

"And he found out you were married," she whispered. "He's daring you."

"He's dared the wrong men."

Keiley flinched at the murderously cold smile that curved at her husband's lips. And she didn't miss the plural at the end of that declaration. The wrong men. She turned her gaze to Jethro and caught her breath. If Mac was murderously cold, then Jethro was icy. His eyes were like winter frost, his expression merciless.

"What are you going to do?"

"We're going to catch the bastard," Mac assured her, his voice silky smooth but with an edge of violence as he turned to Jethro. "Do you still have the tracing program on your laptop?"

Jethro nodded.

"Hook it up to the computer in her office in the morning," Mac ordered him. "I'll put her to work on that program she installed on my laptop and see what we can pull up. I want you to call the director, let him know what's going on, and have the files sent here by overnight courier. This time, that bastard is mine."

"We can do all this in the morning, Mac," Jethro said quietly, nodding toward her. "She's exhausted, and I'm betting she still hasn't eaten."

Keiley shook her head quickly. "I'm not hungry. I want to know what's going on first."

"You're too tired to make sense of it, Keiley. And we're too damned tired to go any further tonight," Mac sighed, moving across the room as Jethro began to pack up the equipment. "We have the prints from here and the balcony door. Tomorrow we'll courier them out to the Bureau and see if he got sloppy."

"I can't sleep." Keiley shook her head quickly, panicking at the thought of even trying to sleep.

"You're going to eat first." His arm went around her, and the warmth of his body immediately began to seep into her. "Then we're going to lock the doors, rig a few alarms, and pile into Jethro's bed. Jethro and I will take turns listening for anything and you will sleep."

She shook her head again.

"Grab the pizza, Jethro. We'll eat in the kitchen. I need to check on the dog anyway."

"Pappy?" Keiley glanced at him in concern.

"I just want to make sure he wasn't hurt. I just remembered that he tried to attack the bastard."

He should have thought about the dog earlier. If anything happened to the mutt, Keiley would be inconsolable for days.

"Stay here, Kei." He pushed her into a kitchen chair and bent to her, staring her directly in the eye. "Right here. You don't move. Are we clear?"

She grimaced, her lips pursing in defiance.

"Keiley. Don't push me right now."

Her jaw clenched. "Fine. But you better hurry."

"Mac, the dog is right by the door," Jethro informed him. "I'm going to let him in long enough to check him out."

Mac turned, watching as Jethro opened the door and clicked to the dog to enter.

Hesitant, watching the room warily, the shepherd mix crouched and slunk into the kitchen. Closing the door, Jethro ran his hands carefully over the dog's large body, checking for wounds or any sign of pain.

"He's fine." Jethro opened the door.

Pappy had no intentions of leaving as easily as he had entered, though. Whining, he crouched again and pushed himself further into the room.

"Let him stay," Keiley ordered them both. Her voice wasn't pleading and she wasn't asking. It was a demand.

Mac stared at the animal. Sure as hell if he let it stay in the house tonight he would never get it back out of the house.

"Keiley—"

"Forget it, Mac. I'm not leaving Pappy out there for some crazy idiot to take potshots at. He's staying in the house."

The dog disappeared under the table, his head showing up on Keiley's lap as he whined again, his brown eyes adoring.

"Hell."

"Live with it," she whispered. "I won't let him get hurt."

"All right, he stays in the house."

He glanced at Jethro wryly as Keiley opened the pizza box and slipped the dog a slice of pepperoni, mushroom, and double cheese.

"And stays, and stays, and stays." Jethro grinned as he locked the door and dragged a chair from the table before pulling another slice of the pizza free and pushed it to Keiley. "Now you eat. And don't argue." He held his finger up as she started to do just that. "Eat or I'll personally escort that mutt into the garage and lock him up there. Unlike Mac, it doesn't break my heart when you don't get your way."

Her eyes narrowed. "I am not spoiled."

"Of course you are, sugar." He grinned, causing Mac to stifle his laughter. "He has you spoiled worse than a Christ-

mas puppy, and that's how he loves you best. But not me."
He leaned back in his chair lazily. "I'm a hardass. I can take
the heat. Fight with me all you want, I know how to spank
you and make you like it."

Mac tensed, but not in anger as he should have. The
thought of watching Jethro deliver one of his erotic spank-
ings to Keiley's rounded little rear was enough to arouse
him despite the threat they had just avoided.

"Are you going to let him talk to me like that?" she asked
Mac incredulously, turning to stare back at him with narrowed eyes.

Mac couldn't help but grin. "He can make you come
when he spanks you. What do you think?"

"I think you're both perverts," she snapped back.

Mac arched his brow in surprise as he pulled a chair
from the table and took his own seat. "Are you just figuring
that out, sweetheart?"

She stared back at him intently before her gaze shifted to
Jethro. Mac saw the thoughtful look in her eyes, the way she
focused, as though she were seeing deeper than any of them
knew.

"No," she finally answered, turning back to meet his gaze
with a mysterious little smile. "I already knew."

And that was a scary thought.

Hours later, Mac sat in the recliner across from the queen-size
bed where Jethro held Keiley. There was something oddly intimate about the way his friend had wrapped his body around
Keiley after Mac left the bed. Something Mac hadn't noticed
before with the other women they had spent the night with.

Jethro held her much as Mac did himself. He surrounded
her. She was tucked into the curve of his body, the loose
t-shirt and cotton pants she wore doing nothing to dispel the
sensual, erotic sight of Jethro wrapped so snugly around her.

They were all dressed in comfortable clothing. Jethro was
in sweats and a gray t-shirt. Mac himself still wore his jeans,
a shirt, and sneakers.

They were prepared, though the odds were that they were

prepared for nothing. But Keiley had refused to undress. The stark fear that had filled her eyes when he suggested it had prompted him to let the subject go.

He watched curiously as Jethro shifted, drawing Keiley closer, her head tucked beneath his chin, his hand pressing against her stomach, drawing her tighter into his thighs.

He should be jealous, Mac thought. No one had ever held Keiley like that with the exception of himself. And he was observant enough to note the fact that Jethro was holding her as he had never held another woman in Mac's presence.

He rubbed his finger thoughtfully over his cheek, wondering at the lack of jealousy, the lack of possessiveness. He was like a dog over a bone when it came to other men being around Keiley. He knew the strength of his possessiveness where she was concerned and he knew he should be worried that it was absent now.

What the hell was up with that? he wondered. He was sitting here, watching another man hold her, and he was as aroused as he had been watching Jethro go down on her earlier that night.

He breathed out heavily and stared toward the curtained window reflectively. For the past ten years, Jethro had almost exclusively been the third he brought to the bed with his lovers. For some reason he seemed to provide the perfect counterpoint that Mac had been looking for to bring to his women. Mac cared for them; Jethro lusted. Gentle dominance and dark power, that was what they provided as a team for the lovers they had shared.

They were partners at the Bureau, the perfect team for the investigations they worked. They were also the perfect team for the women they shared.

And now, the woman they loved.

The insight came to him slowly as he turned his gaze back to the bed. Jethro was beginning to care for Keiley, and Mac hadn't expected that. But neither was he regretting it, nor was he worried about it.

Especially now. She was protected in ways he couldn't

protect her on his own, and in the past years he had worried about that. Providing the protection she would need if one of his past investigations ever managed to come back and haunt him as it was now.

The Playboy was good. Damned good. And he had so far eluded every law enforcement officer who had investigated the individual cases. And with each successive strike, he was growing more violent.

"We'll protect her, Mac." Jethro's voice was a quiet whisper, pitched just low enough to keep from disturbing Keiley. "He won't get away this time."

Mac stared back at his partner, seeing much more than he bet Jethro thought he could see. Mac could sense the emotion in the other man, the same fiery response to Keiley that Mac had known since the first day he met her. There was no turning away from her. There was no chance to avoid the effect she had on a man once he touched her. There was only the sure and certain knowledge that life would never be the same without her.

"Yes, we'll protect her," Mac agreed, feeling the burning rage building inside him once again.

Tonight had been too damned close.

"You need to train her to work with us," Jethro said then. "Teach her how to protect herself and how to back us up."

"Teach her how to stay put," Mac muttered.

"She's never going to stay put. You know better than that. You're her husband. Her heart. She'll no more stay put than you would. Think about that one."

Mac grimaced tightly, knowing he was right.

"She'll follow your lead, but she'll never let you lock her away. She proved that tonight, and we all nearly paid for it. Teach her, Mac. Or I will."

Mac stared back at his friend through the darkness of the bedroom, discerning the shadow of his body alongside Keiley's and the glitter of his eyes.

There was nothing to be heard outside but the sounds of the night. Beyond the locked bedroom door, Pappy lay on guard, an early warning should anyone breach the house again. But he still wondered why the animal hadn't sounded the alarm sooner. That question and the determination in Jethro's voice pricked at him.

Keiley was smart enough, in control enough, to back them up if she had the proper training. But there was no time to train her properly.

"We'll take turns covering her," he finally said softly. "Instruct her as we can. But this isn't going to go down easy, Jethro, I can feel it. He took a chance last night and got away with it. He'll make a move again soon."

"And he's escalating," Jethro murmured. "The next move could be completely unlike the ones he's made before. We need to keep her in the house. Keep the windows shuttered."

Mac let his gaze drop to Keiley. How long could he keep her out of sight and still draw the stalker in?

"He knows we're on guard now," Mac murmured. "If he's smart, and we know he is, he'll wait and watch."

"So will we." Jethro's voice was pure death. "This time, we'll get him."

This time they would get him. Mac wiped his hands down his face before rising to his feet and shucking his jeans. The rest of the night would be quiet, he could feel it. He was exhausted and Jethro was awake now.

"Give me two hours," he told his partner as he crawled into the bed and dragged Keiley into his arms.

She muttered sleepily but cuddled against his chest like a sleepy little kitten and drifted off once again.

"I'll sleep in the morning," Jethro told him quietly as he moved from the bed. "Go ahead and rest, man. You're the one who's been out of the game for three years. Not me."

There was an edge of amusement to Jethro's voice that had a grin tugging at Mac's lips. Yes, he had been out of the game, but he wasn't nearly as rusty as Jethro was accusing him of being.

"I can still kick your ass," Mac assured him.

Jethro stretched lazily. "Expect to back up that claim, my friend, because this week we'll be sparring."

Mac grinned as he settled deeper into the pillows, his arms holding, sheltering Keiley as he drifted off to sleep. He trusted Jethro to watch his back. But even more, he was starting to realize that he trusted Jethro to watch his wife's back, which was infinitely more important.

CHAPTER THIRTEEN

The next morning, towel wrapped around her and fresh from the shower, Keiley left Jethro's bathroom with every intention of going to her own before dressing.

Her essentials were in her bathroom, her lotions and scents and the light makeup she wore through the day. But the minute she walked out of the bathroom, she knew she wasn't going anywhere for a while.

She faced the two men who had broken through barriers she hadn't known she had last night. Men who had touched her with a passion and hunger she hadn't expected, then protected her through the night with a dedication that had left her shaken.

She stared at her husband as he slowly pulled the dark t-shirt from his body, revealing the finely sculpted muscles of his chest with the light scattering of black hair across it.

On the other side of the bed, Jethro followed suit. He wasn't as heavily muscled as Mac, but the mat of hair was a little thicker, his hard body leanly muscled and compact.

A scar she hadn't noticed the night before ran from his chest to his abs. The wicked mark against the darkly tanned flesh reminded her of the dangerous career he and Mac had chosen.

Flicking her gaze between them, her hands knotted on the towel covering her as she cleared her throat with a hint of hesitation.

"I'm a little sore," she said breathlessly, her rear clenching at the slight ache that had been left from last night's excess.

"There are other ways." Mac's voice was low, but nothing could disguise the hunger in it. It lent a rough edge to his tone, a dominant strength that had a tremor racing down her spine.

Her gaze moved to Jethro. He had held her as she slept, she knew. She remembered drifting awake several times to feel his arms around her, to smell his scent enveloping her.

"This sort of relationship is all about trust, Kei," Jethro said then, moving closer, his blue eyes heavy-lidded. "There are no recriminations and there never will be. No guilt. No pressure. If you want to call a halt, then all you have to do is say the word."

"And if I say the word?" she asked curiously.

"Then I back off." He shrugged as he moved slowly around her, stopping as he stood at her back. "It's that simple. And when you're ready again, all you have to do is say so."

She stared back at her husband. Jethro might back off, but she could see the flames burning in Mac's eyes. She was finding that when it came to this particular hunger, he was resolute.

She could see the pleasure in his eyes as Jethro's hands touched her shoulders. They were calloused, but not as roughly as Mac's. Still, though, they rasped over her flesh as he smoothed them over her shoulders and down her arms to her elbows. There he pulled her arms back, forcing her to release the towel and to curl them around his neck instead.

"Damn, you're beautiful," Mac growled, watching. Watching as Jethro slowly pulled the towel from her body.

Keiley gasped as the cool air in the room and the heated sensation caused by Mac's gaze on her suddenly tightened nipples sent a wave of helpless pleasure racing through her.

Mac didn't move from where he stood, but the lithe flex and ripple of muscle as he shed his sweatpants and revealed the steel-hard erection beneath them was too arousing. His fingers curled around the base, his biceps flexing as he tightened his hand on his cock.

"I want to watch you, Keiley. You and Jethro. I want to watch the pleasure suffuse your face, your body. I want to see what I'm always too dazed by pleasure to watch when I'm taking you."

Her eyes widened as Jethro's hands slid to her waist before flattening on her stomach. Her arms started to fall from his neck.

"Keep them there," Jethro growled, his honeyed voice firm and resolute. "Don't move your arms. Stay where he can see you."

"Mac." His name was a whispered protest.

Mac shook his head slowly, the midnight strands of hair caressing his shoulders as he watched her with lashes half lowered over his steel-gray eyes.

"Just feel, Kei," he said. "Just let me watch. Let me see your pleasure. Do you know the high I get watching you come undone? Watching the pleasure mount and mount until you're helpless beneath the rush of ecstasy?"

Keiley was shaking. She could feel the tremors racing through her body, helpless beneath the astounding wash of hunger that his words evoked.

How could anyone deny the look in his eyes? Possessiveness, it was there. Keiley had a feeling that once Jethro walked out of their lives, what they had now would never happen again. Burning hunger blazed in his expression. For whatever reason, he needed this. Like other men needed a kiss, needed the words of love, Mac needed this. It was affirmation of some sort to him. And it raised questions Keiley knew she would eventually have to ask.

And there was love. She could see his love for her glittering more fiercely now than ever before. There was no way she could doubt it. He might be allowing another man to touch her body, but at that moment she could feel Mac touching her soul.

"I want to watch him take you, Kei."

A breathless moan slipped past her lips as Jethro's hands smoothed higher, his palms cupping the undercurves of her too-sensitive, swollen breasts. He lifted them as though in offering before his fingertips rubbed over the tips with heated precision.

Her knees weakened. Fire rocked through her veins. Then, just as quickly, she was being turned, lifted into Jethro's arms, and laid carefully in the center of the bed.

She watched as Jethro stripped his pants from his body, his erection springing free, tipped with moisture and flushed with lust. Mac's cock was a bit thicker, Jethro's was a bit longer. Both men were impressively endowed with the sexual expertise to use it effectively.

Narrowing her eyes and flickering her gaze between both men, Keiley arched on the bed, her hands sliding up her stomach and down again as the heated ache between her thighs began to increase.

"You could join us," she whispered to her husband.

She wasn't certain how she felt about this, having him merely watch as another man touched her, kissed her, possessed her. She couldn't control her responses, couldn't control the eroticism that rose inside her as she glimpsed the approval in Mac's gaze.

"I want to watch," he murmured. "I want to see you taken away by the pleasure. How you look when you hold nothing back."

She licked her lips nervously. "I've only done that with you, Mac."

"And I'm here," he assured her, moving closer to the bed as Jethro came down beside her.

"It's not the same." She jerked as Jethro's lips touched her shoulder, his tongue licking over the flesh and sending a spike of electric sensation racing through her.

She had only ever responded to Mac this way. Now, beneath his gaze, her body was responding to another man, the flares of sensation tearing through her, clawing across her nerve endings in violent hunger.

And his touch wasn't like Mac's. His lips were a little rougher, his tongue just as adventurous, but the texture of it rasping more than her husband's.

It didn't stop her from responding, from moaning with the sensuality racing through her.

"It's not supposed to be the same," he whispered as Jethro leaned over her, his fingers touching her jaw, turning her face to him. "It's supposed to be hotter, more intense. It's supposed to make you weak with need, Keiley. It's supposed to make you wet and wild. That's what I want to see. That's what I need to see."

The truth of it was in his gaze, in his voice so filled with hunger. Her chest clenched with a sudden shaft of pain. What had happened in her husband's past to have caused this? Surely something darker and more vicious than he had so far told her.

She stared up at Jethro helplessly then.

"Shh," he whispered, as though he could see into her, could see the sudden fear that grew inside her for her husband. "There's no pain here. Only pleasure."

Only pleasure? A pleasure derived from the need to escape the pain?

Her hands lifted, touched his face, her fingertips skimming over his high cheekbones, the dark brow, then into his overly long hair.

Hair nearly as black as Mac's, but with dark brown shades threading through it. It wasn't the silky softness of her husbands, it was coarser, though not as thick.

She watched as his expression tightened with her touch, an almost desperate light filling his gaze before he swiftly closed his eyes for a long second.

When they reopened, it was gone, but the blazing hunger remained. In his gaze and in his kiss.

The kiss caught her off guard. It was like Mac used to kiss her. Without apology. Without asking. Without the natural gentleness that came with three years of marriage. It was the kiss of a man who made no apologies for his desires and no excuses.

"You like that, don't you, Kei?" Mac whispered. "I see how he's kissing you. You like having your lips taken."

She couldn't deny it. She couldn't affirm it. She was too busy fighting the response that threatened to swamp her.

"Don't fight it, sweetheart." Mac's voice was a low, rough growl of rising hunger. "Let me see your pleasure. Your need. Give in to it."

She whimpered as Jethro nipped at her lips, stroked them with his tongue, and pushed his fingers into her hair to hold her head in place. He was restraining her movements, but not her response. Where it welled from, she wasn't certain. From some dark inner part of her soul that reveled in the extremity of taking another man as her husband egged her on. In letting her own sensuality free, letting it rule rather than being concerned with how he might look upon her for being ruled by it.

Her arms wrapped around Jethro's shoulders, her fingers playing with his longer hair, pulling at it, tugging his lips closer as her tongue touched his.

As though she had struck a match to gasoline, Jethro's response exploded over her. His muscles tightened and flexed, his cock jerked against her hip, and one long leg tangled with hers.

Suddenly the flaming need was whipping around her, through her, over her. Her lips parted further, taking his kiss and returning it, drawing it into her before giving it back.

Lips and tongues battled in a dance of erotic fervor. Hands stroked sensitive flesh. His were broader, cupping her breasts, tweaking her nipples, hers smaller, stroking up his back, tangling in his hair, feeling the muscles shifting in his shoulders.

Her nails scraped over his flesh, and he groaned in response. His lips tore from hers, stringing heated kisses down her neck as she arched and silently pleaded for more.

She forced her eyes open as Jethro's lips moved to her breasts, only to whimper in rising heated desire. Mac still stood by the bed, slowly stroking his cock, his gaze dark, his expression clouded with pleasure and approval. With a surfeit of love as his gaze met hers, and wicked, carnal knowledge, his eyes dropped to where Jethro's tongue was slowly curling around her nipple, sending a whiplash of naked fire to flay her nerve endings.

God help her, just as he wanted, she was coming undone.

Mac watched as Keiley's eyes began to glaze over, then dropped to where Jethro ministered to her nipples with seductive abandon.

Broad male hands cupped her breasts, lifting first one, then the other to the wicked lash of his tongue, then to his suckling mouth. Her nipples darkened, becoming cherry in color rather than the innocent pink of pre-arousal.

The delicate tip disappeared into Jethro's mouth as his cheeks began to draw deeply. Mac knew what pleased his wife, just as he knew from watching his friend repeatedly how he tormented tender, sensitive nipples.

His tongue was lashing at it. Keiley jerked with each flick of a tongue against her highly sensitive nipples. She was trembling now, shuddering, her nails creating indents in the hard muscles of Jethro's naked, tense shoulders.

Moans slipped from her lips as Jethro began to slip down her torso. He strung kisses along her perspiration-slick flesh. Tender skin that shimmered with life and moisture. His tongue licked over the lightly salty essence of her, causing her to shudder as her hands pushed him lower.

Mac grimaced with rising hunger, his hand tightening on the shaft of his cock at the sight of Keiley pushing Jethro to the soft folds between her thighs.

She loved having her pussy licked. She kept the soft curls that shielded it trimmed to the perfect length so they were still soft, yet didn't impair the pleasure Mac found in going down on her.

Jethro would appreciate that, though Mac knew that eventually he would press her to have the plump little mound waxed. Something Mac had put off, waiting, he knew, for Jethro's arrival.

Jethro eased lower, spreading her thighs wider, wedging his shoulders between them and revealing the glistening curls to Mac's gaze.

His friend's eyes lifted, a question in them. Mac grimaced in rising lust. Watching this, having the chance to watch Keiley's pleasure, knowing that the intensity was greater for the extremity of the act, had his own pleasure spiking higher.

He could watch her. Gauge her response. See her coming apart and know that the pleasure she was receiving was greater than any he could give her alone. He wasn't sharing her. He was giving to her.

He nodded slowly to Jethro, finally answering the question in the other man's eyes. They had done this so many times before that Mac felt a shimmer of amusement that the other man would ask permission to continue at this point.

But once that permission was given, Jethro didn't hesitate. With his thumbs he parted the soft folds, revealing the glistening pearl-pink flesh saturated with sweet female syrup. It was thick, sweeter than candy, slick, and Mac knew that the fresh, soft scent of it would make Jethro crazy.

The other man loved eating pussy. He loved the taste, texture, and exciting heat to be found only between soft thighs and aroused folds.

His head lowered, though he was careful to make certain Mac could see every lick, every promise he gave to the trembling flesh.

Keiley's clit was swollen now, glistening nearly red with the aroused fervor whipping through her. Jethro rimmed it slowly, then closed his lips over it and suckled with delicate greed as one hand moved lower.

"Oh God! Jethro!" Keiley cried out, her head whipping from side to side before her eyes suddenly jerked open and she tensed, her eyes moving to him.

As though she had just realized she had screamed another man's name.

Jethro didn't ease in his caresses. Mac watched the battle on her face, the fight to stare back at him versus the need to close her eyes and let herself fly.

"Let go," he whispered, moving closer to her, kneeling on the bed to touch her cheek, his thumb whispering over her lips. "Let me see you let go. It doesn't matter whose name you scream, baby. We're both here."

Her hips jerked, arched. Mac gritted his teeth against the hunger tearing him apart. He knew what that meant. Jethro's fingers were filling her, stroking inside her, fucking her with slow, sweet strokes as she began to shake with the need to release.

"I know what he's doing to you," he told her as she stared back at him, helpless. "He's fucking that tight pussy, his fingers filling it, burning with the grip you have on them."

Her lips parted with breathless pleasure as he glanced down her body once again. Jethro's eyes were closed, his tongue dancing around her straining clit, licking, drawing the heated syrup to his lips until it clung to them with glistening sweetness.

Mac lowered himself to the bed, his arm going beneath her neck, holding her head to his chest as he continued to watch. Watched the sweetest pussy in the world as it creamed for Jethro's mouth. Watched as her clit disappeared inside the other man and, seconds later, she screamed his name, jerking, writhing as Mac held her to him, feeling her orgasm ripping through her.

"I need her." Jethro jerked to his knees and tucked his cock against the fragile folds of Keiley's slick flesh.

Jethro pressed her legs further apart, opening the plump lips further to reveal the dark pink flesh hugging the tip of his cock.

With one arm Mac held Keiley close as he stroked his own dick with his other hand. Son of a bitch, he was going to be lucky to last until she came again.

He was going to be lucky to last until Jethro buried fully inside her.

He was working his cock in, the head disappearing, then reemerging, slick and glistening with her inner juices before disappearing again.

Keiley's sharp little teeth bit into his chest as he watched Jethro wedge inside her a little deeper with each stroke.

"Ah God. She's so fucking tight." Jethro breathed roughly.

"So hot. So tight. God help me." He impaled her farther, pulled back, the sweet juices clinging to his cock like threads of damp satin before he penetrated once again.

It seemed to take forever. With each stroke inside her Mac's fingers tightened on his cock, stroking it, feeling the blistering heat of her pussy through memory alone.

Jethro felt his soul rocking. He stared at where he was penetrating Keiley, barely half-impaled, and he was ready to release. He could feel the pre-cum welling from the head of his cock before he suddenly stilled. He stared at the naked length of his erection that he had yet to bury inside her before his gaze jerked to Mac.

The knowledge that he wasn't wearing a condom was in the rueful, amused glimmer of his friend's eyes.

Jethro swallowed tightly. God, if he had to pull free and sheathe himself, lose the feeling whipping through his dick, he would die.

"I'm protected," Keiley said breathlessly. "I won't get pregnant."

His hips jerked, driving full-length inside her as he felt agonizing, clenching pleasure tighten his balls and rip up his spine.

"Ah, fuck!" he groaned.

He was doomed. Dead man walking.

He shook his head, fighting against the incredible power of the pleasure rocking him to his soul.

"It's like being inside a dream, isn't it?" Mac rasped softly. "A wicked dream so hot, so searing, that you know if you wake up you're going to die."

Jethro's hands tightened on her thighs as he fought to breathe through the rippling, clenching pleasure racing from his cock to his chest.

Beneath him, Keiley was arching, screaming his name, her juices heating her pussy until he swore they would both combust from the pleasure of it.

As good as it was, as shaken as he was, he couldn't stay still. He jerked back, impaled her again, watching as the plump folds of her pussy parted, then closed around his cock, feeling the viselike grip of her inner muscles stroking over him.

Then he was moving, thrusting harder, coming over her as Mac eased back, pulling her into his arms, feeling her nails biting into his flesh as he began to pump inside her.

Her legs wrapped around his waist, her hips arched, her pussy tightened—ah, God, she was so tight—and a second later he felt heaven. He felt her lock down on him, tiny muscles clenching and stroking his cock as he buried himself inside her over and over again. Felt the tight little channel pulse, clench, then explode around him.

He meant to pull out. He meant to hold back his own release to spill to the blankets, but she caught him off guard. Screaming his name, her arms tight around him, her hard nipples searing his chest as her pussy burned along the length of his cock.

Before he could catch himself, he was spilling inside her. Pumping hard and desperate as spurt after spurt of semen filled her willing flesh.

He gasped her name, pressed his lips to her neck, clenched his eyes tight, and prayed for a miracle. A miracle because he was falling in love with his best friend's wife.

He was aware of Mac's shattered groan at his side and knew his friend had found his own release. Jethro collapsed, barely managing to catch his weight with his elbows.

He had to force himself to stop whispering her name into her neck. Had to force himself to push his own fractured emotions deep beneath the now-shattered shield he had once erected around his heart.

He had to force himself to remember that he was just there for the fun. That was it. That was all. Just for the fun.

CHAPTER FOURTEEN

Keiley stared at the computer screen, the program pulled up, the code she was attempting to finalize, and gave a weary sigh before lowering her head and rubbing at her forehead.

She didn't have a hope of keeping her mind on what she was doing. The events of the night before were playing before her mind. Like shadows on a dusky summer evening, whispering over the memory of her own pleasure, the excitement that tore through her, the shuddering ecstasy, the emotions—

This wasn't happening.

Keiley clenched her fingers in her hair as she pressed her lips together, fighting through the confusion rising inside her.

None of it made sense. She was certain this wasn't what it was supposed to be. It was supposed to be fun, right? Mac didn't intend for this to go on indefinitely. He didn't intend for her to care for anyone other than him.

But she was beginning to care, and that wasn't acceptable. It was a betrayal.

She shook her head, forcing herself back to the program, to the job she had been hired to do, rather than the mess her husband was making of her emotions.

As her head lifted her gaze was caught by Jethro's laptop, its slender connection attaching it to her computer, running programs within programs and tracking and tracing any incoming messages or e-mails. Jethro had told her quite specifically to stay off-line and let the program do its work. They didn't want the stalker actually engaging her in communication. They wanted to make certain there was no access to her. No way to track her. No way to harass her.

"Stay off the computer, Keiley." Mac walked into the office for the fourth time in an hour, his voice firm as Keiley stared at the computer.

"I have work to do." Saving her work, she shut the program down before staring at the minimized chat and relay programs she normally ran on a regular workday.

She was logged into two open forum conferences, though her message bar was set to *away*. Her private communication programs were open, as was another chat line. But Keiley wasn't there. She was staring at her desktop instead in disgust.

"The Playboy gets his kicks out of terrorizing the wives of his victims," Mac repeated.

"Don't give him access and he'll have to change his tactics, therefore making him easier to catch," she finished in irritation. "I know that, Mac."

She pushed away from the desk, straightened, and moved around the desk.

"I can't just sit here and stare at an empty computer screen, and I can't stand to work wondering what the hell is going on in my conferences." She heard the anger in her tone even as she found herself unwilling to push it back further.

"Hey. It's okay." He caught her in his arms as she moved to pass him.

From behind, he wrapped her in the strength and warmth of his body, and she wished it were comforting her. She wished she could find some peace within the confusion twisting through her mind.

"Too much too fast," she whispered brokenly, her hands latching onto his wrists as she leaned back into him, trying to absorb his strength, to hold onto it.

"I know." He kissed the top of her head and held her safe.

But she had found that she could find the same feelings that she found with Mac in another man's arms.

Keiley tensed at the thought, suddenly desperate to get away from him, desperate to clear her head of his scent and his warmth to make sense of the emotions she couldn't seem to get a handle on.

"You don't know, Mac." Tearing from his arms, she lifted her hand in a halting motion, feeling him reach for her again, feeling her own weaknesses overwhelming her. "You don't know what I'm feeling. And you don't how frustrating this is. How could you? It's not you that bastard is using as a tool to test you."

"And you think watching him tear you apart doesn't tear me apart?" His voice deepened, grew rougher. "You're my wife, Keiley."

"Am I?" She turned back to him, her breathing rough, the anger and the frustration boiling inside her. "Am I your wife or a toy you've grown tired of playing with, Mac? Personally, I'm starting to feel more and more like the toy."

She watched his jaw flex, the way his eyes began to brew with the turbulence of emotions suddenly boiling beneath the surface.

"You were never a toy, Keiley," he said. "And you can't deny you found something you were looking for yourself when Jethro came to our bed. Don't belittle us both by denying it."

She wanted to lie. She wanted to scream out a denial in his face and strike out at him for the emotions she could no longer make sense of. She wanted to make him pay for the turmoil in her heart, and in her head.

He chuckled then, lighting a fuse to the anger raging inside her, the arrogance in his expression, the knowing sensuality and certainty in his eyes setting a blaze inside her head that threatened to turn into a conflagration of fury.

"Keiley, it's okay," his voice gentled. "You've sat in here by yourself, thinking about it, remembering it, knowing you can't escape it, and I know you're scared." His jaw clenched as his expression softened. "Nothing's changed."

"Thats not true!" Her voice began to rise.

"What's changed then?" he asked. "Tell me how it's different, Kei. I'll make it better."

"Everything!" she cried. "This—this is too much, Mac."

"What's too much, Kei? The emotion? The need? Finding out that there's more to us than you imagined? You always knew that. If you hadn't, you wouldn't have been pushing when you began to realize you weren't getting all of me," he told her fiercely.

His eyes. If they had been angry, if he had been angry, she could have fought. But she couldn't fight his gentleness or the truth that he made her acknowledge. That it was more than she imagined. More pleasure, more hunger, more emotion than she ever wanted to lose.

"Look at you," he said then. "Your eyes are nearly green with the heat inside you. You make me so damned hard I can barely breathe when you try to fight what I know we both want."

He moved forward. Keiley retreated.

She wanted to beg him to stop, she wanted to beg him to take her. She wanted to scream in frustration and whimper in arousal.

"Stop, Mac." She stopped. Holding her ground as he paused in front of her, his head tilting toward her, watching her with a small quirk to his lips, almost a smile, full of knowledge.

This part was the Mac that held her soul. Gentle loving. It was being brought back to her that she had sensed the depth of his sexuality during the beginning of their relationship, had sensed the secrets he held back from her. And she had ignored them. She had pushed aside her own wariness and let him hide from her. She was at fault as much as he was, yet acceptance wasn't as easy for her.

It wasn't Mac she was having problems accepting, though, and she knew it. It was herself. It was realizing that this wasn't going to be a game. It wasn't just an interesting episode in their lives. It was going to change them all.

"Look at your face," he said, his voice soft. "Do you have any idea what it does to me to see that battle raging in your eyes? To watch you learning yourself, Keiley?"

"Learning myself? I'm not learning myself, Mac, I'm destroying myself."

She turned and left the room, left him before she revealed more than she wanted to, more than either of them could handle.

In running from Mac, she ran headlong into Jethro, though. Dressed in snug jeans and no shirt, barefoot and leaning against the kitchen counter with a cup of fresh coffee, his gaze searching as he watched her, then flicked behind to Mac.

"Everything okay?"

He couldn't just keep his mouth shut, could he?

"Everything's fine."

Or it would be if her breasts weren't swollen and sensitive, if her sex weren't heated and slick with the warmth of the hungers raging through her. If she could just get the image and the memory of him kneeling between her thighs, entering her, stretching her, and burning inside her womb as he thrust inside her.

If she could forget that she had felt his semen filling her, rocking her higher, and pushing her own orgasm past endurable limits.

"Everything's fine, Jethro." Mac lent his own voice to the assurance, which only pissed her off further.

She continued through the kitchen and headed briskly for the doorway. She had to get away from them. Escape. She had to escape before she humiliated herself. Before she begged them to take her.

She couldn't live like this, she told herself as she rushed for the stairway. She couldn't feel torn between her husband and another man. She couldn't have her emotions destroying her like this, because as God was her witness, she would end up destroying them all.

"No, Keiley." Mac caught her at the first step. "Don't run from this, baby."

His hold was gentle, pulling her into his thighs and off her feet as escape was so close within her grasp.

"Mac, please—," she whispered, realizing that he was heavily aroused.

She could feel it. Smell it. She was weakened by it.

"No!" She couldn't. Not again. She couldn't let the insidious emotions creeping inside her take room. And they would. One more instance of her husband allowing another man to take her and she would lose the battle she could feel beginning inside her.

"Just no?" he whispered at her ear, his voice and his hold so gentle it sapped her strength.

She could feel him behind her, thick and hard, pressing against her buttocks as his lips caressed her neck with heated demand.

Her eyes closed as the need began to overwhelm her. Feeling Mac lift her, cradling her in his arms as he moved up the stairs.

"You promised," she whispered into his neck.

"To love you, protect you," he murmured. "Do you really want me to let you go, Kei?"

He gently laid her on the bed seconds later, but as her frantic gaze moved over his shoulder, she didn't see Jethro. She didn't see the dark visage of the man whose eyes haunted her with shadows.

At least she knew some of Mac's demons. Parts of the brutality of his past. She had lived long enough in Scotland Neck that what Mac hadn't told her, others had.

She knew his pain. She knew his need for comfort when the demons rose within him. Jethro's struck her deeper, harder, for the very fact that she knew so little about him.

"What are we doing to our marriage, Mac?" But she wasn't moving, she wasn't attempting to escape. Instead, she watched in rapt attention as he quickly undressed.

"Making it deeper, Kei, stronger," he whispered sensually, suddenly stilling and staring back at her silently as she gripped the hem of her shirt and jerked it over her head.

She needed him. She needed her husband. She needed to know that the desire was just as sharp—no, sharper, hotter—than it had been with Jethro. She needed to know she wasn't losing the dreams she had woven around them, that she wasn't losing the man she loved.

As he watched her, she felt the hunger rise inside her, hotter, stronger. She scooted to the edge of the bed, her legs draping over it as her fingers went to the snap and zipper of her shorts.

"You're falling behind, Mac," she breathed out imperatively as she glanced at the erection straining beneath the fly of his jeans.

She was skimming the shorts down her legs and dropping to her knees in front of him as he tore the belt loose. Brushing his fingers aside with frantic need, she tugged at the metal clasp, then eased the zipper down.

The material smoothed down his legs along with his underwear, leaving the thick, heavy length of his cock to her avid gaze.

"Just us," she pleaded, filling both hands with the heated length of male flesh as her tongue licked over the dark, heavily flushed crest while she stared up at him.

His gaze moved over his face as his fingers threaded through her hair.

"We're the only two here," he assured her before his fingers slid through her hair. A grimace controlled his face as she allowed nothing but her tongue to touch the engorged head of his cock.

She stared back at him, fighting to hold onto her control as his fingertips touched her cheek gently.

"Just us," she said desperately as she lifted her head.

"Yes. Just us."

Keiley stared back at him desperately as her mouth covered his cock head once again, filling her mouth with his flesh. She should have been nervous, frightened. She should have come to her feet and told him to jack off instead. But she couldn't. She couldn't because she needed this just as much as he did.

Leaning back, she licked her lips slowly before trailing her fingers over the upper mounds of her breasts, then glanced over the tight, hard nipples as he stared down at her.

"Like this?" she whispered breathlessly needing to tease, to tempt.

This she liked. Her fingers surrounded her hard nipples, adding a heavy pressure, caressing them with enough strength to redden the hard tips.

His eyes dilated as she breathed in roughly. He slid his hand into her hair before wrapping the fingers of his other hand around the base of his erection.

She knew what was coming, felt it burn through her nipples as she tweaked them erotically, felt it clench in her womb and spill slick heat between her thighs.

"Which way do you prefer?" His voice was husky. Wild.

"This." Her fingers tightened on her nipples until it felt like teeth were nipping the tight buds, causing her lips to part helplessly with pleasure.

A move Mac took full advantage of. With his gaze still on her trapped nipples, the head of his cock sank into her mouth.

Keiley moaned as she heard Mac's guttural growl. Her lips closed on the head of his erection and sucked with delicate greed as she pinched and caressed her own nipples.

She stared up at Mac, watching his expression tighten, the hard, hungry grimace on his face as he held her in place and pulled back, removing his cock from her possession.

She licked her lips, pursed them, and blew over the damp head.

And she watched the control he was relying on so heavily break. But it didn't break in any way that she had expected. She expected him to fall upon her in desperate need. To spread her thighs and fuck her like the conqueror she could see glittering in his eyes.

When Mac's control broke, though, it revealed more than

a conquering sex god. It revealed the man who knew how to love.

He pulled her quickly to her feet, his hand once again shackling her wrists behind her back, his head lowering, his lips covering one hard, exquisitely sensitized nipple.

He didn't just suck it into his mouth. His teeth scraped, nipped, his tongue swirled and licked as he held her before him. Each caress was diabolically laid, performed and practiced with sensual precision. His free hand, calloused fingertips flat against her flesh, smoothed down her abdomen and tucked between her thighs.

Before Keiley could catch her breath or gather herself for the coming thrust, two of Mac's fingers began to work slowly, gently, inside the wet, hot depths of her core.

"You like that," he groaned, his head lifting as she arched in his arms.

"Yes." She writhed on his fingers. "Oh God, yes."

"My fingers fucking inside you, caressing you." His words followed suit, his fingertips curling, caressing with devastating results while he held her practically immobile with his hard body and restraining hand.

Rapid-fire bursts of pleasure exploding inside her body as Mac bent her over his arm, his lips lowering to play with her nipples again as his fingers moved inside her, stroking deep, caressing her, burning through her mind.

There were other things burning inside her as well. The fierce, blazing heat was followed by the knowledge that something wild, something untamed, was growing as well. Despite his gentleness, his emotion, she was burning higher.

She had once been content to let Mac direct their lovemaking; now she strained against him, needing to establish her own dominance.

He chuckled at the movements, ignoring her harsh cry as his fingers slid from between her thighs while he deftly turned her, bending her over the high mattress of the bed.

"Now, this is a pretty sight." His hand caressed over the

rounded curve of her buttocks, stroking them, causing her to shudder at the submission of her position.

"You're a pervert," she accused breathlessly.

"Oh darlin', you have no clue," he murmured, his roughened voice stroking over her senses as she bucked against him.

Keiley could feel the familiar, blistering heat surrounding her as Mac's hand cupped beneath her thigh, lifting her leg until her foot was braced on the wooden frame of the high bed before she felt his cock pressing against the hot, wet folds of her sex.

"This is the sweetest pussy in the world," he groaned behind her as she caught her breath at the pleasure.

He was stretching her, working inside her with slow, heavy movements that had her crying out his name.

"Do you like this, Kei?" Bending over her, his lips moved to her ear as his erection pressed deeper inside her. "Do you feel how tight and hot your pussy is around me? How sweet and wet you are?"

She could feel. She could feel every inch of his cock throbbing inside her, stretching her. The broad head parted her flesh, making way for the heavy stalk behind it to fill her. And she could do nothing to hurry him along.

The sheer impact of the submissive position combined with the powerful strength behind her shouldn't have made her hotter. It did, though. She could feel her juices gathering and flowing, slickening her, easing his way as he drew back until only the broad crest remained within her grip.

A second later he plunged inside her.

Keiley arched, crying out his name, trying to writhe beneath him as the incredible pleasure threatened to explode inside her. She wanted it to explode inside her. The knot of tension gathering in her womb was agonizing, the pleasure of it building until it bordered on pain, until the need to orgasm was ripping through her mind.

"God, I love fucking you," Mac whispered at her ear. "Feeling you tighten on my dick, your pussy sucking it inside you and rippling around it like the tightest fist."

His voice was harsh and guttural, his hands less than

gentle as he held her, his hips gathering speed, gathering in power. His cock plunged inside her, worked through the snug tissue, stroked and caressed, burning her with the strength of his passion as her own burned inside her.

She couldn't handle it. She felt stretched until pleasure and pain combined, until the need for release had her hands fisting in the blankets beneath her.

"Mac, please," she panted, barely able to breathe.

He was moving deeper now, harder, his breathing a dark rasp behind her as she felt her womb begin to ripple with the warning tremors of orgasm.

"So sweet and hot," he groaned again, pumping faster. "So tight and sweet."

Heat surrounded her, pulsed through and around her.

"I love fucking you," he groaned. "I dream of fucking you. I ache when I'm not fucking you."

She was crying out for him now, incoherent, lost in a world that centered on his thrusts inside her, his fingers sliding over her hip and delving between her thighs.

The swollen bud of her clit pulsed and throbbed as his fingers surrounded it, welcoming the touch as perspiration soaked her flesh and the demand for release pulsed in her veins.

His fingers stroked, his cock thrust, and within seconds Keiley felt the burn begin exploding throughout her body. First in her clit. An exquisite burning sensation erupted in the tight knot of nerve endings and tore her mind from her body. It echoed into her womb, then into her vagina, then throughout her body as a harder, deeper explosion ripped through her.

She bucked beneath him, trying to scream, trying to escape the intensity, the power of her orgasm until the violence of her pleasure ripped through her mind and sent her senses spinning. Flying. She was flying, lifted and flung into a world of kaleidoscope colors and an ecstasy she never grew used to.

Dimly, she felt the last hard thrusts slam through her before Mac poured his release inside her with a shattered male groan and the feel of his teeth at her shoulder. They were both shaking, shuddering, fighting to find their breath and their senses as he surrounded her with his arms and pulled her fully up onto the bed before stretching out next to her.

CHAPTER FIFTEEN

Keiley drifted in a haze of pleasure, pushing back the niggling little reminder that they had indeed been alone.

"It's not the same now, is it?" he whispered against her ear, satisfaction and dark knowledge filling his voice. "You know the difference. You feel it. And you miss it."

Her eyes opened, her gaze immediately caught by the wooden panels that covered the hole left by the shattering of the French doors.

"I can live without it." Her voice was quiet, reflective. Because she had heard those same words from Mac before they ever left Virginia.

What were they going to do when Jethro left? He couldn't stay forever. He had a life, his own interests, and one day he would fall in love himself. Where would that leave her then?

"It's different," she finally said, her voice low, thoughtful. "But I couldn't do this again." She knew that with a certainty. "When Jethro's gone, it will be over."

She expected an argument. Instead, she felt the smile on his lips that were pressed against her shoulder.

"When Jethro leaves, it will be over," he agreed.

Keiley rolled over, staring into his eyes with a frown. "I'm serious, Mac."

"I know you are, Keiley." He cupped her cheek with his palm. "I never imagined or considered sharing you with anyone else. And I never will."

"Why Jethro?"

He shook his head. "Because he suits us both," he finally said.

And that was all she was going to get out of him. He was so damned closemouthed about this that she felt as if she were walking through shadows alone, feeling her way through this strange new relationship.

"I love you, Mac," she said as she turned and rose from the bed before turning to stare back at him. "I love you more than my own life, but you're starting to worry me."

"How am I worrying you, Kei?" He turned on his back, lusciously nude, powerfully sensual, that arrogant quirk on his lips drawing a frown between her brows.

"Because you're playing games." She leaned forward, placed her palms on the bed, and stared him straight in the eyes. "It won't take me long to catch on to this new side you're showing, husband mine. And once I figure it out, this sexy little battle you're starting will even out. I promise you that."

His gray eyes lit with challenge and humor.

"I look forward to it," he drawled with a sensual smirk. "You have no idea how much I look forward to it."

She opened her lips to inform him how little she appreciated the arrogance when the soft trill of the doorbell interrupted.

Keiley jerked back as Mac suddenly surged from the bed and grabbed his jeans, jerking them on quickly.

"I wanted a shower," she said mournfully as she grabbed her clothes and rushed to the bathroom.

The slick warmth of sex still coated her thighs, reminding her of the excess of moments past. She hastily cleaned up before dressing and rushing back into the bedroom, where Mac was waiting impatiently.

"It's Maxine," he informed her as he glanced out the side of the curtains to the driveway.

"Maxine?" Keiley pushed her feet back into her sandals.

"Jethro let her in." Mac sighed, his expression rueful. "We'd better get back down there."

Keiley stared back at him with a measure of concern.

"What will Jethro do?"

He snorted. "With Jethro, who can be sure? It's according to the mood he's in."

Keiley stepped into the living room behind Mac to see that Maxine Bright hadn't arrived alone. She was accompanied by her quiet husband, Joseph.

Joseph wasn't rough and rugged, and he wasn't altogether handsome. But his quiet blue eyes and warm smile were steady and dependable. And his reputation for spoiling Maxine was legendary.

Six feet tall, lean rather than muscular, but with a surprising male grace, Joseph Bright was the complete opposite of his wife. Until Keiley had met his wife, she had imagined he was staid, stuffy, and self-righteous with his carefully combed thinning brown hair, light blue eyes, and carefully controlled lips.

As she had gotten to know the couple, she had learned that Joseph had a wicked, quiet wit, and that he was the perfect counterpart for his vivacious wife.

"There you are." Max bounced from the couch where she and Joseph had been sitting talking to Jethro. "We've been talking to your guest." She turned to her husband with a grin. "Why don't you ever have such good-looking friends visit?"

"Because they know you," he snorted. "You terrify them."

Keiley smothered her laughter at the frown that pulled at Max's pretty face and the little pout that pulled at her lips.

"You'll pay for that, Joseph," she warned him.

He winced, though there was an edge of laughter in his gaze. "I'm sure I will, Maxine."

He rose to his feet to meet Mac's outstretched hand then. "Mac." He nodded to Keiley. "Keiley. It's good to see you two. I hope we aren't disturbing you. Maxine was supposed to have called you before we arrived." He gave his wife a mocking glare.

"Oh, dear. Did I forget?" Maxine blinked innocently. "How rude of me."

Mac laughed. "You're always welcome, Max. I see you've met Jethro."

"We have indeed," Max drawled. "I'm impressed, Mac. He's actually very charming."

"What did you expect?" Mac chuckled as Jethro rose to his feet as well.

"Well, according to Delia, your houseguest was a cross between a pit bull and an ogre. Of course, I just had to find out for myself." Her tone gave every appearance of friendly laughter, but Keiley heard the anger just beneath it. "And can you imagine?" She turned to her husband, meeting his wary gaze. "We must have missed the orgy, honey. Do you think we should come back later?"

Joseph's expression tightened for an instant before he turned back to Mac with rueful amusement.

"She promised to behave."

"Yes, I did." Maxine turned to Keiley. "Where the hell have you been? You missed last night's meeting and Delia is telling everyone far and wide it's because you're having orgies out here, and evidently the whole damned FBI agency Mac was a part of is participating. Really, Keiley. You didn't invite me."

"I would have." Keiley shook her head mockingly. "But you know how it is, Max. I had to try them out myself before I introduced them to you. I know how picky you can be."

Max's green eyes twinkled with merriment as a spurt of laughter left her throat.

"I am very picky." She cast her husband a teasing glance before moving to Keiley. "Let's go discuss their fine qualities while Mac and Jethro entertain Joseph." She gave Mac a warning look. "And be nice or he won't play with me later. I wouldn't like that."

"Yes, Maxine." Mac was obviously restraining his own laughter. "I'll be very gentle with his delicate sensibilities."

"You do that." Maxine nodded as she pulled Keiley from the room. "And remember, he blushes easily. So don't embarrass him."

Keiley couldn't help but smile as Maxine pulled her across the foyer and into the kitchen before releasing her arm and heading for the refrigerator.

"You know, Keiley," she commented as she pulled a drink free from the interior and popped the cap. "We're going to have to have a little talk about the best way to weather gossip. Hiding out at home isn't going to do the job."

"I had no idea there was any gossip, Max." She stared back at her friend, at once amused and concerned.

Maxine was furious beneath the amusement. She had to be the only person Keiley knew who could be equally amused and angry at the same time.

"Figures." Max plopped into a kitchen chair and stared back at her with a grin. "All those orgies take time, I imagine."

"She's really saying that we're having orgies?" Keiley winced.

"I don't know if she started it or if she's just pushing it along." Max shrugged then. "But it's working its way through the charity committee and likely through town as well. Thankfully, no one is really taking it seriously. What's happened to the world? Ten years ago, we would have all been suitably horrified by the prospect and blacklisted you immediately."

"Progress. Go figure." Keiley laughed as she sat down across from her friend. "Maybe orgies just aren't fun enough anymore."

"Or too tame," Max snapped, the edge of anger showing in her voice again. "Delia's becoming a problem, Kei. She's managed to even surprise me. Did you know she's trying to have you thrown off the committee?"

"She's been trying to do that since my first year there." Keiley shrugged as she tucked her leg beneath her on the chair and leaned her elbow on the table. "Come on, Max, she's harmless. She's just jealous."

"Jealous, you say," Max snorted. "I swear, she had a nipple hard-on when she was talking about immorality within the committee ranks, and if she didn't cream her tight-laced panties when she said the words *ménage* and *orgy,* then I don't know my body language." Max paused. "We both know I know body language, right?"

"You do know your body language," Keiley agreed.

"It was gross." Max gave a mock shudder. "She was standing at the podium during the meeting last night getting wet at the thought of hurting you and Mac. The woman is rabid."

"She's sad." Keiley shrugged again. "I signed the contract; they took my money. They can't take me off the committee and their petty shit doesn't affect me."

"Keiley, can she have any kind of proof?" Max asked her softly then. "I don't care what you do here in your own home, and if you were getting it on with both those lean, mean hunks in there, then more power to your energetic ass because you have a hell of a lot more stamina than I would have. But Delia is too confident that she can have you voted out."

"Delia's alway confident and never successful," Keiley assured her. "She's making a lot of noise, Max, and noise is something better off ignored. She'll get tired of it eventually, as she always does, and go away."

"You can't keep missing meetings." Max shook her head. "Promise me you won't. You have to face them, sweetie. I know how hard it is, hell, poor Joey, he goes through hell because of me and I know it. But I can't be someone I'm not and still be happy. That's how I know you can't hide from it."

"I'm not hiding from the gossip," Keiley assured her.

"Keiley, listen to me." Max leaned forward, her green eyes compassionate. "You're one of my best friends and I know you. I know what you told me about your past with your dad, and I know how gossip hurts. You're hiding."

"Not from the gossip." Keiley breathed out roughly the minute the words left her lips.

Damn it. The last thing you did was give Max a lead when she was in protective mode. The other woman was like a protective mother wolf when it came to her friends.

"Then what?" Max frowned. "What the hell is going on, Keiley?"

"Keiley has picked up a stalker, Max," Mac said from the doorway as he, Jethro, and Joseph walked into the room.

Silence filled the kitchen.

Joseph moved around the table, pulled out the chair beside his wife, and sat down beside her, his arm going around her as Mac sat down beside Keiley and Jethro moved to the refrigerator.

"Mac just explained everything to me, Max," Joseph told her, his voice soft as Max stared back at her in horror. "It's an old case that Mac was working on. It's followed him here."

Jethro sat out three beers as Keiley stared back at Max. Then she shot Mac a disapproving frown. "I could have handled this, Mac."

"Oh, listen to Superwoman here." Max threw her hand toward Keiley as her green eyes glittered damply. "You could have handled it. Well, God bless your heart."

Keiley winced. It was never a good thing when that comment came out of Max's lips.

"Now, Max."

"Don't you 'Now, Max' me, Keiley McCoy," she snapped. "I'm glad you're handling it so damned well by yourself because honest to God, I just felt my heart fall to my stomach and it's not in the least comfortable buried down there."

Keiley's lips twitched. That was Max, dramatic to the end.

"I could have handled telling you myself," Keiley explained. "Mac and Jethro are taking care of things, Max. It's going to be okay."

"That bitch, Delia," Max muttered then. "She's a viperous little wannabe slut with no way out from beneath her mommy-in-law's eagle little eye. You know she's doing this because she wants in Mac's pants. Right?"

"She's welcome to try." Keiley shrugged. "I just can't promise she'll have a hand left when I get finished with her."

Max sniffed as an unwilling laugh roughened her throat. "Don't make me laugh, Keiley. I'm too horrified to find any amusement in this."

Then her gaze shifted to Jethro as he took his seat on the other side of Keiley.

"I liked the idea of the ménage better," Max sighed, staring back at Keiley sadly. "That sounds like a lot more fun."

She had no idea just how much more fun it was.

"Mac, is there any way we can help?" Joseph asked then.

"Stay away," Mac warned him. "I don't want him to find another victim to focus on, Joe. And keep your ears open. I don't like the way this rumor of a ménage has suddenly flared up. See if you can hear where it started."

"I can find that out." Max glared back at Mac. "Trust me, Delia can't keep a secret, and I know she's behind this. I'll find out where it started or if she just started it on her own."

And Max could do it. The woman was a dynamo. She could widen her green eyes with naïve innocence and play the clueless Southern belle with just the right touch of realism. False realism, but it worked.

"See what you can find out for me, Max." Mac nodded as Keiley glanced over at him. "And don't say anything about the stalker. I'd like to keep this quiet if we can."

That was all it took. Maxine might give the appearance of flightiness, of cluelessness, but it hid a mind as sharp as a razor and a loyalty as deep as the oceans.

"Of course we'll keep it quiet." Max stared at Mac as though he had lost his mind. "You think I want Delia Staten to get her hands on this information? She would find the bastard and help him out."

"Max," Joe chastised gently.

"You know it's the truth," Max pouted back at her husband. "And Keiley knows it as well. Delia would do anything for a chance to get in Mac's bed." She turned to Mac. "Why didn't you just give her some before you left town fifteen years ago instead of leaving her in suspense?"

Joe lowered his head and shook it, helpless as his shoulders shook in silent laughter.

Mac stared back at her with brooding mockery. "And how would that have helped me?"

"Well." Max waved her hand blithely. "We all know how inexperienced eighteen-year-old jackasses are. She would have never looked at you twice when you came back."

"Max," Joe groaned in protest.

"Joe, you're lucky someone didn't steal your wife away

before you ever moved back here and rescued the rest of the male population," Mac laughed.

"I'm lucky someone didn't kill her," Joe grunted, though his expression was filled with pride, his eyes alight with love when he looked at her. "Come on, wildcat. Let's do as Mac suggests and get out of here."

"You have to be at tomorrow night's meeting," Max all but ordered Keiley, rising from her chair and pinning her with an eagle stare. "Other people will end up coming out here to check on you if you don't. I was just elected as the advanced strike."

Keiley looked back at her in surprise.

"Honey, you have friends here." Max shook her head at Keiley's surprise. "More friends than you know. I've had five phone calls since you missed that meeting, and one came from the old dragon lady Victoria Staten herself. And trust me, she doesn't normally call and check on anyone."

"I'll be there," Keiley promised, rising to her feet as Max moved around the table. "And you take care yourself."

As their goodbyes were said and Keiley accepted a fierce hug from her friend, she stood back while Mac led the couple to the door and walked to the car with them.

Behind her, she felt Jethro, far enough away for decency's sake, near enough to remind her of the warmth and strength of his body.

"I'm going to have to go to that damned meeting," she muttered. "I really don't want to have put up with Delia Staten this week."

She was still too raw, too aware of the truth behind the gossip. She would have much preferred to hide in the house and pretend that the world outside had ceased to exist.

"You can't hide forever."

Keiley swung around, meeting his dark blue eyes, seeing the fall of his black hair over his brow and the wicked, sensual dip of his thick lashes over his brilliant eyes.

She pushed her hands into the pockets of her shorts before moving around him and heading back to the kitchen.

"I'm not in the mood to argue with you. I've already been there with Mac and once a day is enough."

"Keiley, am I hurting you?"

She turned back to him quickly. He stood framed in the doorway, watching her with an assessing gaze, his expression cool, almost forbidding.

"Do you want to hurt me, Jethro?"

"I don't want to hurt you. If it's hurting you, I'll leave."

"You're not hurting me." Confusing her. Making her question herself. But it wasn't pain. She wondered if the pain would come if he left, though.

"I need to go back to work." She shook her head as he stepped closer. "I just need to get away from you and Mac. Just for a little while. Just—just for a while."

CHAPTER SIXTEEN

The next day Keiley sat in the garage, stretched out on the old sofa she and Mac had discarded the year before, and worked on the data program she was still tweaking on Mac's laptop.

She could have worked more much effectively in her office, but Mac refused to allow her to work there alone, and he and Jethro were busy "sparring." It looked more like they were busy trying to kill each other.

Wearing only a few pads at elbows and knees and lightly padded headgear, they went at each other with fists, kicks, and heavy male grunts in the center of the thick mat Mac had unrolled across the cement floor.

She winced as Mac landed a hard blow to Jethro's gut, then closed her eyes as Jethro landed a double-fisted blow to Mac's back that nearly took him to the floor.

That had been going at it for over an hour, with neither man appearing to get the best of the other. Mac was more muscular. The heavy farmwork he did on a daily basis had given him a solid, thickly muscled physique. Jethro was as tall, but not nearly as broad or physically strong. He made up for it with speed and adaptability. Not to mention striking with carefully aimed blows for the weakest parts of Mac's body.

She had a feeling she wouldn't have to worry about sex because they would be too sore to move.

They had been at this off and on for two days now. Pushing

each other, daring, challenging, taking out their aggressions in what they called "preparation" until they could take them out on the stalker who had decided to begin e-mailing with fanatic intensity.

The smug dares he had issued to Mac and Jethro were insane. Declaring both men incompetent, unable to protect her. That she needed a man better able to secure her welfare because obviously Mac couldn't. Making his knowledge of the building relationship between her and the two men clearly apparent.

In the past two days, there had been over six e-mails, and even now Jethro's tracking program was working its way through the bouncing Internet signal the stalker was using to send them.

The e-mail account was from an anonymous mailbox, and the origin of it was ghosting through Internet hosts all over the globe. And while Jethro attempted to track him, his e-mails were escalating in anger to the point that he was now berating Mac and Jethro about their sexual relationship with her.

At that thought she sobered, trying to push back the niggling discomfort moving inside her. Not that having sex with the two men together was bothering her; that part she thought she was handling reasonably well. What had begun rippling through her with nervous intent was the awareness that something more than sex was growing between her and Jethro, though.

In the past days she grown aware of a thread of feeling, an emotion that had first begun between her and Mac during those first weeks of courtship. It was growing between her and Jethro now, though it didn't seem to be detracting from the bond she had with Mac.

She was certain Mac couldn't want this to happen. Could he? He had always seemed so possessive of her, so determined to keep other men from encroaching on her attention, that he was suddenly confusing her.

He was throwing her and Jethro together, giving the other man every chance to touch her however he liked, even to the point that often Mac found his release with his hand or buried in her mouth rather than within her body.

Shaking her head, she turned her attention back to the final adjustments she was making to the program Mac was using to scan the Internet, forums, and chat boards for the stalker. Key words were tweaked with regularity, and the processing ability of the program was now working with one hundred and ten percent efficiency and speed.

It wasn't going to make its round of scans overnight, but it would do it much faster now than it had before.

As she set the program to run in the background of the laptop she looked up as Mac and Jethro collapsed, panting, onto the mat, obviously calling a draw once again.

"You two are going to kill each other," she told them as she set the computer aside and rose to her feet. "You're exhausting me just watching you."

They turned their heads to stare at her for a long moment before groaning and turning away once again.

Keiley leaned back on the sofa and watched them with a smile. "How much longer are you two going to go on like this before you realize you're equally matched?"

"Not true," Jethro muttered. "I'm faster than he is."

"Bullshit," Mac groaned. "I'm stronger."

"Yeah yeah yeah, and you're both mean as a junkyard dog and twice as cunning. Now get your butts to the shower so I can fix lunch. I'm hungry and I'm tired of watching the two of you beat each other up."

She absently ruffled the fur of the rather large Pappy as he laid his head on her lap now that the laptop was moved to the side. "You're even making Pappy tired."

Mac turned his head again to stare at the dog with narrowed eyes. "Damned mutt. He's never going to go back outside, is he?"

"Probably not." She smiled back at him consolingly. He preferred having pets outside rather than in the house. "Content yourself with the fact that he seems housebroken."

Mac grunted at that before levering himself upright and watching as Jethro did the same.

"You should have never let that damned dog in the house," he growled.

Jethro just shook his head. He hadn't said much in the past few days, brooding over his computer instead and conducting several net meetings with agents in the Bureau's D.C. office.

Keiley stood on her feet. Pappy rose as well, trotting behind her as she headed for the door. "Go shower," she told the men.

The dog pushed in front of her, moving through the short hallway ahead of her as she entered the house, his ears cocked as though listening for anything unusual.

Keiley was aware of the small pistol resting in the pocket of the dress she was wearing today and the knowledge that she couldn't be too careful now, even in her own home.

"Hold up there." Mac caught her arm as she neared the entrance to the living room and moved ahead of her.

His weapon was in his hand, and as she glanced behind her at Jethro, she saw that he carried one as well.

"This house is rigged with so many damned alarms and booby traps now that I'm afraid of being caught in one myself," she snorted. "I doubt anyone is going to slip in."

They sure as hell weren't slipping into her bedroom anytime soon. Mac and Jethro had nailed planks of plywood over the French doors until the new doors could arrive within the next few days.

"Let's just make certain," he murmured as Jethro moved around them and they began a careful, quiet search of the house.

Keiley just shook her head at them, though she followed along quietly until they were back in the kitchen.

"I have to go take care of the stock," Mac said as he gathered clean clothes from the washroom and headed for the shower attached to the washroom. "I won't be gone long. Keep her in line, Jethro."

Keiley turned carefully to Jethro, lifting her brow mockingly.

"I'll do my best." Amusement laced his voice, but little of it reached his eyes.

Dragging out a cooking pot, Keiley set it on the stove before moving to the refrigerator and pulling out the small roast she had placed in the fridge to defrost the afternoon before and vegetables free of the crisper drawer.

As Mac showered, Keiley cut the roast into chunks before tossing them in the pot, covering them with water, and setting them back on the burner.

That taken care of, she set about cutting and chopping the vegetables for the vegetable soup she had planned to fix.

"You're a good cook," Jethro suddenly announced from behind her, causing her to glance quickly over her shoulder.

He was staring at her broodingly, much the way Mac looked when he was debating a problem.

"Thanks."

"Did your mother teach you how to cook?"

Keiley paused in preparing the vegetables, staring down at the celery she was destringing before a sad smile tugged at her lips.

"Mom was an excellent cook."

She had been. The perfect homemaker, a good wife and mother until her life had gone to hell.

"You look like her," he stated then.

Keiley froze before turning to face him slowly.

"I ran a check on you when I saw how fast Mac was falling in love with you." There was no apology in his expression, just that brooding, questioning gaze.

"Great," she muttered. "Thanks for letting me know." It was information she could have done without.

"You rose above their mistakes." He leaned back against the wall lazily, though his expression didn't change. "It must have been hard, though."

"What must have been hard? Not embezzling when I had the chance? Staying away from the liquor when things got hard? Sorry, Jethro, but it was no chore at all." She sliced the celery with brutal strokes. "It was actually pretty damned easy."

"You were eighteen when your mother committed suicide. Your father died of a heart attack a year later, in prison.

From what I learned, the community you lived in pretty much ostracized you."

Yes. They had. They had talked and gossiped and made her life hell by turning their backs on her and whispering whenever they saw her.

"I survived."

"Beautifully," he said calmly.

"What's the point behind this, Jethro?" She laid the knife down carefully before turning to him and meeting his gaze directly. "Do you torture your lovers for the hell of it, or is it an added bonus?"

His gaze flared. Brilliant pinpoints of glittering arousal suddenly filled it as his eyes raked over her body.

"Are you my lover?"

Keiley blinked back at him in surprise. There was a darkness in his tone that had her stepping back, a fierce, sudden vein of possessiveness in his voice.

"I'm Mac's wife," she whispered. "But I would assume what's been going on here in the past few days makes me your lover as well. For now."

His lips quirked with a hard edge. "Yes, for now."

The tension emanating from him was thick enough to make her catch her breath.

"What about you?" She tilted her head curiously. "What would you call it?"

"Disastrous," he suddenly stated, raking his fingers through his hair and pulling free the elastic band that had held it behind his neck. It framed his face now, laying longer than Mac's, and giving his expression a harder, more savage appearance.

"I'll agree with you there." She turned back to the vegetables, willing her heart to slow down, her pulse to stop choking her with the fierce, hard throbs she could feel at her throat.

"Then why are you allowing it?" he suddenly snarled. "You're sleeping with your husband's best friend. You're not even cheating, Keiley. You're letting him pawn you out like a favorite shirt."

"God damn you!" She rounded on him, the knife still gripped in her hand, fury racing through her now. "If you don't like it, then pack your shit up and leave. I didn't ask you to come here. I didn't ask you or Mac to begin this debacle, and I'll be damned if either of you will punish me for it."

His curse was blistering as he turned away from her and paced across the room. "You didn't deserve that. I'm sorry."

"No, I didn't," she snapped back. "And you can shove your apology. If it can come out of your damned mouth, then you can stand by it."

He swung around on her. "I apologize."

"I don't want your apology," she informed him in disgust. "Let me give you a clue here, Jethro. The same one I gave Mac years ago. Just because you're here, just because you're sharing my bed, does not give you the right to spill trash out of your mouth and excuse it with an apology. Make that mistake again and you'll leave."

His eyes narrowed. "Will I now?"

"Oh hell yes, you will," she informed him. "All that he-man alpha stuff is real arousing. It's even cute sometimes. But you can take your attitude somewhere else, because I'll be damned if I'll put up with it."

And she meant it. Jethro stared at the anger in her eyes, the flush mounting her cheeks, and he would have smiled if she weren't holding that knife like a weapon rather than a tool.

His gaze flickered to it. "Are you going to use that?"

"Don't put it past her." Mac stepped into the room, his gray eyes gleaming with amusement but also a hint of anger. "What did you do to piss her off?"

"Nothing." Keiley turned and began attacking the vegetables, as Jethro suspected she wanted to attack his head.

"I said something stupid," he answered for her. "She seems unwilling to accept my apology."

He started back at Mac, meeting his friend's eyes, knowing he had done Keiley an injustice even as those earlier words had slipped past his lips.

"She's bad for that." Mac shrugged. "She tossed me out

of my own apartment at two o'clock in the morning before we even started sleeping together."

Jethro watched as Mac eased over to her, his arm going around her, his lips at her ear as he whispered something that had a snort of a laugh erupting as she pushed him away with a look filled with exasperation and amusement.

"Get out of here," she ordered. "And take him with you." She pointed the knife over her shoulder at Jethro.

"He stays," Mac informed her, his voice firm. "I'm not leaving you here alone."

She glared over her shoulder at him. "There might be bloodshed."

"Just be sure to leave him in fighting shape." Mac shrugged. "If he's dumb enough to tempt a woman wielding a knife, then he deserves everything after that."

But he cast Jethro a warning look. Jethro folded his arms over his chest and stared back at him coolly before frowning at the knowing grin Mac finally gave him.

"I'll let you two fight it out, then." He patted Keiley's butt, jumping quickly out of the way as she slapped at his hand.

Still chuckling, he pulled his shirt on, buttoned it, and tucked it quickly into his jeans before pulling on his boots.

"I'll be around the stables and barns," he informed them both. "I let farmhands leave a few hours ago and I want to make certain everything's running smoothly before this evening."

"I told you I would cancel that, Mac," Keiley muttered.

"She has a meeting with her charity committee tonight for an hour or so," Mac said to Jethro. "We're going with her."

"That is not going to work," she snapped.

"We'll sit in the truck and wait on you. You are not going by yourself and you're not missing it. You look forward to this all year, Keiley. You're not going to let Delia's poison ruin it for you."

"And you bitch about it all year," she argued back. "So you can get out of it this time."

"The hell I will!" Mac glowered back at her.

The interplay was interesting, fiery, yet Jethro could detect the respect and bonding Mac and Keiley had developed over the years. It made him ache. Made him want to be a part of it even though he knew it was never going to happen.

"Keiley, I'm not letting this bastard steal this from you." Mac's voice suddenly softened as he stared back at her profile. "We'll go to the meeting and then catch dinner in town. We're not hiding."

"Delia will be there."

Jethro watched her fist clench on the counter.

"So Delia will be there. I'll be damned if I'm going to pretend you're not my fucking wife for that bitch. Get that off your mind. If she hasn't accepted the fact that it's not going to happen between me and her in fifteen years, then you can pretty much bet she's not going to figure it out, and you can go on with your life."

She looked over her shoulder at Jethro. "She'll be rude."

"And then me and Victoria will have a little talk about the nature of the Bureau and exactly what she doesn't want my friends looking into." Mac shrugged then. "Big deal. Do you want to hide for the rest of your life from the likes of her?"

Keiley muttered a little curse that had Mac's brow lifting and a smile tugging at his lips. "That's my girl. I'll be back in a little bit. Mind Jethro. He's an asshole, but he knows how to protect you."

"Thanks for the reference," Jethro growled.

"Welcome, bud." Lifting his hand, Mac punched in the alarm code before opening the back door, calling Pappy to him, and leaving the house.

Moving behind him, Jethro reset the code and turned slowly back to Keiley.

She was dumping the vegetables into a large bowl of water, her back still to him, the knife laying harmlessly on the counter.

"Would you really use the knife?" he asked her.

The look she gave him wasn't a compliment. It was the look a woman gave a man she considered less than an imbecile.

"No. I wouldn't use the knife on you."

"Mac seemed worried enough about it."

"Because Mac knows I'll brain him for being a moron," she snapped. "I don't handle the big strong male being stupid very well."

"I was being stupid," he agreed.

She stared back at him silently, her expression pulled into lines of weary acknowledgment.

"Maybe I deserved it," she finally whispered as she turned back to the sink, dampened a cloth, and began wiping the counter down.

She didn't deserve it. She deserved a man who recognized what a treasure he had. A treasure that wasn't meant to be shared.

"Why do you say that?"

He watched as she breathed in deeply before turning back to him.

"I knew about Sinclair's Club before I married Mac." She shrugged, the cloth clenched in her hand. "After I learned he was a member, maybe I let my own fantasies weave around it too much."

Jethro felt his expression flinch. "What are you saying?"

"I knew about you and Mac," she snapped angrily. "I heard the rumors about the two of you, then I heard the rumor that he was a part of the club. Mac didn't force me into this, Jethro. Mac hasn't made me fantasize about it. And he didn't pawn me off like an old shirt. I knew what I was doing."

"You fantasized about me?" That surprised him. He hadn't seen her since the first months after her marriage to Mac, and he had made certain not to so much as flirt with her during that time.

"Sometimes." Her shoulders shifted defensively. "Look, Jethro, I love Mac. Heart and soul. He's my life—"

She broke off, her teeth biting at her lower lip as she quickly turned away.

"But?"

"But I knew this was a part of him when I married him," she said softly. "I sensed it was a part he wouldn't be able to leave behind him."

Admitting that to herself was something that had been hard for Keiley to do over the past few days. Looking into herself and seeing that she had known this path was coming, whether she let herself realize it or not, hadn't been easy.

"You're too good for this."

Keiley could hear the anger in his voice. Like Mac, he hid it well. It came out as a gruff rasp that could have been many other emotions. But it was anger. Anger and self-disgust.

"Don't fool yourself." She tossed the cloth in the sink before turning back to him and staring him squarely in the eye. "And don't turn this into something it isn't. I'm not the delicate fairy Mac keeps wanting to see me as. I have my own needs as well, Jethro, and I'm not above admitting to them. I don't know if it's Mac's hungers that make me wild, or merely my own in the face of his acceptance. Whatever the reason, I'm not going to lash into myself or Mac over it. And I'm definitely not going to blame you. I've never walked the same path other people found comfortable and I'm not going to start now."

"That's not exactly true," he pointed out with an edge of humor. "You're not known for being a wild card, Keiley. You wouldn't have the solid reputation you have in business if that were the truth."

Keiley shrugged off the compliment. "It doesn't change the truth. I've known this was coming. Just as I knew it would be you he chose when he brought someone else to our bed."

"And you knew that how?"

She saw the frown, saw the edge of anger in his eyes, but she saw something in him that she had seen in Mac when she first met him. He was as lost inside as Mac had been.

"Because you're like a brother to him," she said gently. "He's missed you these last three years. Missed working with you. Missed sparring with you. Mac doesn't trust many people, you know."

Jethro shifted uncomfortably then. "Yeah. I know that."

"And neither do you," she pointed out. "I've stood between the two of you for three years as I've tried to find my own footing with Mac and who and what I am within our marriage. I can't be the good girl all the time. I wanted to be. I thought I could be."

"You married a man who lets you be free," he stated.

"Maybe too free." She shook her head at the thought. "Whatever the reason, Jethro, don't think I'm being coerced into what happened. I accept who and what I am. That's something you'd better do as well. I'd prefer you called me a whore than to blame Mac for something he didn't initiate."

"Never say that again," Jethro suddenly snarled, moving quickly across the room, reaching for her and jerking her into his arms as he glowered down at her, angry flames licking in his blue eyes. "Never say that word in reference to yourself again or so help me, I'll paddle your ass in a way that you won't soon forget."

CHAPTER SEVENTEEN

Keiley stared back at Jethro in shock. His arms were tight around her, holding her flush against his hard body, his erection pressing demandingly into her stomach.

And she was aroused. Panic began to consume her. Mac wasn't here, and Jethro was holding her. His fingers were digging into her hair, jerking her head back, his head descending, and Mac wasn't here.

She whimpered in distress, her fingers curling against his chest as his lips covered hers. Covered them. Possessed them. Rocking the foundations of her belief that she only gained pleasure from this because of Mac's pleasure. That it wouldn't happen without his presence. That it wasn't disloyal. That it wasn't Jethro.

Sensation swamped her as he forced her lips to part, as he dragged her closer, lifted her, and pressed her tightly against the wall.

Lust tore through her. Her hands were suddenly gripping his neck as his hand lifted her leg, wrapping it around his hips before his fingers moved between her thighs.

It was happening so fast. Too fast to stop it. Too fast to control it. Jethro's lips slanted over hers as a rough male groan of hunger shook her to her core and vibrated through her with an answering passion.

She should be pushing him away, but she was holding on to him, crying out into the kiss as she felt his fingers rubbing over the silk that covered her sex. Imperative, desperate fingers that pulled at the material until they revealed the silky heat blooming between her thighs.

A second later they were filling her.

Keiley arched, screaming into his kiss as she felt the impalement. Her muscles locked around the two fingers inside her, her hips arching, riding the incredible pleasure he was stroking into her as his lips traveled down her neck.

Questing. Commanding. He refused to ask for permission. He was demanding her response and receiving it, and she was helpless beneath it.

Helplessly, agonizingly responding to the hard thrusts inside her quaking center as her juices began to flow in demand.

As he pushed her past reason with the invasion the other hand tore at the bodice of her breasts, popping buttons, revealing her bare breasts and the hard nipples standing out like beacons of lust.

"God, I can't touch you enough," he bit out against one swollen mound. "I can't fuck you enough. Can't kiss you enough."

His lips covered an aching peak as Keiley moaned in helpless surrender, her arms locking around his head to hold him in place as she rode the waves of pleasure racing through her.

It was like this with Mac. It was only supposed to be like this with Mac. Not with Jethro.

"I fucked you without a condom the other day," he suddenly groaned as he released her nipple. "While Mac watched. You were so hot. So tight. And I haven't forgotten, Keiley."

She shook her head desperately. She had known he was bare and hadn't wanted to face it. Hadn't wanted to think about it.

He nipped at the tender flesh of her breast. I want that again. I want inside you, bare, burning, pumping my release inside you and feeling those delicate little ripples of your release on my dick."

She was shaking her head desperately, aching, feeling her juices flowing harder, faster at the thought of the pleasure his words evoked.

"Oh God," she gasped as his fingers impaled her harder, deeper.

He wasn't taking her gently and she found she didn't want gentle. He was taking his pleasure, slamming it into her, and she was loving it. Creaming for it. Tightening around the invasion as her body tightened further in the need for release.

"It was like fucking a dream." He licked her nipple before lifting his head, snaring her gaze as he thrust his fingers inside her again. "Like fucking hope."

She shook her head again, feeling emotions rising inside her that she didn't want to face, didn't want to acknowledge. But they were there. Staring her in the face as they blazed from Jethro's eyes, and slamming into her chest as they welled from within her.

"No," she gasped. "No."

Terror suddenly gripped her, a fear unlike anything she had known in her life. She pushed at his shoulders, beat at them until his expression twisted in agony and he released her with a quick, sudden move.

"Keiley." He stared back at her, grimacing painfully. "Baby—"

"No!" Her fists clenched as anger rocked through her. Anger and sudden fear as her gaze moved to a flicker of movement by the door.

She paled. She could feel the color washing from her face as she stared at Mac's thoughtful expression. She could feel herself shaking, trembling, as Jethro cursed beside her.

"It's not her fault, Mac." His voice was dark, edged with a potential for violence.

Mac's gaze sliced to his friend, the gray eyes calm, his expression placid if curious.

Keiley shook her head, feeling the tears that filled her eyes, the knowledge of the betrayal she had just dealt to her husband. It was one thing to let Jethro touch her while he watched, another to do so while he was out of the house.

"Oh God. I'm sorry," she gasped, the tears suddenly breaking through her control as he straightened, moving his

shoulders back from the wall he had been leaning against.
"Mac—"

"Stop apologizing, Keiley," Jethro snapped, moving in
front of her, between her and Mac. "It's not your fault."

She could feel her world shattering around her. Right
there, she stared at her husband, feeling everything she had
ever dreamed of crashing upon her.

She might as well have been cheating on Mac. She knew
the unwritten, unvoiced rules. The rumors of them had
abounded in Virginia. Only when the husband was present.
Only as a threesome. Never as a couple.

She stared between the two men, shaking to the point
that she wondered if she could stand.

"Keiley, sweetheart." His voice was anything but angry
as he moved toward her.

Suddenly Jethro was pushing her further behind him.
Keiley gripped his arm in shock, in pain.

"Stay back there, damn it," he snapped as he faced Mac.
"He won't blame you, Keiley. I won't let him."

"Stop this!" she screamed out tearfully. "Oh God. What
have I done?" She stared between the two men, watching as
Mac's expression suddenly shifted. Concern or anger? He
had every right to be furious. To be betrayed.

And she had no right to suddenly feel torn between the
man she loved, and the man she was terrified she was beginning to love.

She retreated, stumbling back as she stared between the
two men, shock and horror at her own actions filling her. She
couldn't look Mac in the eye, she couldn't bear the knowledge that in a single second, she had betrayed both men.

"Keiley," Mac called out as she spun away and raced from
the room. She had to get away from them, she had to escape.
If only she could escape her own actions as easily as she was
escaping what she knew was Mac's coming feeling of betrayal.

Mac moved quickly as he saw Keiley turn and run, attempting to push past Jethro to get to her. Unfortunately, it seemed

that protective instincts he had only suspected the other man possessed rose to the fore.

"It wasn't her fault." Jethro slammed him back, standing defensively, poised to fight.

"Of course it's not her damned fault," Mac snarled. "Son of a bitch, Jethro, do you I think I didn't know my wife was going to end up loving you?"

He watched as Jethro staggered back.

"Get the hell out of my way," Mac snapped then. "Let me take care of her, then I'll take care of you."

He hadn't expected to walk in on the scene between Jethro and Keiley, but he hadn't been surprised by it. He had been damned turned on by it. There was nothing as arousing as Keiley helpless beneath her own desires.

Taking the stairs two at a time, he moved quickly through the hallway to their bedroom, his jaw clenched tight at the fear, horror, and pain he had seen in her face.

She had, perhaps understandably, jumped to the wrong conclusion, and now he had to fix it. It seemed he was going to have to fix it not just with his wife, but with his best friend as well. Neither, it appeared, seemed to see where this was heading.

As he stepped into the room, he came to a stop, staring at Keiley as she stood before the shaded window. Her arms were wrapped around herself, her shoulders straight and tight.

"I can't even stare out the damned window," she said roughly. "I can't move around my own home." Her head lowered as she pushed her fingers roughly through her hair. "And I'm scared." The last was whispered in a voice rough with unshed tears.

Mac moved across the room, wrapping his arms around her even as she flinched as though surprised that he would hold her.

"I expected it," he whispered in her ear then. "Do you think I would bring another man into our bed and place rules on it? That I would chastise you, or punish you for being the warm, passionately exquisite woman you are?"

She tensed in his arms, then jerked away from him, turning to face him furiously.

"What are you saying, Mac?" Incredulous anger filled her voice as her eyes widened and he watched knowledge slowly fill them. "You intended for me to—" She swallowed tightly. "To care for Jethro."

He saw the betrayal in her eyes, the fear. Hell, he hadn't expected to have things become so damned complicated. But they were. She had every damned right to be outraged.

"I knew you would never take another man into your bed without it," he told her then. "Keiley, you're not a casual woman, I always knew that. From the first day I met you, I knew you would never be the type of woman to play games like this with a succession of different men. And I knew I could never handle that."

"You couldn't handle that?" she grated out, staring back at him as though he were a stranger. And perhaps he was. He had never shown her the parts of himself that mattered. He had kept them hidden away, kept them tucked carefully in a dark little box until they had grown too hungry to stay put any longer.

"What's going on here, Mac? Did you suddenly decide you've had too much of married life and decide to find a man you approved of for me? Are you ready to leave? Are you missing something I'm not giving you?" Her voice rose with each question, betrayal and pain filling her tone as his eyes narrowed on her.

"Never," he bit out, reaching out for her, gripping her shoulders with his hands as he gave her a small, firm shake. "Do you hear me, Keiley? I will never let you go."

"Stop manhandling me." She tore out of his grip, putting distance between them once again before turning back to glare at him. "What did you think you would accomplish here, then? Is there something going on between you and Jethro that I need to know about? What?"

Mac's head jerked up incredulously. "Are you asking if me and Jethro are bisexual, Keiley?"

"I think that about sums it up, Mac." Her arms crossed over her breasts as she threw her hip forward in confrontation.

She had no idea how hot it made him, having her defy him, having her anger meet his dominance head-on.

"Not even a chance in hell." He grinned tightly. "The only ass I have a mind to fuck is yours, sweetheart."

"Not even in your greatest fantasy." Her arm struck out, her finger pointing back at him furiously. "You can shove your dick up your own ass for all I care. If you're not bisexual, then what the hell did you hope to gain? Is your wife loving you too much pressure? What? What in the hell would possess you to attempt to make me fall in love with another man?"

"I'd like to hear that answer myself." Jethro stepped into the room, his arms crossed over his chest, his expression controlled, his eyes glittering with anger.

Mac almost smiled. These were the two people he loved most in the world. Jethro was like a brother to him, and Keiley, hell, she was his soul, but Mac knew himself. Just as he knew his friend.

"How many women have you shared since I got married?" Mac asked him.

"That has nothing to do with this, Mac."

"Answer the damned question," he snapped. "How many?"

Jethro glowered back at him. "None."

He turned back to Keiley. "When he's gone, will you let another stranger in your bed? One I'm not certain how far to trust with my wife rather than a lover? Don't you think you'll sense that discomfort?"

"As Jethro said, what the hell does that have to do with anything?"

"Connection and bonding," Mac snapped back at them both. "Sometimes it takes three to make a whole. There's only one man I trust enough to hold you without me, and that's Jethro. And I know Jethro. He was half in love with you when I met you and too damned stupid to do anything about it. This way, we all get what we want and we're damned happy with it."

"Happy with it because it's what you decree?" Keiley yelled back.

"Hell, yes!" That one shut her up. She stared back at him, her lips parted in shock, her eyes wide with it. "I'm sick to death of denying what I am. And by God, you try telling me you'll ever let any other man in your bed with us!"

"And what about Jethro?" she cried out. "Don't you think he deserves a woman who loves him? Just him?"

"Is that what you want, Jethro?" Mac asked him.

"I have what I want," Jethro answered softly.

"What about me?" She was seething now, like a volcano ready to blow. "Do you think I want to live my life putting up with two fucking pricks rather than one? Well, you have another damned think coming, you son of a bitch. At this moment, I'll be damned if I'll let either one of you back in my fucking bed."

Damn, he was in trouble now. She wasn't just screaming, but her face was flushed, her eyes a chocolate brown, and she was cussing. A lot. Keiley wasn't much of a cusser until she was ready to brain some idiot male who had finally pushed her patience to the limit. Even Jethro was watching her warily now.

"You could have tried discussing this with me first," Jethro muttered.

"Wouldn't have been as effective." Mac shrugged, keeping his eyes on Keiley as she stared between them as though observing some strange, alien set of creatures.

"I'm married to a crazy man," Keiley muttered, shaking her head as she continued to stare at him in dumbfounded confusion. "Mac, have you lost your mind somewhere in the cow shit lately?" Her voice sliced through the air like a razor.

His lips twitched. She was at her most confrontational, her most defiant.

"Not lately," he assured her.

"Somewhere in the past, then, and I didn't notice it?" she asked with false sweetness.

His eyes narrowed on her further as he heard the anger in her tone, her confusion.

Keiley glanced at Jethro. This time, he was the one leaning lazily against the wall, watching the exchange thought-fully. But Jethro's thoughtful expression was a bit more menacing than Mac's.

Keiley breathed in deeply, smoothed her hands down her dress, then stared back at her husband as confusion swamped anger and left her helpless before the regret she saw in his eyes.

"Why, Mac?" she finally whispered. "Why in God's name would you want me to love another man?"

"Because it completes all of us," he answered her gently. "Because it's the only way I can be certain that no part of the past remains inside me. It's the only way Jethro can fully give himself. And it gives you a balance, a freedom you wouldn't have otherwise. Because without it, I wake up shak-ing with the thought of what I could do to both of us. Without it, Jethro would continue on the same damned path he re-turned to when I left. Not giving a damned damn about life, one way or the other, because the balance is gone."

"And you think you can just make this decision for us on your own?" She shook her head, staring back at Jethro as he lowered his head, his expression rueful as he shook his head slowly.

"Do you love her, Jethro?" Mac didn't take his eyes off her.

Jethro's head jerked up, and Keiley saw it. She saw the emotions raging through him, things she hadn't wanted to see before.

"If he left tomorrow, Keiley, would you cry?"

"That's not love, Mac," she whispered, shaking her head herself now. "That's not love. And I'm not playing this game with you. Not anymore."

She turned and walked out of the bedroom, moving slowly, aware of the two men following her, their expressions counterpoints to each other.

Counterpoints. Balances. A team in a way Keiley had never imagined and couldn't fully understand.

She moved down the stairs, aware of Jethro edging around her, moving in front of her, checking each room be-fore she entered it. But the knowledge was distant, just as the awareness of the two men was distant. Suddenly, Keiley felt more alone than she had ever been in her life. Held suspended, watching events that she couldn't understand how she had become a part of.

As she moved to the stove to check the roast boiling merrily, she was aware of Jethro leaving out the back door, but Mac stayed behind. Her house was becoming a merry-go-round of two men shifting and revolving around her.

Behind her, Mac pulled out a chair, and she heard his sigh as he sat down.

"I was five when I first realized what hatred was," he suddenly said.

Keiley swung around in surprise. He always refused to discuss his childhood.

"Dad was insistent that I make friends with this kid on the other side of town. Tobias Blackwood." He wiped his hand down his face. "A shadow of a kid, though I didn't realize then the ghosts he lived with or the reason my father insisted on the friendship. See, Dad liked an audience when he really got wound up, and showing another kid what a pussy his son was made him feel like a man."

Keiley felt the horror reflected in Mac's eyes.

"It was late. After dark. Tobias and I had stayed outside as long as we could. We didn't talk much, batted around the hills some, played some halfhearted basketball. But then we couldn't put it off any longer. It was time to go in.

"He got started on Mom during dinner. He asked her what she had done that day. See, he had sent her to the store for groceries while he did chores outside." His expression became distant. "She told him what she did, who she saw, how much the groceries cost, and the state of the damned vegetable bin. And I could see the fear building in her eyes. Was the owner there, he asked her. She shrugged and said she hadn't seen him. And that crazy light lit his eyes. And I knew what was coming."

As Mac spoke, he stared around the kitchen. Once, the table had sat where the washroom was now. His mother had kept eating, small bites that she pushed into her mouth as her husband accused her of fucking the grocer. How long had it taken? How many times did she think she could do it and not get caught? He couldn't walk in the store without the grocer smirking in amusement. Didn't she know what a whore she was? An embarrassment.

Mac had chanced to look up at Tobias. The motherless boy was staring at his plate, his hands in his lap, unable to eat. And then Mac's father had glanced at him.

You fucking bitch, look how you've ruined that kid's meal. You ruin everything. I'll have to go to another town just to buy groceries because you can't keep your skirt around your fucking knees.

Tears had streaked her face and he had raged over that. As the meal drew to a close he turned to Mac. *Johnnie, make sure your woman's not a whore when you get one.*

Then he had just stopped. His expression had evened out, and he began talking as though he hadn't been raging for nearly an hour. As though he hadn't just revealed the hell Mac lived with in front of another kid. A kid who could tell it. Who could go to school and relate his mother's shame.

"He never said anything." Mac shook his head. "Tobias never told, and I made sure I never had company after that again. But I learned hatred. And I swore it wouldn't happen to me, Kei."

He didn't whine. He didn't beg. He lifted his head and he stared back at her, his jaw clenched.

"I'll never speak of this again. I never want to discuss it, ever again. Over the years, it grew steadily worse until one day Mom got sick." He couldn't look at her. He inhaled roughly, remembering his fragile, timid little mother. "She got a fever and tried to say it was just a cold. Three days later she couldn't get out of bed. Dad picked her up and carried her to the truck and took her to the doctor. They wanted her in the hospital, but he wanted her home. So she came home. She died the next evening."

"It wasn't your fault," she whispered. "She should have left him. She should have killed him."

His lips twisted. "I told her the same thing." He raised his gaze to hers, the pain and fury at the pain crashing over him. "She said she made the vow. It was her mistake. In sickness, in health, for better or worse. It was her mistake and God would take care of her when she couldn't live with it any longer."

"God!" Her hand capped over her lips as she stared back at Mac, horrified.

"I have him in me," he said softly. "That filthy bastard's blood runs through my veins. After Mom died, I left. I left him alone. And I swore I'd let him die alone. I went to college on a scholarship. Being away from him, I didn't have to hide girlfriends. I was free. Or so I thought."

His first lover had been a tall, slender blonde. She had been a sexual adventurer and filled with life. And the first time Mac had seen her talking to another man he had terrified himself. The words had been hovering on his lips, the insults in his mind, the destructive paranoia blazing through his consciousness.

"A friend of mine saw it," he said softly. "He was a few years older than I was, and he knew something about the darkness that inhabits men's souls. And he introduced me to my first ménage."

He leaned back in his chair, staring around the kitchen. After his father's death he had had the place completely renovated. It looked nothing like the dark, squalid home he had lived in as a child.

He could still feel his mother, though. When his father wasn't around, she would laugh. She played games with him as a child and talked to him as a teenager. Her gentle voice still filled his dreams sometimes. Her tears filled his nightmares.

"How did it evolve to this?" She waved her hand to encompass the situation they were in now.

"Jethro." A mocking smile twisted his lips. "I met him at the Law Enforcement Academy. We applied to the FBI the same day. He was like this other side of me. The darkness I kept hidden showed on his face. The softness he kept hidden, I knew how to give my women." He shrugged tightly.

"It just evolved. When you and I married, I thought it would go away. I thought I could force it away."

He stared back at her forcefully then. "I haven't let you see or know what raged inside me because I love you, Kei. I love you more than any man has a right to love a woman."

"Mac." She swallowed tightly. "The past is no excuse—"

"The past isn't why I do it now." He shook his head. "It's not some kind of damned crutch, Kei. And it's not just a handy excuse. That's what started it. That's how it evolved. When we married I left it, and I learned some things about myself. I learned that I missed it. I learned that I can't watch your pleasure and give it to you at the same time. I learned that I need the balance I had left back in Virginia. My psyche was warped before I ever shared the first woman, and age only intensified it. You have all I am now. It's up to you whether you can live with it."

"You're asking me to love another man." Her voice was filled with helpless confusion. "This isn't just sex you want, Mac. Think about this. If I ever have children, you'll never know if they're yours. Our children would endure the gossip and the talk Mac, what you're asking is impossible."

"Is it? Or do you just want to think it is? How we deal with it is what matters. How you want to deal with it. I can live without it, but I won't deny I want it. I want you to share not just your body, I want you to share your heart."

"Why? Damn you, you haven't given me a reason why."

"Because he's as lost as I was before you loved me. Because he's the only fucking brother I've ever had. Damn it, Keiley, because it brings us all three of us pleasure and it by God completes us and you know it."

Mac came to his feet, fighting the surge of frustration eating through his soul. He inhaled roughly.

"I've lived a violent life. I've made enemies. I've been undercover so many times, for such long periods of time, that sometimes I wondered who I was. Jethro was always there. He was always a reminder. And he's here now, protecting you when I can't. Covering my back and yours. You're not losing anything if you accept this, you'll only gain, Keiley.

You'll be loved until the walls are bursting at the seams with emotion. Loved and sated, completely. Think about that. Think about it, and then let me know if you really want to lose it."

"It's not a good enough reason," she cried out.

"It's the only fucking reason I have, Keiley," he yelled back. "I need you. I love you until it burns through my soul, but son of a bitch, I love you even more when I see you with him."

"Why? Why?" she screamed.

"God damn it, I don't know why," he snarled back, raging, an inner fury she had never seen in him before burning through his eyes, his expression. A pain, a blistering agony that Keiley felt ripping through her soul. Because she had never known it existed.

CHAPTER EIGHTEEN

"Do you know what I see when I see him taking you?" He advanced on her, his larger body taut, tight with tension with a sudden lust she had never glimpsed in him before.

He backed her into the counter, his arms bracketing her, his chest raking her breasts through the dress she wore as his breath sawed in and out of his lungs. The eroticism of the position stroked along her senses like invisible fire.

"I see perfection," he growled. "I see his hands touching you. And I don't see a whore. I see beauty. I see life. I see you giving into the most perfect passion ever created. And I get to watch it. I see a woman so filled with passion and love that she gives herself to it. I *see* love, Keiley."

His head lowered, his lips drawn back from his teeth in a grimace of remembered pleasure as his eyes darkened and gleamed with it. Remembrance marked his expression. But it also marked her arousal. It was burning through her, reminding her of the fantasies she had allowed to build over the years and the hunger Mac was brewing in her now.

"Mac—"

"Deny that the nights it takes me all night to sate the arousal inside you, you don't wish for more." Knowledge tightened his expression. "I see your eyes then, baby. I see the need. I see the fires burning inside you. Don't tell me you haven't craved it."

She wanted to whimper and only barely managed to hold

it back. Sometimes she knew he saw too much, knew him too well.

"Fantasy." She swallowed tightly before licking her lips to ease the nervous dryness. "Fantasy shouldn't count."

"Fantasy always counts, Keiley," he crooned, his smile slow and heated. "You're fantasies mean everything. Anything you want. Everything you need. It all matters to me, darlin'. Don't you know that? Your fantasies." His lips smoothed over her brow. "Every hunger." His voice deepened. "Every dream."

A tremor raced up her spine as she drew in a hard, deep breath.

"He's taking what's yours," she whispered, feeling the heaviness in her breasts, between her thighs, at the memory of Jethro taking her, at the feel of Mac against her.

Mac shook his head slowly. "I don't possess you. I don't want to take from you, Keiley. I want to give to you. I want to give you enough pleasure to wipe every preconceived notion of passion out of your head. And I want to watch it. When I fuck you, I'm sucked in. Sucked into that sweet hot pussy. Sucked into your kiss. Sucked into your heart. I can't see or feel anything but the explosions of sensation in front of my eyes. But when he touches you, when he takes you, I can see. And I can see it turns you on. It makes you burn. You love it. Admit you love it."

His lips were hot, rasping with such pleasure that it sent shudders racing through her as he stroked them over her jaw. Soft kisses, black velvet rasping over sensitive flesh.

"I love it," she panted, breathless as one hand dropped from the counter to her thigh. "But it's not natural."

"Says who?" His lips brushed down her cheek, his voice guttural, savage. "Does it feel natural, Keiley? Does it feel like he should have been here all long, loving you with me? Keeping you warm from one end to the other? Keeping you sated, held?"

It did, and that terrified her.

"Someone's going to get hurt," she whimpered. "I don't want any of us to get hurt. I don't want to be hurt."

The thought of the gossip, the rumors, of everyone knowing a part of her intimate life, was worrisome. It wasn't panicking her, though, and it should have. She should be half hysterical at the thought of people whispering about her sex life. About acts that were considered beyond the norm. Beyond respectable.

But she wasn't. What was more frightening, the fact that she wasn't frightened? Or the implications of that lack of fear? The implications of the fact that she was already half convinced?

"We'll keep it quiet," he promised roughly, dragging the skirt of her dress up her thighs.

Breathing was becoming difficult. The feel of the material sliding up her legs, of his palms caressing the flesh it revealed, was too much for her weakened defenses. They were collapsing, shattering, and drawing her into a world rich with the promise of more of the incredible pleasure she had known to this point.

She shook her head weakly. "It won't work like that."

She knew she needed to argue. She needed to convince him, but she couldn't find the words to convince him. She couldn't find the will.

"All you have to do is enjoy it," he crooned, his lips caressing her ear as her head fell back, weakening desire flooding her body. "All you have to do is let us love you. No pressure, baby. No expectations. Let me take care of the logistics. I'm good at that. Remember?"

She gasped as he lifted her, placing her on the counter before his hands gripped her panties and pulled them from her legs.

The silk slid slowly from her body, pulled away by the experienced, knowing touch of the man leading her into the promise of things she would have never imagined she would feel.

"Mac."

He reached over, flipped off the stove, then knelt in front of her.

It was wicked. It was so damned sexy. It sent the blood racing through her veins with fiery pleasure.

Kneeling before her, he parted her thighs further, his fingers feathering over the wet curls that shielded the folds so aching for his touch.

"I watched him eating this sweet pussy," he crooned as he spread her legs. "I watched you creaming for him, and all I could think was how beautiful you were. Watching you makes me crave the taste of you, the feel of you, even more. It makes the desire sharper, the hunger deeper. When I finally get to taste you—" His tongue dragged through the silky, drenched slit between her thighs as she cried out his name. "All I can think about is how perfect you were as we held you between us. All I can think about is how sweet and pure you taste."

"Mac, this is depraved," she whimpered, then gasped as he delivered a hot, sucking little kiss to her clit.

It wasn't a lick or a stroke. It was a kiss. He was kissing her clit, sucking it into his mouth for a quick lick before releasing it, and starting all over again.

They were explosive, heated kisses. They tore restraint from her mind and left her lost in her attempt to find an objection to what she knew was coming in this new relationship.

Instead, she leaned back, bent her knee until one foot rested on the counter, the other over her husband's broad shoulder as she watched his lips and tongue caress her slick, juicy flesh.

He drew back, flicked his tongue over her swollen bud, then leaned back for another kiss. His palms splayed on the inside of her thighs, holding her apart for caresses that were burning through her soul.

"I love your lips on me," she whispered with a mewling little whimper as his tongue circled her aching clit. "Your tongue."

His black hair caressed her inner thighs, the stubble on his cheeks smoothed over her flesh, his hands pressed her thighs wider, allowing her a better view of his caresses.

A view of his tongue slowly circling her straining clit, flickering over it, kissing it, her juices clinging to his lips like silky threads.

"Oh, Mac. Yes," she sighed as his lashes lifted, his gray

eyes dark, gleaming with lust and emotion as his tongue reach out, licked, laved, then his lips surrounded the little bud for another exotic kiss.

"I'm going to come," she moaned, her hands on his head, holding him to her. "I'm going to come so hard, Mac."

"Come for me, baby," he growled.

"Lick me, Mac. Harder. Suck my clit harder." She arched her hips to him. "Oh, God, your lips are so good. Your tongue is so good. Oh, God, I'm going to—" She gasped as he pressed two long fingers inside her, thrusting demandingly, not bothering to work his fingers inside her, burning her instead with a fierce, quick thrust. "Come—"

She shook violently. Pleasure tore through her, exploded inside and out as she screamed and bucked, and then for the first time she heard the explosions vibrate from outside the house.

In the next second she was trying to figure out why the world was spinning around her. Why Mac was cursing and she was crouched between the counters on the floor rather than feeling her husband's cock driving inside her.

"Stay down!" he yelled as she heard another explosion.

Gunshots.

Shock whipped through her.

"Jethro's out there!" she cried hoarsely, her horrified gaze meeting Mac's.

"You stay put." His finger was in her face, his expression fierce as he suddenly dragged her along the floor, moving her into the washroom, then the inner small bathroom.

"In here." He pressed a gun in her hand, his expression so savage he terrified her. "Leave this room and I promise you, I'll tan your bottom. Do you understand me?"

She nodded fiercely.

"Jethro," she whispered. "Hurry, Mac. Please hurry."

A reluctant smile tugged at his lips as his gaze suddenly gleamed not just with fury over the attack but with an inner satisfaction.

"I'll be right back, sweetheart. Stay put for me, baby. I'd lose my soul if I lost you."

"Right here," she promised, then cried out in fear as another shot sounded.

Mac slammed the door, and Keiley heard nothing after that.

Mac stopped long enough to pull the Glock he kept hidden in the pantry closet free. He checked the extra cartridges as he ran through the kitchen, jerked the door open, then jumped and rolled across the patio until he came to rest behind the thick shrubbery growing at the corner.

He scanned the yard before moving, staying behind the carefully planted ornamental trees, thick shrubbery, and decorative cement pieces.

He came up behind Keiley's favorite cement gargoyle, a huge black monstrosity nearly as tall as he was, thick, heavy wings outspread.

He scanned the area again, grimacing when he saw the shadowed outline of his friend beneath the thick spruce tree growing at the boundary of the yard.

Damn, why hadn't he thought to get radios?

"Jethro," he called out when he saw Pappy slinking from beneath the other side of the tree. "You okay, man?"

Jethro moved as the dog, evidently smarter than its human counterparts, kept its belly to the ground as it made its way along the edge of the yard and begun coming up to the house behind the same border of cover Mac was using.

Following Jethro's hand signals, his gaze moved past the barns and stables to the hill rising above the house on the other side.

Squinting, he tracked the land, seeing nothing but the soft breeze playing through the trees.

"I have you covered!" he yelled back, keeping his eyes on the area. "Work your way in."

He watched, his eyes piercing the thick woods, but he couldn't see a damned thing. Long minutes later he shifted his gaze away enough to catch Jethro moving to his side.

His shoulder was bloody, a thick furrow slicing across the bicep.

"You okay?"

"Bastard winged me," Jethro cursed. "I was able to spot where the first shots came from, but after that I lost him."

"Get ready. We need to get in the house." Mac was tense, worry for Keiley obliterating everything else.

"I'll go first, then cover you." Jethro started to move when Mac gripped his shoulder and pulled him back.

"You're already hit. I'll go first."

"Like hell. The last thing Kei needs is a bloody husband. A bloody third is another damned thing."

He heard the shade of bitterness in his friend's voice but let him go, his eyes on the hill until Jethro made it across the patio.

With his weapon raised, Jethro covered Mac's quick sprint across the open portion of the patio before they both moved hastily into the house.

Mac closed the door, reset the alarm, then moved quickly to the bathroom door.

"Keiley?"

The knob turned. Mac stopped the opening of the door in time to keep her from seeing a bloody Jethro.

"Jethro's fine. Lock yourself back in while we check the house."

Her face was pale, her eyes dark in the paper-whiteness as she nodded quickly and hurriedly reclosed and locked the door.

"The alarm was off while we were outside. We check the house first."

Jethro nodded quickly, wiping a smear of blood over his forehead before moving in front of Mac. Blood stained the short sleeve of his shirt and had run along his arm. Jethro wiped his hand on his pants, smearing more blood, before they began canvassing the house.

Mac grimaced at the thought of Keiley seeing the wound or the mess it was making. It wasn't life-threatening, just damned messy, and sure to upset her.

"I'm getting tired of this bastard!" Jethro snapped as they

finished the upstairs and began making their way back down. "He's pissing me off, Mac. He was after you. There's not a doubt."

"I came in early from checking the place," Mac murmured as he glimpsed Pappy lying in the foyer.

The dog had slid into the house between him and Jethro, so quickly and quietly that Mac had only distantly noticed the move.

"What happened out there?" he asked.

"I saw Pappy huddled under the trees. He didn't come when I called to him, so I went to see if he had been hurt. The shot caught me about middleways across the yard. By the time I found cover I was closer to the treeline and out of the line of sight than I was to the house."

"Rifle or handgun?"

"Handgun. I'm betting a rifle will be next."

Mac shook his head. "He would have used a rifle first time. He wants to keep the odds even."

"Hell of an observation," Jethro grunted as they entered the foyer and Mac moved quickly back to the bathroom.

"Fact. Based on the files of the victims. He kept his playing field even. It's a test. To win he has to play fair. You should have come back into the house before checking anything."

He caught Jethro's grimace. "She needed you worse than I did."

"She wasn't being shot at," Mac pointed out logically. "And there was no danger of her leaving because of a realization that hurts none of us. I could have dealt with that later."

Jethro caught his arm as he started to move through the foyer.

"You should have discussed this with me first," he snapped, his eyes narrowing angrily.

Mac grinned with an edge of mockery. "You already loved her, Jethro. You think I missed it before we left Virginia? Do you think I didn't hear it in your voice every time you got around to asking about her whenever you called?"

"I was handling it." Jethro's expression was tight now.

"Handling it so well you haven't shared a woman since we left town?"

"I was handling it." His voice lowered in warning. "I wasn't in love with her, Mac, until you began playing your little games."

Mac sighed at that. "Sometimes you have to go with your gut, Jethro, I keep trying to tell you that. You'll hit an investigation with both feet forward and your gut all but getting you killed. When it comes to women, you act like you're using a damned manual until you get them into the bed. You won't find love that way."

"I wasn't looking for love."

"No, you weren't. You'd already found it. Unfortunately, someone else beat you to her first."

"If I wanted her that bad I would have done something about it."

Mac shook his head. "You're a lousy liar, my friend."

"Stop bitching, Mac, you're starting to sound like someone's father," Jethro growled.

"As long as I don't sound like mine," he snarled, pausing once again at the bathroom door and tapping at it lightly. "It's safe, Keiley."

The door opened slowly. Her eyes went quickly over Mac, then turned to Jethro. She swayed, any color she could have possessed leeching from her face as she stared at the blood.

"It's just a flesh wound." Jethro started in surprise at the horror that washed over her. "It's okay."

"Just a flesh wound?" she snapped, lifting her gaze to meet his. "For God's sake! You're bleeding all over my house. At least try to act concerned."

CHAPTER NINETEEN

Keiley stood in front of Jethro as he sat at the kitchen table, the first aid supplies laid out on the table as she cleaned the wound on his arm.

"You need to go to the doctor," she said fiercely. "You need stitches."

He was as stubborn as Mac. He had refused to go to the hospital or to allow her to call the paramedics.

"Slap a bandage on it and stop fussing over it," he had ordered uncomfortably, as though her concern made him edgy.

And it probably was. He kept shifting in his seat worse than a kid eager to get back outside and play. Or a grown man determined to rejoin a fight.

"You're not Superman."

"I'm not bleeding to death, either."

She looked in his face then, her lips trembling at the tenderness of his expression, the gentle light in his blue eyes as he reached up and cupped her cheek.

"You and Mac are driving me insane, you know," she informed him, attempting to chastise him for his recklessness. "I'm not a doctor or a nurse, and patching up grown men who should have enough sense to see one makes me irritable."

"I wouldn't want to make you irritable," he assured her, his voice filled with a hesitant gentleness.

Jethro didn't have the first clue about how to handle the emotions that were raging between them. Not that Keiley claimed to know how to handle it herself, but Jethro's attempts to get a handle on them were endearing. And, unfortunately, only made her own seem stronger.

If his expression of male confusion and wariness was anything to go by, he was still struggling to hold them back, despite Mac's awareness of them. And that made her wonder how he would eventually handle the other emotions that could end up cropping into this relationship Mac had orchestrated. Especially the emotions she knew Mac would have a hard time dealing with.

"Are you a jealous man?" she finally asked, feeling her fears of the future edging into her voice.

"I would kill any man but Mac who dared to touch you." He sighed, his thumb touching her lips as they trembled again. "He was wrong, though, when he said I was half in love with you before he won your heart. I wasn't. I already loved you fully, Kei."

"Don't say that." She tried to keep her voice firm, her emotions under control. "The two of you ask too much of a woman."

"Yeah. We do," he finally agreed, his gaze hooded, intense. She had always felt that Jethro, like Mac, saw too deep into her soul.

Mac was sneakier than Jethro, though. He hid that dangerous part of himself behind layers of control and charming smiles. A person could sense the danger lurking beneath his quiet exterior, but as with all illusions it eased beneath the carefully controlled façade he presented.

Jethro, on the other hand, had never pretended to be anything other than exactly what he was. Dangerous to anyone who dared get in his way, an emotional risk to any woman who dared love him.

Until now.

Now, the cool purpose that had once been in his brilliant blue eyes was gone. In its place she could see the charisma he kept hidden, the emotions he tried to deny even to himself.

She breathed in shakily before applying a coat of antibiotic salve to his arm and wrapping the gauze over a wide folded bandage. The white of the gauze glared against the sun-darkened flesh of his arm while the muscle beneath flexed experimentally.

"Stay still," she ordered quietly. "You'll start bleeding again."

"Who cares?" His other arm came around her hips, pulling her close as he suddenly buried his head against her breasts.

Surprised, Keiley gripped his shoulders, staring down at the coarse black hair that fell down the back of his neck.

"What do you want me to do?" he asked, his voice muffled by the cloth of her dress.

"About what?"

"About this." He pulled her forward, dragging her leg over his thighs and forcing her to straddle him as he lifted his head.

"This" was the straining erection beneath his jeans and the hunger in his gaze.

"You can't love me," she whispered. "You and Mac, you were too good as friends, as agents working together. That's all it is."

"I saw you first, Kei. Remember? The parties you were invited to the week you met Mac. I made sure you were there. I knew you. I wanted you."

Keiley shook her head. She did remember those parties, and she remembered seeing him. Remembered those blue eyes following her, the feeling of feminine awareness, the knowledge that he was more than she could ever handle.

She had no idea how right she had been.

"I knew Mac would love you, too." His hands gripped her hips, jerking her closer, pressing his cock deeper into the cradle of her thighs. "I knew he would make you love him. I knew he would love you. I thought." He paused, staring back at her as he grimaced tightly. "I thought, a month or two, and he would invite me in. When the invitation didn't come, I went on. Because I couldn't risk hurting you. Or Mac."

"Why would you do that, Jethro? Why would you give him what you wanted?"

These two men confused her. There wasn't even a hint of sexual frustration toward each other. All their sexual heat was centered on her alone. There was no feeling that bisexual urges tormented them, no feeling that they wanted or loved anything but her. Yet they knew each other so well.

"One of these days, I'll tell you a story." He laid his forehead against hers, his gaze darkening painfully. "A story about a boy without a home, without a family. About a kid tossed out like so much garbage and then shuffled through a system as cold and unfeeling as the streets. Then I'll tell you about how a man, one with his own shadows, befriended that boy when he became a man. They had a lot of adventures together. But then man saw the woman he was going to love and he knew he could never love that woman without scaring the hell out of her. Without sharing her. Without pushing her too soon, too fast, because of his hungers.

"I know you love Mac heart and soul. But I know you care about me. In time, I think, you could love me, Kei. And I would die for that love."

"Love is possessive, Jethro," she said desperately. "If I let this continue, I couldn't share you. The day would come when you found someone you could really love. What happens to me then? If I love you just as deeply, just as possessively, as I love Mac?"

His hands tightened on her hips as his expression turned feral with hunger. "You could love me like that, Kei?" He asked, his voice guttural. "Could you love me like that?"

"What do you two think you are doing to me?" she cried, struggling from his lap. "One of you should be jealous."

"Why? Mac wouldn't have invited me here if there were

a chance that he would regret your loving me. Both of us, Kei, we grew up alone, shadowed by the actions of others. We found a connection as friends, a bonding as we shared our lovers. I know the man he is, and he knows the man I am. It has nothing to do with sexual feelings for each other and everything to do with needing something more out of a relationship than other people do. Of knowing each other so well that there was never a chance that we would love separate women."

And strangely, that made sense.

"Mac's controlled. He thinks before he acts. He never makes a move without knowing the consequences," he continued. "He knew what he was doing."

She closed her eyes and let her head rest on his shoulder, hiding the tear that fell from her eyes as her arms tightened around his neck.

If one of them, just one of them, had acted jealous of her, if one of them had seemed hesitant about this relationship, she could have denied both of them.

But they were two parts of a whole. Separate, yet complete when they were together. When they were with her. And she felt complete. That edge of darker eroticism that she had known rode inside her was sated with it.

"I could love you, so easily, just as intensely as I love Mac."

She felt him tighten to the breaking point, his arms contracting around her back.

"But be certain of this, Jethro." Her eyes opened, snared instantly by Mac's gaze as he stood in the doorway. "Be very certain this is what the two of you want. Because heartbreak isn't something I deal with well."

Mac's lips tilted, his head inclining in acceptance as Jethro buried his head against her neck, a shudder racing through him.

"Copter's coming in," Mac said then. "The director was in Raleigh and he came in with the two agents we requested."

"Hell," Jethro breathed against her neck, bestowing a kiss so gentle there that it brought tears to her eyes. "Come on, sweetness. It looks like I'm not going to get what I need right now."

He lifted her easily from his lap, setting her back before dragging himself to his feet. His face was pale, his eyes standing out like gems behind his dark lashes.

"You need to rest at least, Jethro," she sighed. "That was a pretty bad wound. It needs stitches."

"I don't like stitches." He shook his head as he lifted his weapon from the table and tucked it in the back of his jeans.

She turned to Mac for help, only to get a narrowed warning of his eyes and a subtle shake of his head.

"Fine. Fall flat on your face. See if I care." She turned to the stove and surveyed the roast she had turned back on. "I'm canceling the meeting tonight. It's too late to try to go anyway. We'll have the soup for supper and see if we can't get some sleep tonight."

She could feel her system dragging, reminding her that the last few days had been filled with too much darkness, too much danger.

"We'll make the meeting," Mac informed her. "You go get your shower and get ready. I'll meet with the director and Jethro can stay upstairs with you. The only way to draw this bastard out is to go out."

"And let him take potshots at us?" she asked angrily. She couldn't believe he would dare suggest anything so dangerous.

"The sheriff is on his way, too, Kei. There's no way to keep this under wraps now. I'd rather answer the questions in town than to have everyone we know descend upon us like a pack of gossiping old women. Now go get dressed."

"Don't use that commanding tone of voice with me, Mac. I have supper on. I am not going out."

Their gazes clashed.

"Fine," he said softly. "But think about this. Delia Staten will show up with her mother-in-law. Victoria, despite her daughter-in-law's faults, always thought very well of me. If they arrive here, God only knows how long they'll stay. We'll have a steady stream of visitors for days. Is that what you want?"

"Tell them to go home," she gritted out.

His brow arched. "Think that will work, do you?"

"I hate it when you're so damned logical." She felt like stomping her foot. "Don't answer the damned door. Let Jethro answer it."

Mac winced.

"Yeah, I'll just shoot them," Jethro muttered. "What's a little more bloodshed?"

She turned back on him, beginning to feel defeated, closed in.

"You would not."

"No, but I don't have a whole lot of tact," he informed her. "I'll tell them to get fucked quite succinctly without even thinking of the consequences. Is that what you want?"

"I want you two to be sensible." She felt like pulling her hair. She contented herself with clenching her fists at her side.

"We are being sensible. Now go shower. I'll put the food up here while I talk to the director. Jethro can give his report when you come back down. And don't take all day. We need to get out of here and get this done."

"This is stupid," she muttered.

"The sooner we get it done and over with, the quicker we can get home and try to get some sleep. The extra agents will take up watch outside tonight and tomorrow and give us a chance to rest. Then, we go hunting."

"How?" She didn't like the sound of that.

"Very discreetly," he said firmly. "We'll discuss it later. Now go."

"Now go," she muttered. "It's occurring to me, Mac, that you have a streak of stubbornness that is starting to piss me off."

She caught the surprised look Jethro gave Mac. Veiled, rife with male amusement and a hint of surprise.

"She's just figuring this out?" he asked Mac. "Hell, you've been spoiling her, Mac."

"And I've done so with great joy." Mac's expression became heavy with sensuality then, the effect of it tightening her womb despite the frustration and fear of the situation she found herself in.

"So keep spoiling me and fix this."

"I am fixing it." His expression assured her that it wasn't going to be fixed her way. "Get ready for that meeting, because you're not missing it. You have an hour and then you're walking out of here, under your steam or mine, take your pick."

Her eyes narrowed on him. "That marriage license didn't make you my boss, Mac."

"No, in this situation that marriage license makes me more than your boss, Keiley. And you will do whatever it takes to keep you safe. Do you understand me?"

"This meeting has nothing to do with safety."

"Do you understand me?" His voice hardened, as did his expression.

She could argue all she wanted, but Keiley knew in that instant that if she wasn't ready to go in an hour, Mac wouldn't be above carrying her out of the house kicking and screaming.

"You're impossible," she snapped. "When this is over, we're having a talk about this sudden inclination to give orders, Mac."

"As long as you wait until it's over." His eyes gleamed with sudden male appreciation and approval. "I'll be waiting down here for you." Mac turned to Jethro then. "The director will want to talk to you before we leave, so don't delay up there to avoid it."

In other words, no sex. Keiley rolled her eyes and gave both men a cool, firm look.

"He'll be available," she promised her husband.

Keiley stared back at Jethro's suddenly closed expression and ached at what he had told her earlier. The boy that had been tossed out like so much garbage, shuffled through the system, and ignored until Mac befriended him.

"Come on darlin', let's get you ready for that meeting." Jethro held his hand out to her as Mac watched his friend in concern.

And Keiley understood that concern. Jethro's face was pale, his gaze too bright, too unsettled.

"He needs to rest, Mac," she told her husband fiercely. "He was shot."

"I was nicked and I'm fine." Jethro's voice became graveled, darker. "You're going to that meeting Keiley. Mac's right, this is the best way to deal with this small-town bullshit. Face them and tell them to fuck off before they have a chance to blindside you."

She stared at him in surprise as his jaw suddenly clenched and he gave his head a brief, hard shake.

"Let's do this, Kei. Then when we get home, I'll rest. I promise." He was making an obvious effort to restrain his impatience and his anger.

Keiley glanced at Mac, seeing the heaviness in his gaze, the worry as he watched his friend.

Damn him, he deserved to worry. By bringing Jethro into this relationship as he had he was awakening demons that the other man had obviously forced into hiding.

"You're damned right you'll rest," she muttered as she took his hand and let him lead her from the kitchen. "Or I'll knock you out."

He didn't answer. Instead, his hand moved from hers, allowing it to settle in the middle of her back as they moved up the stairs. She could feel the heaviness of his emotions, a weariness that had her glancing at him nervously.

"I'm not going to hurt you," he blew out roughly as they entered the bedroom.

"I never imagined you would hurt me, Jethro," she sighed. "But you're hurt—"

His head lifted, his gaze spearing into her, silencing her. She could see so much more now that they were no longer with Mac. Arrogance, definitely. There were no two men more arrogant than Jethro and Mac could be. But she saw more. Years of loneliness, of aching dissatisfaction.

He reached out and touched her cheek gently, his calloused fingertips stroking her flesh almost in regret.

"I wish I knew how to show you what I feel," he whispered then. "How to touch you so you know how deeply you touch me, Kei. How to know the right words to make you understand the gift you give me."

Her lips parted in surprise. "Jethro—"

He laid his fingers against her lips.

"From the moment I saw you, suddenly I wasn't a ragged five-year-old anymore. I didn't feel the disassociation I had to force on myself to endure living with strangers, all the while knowing there were those who shared my blood, who my parents trusted to watch over me if anything happened to me. The ice that had grown inside me over the years melted the night I met you, and I haven't known what to do with the emotions you made me feel."

"What are you saying?" she whispered in horror. "You had family? And they left you alone?"

"Family." The bitter curve of his lips was anything but amused. "Family sticks together. These people were related by blood. My father's brother. My mother's mother. They signed the papers that turned a five-year-old still covered in his parents' blood over to the state. I attended my parents' funeral with my social worker, while those exalted family members wept over my parents' caskets."

Jethro pulled his hand back from her, raking it through his hair as he turned away from her. Hell, he wasn't a kid anymore. Those years were long behind him. But the moment he saw Keiley more than three years ago they had risen inside him again with a force that had terrified him.

As a child he had forced himself to disassociate from his emotions. To watch and analyze others'. To understand what drove them rather than to participate in their emotions or their lives.

When he met Mac, the other man had forced him to view life with a bit more participation. He pushed, he manipulated, and he bribed Jethro with the tender emotions of the lovers they shared. But not until Keiley had he actually been forced to love.

"What happened, Jethro?" He stiffened as he felt her behind him, felt her arms wrap around his waist as she laid her head against his back.

"My father had a brain tumor. It was affecting his emotions, his perceptions of reality. No one knew how bad it was until the day he killed his wife and then himself." He frowned, remembering his parents with a clarity that often raged inside him.

His mother, Lucia, had been gorgeous. Long black hair, laughing blue eyes, and a smile that lit up the world. His father had been tall, strong, invincible, until the day he turned a gun on both his wife and himself.

He heard himself talking, whispering the words to Keiley, but the memories held him.

He had been secure. Happy. He had lived in the big brick home on a hill and his father had been building him a tree house when his world collapsed around him.

"And when they were gone, everything was gone." He was finished, frowning at the lack of emotion he detected in his own voice. It should have been raging with emotion. It should have been an animal's snarl of rage for all he felt as he let himself remember. "My parents had discussed what would happen if anything happened to them. Their will gave my uncle care and custody of me and anything they had. The state took the house for taxes and debts. But everyone I shared blood with washed their hands of me and let the state take me as well."

"Everyone?" She heard the pain in his voice. "There was no one?"

"No one." He turned, easing from her hold as he breathed in heavily. "I survived, though. I stopped caring." He stared back at her then. "I made myself stop caring. I couldn't afford to hate, to hope, or to love. I wiped them out of my mind and I set about surviving from one foster home to another. Until I graduated and went to college." His lips edged into a grin then. "Then I met Mac. Mac doesn't do anything by half measures, and I think the fact that I refused to feel just irked the hell out of him."

He sat down, feeling an edge of weariness creeping over him. Then he reached out, amazed at how easily Keiley moved to his lap, allowing him to hold her, holding him in return.

"Mac can be like that," she said gently, her head at his shoulder as he buried his hand in her hair and held her to him.

The soft weight of her, the warmth of her, it speared into his soul like sunlight.

"Then came Keiley," he whispered. "I took one look at you and felt the last of my defenses melting away. I couldn't speak to you. I couldn't go near you. You terrified the hell out of me, so I guided Mac to you."

Because he had known Mac would complete her more than he ever could. She had the shadows of lost dreams in her eyes, and a wariness he knew he would only make worse. A wariness Mac could heal.

"I thought he would call me within a few weeks. A few months. 'Hey Jethro,' he'd say, 'come on over and play.'" He felt his expression twist at the memory of the loss he had felt when that call hadn't come. "Instead, he called and told me he was marrying you."

"And you just accepted it?"

"Yeah. I did." He nodded, heavily. "Because I love you both, Kei. Mac is my only true family, and you were my heart. You two suited each other."

"You were too scared."

Trust Keiley to get to the heart of the matter.

"The big tough agent was too scared of a girl to even speak to her." Her voice resonated with the beginning heat of anger.

"Yeah, he was." He could grin now, though it hurt. "You scared the hell out of me. Because you made me feel. With those big hazel eyes and that wary smile. Mac, though, he knew how to fix what hurt you, whereas I would have pushed and hurt you worse. A part of me knew I just had to wait. Mac and I—we balance each other out. We're both scarred, Keiley, but you heal us. I always knew you would heal us."

"I'm possessive, Jethro," she said then. "I'm so scared you're going to realize this isn't what you really want. That you need your own woman, one you don't have to share. Your own family."

"I have my family." His arms tightened around her. "You and Mac are my family, Kei. You made me feel things I swore I would never feel. You made me dream of warmth and forever. Don't take it away now, not if it's in you to love me."

Keiley heard the reservation in his voice then, the automatic defense against rejection and wanted to weep. God help her, what she was going to do with him and Mac? They were breaking every rule ever created for a relationship and making her think it could work.

"Come on, you have to shower." He lifted her to her feet, rising behind her as he pushed her toward the bathroom. "Get in there. Or you'll be late.

She turned back to him instead. "I—"

He laid his fingers on her lips. "You just needed to know the why of it, Keiley. Don't make any decisions. Don't worry about any of it. Decisions can wait, but sometimes, they come easier later if the understanding is there. I just wanted you to understand."

Understand that everyone he should have been able to trust in as a child had betrayed him. As they had Mac. As she had been betrayed.

"Damn, we make a hell of a trio," she sighed. "I think dysfunction is going to be our middle name."

A grunt of a laugh surprised him. She made him laugh. She made him smile. She made him forget the shadows that had followed him the better part of his life.

"I love you, Kei," he said softly then, watching the somberness that filled her gaze. "If you can't love me, I'll live. But nothing will change what I feel for you. And only for you. Now get that shower before the director demands my presence. Mac and I don't have a problem sharing you between us, but if that bastard sees you naked and soft I might have to kill him."

He pushed her gently toward the bathroom. "Go on sweetheart. Remember, decisions are for later. For now, we have the ogre of the Bureau to face."

CHAPTER TWENTY

"Director Williams, you remember my wife, Keiley." Mac held his hand out to her as she stepped closer.

"Hello, Director Williams. It's good to see you again."

Richard Williams was a broad, rounded little man. He could have been a perfect St. Nick if his hair had been a bit more gray. His smile was wide, his cheeks ruddy, and sky-blue eyes twinkled back at her as he shook her hand.

"It's good to see you again, Mrs. McCoy. I'm just sorry it was under these circumstances. As I was telling Mac, I've sent several agents onto the property to check for any evidence the shooter may have left. I know he was uncomfortable leaving you here alone while he and Jethro took care of it."

"Mac and Jethro will handle the circumstances," she responded, aware of Jethro moving just behind her shoulder as Mac stood at her side. "But I appreciate the help."

"Jethro." The merriment in the director's gaze chilled as he glanced over his shoulder. "You were supposed to be on suspension, if you recall."

"I'm enjoying my vacation greatly, Director Williams."

She wondered if the director caught the slight edge of tension in his voice, though.

He grunted at Jethro's comment before turning back to Mac.

"Tell me what you need," he ordered then. His deep voice

would have been booming if it weren't for the control Keiley heard in it.

"The files I requested as well as access to the Bureau's database. I want to catch him while he's here, Director. It's time to end this."

"I'm sure his other victims feel the same." Williams nodded as he pushed his hands into the pockets of his slacks, pulling his jacket back as he stared back at them. "I've reinstated Jethro for this. We don't need any problems once the Playboy is in custody. We'll discuss the disciplinary measures you ignored when you return to D.C.," he told Jethro.

"Discussion is the spice of life, Director. You know how much I enjoy it."

Keiley winced. There was no mistaking the edge in his voice this time.

The director shook his head reprovingly before turning to Mac. "Do something with him."

"I'm not his boss." Mac shook his head with a laugh. "I'll leave that up to you when this is finished. For now, I appreciate the help."

The director rubbed his whiskered chin thoughtfully. "I'm sending Agents Heinagen and Sheffield back in the morning. Heinagen will take a room in town and see what he can learn. Sheffield was raised on a farm. Hire his ass and don't give me any lip over it. He'll watch your back and your wife's and allow you to investigate what you need to while protecting her."

Keiley glanced up at Mac before staring at the two agents. She had never seen two men least likely to have been raised on a farm.

"Agents Gregory Heinagen and Casey Sheffield," Director Williams introduced her to them. "They'll fly back with me to Mount Pilot and rent their vehicles before returning here early tomorrow. I agree with your assessment. The stalker won't return tonight, and with both of you in the house, it's doubtful he can breach the premises. Get this cleared up, though. I don't like having one of my agents targeted."

"Former agent," Keiley reminded him with a cool curve to her lips and a warning glint in her eye.

"Former agent," he agreed, but she knew, she could see the calculation in his eyes. He intended to have Mac back at the Bureau along with Jethro.

She pressed her lips together and stepped to the side, glancing back at Mac, then at Jethro.

"I forgot my shawl upstairs and we need to be leaving soon if we're going to get to that meeting on time."

She didn't give him time to accept or reject, but swung on her heel and moved for the foyer before heading up the stairs. There would be no return to the Bureau for Mac as far as she was concerned. And Jethro—her chest clenched at the thought of what he would do. Stay or leave, either scenario held the power to break her heart.

She was aware of the agent moving behind her, following her from the living room and up the stairs, just as she was aware of the tension she was leaving behind her.

Sheffield, Casey Sheffield, she remembered the agent's name. Short sandy hair, lean compact frame, and piercing brown eyes. He moved silently but efficiently. But he still moved like an agent. He wasn't going to fool anyone. Least of all a stalker.

"Well, Mac, it seems I might have upset your wife." The director turned back to them after motioning one of the agents to follow Keiley upstairs.

"She'll be fine." And she would be, as soon as he assured her that there were no incentives the director could give him that would bribe him back to the Bureau. He was perfectly content right here on the farm, living and laughing with Keiley without the additional risk of a dangerous occupation.

The director's gaze went to Jethro then, and Mac could see the suspicion in the other man's eyes. He knew the rumors, hell, he knew the facts of the lifestyle he and Jethro had lived. Mac had no doubt in his mind that Williams was putting two and two together and coming up with a very pleasurable three.

"You should have told me you were heading this way, Jethro." The director's voice held a hint of reproval.

"Why? I came out here for a vacation. The stalker didn't show his hand until after I arrived."

"Mac, aren't you afraid rumors of an additional relationship here might push that stalker further than you anticipate?" the director inquired then.

"What the hell do you mean by that?" Jethro snapped, his gaze slicing to the other silent agent as Mac crossed his arms slowly over his chest.

Mac restrained a smile. He could see the protectiveness rising in Jethro. Jethro knew Keiley well enough to know that she wouldn't appreciate a discussion of certain aspects of her private life. Especially those aspects that included a ménage.

"Director, let's not play games while we're standing here," Mac warned him. "I have a meeting to take my wife to and a stalker to stop. I don't have time to wade through the bullshit. Any extra relationship won't matter either way, and quite simply is none of you business."

"The bullshit," the director sighed. "Fine. I want you back. You were one of our best agents."

Mac was shaking his head before the words were out of the director's mouth.

"No way. This is where I'm happy. This is where I'm staying."

Williams turned to Jethro then, his gaze cool, hard.

"You'll be back as soon as this is over. Correct?"

There was a hesitation, just enough to have the director's eyes narrowing before Jethro nodded sharply. Mac restrained his smile. He had a feeling Jethro wouldn't be going anywhere. The hours he and Mac spent working the farm of the mornings were beginning to settle into the other man. Mac could see the peace gathering inside him. The farm had a way of doing that. Building inside a man, showing him what he could do with his own two hands and the sense of satisfaction that came from it.

"Well, I think I hear your wife, Mac," Williams breathed out heavily. "Keep me apprised of your progress here. I'll make sure you have everything you need to catch this bastard."

"I appreciate it, Director." Mac accepted the director's handshake, noticing that the other man pointedly ignored Jethro as he turned to go.

"I'll drop Heinagen and Sheffield off in Mount Pilot. They'll be back here in the morning sometime," Williams reminded them as they stepped into the hallway.

Keiley was stepping into the hardwood foyer, a creamy silk cobwebbed shawl over her arm and her purse over her shoulder. Her eyes were cool and challenging as she met the director's.

"Good evening to you, Mrs. McCoy." He inclined his head cordially. "It was good to see you again."

"Good evening, Director. I'm glad we had a chance to visit for a moment."

Mac had to smother his laughter. She was facing the director like a little terrier, determined to hold onto what she had claimed.

Stepping to her, Mac allowed his arm to curl around her before pulling her against his side. The steady warmth of her, the way she melted against him, the sweet acceptance she had always given him filled him once again.

He couldn't keep from tightening his hold on her, hugging her perhaps a bit closer than normal, inhaling the sweet scent of her. And he couldn't keep his body from responding to her. He hardened to the point of pain, to the point that he had to remind himself that the meeting had to come first, then the pleasure. So much pleasure and a sweet, hot, giving ecstasy that he had only found in her arms.

Nodding easily, Director Williams opened the door just as one of the investigative agents who had been sent into the treeline rang the doorbell.

"Director." The blond haired agent nodded respectively.

"There was nothing there soon. Tracks were brushed out and no casings were left. It's clean."

"No more than we expected." Mac wrapped both arms around Keiley, holding her closer, wishing he could shelter her from all of the nastiness of the world. "He's never left evidence lying around before."

"He's never moved this fast, either," the director pointed out. "You've made him angry, Mac. Be careful."

"Always, sir." Mac nodded, feeling Keiley's nails biting into his arm as the director turned and left the house, followed closely by Heinagen and Sheffield.

"I don't want to go to that stupid meeting," Keiley snapped as the door closed behind the last agent.

She pulled herself from Mac's arms, turning on him angrily and glaring back at him.

"We're going to the meeting, Keiley." Mac's voice was firm, that commanding firmness that made her so crazy. That said he had made up his mind and that was that.

"This is insane, Mac. He's out there waiting on us. You know he is." She turned to Jethro for help. "Talk to him."

"I have, darlin', and I agree with him."

No help there. She felt her upper lip tremble, just a bit, that little movement that Mac always teased her over as a being a twitch. He claimed he was wary of it, but looking in his eyes at the moment, she saw no wariness, not so much as a hint of weakness.

"What if he gets in the house?" She looked from Mac to Jethro. "There's no one here to protect the house. He could be waiting in any room when we arrive."

Mac leaned close, his lips settling at her ear. "If he shows up, if anyone is in the house, then we'll know it. And we'll have him."

She jerked back, staring up at him in surprise.

"Shh," he warned with a grin, dropping a kiss to her lips. "I'll explain later, sweetheart." Then he turned to Jethro. "Get us a jacket, Jethro. Let's head out of here and give Delia Staten something to gossip about." Keiley didn't like the vengeful light she saw glittering in his eyes then.

"Mac, what kind of game are you playing?" she whispered.

"One that I know how to win." That assurance made her stomach tighten with nerves. "I promise you, sweetheart, this is a game I surely know how to win."

CHAPTER TWENTY-ONE

Explaining the particulars to Keiley hadn't been easy. As they drove to the Staten mansion, Mac outlined the silent alarms he had set in each doorway of the house. The motion-activated alarms were silent and programmed to notify the handheld sensor he carried with him.

Mac had designed the alarm system himself in the event that one of his cases ever managed to follow him. The handheld sensor would track anyone in the house from room to room, showing entry and exit as well the path taken. Other sensors tracked body heat through each room, while still others would trigger an alarm for any electronic explosives set.

The security system was one of the greatest expenses of the complete renovation that Mac had done to the house after his father's death.

That didn't mean Keiley was in the least bit happy with his plans. As he pulled into the circular driveway of the Staten mansion she was coldly silent, disapproving, and, he knew, frightened.

"I don't like this game, Mac," she told him as she opened her door, her gaze swinging to the backseat of the pickup truck where Jethro lounged with lazy abandon. "You're risking yourself, and that's not acceptable."

"What would you suggest, then?" he asked her, laying his forearms on the wheel and turning his head to stare back at her. "Why don't we run, Keiley? We'll sell the farm, set up somewhere else and wait on him to find us again. How does that suit you?"

"Don't be a smartass, Mac."

"I'm just being honest. We have to stop here. He'll only follow us if we don't."

Her upper lip twitched. That made twice. He was in for it later and he knew it. The minute it was safe for her to tear into him, then his little wife was going to skin him alive. It made for some great sex later, but he was well aware of the fact that right now, Keiley was hurt, confused, and angry. And that wasn't what he had ever wanted their life to be.

"Keiley."

Mac's gaze shifted behind her to where Jethro sat forward on the backseat.

"What, Jethro?" she snapped back, though her gaze stayed on Mac's.

"Remember when I told you I didn't have a problem not letting you have your way?"

Mac watched her delicate nostrils flare as she shifted her gaze back to Jethro.

"So?"

"So, get your pretty butt up to that meeting before I have to get out of this truck and give Delia Staten something to gossip about."

Mac restrained his smile as a hard wash of fiery color filled her cheeks. If she had been embarrassed or hurt, he would have pulled Jethro back. He wouldn't have given a second thought to it. But as he spoke, Mac watched the fear and confusion leave her gaze, to leave it filled instead with full feminine awareness of the male awaiting a chance to get his hands on her.

She swung her gaze back to Mac. A silent demand that he do something about Jethro. It was all he could do to contain his grin. He spread his hands in a gesture of compliance. "I guess you'll just have to deal with him later, darlin'," he told her. "For now, though, you might want to do as he suggests. I think you know neither damned one of us cares if the whole world knows who shares your bed. But I know you do. For now."

Rather than giving her a chance to argue further, Mac moved from the truck, aware of the women who stood outside the house watching them. He moved to her door, opened it, and stared back at her.

"For now?" she hissed incredulously as she was facing him once again, refusing to accept his hand in getting from the truck. "Is insanity rubbing off this week?"

Jethro shifted behind her.

Mac watched as her eyes widened just enough to assure him that she had felt the sensual threat behind her. As Mac gripped her waist and set her gently on the pavement, he was aware of the feminine nails pricking into his jacket, reminding him that he had every intention of joining that meeting until she convinced him to await her outside.

"This isn't going to work." She watched Jethro warily as he unfolded his long legs from the pickup and stepped out.

Right there in full view, he shrugged his jacket off, turning his back to reveal the holster-encased pistol at the small of his back.

Twitters of gossip sounded behind them as he threw the jacket to the backseat and turned to Keiley with a rakish smile.

"Oh God," she whispered, rolling her eyes as she glanced back at the women gathered together at the entrance to the house. "Jethro, I'm going to kick your ass."

"You can try." He shrugged as he moved to the front seat and lounged back. "Sure you don't want us to go in with you?"

"And cause even more of a scene?" she muttered. "I knew that the two of you together were trouble."

"It was a given." Jethro smiled. "We'll wait right here on you now."

Mac stared back at the house at the sound of the door opened, watching with narrowed eyes as Victoria Staten stepped elegantly from the house, followed closely by her daughter-in-law, Delia.

Mac had known there wasn't a chance Victoria would let him get away from there without seeing him. She might be the queen bee in Scotland Neck, but she had a heart, unlike her daughter-in-law.

"John McCoy. What kind of trouble are you causing now?" she asked as she stepped down the wide stone steps, as slender and graceful as she had been for as long as he had know her.

"I hate both of you," Keiley muttered as Victoria and Delia came closer.

"Be a good girl now, Keiley," Mac told her softly. "You can kick us when we get home."

"John, you rascal." Victoria's voice was filled with affection as she neared him, lifting her hands to accept his as he moved closer to her. "You have all the ladies atwitter here tonight. Please tell me that you and your very handsome friend intend to wait on Keiley rather than joining her? All that testosterone in the same room with those women might be too much for them to handle."

Her smile was as gentle and warm as it had been the night she found him, cold and hungry, curled beneath a bench in the park in town when he was barely fourteen.

"Victoria, you're as beautiful as the day I met you." He kissed her wrinkled cheek gently, aware of the frailty of her body when before she had seemed as strong and enduring as the mountains around them.

"Flatterer." She reached up, patted his cheek with a soft hand, then turned and lifted a brow as Jethro stepped from the truck. "And who is this handsome fellow?"

"Victoria, meet a good friend of mine and my previous partner in the Bureau, Jethro Riggs. Jethro, this is Mrs. Victoria Leia Staten, the most gracious lady to ever step foot in North Carolina."

A light flush mounted her cheeks as her green eyes sparkled merrily back at Jethro.

"Mr. Riggs, you have my ladies gasping," she informed him as he took he hand and bestowed a flirtatious kiss on the back of it.

"That happens a lot," he whispered back at her, wicked charm glittering in his eyes as Mac caught Keiley closing her eyes helplessly. There was no doubt that she wasn't ready to strangle them both now.

"I bet that nasty gun at your back helps." Victoria leaned closer with a smile that assured both men that she knew what a man was, and she knew well their weaknesses.

"It does seem to leave an impression," Jethro chuckled as she stepped back and he released her hand.

"Mac, you remember Delia." Victoria introduced her as Delia cleared her throat rudely. "My daughter-in-law."

Delia flushed at the reminder, her brown eyes darkening with anger as her flat cheekbones flushed.

Delia was as pretty as she had ever been, but Mac sensed she was more vicious than he had ever suspected her of being.

He nodded. "Evenin', Delia."

Jethro leaned against his hip, watching the scene with a sense of mounting fury. He could see the edge of cruelty in Delia Staten's lips and in the vengeful glitter of her eyes as she glanced at Keiley.

"We heard you had a friend staying," Delia drawled, brushing back a strand of long silken brown hair over her shoulder. "Keiley's been very greedy keeping the two of you to herself."

Jethro's jaw clenched at the veiled insult of her voice and watched as Mac tensed. Keiley's chin lifted as her hazel eyes narrowed and Victoria Staten seemed resigned.

"Delia, dear, why don't you round everyone up and get them into the ballroom?" Victoria suggested. "Keiley and I will be up momentarily."

It was a very polite, very pointed command.

"Of course, Victoria," she gritted out. "Do hurry, though, we can't begin the meeting without you." Her gaze when it flicked to Keiley promised retribution.

Jethro watched as the woman turned, graceful, furious, her back ramrod-straight, her chin held high as she stalked off.

"Mrs. Staten, no offense intended, but that young woman could do well with a nice little spanking."

Victoria's eyes widened as Keiley gasped. A second later, a rich, feminine laugh filled the air.

"You could be right, Mr. Riggs. Unfortunately, my son seems unable to apply the punishment as needed, I fear."

"Poor guy." He shook his head disparagingly. "She runs right over him, huh?"

Victoria turned to Mac. "Your friend is a bit of a rogue," she informed him with the cutest little bow-shaped smile for a woman her age.

"He's a bit of something," Keiley muttered behind her.

Jethro arched his brow as he caught her gaze, promising her, promising himself, later, he would show her the fine art of heating up her backside as he heated that hot little pussy.

"Now, Keiley, I think he seems like a fine young man," Victoria disagreed. "Like Mac. Powerful and very aware of his own charm."

Jethro wasn't certain if that was a compliment or an insult. He glanced back at her, a grin tugging at his lips as her astute gaze went over him once again.

"I can guess why the two of you are escorting Keiley." The laughter left her face as she glanced first from him to Mac. "These ugly rumors making their way around?"

"I hear Delia's behind much of the commotion, Victoria," Mac stated softly. "I want it stopped."

Victoria sighed at the rebuke in his voice. "I have no idea where she's getting her information from. I've made my son aware of the problem, and he's promised to take care of it. If he doesn't, then I shall," she promised. "But remember, John, this is a small community. Games played in private are rarely ever kept in quiet."

Mac stared back at Victoria. He could see the knowledge in her eyes, her awareness of the tension that existed between him, Keiley, and Jethro. She wasn't a dense woman. She knew men and she knew women, and she knew that the nature of gossip began from a grain of sand and revealed the mountain in the mist.

"And you know I don't give a damn about gossip," Mac reminded her, his voice hardening. "But I won't have Keiley hurt."

"And what makes the two of you think I need you stepping in to fight my battles?" Keiley stepped away, flicking both of them an irate look at that point. "I'm going inside. You can play the badassed agents all you want. I've had enough of it."

"Your language, dear," Victoria reproved gently. "A lady never curses in public. There are much better ways to handle the delicate male ego."

Keiley paused. "With a two-by-four?" she asked.

Victoria's lips pursed as a smile tugged at her lips.

"Only as a last resort," she murmured humorously. "And never in public."

Keiley shook her head. "If your delicate male egos will excuse me," she said mockingly, "I'm going inside. I can deal with the gossips easier than I can you two."

Mac watched as she turned and headed for the wide stone steps that led to the porch and the double doors into the mansion.

His eyes were on her butt. Those sweet swaying curves that he swore had to be bare beneath that dress. He couldn't see a hint of a panty line.

"You've been married three years, John McCoy," Victoria's amused, chastising voice had his gaze snapping back to her. "You ogle your wife's backside in public now."

His brow arched.

"And your friend shouldn't be ogling it at all." She turned a frown on Jethro, who at least had the grace to lower his gaze despite the grin that tilted the corners of his lips.

"Rascals," she accused fondly. "You've definitely livened up these meetings of late. The ladies are all speculating on the exact reasons why Keiley has been absent. But I think I'm more interested in the exact reason why a helicopter supposedly bearing FBI markings landed at your farm earlier." Her gaze chilled over and her expression became warning. "Don't make me have to strain myself to get the information, John. You know I won't be pleased."

That was Victoria. Equal parts demand and gentle humor. Jethro stared back at her, surprised. "How did you know?"

"My dear boy." Victoria's smile was sugar-coated steel. "I know things that would make your hair turn gray. Most really doesn't interest me, such as your relationship with John's wife. But if she's in any danger, then this does interest me. I'm rather fond of the child, and I'm rather determined to have my answers. So do be brief and do be honest." She stared back at Mac knowingly. "Remember, son, I can pick out a lie a mile away. Now start explaining."

The minute Victoria Staten entered the ballroom, Keiley knew Mac had told her about the stalker. It wasn't anything she did or anything she said. It was the way the other woman looked at her, piercing, compassionate. It was enough to cause her to grit her teeth in frustration.

Keiley was well aware of the affection the older woman felt for Mac. Victoria had made it clear to her three years before that she had a soft spot for Mac and that she expected any wife of his to take her place within the social sphere governed by the Statens. Mac's farm was one of the more prosperous properties, and she considered social acceptance to be the forefront of personal acceptance. She demanded that Keiley have her hand in several different committees. Committees that would shield her from Delia's viperous tongue and gossiping snideness while ensuring her social acceptance whether Delia wished it or not.

Keiley was well aware that Victoria had added her own subtle approval to her fledgling efforts to fit into the county's evolving social structure. And she appreciated it. Keiley had always appreciated what Victoria Staten had done for her, but she had been careful to keep a very steady distance from her.

First and foremost had been the early information that Delia still lusted after Mac, and the fact that Delia was Victoria's daughter-in-law, Keiley knew, placed the older woman in a delicate position. A position she didn't want to have to test.

"What in the world is going on?" Maxine muttered beside her as Victoria's gaze lingered on Keiley before turning away.

"Who knows?" Keiley answered on a sigh. But she did know, and Keiley had a bad feeling she might know more than Keiley wanted her to.

"Mac's told her something, hasn't he?" her friend asked.

Keiley snorted. "Do you honestly think Mac could keep a secret from her?"

"Only if he really wanted to." Max shook her red head. "They have a soft spot for each other that goes way back. I swear, if it hadn't been for Victoria's intervention when he was a child, Mac's father would have destroyed him along with his mother."

Keiley knew about that intervention. How Victoria had befriended Mac and applied subtle pressure to his father, of the financial sort, to ensure that Mac wasn't hurt. At least not physically.

"Well, he must not have wanted to keep his silence, then," Keiley sighed. Not that she resented the older woman having the knowledge. It would stay silent, secure. Victoria would do nothing to harm Mac in any way, and Keiley knew it.

"Is he any closer to catching that creep?" Max kept her voice low, her gaze carefully tracking anyone who would have listened.

"Let's hope so." Keiley nearly shuddered at the memory of the shooting. Her system was still frayed, her nerves ragged. She didn't need to be here. She needed to be with Mac. She needed to know he was okay rather than in full view of a bastard with a gun. "Let's pray so."

Max's hand settled on her back, her touch compassionate, sympathetic, but Keiley had never felt so alone.

As Victoria took her place at the small podium at the front of the room and called the meeting to session, Keiley found her seat, sat back, and tried to relax. As she faced the women of the charity committee, she realized she didn't give a damn about the gossip. Let their tongues wag. Let them talk. The gossip meant nothing. Hell, even if they knew the truth, it meant nothing. There were two men awaiting her outside, both determined to protect her, to keep her secure. Both supremely confident in their abilities to do not just that, but also to love her equally, to share her without remorse, without bias.

How many women had the chance to hold the hearts of two men such as Mac and Jethro? As the meeting progressed around her, Keiley admitted that for the first time since her father's suicide, she didn't care what those around her had to gossip about. She definitely didn't care if they suspected what was going on in the privacy of her bedroom.

That was her bedroom. If she held the hearts of two men, two men willing to share her love, then it was her business. It wasn't theirs. And if they wanted to make it their business, then let them have at it. She had seen too much, known too many lonely days and nights before she met Mac, to ever want to return there. She wasn't throwing away something she wanted, something she needed, because of gossip.

Finally, blessedly, the meeting came to an end. Victoria Staten released them with a graceful nod to the buffet and snacks set up in the back of the ballroom with a pointed reminder that everyone should attend the next meeting, which would finalize the details for the booths.

Keiley rose hastily to her feet, waiting impatiently as Victoria left the podium and moved for the ballroom doors as a maid moved to open them.

"I have some things to see to for just a moment," she informed the room at large. "I'll return in a bit."

And Keiley had every intention of escaping. But seconds after Victoria left, Delia stepped in front of her.

"Keiley, could you come to the committee board?" She extended her hand to the long table where the women of the committee still stood. All but Victoria Staten.

"Of course," Keiley murmured before following the other woman suspiciously.

She didn't trust Delia, and she didn't trust the glitter of triumph in her gaze.

"Hello, ladies." Keiley nodded to the six women who hadn't bothered to stand as she approached. "What can I do for you?"

"You can resign from the committee." Delia laid a resignation form on the table in front of her as Keiley stared back at her, trying to hide her incredulity.

"Resign? Delia, why would I want to do anything so insane?" She would lose heavily if she resigned now. Not only would she lose the money she had invested in the charity booth, but she would have to pay a heavy loss for walking away.

"I believe you'll consider it in your best interests when you see this." The other woman removed a picture and slapped it down on the table in front of her.

Keiley felt the blood drain from her face. For a moment, the room darkened, and she had a horrifying fear of losing the strength in her legs.

Nothing could be more incriminating. The picture had to have been taken from a crack in the curtains over the wide living room windows of her home. It was positioned perfectly to catch the full view of Mac, Keiley, and Jethro. Naked. Obviously engaged in a full ménage act, their expressions tight with ecstasy.

Keiley picked up the picture, watching the print shaking in her hand and realizing her fingers were trembling violently.

"Where did you get this?"

"Does it matter where I got it?" Delia questioned snidely. "I have it. And so will everyone you know if you don't sign that paper."

They would have it whether she signed the paper or not. She lifted her gaze and met the condemning stares of the other head committee members.

She could feel the heat of humiliated anger rising in her face and refused to bow down to it. This picture was an invasion of her privacy, of her home, of her life.

"Are you truly this vindictive, Delia?" she asked, even

though she knew the other woman was. "Is your life truly so pitiful that you have to destroy others to make it seem worthwhile?"

She looked at the other woman, watching as a flush of fury mounted her cheeks.

"You're not wanted here, by any of us," Delia snapped. "You should have never married Mac and you should have never come here. You don't fit in and sluts like you are not wanted."

"What about the slut who is so hot for another woman's husband that she'll resort to this?" Keiley retorted, indicating the picture as she stared back at Delia. "Do you think for one second you'll ever have Mac?"

Her lips thinned, and for a moment Keiley glimpsed the gloating satisfaction in Delia's gaze. Delia didn't care at this point if she managed to snag Mac to her bed or not. The point was, Mac had rejected her all those years ago. He was the only man to have done so, the only thing she had wanted that she couldn't have.

"I'm not resigning."

"Then this picture will hit the Internet within hours," Delia drawled smoothly. "Everyone in Scotland Neck will see it and they'll know you for the whore you are."

"You're such an amateur, Delia." Keiley shook her head sadly as she folded the picture and secured it in her purse. "You should be certain when blackmailing a person that they give a damn about the blackmailing material. Of course, I'm just the slut having sex in my own home. I'll be sure to give Mac your demands and see how he feels about it."

Keiley watched her composure slip marginally then. Delia hadn't anticipated this. Though why she hadn't, Keiley couldn't understand.

"If I post that picture he'll be humiliated," Delia snapped.

Keiley shook her head. "You really don't know Mac, do you, Delia? The first thing he's going to do is come down on your husband's head like a ton of bricks. Then he's going to call his very good friend, your mother-in-law, and he'll come down on her head like a ton of a bricks. And then."

She looked at each of the other members. "He's going to come after the rest of you. You should really research your victims closer and make sure they give a *fuck* about the blackmail material."

Keiley was aware of the fury vibrating in her voice then. She knew it was shaking through her, shuddering violently through her insides. Her stomach knotted with rage and the flashback to the helpless teen she had been when a community had turned against her tore through her.

She could see the nervous uncertainty working through the other women of the committee then. The heads of the charity committee, mostly older women, certain in their morality and their judgments. Certain that Keiley would be as horrified by her secrets coming out as they would have been.

Victoria had made a mistake in choosing these older women, and especially in choosing her daughter-in-law as the only younger member of this group. Because Delia didn't have a clue about her own peers. Alternate sexual lifestyles among her age group were not that uncommon.

"This will ruin you," Delia snarled. "No one in Scotland Neck will work with you and you'll definitely not be wanted within the organizations you're a part of now. You'll be an outcast, Keiley."

"So cast me out." Keiley smiled coldly. "I don't need you or the fine people of this county to work. And I promise you, Delia, my clients don't give a damn who I sleep with. All they care about is the bottom dollar, and I bring that in excellently."

"And Mac?" Delia sneered. "What about him?"

Keiley gave her a pitying glance. "You obviously don't know Mac very well. By time he's finished with the husbands of this fine group, no one will dare ostracize him or me. Get a clue here, Delia. He has friends in the FBI. Friends who, I promise you, wouldn't blink at the picture. Or at the hell they can make your life. And yours." She turned to Victoria's sister-in-law. "Or yours." Victoria's best friend. "Or yours and yours and yours." Each member of the committee was staring back at her in horror. "Cut your losses, ladies," she sneered. "Because if you don't, I promise you, Mac will make certain you wished you had."

She wasn't wasting so much as another moment here. The longer she stood here, the more the demons of the past bit at her. The humiliating memory of trying to be so good, of trying to redeem herself in the eyes of a community where she had never sinned. Of paying for her parents' sins and realizing she would never be good enough, never rise about her father's thievery or her mother's weakness.

She had been so young, too young to understand what she now knew. It didn't matter when people wanted to see a sin. When they wanted to condemn a person, then the condemnation didn't have to make sense. There were no laws to govern the thoughts and hearts of those with petty, vindictive minds.

Keiley refused to try again. She wouldn't lower her head to Delia. She would not give into blackmail. Never again would she be so weak that she would run and hide because those around her thought she should.

She believed in taking responsibility for her own actions, at all times. She enjoyed the path her life was taking. She enjoyed sparring with both her lovers, and she enjoyed the hell out of the challenge that would come in keeping them in line.

Keiley Hardin McCoy was not a fainting miss, she assured herself as the maid whisked opened the ballroom doors for her and she swept into the huge marbled foyer.

"Keiley, you aren't leaving." Victoria's voice called from a wide door at the end of the foyer as she stepped out. It wasn't a question, it was a demand.

"Sorry, Victoria." Keiley lifted her chin. "I believe it's time for me to leave." Getting out of there before she ripped every hair out of Delia's head out was imperative.

A frown instantly snapped between the other woman's brows as her green eyes narrowed.

"Is there a problem, dear?" she asked.

If Victoria didn't already know about the picture, then she would. There was no hiding it now, and Keiley knew it. As the older woman walked toward her, Keiley felt a flash of sudden regret.

"You know I've always appreciated what you've done for me, don't you, Victoria?" she asked.

Suspicion filled the older woman's eyes. "What has Delia done, Keiley? She's fairly harmless, I'm certain whatever ill will she managed to begin—"

Keiley shook her head. She was going to cry if this gentle, proud woman tried to apologize for her vicious daughter-in-law one more time.

"Just know I've appreciated everything. I really have to leave now."

Keiley turned and moved toward the front doors. She could feel her eyes tearing up and she refused to cry. She wasn't going to cry. She wasn't going to be a baby over this. She was going to be an adult. That was what she was going to do.

Leaving the house, she caught sight of Mac and Jethro standing in front of the truck. They straightened as she stepped onto the wide porch, their expressions filling with heat, memories, and equal desire. And emotion.

The emotion in Mac's gaze was fierce, untamed. Jethro's was wild but more controlled and just as damned sexy. They were tall, broad-shouldered, powerful, muscular. They were men that women dreamed of having in their beds. Men with morals and with a conscience, and they loved her.

Both of these men loved her. Mac, she knew, would always love her. Jethro, she wasn't as certain of, but she knew she couldn't deny him. Couldn't deny the pleasure they both brought her. Or the emotions building inside her. She wanted the chance to hold him the same as she held Mac.

As she moved down the steps, Keiley admitted that she knew she should have stayed home tonight. She knew that coming to this meeting was a bad idea, and Mac would be lucky if she didn't shoot him herself for forcing her into it.

But it had been informative. It had forced her to realize how little the opinions of these women mattered. She had sworn years ago that she would never let a community enforce their opinion of her, on her. It would never happen again. And it wasn't going to happen here.

CHAPTER TWENTY-TWO

There was no fooling Mac or Jethro. As she moved toward them their eyes narrowed, their bodies tightened with tension. Each showed his awareness of her volatile emotions in different ways. Mac's hands flexed as though he were holding his fingers back from clenching into fists. Jethro's biceps seemed to thicken beneath the short-sleeved shirt he wore, pumping up, preparing for battle.

They were like warriors, instinctive, aggressive in the face of any threat. And she couldn't mention this threat. Not yet. Not until she got a handle on it herself and her own sudden aggression.

This relationship had changed her. Two weeks ago she would have been in a panic, horrified that anyone could have witnessed anything so intensely private.

Someone had invaded her home. Had taken pictures. Had shared the evidence that Keiley had enjoyed not just the touch of her husband, but also the touch of his best friend.

And she had enjoyed it. Keiley had seen her pleasure in her face. In Mac's. In Jethro's. The intense intimacy, the emotions beginning to bind them. It had all been there in that picture for anyone who cared to look close enough. To notice how Jethro covered her from behind, his lips pressed to her shoulder, his expression twisted with not just pleasure, but a tortured emotion rising from the depths of his gaze.

And Mac, below her, one hand framing her face, staring into her eyes, his face twisted into a grimace of ecstasy.

She stared at the two men now, knowing they would demand to know why she was upset, that if they found out then both would march straight into the Staten mansion and tell every woman there to go to hell.

And she couldn't bear that. Not yet. Maybe next time. For now, she had to figure out for herself how she felt about this and how she intended to deal with the complications that would arise.

There was no keeping those pictures hidden. If they hadn't already made the rounds of the county, then they would tonight.

"What happened?" Mac's voice was a low growl, a warning of the impending anger ready to rise.

"I told you, you should have just fucked her and had done with it fifteen years ago," she told him with a tight smile. "She would be a little rude now."

"Did she make a scene?" he snapped.

God help Delia Staten if she had, because Keiley couldn't lie to him about it.

"She didn't make a scene, just showed her ass in front of her friends." She shrugged. It was basically the truth. "So, did your handy-dandy little gadget show anyone in the house?"

His lips tightened. "Not yet."

"Then let's go get dinner," she stated. "I'm in the mood for Casey's. What about the two of you?"

She was aware of the probing looks she was receiving from both men as she pulled open the door to the truck.

"I thought you wanted to get home," Mac pointed out.

"I don't want to cook, and I don't want to clean up anyone else's mess," she told them both, knowing her mocking smile wasn't fooling anyone. "I need a drink and a hot meal, and I want to dance. We haven't gone dancing in a long time Mac."

"She wants to go dancing?" Jethro flicked Mac a suspicious look. She caught it, she knew questions would come later, but hopefully, they would let it go for now.

"Keiley?" Mac caught her arm, turning her to face him, his eyes roiling, the gray shifting and moving in a thunderous pattern. "What did she do?"

"As I said, she made an ass of her herself." Keiley drew in a deep breath as she stared back at him imploringly. "We'll talk about it later. I promise."

Later. When she could face him with the fact that she had made a decision that should have involved both of them. She had told Delia to shove that picture in a less-than-polite place and walked out, knowing what would happen. Before the end of the night, it would be in every attachment to every e-mail address in the county. If it wasn't already.

"Definitely later," he informed her, his voice hard. "But if you've let Delia escape me while I could wring her skinny damned neck, then I'll paddle your ass."

The wave of heat that overtook her was shocking. It clenched her womb, spasmed between her thighs as silky damp heat spilled to her panties.

"Promises, promises," she whispered, but she was aware that the huskiness of her voice owed as much to arousal as it did to the tears that tightened her throat. "Are we ready to go?"

She lifted herself into the front seat, moving to the middle that she had refused to use earlier as she flipped back the padded console and stared back at Jethro intently.

"Backseats are only good for one thing," she told him. "And all three of us can't fit back there."

His eyes darkened immediately, whereas the thunderous pitch of grays in Mac's eyes suddenly stilled. Sexual hunger stamped their features and knowledge lit their expressions.

Could they feel her building need? Nearly two days without satisfaction, with teasing touches and near desperation, always interrupted before they could find a time and a place to relieve the hunger pouring through all of them.

She wasn't fighting this. The time for fighting was over. It was over the minute she dared Mac to bring Jethro into their home. It was over the day she married him, knowing that this time would come.

She was in love with two men. The potential for heartbreak had suddenly doubled, the risk to her heart was greater, but like she had told Jethro earlier, sometimes a person had to take a risk in life.

She watched as he moved into the truck, his body crowding in close to hers as Mac moved to the driver's side and took his own seat. She was between them, surrounded by their heat, by their arousal. Protected by their strength.

As Mac started the truck, her gaze moved back to the Staten mansion. There, Delia Staten stood in the open doorway, her gaze piercing as she stared at the truck. Jealousy and hatred were reflected in Delia's expression as Keiley met her gaze. And vengeance. The other woman would do whatever she could to destroy her, and Keiley knew it.

"I'm going to take care of this," Mac muttered as he circled around the drive and headed back to the main road.

"I don't need you to take care of this. You can't fight these battles for me, Mac. I have to do it on my own."

"You expect me to just sit back while she makes your life miserable?" he snarled, his head jerking around to glare at her before turning back to the road.

"That's exactly what I expect you to do. This is something I have to deal with myself." To a point, anyway.

She was aware of Jethro beside her, his body shifting, then the sound of paper crinkling. Keiley felt her stomach drop as her gaze jerked around. The picture she had folded had fallen from her purse to the floorboard of the truck. Jethro was reaching for it, his fingers touching it.

"I have it." Keiley jumped, bending quickly, fighting to slap his fingers out of the way, to grab the incriminating paper when he suddenly pulled it from her fingers.

"Give me that." She snapped her hand out, trying to jerk it away from him as she felt the truck come to a resounding stop at the side of the road.

The next thing she knew, Mac had it, holding it easily out of her reach as she subsided, sitting still and silent as she stared back at Jethro with furious fear.

"Who. Took. This." The control in Mac's voice was terrifying.

"I don't know."

"Where did you get it?"

Keiley laced her fingers together and stared straight ahead.

"Where did you get the fucking picture, Keiley?" he yelled.

She flinched, hearing the rage in his voice. The same rage that had filled her, that had burned like a cold unquenchable flame in the center of her gut. Hell, it still did.

"It doesn't matter where it came from," she finally answered. "I would say it's a pretty good guess that everyone in the county has one by now, though. Wouldn't you?"

"Son of a bitch." His hands slapped into the steering wheel before he gripped it violently, his anger filling the interior of the truck. "Why didn't you tell me? When did you get it?"

"She got it at the meeting," Jethro said knowingly. "I think we both know when she got it. We can guess who gave it to her. I'm just wondering what she thought she would get in return for showing Keiley she had it."

"Delia did this?" Mac yelled.

Keiley risked glancing at his face and jerked her head forward once again. She fought the trembling in her lower lip, fought the pain that bloomed in her chest.

"I'm sorry," she whispered.

Silence filled the truck.

"What did you just say?" Controlled, icily furious. She flinched once again at the tone of Mac's voice.

"I'm sorry," she said again, lacing her hands in her lap. "I don't know how they got the picture." She swallowed tightly, feeling panic welling inside her then. Black, oppressive, the guilt was suddenly strangling her. "I don't know how to fix this yet. I was going to tell you." She fought the trembling in her voice. "I was going to tell you, but I had to figure out what to do first."

"You mean you had to figure out how to keep me from killing that vindictive little bitch?" he asked, surprisingly calm.

Keiley licked her lips and looked at him again. His voice might be calm, but his expression and his eyes were anything but calm.

"I didn't say it was Delia." It took every once of control she had to firm her voice, to push back the fear, to remind herself she was no seventeen-year-old again. She was a grown woman. A strong woman. A woman capable of accepting the consequences of her actions.

"You're going to rub their fucking noses in it," Jethro drawled then, incredulously. "That's why you wanted to go dancing."

She risked a glance at his face only to stare out the windshield once again. It was just her luck, both men looked like volcanoes ready to explode. There wasn't a chance she was taking either of them out in public tonight.

"That would be unwise." She finally cleared her throat uncomfortably. "Maybe going home would be better after all."

It took her a second to realize that rubbing their noses in it was exactly what she had intended. By morning, that picture would be on the tip of everyone's tongue, and she would be damned if she was going to show any shame. She had intended to strike first.

She was aware of both their eyes on her, especially Mac's. She swore she could feel him watching her, his gaze touching her with incredulity.

"Keiley? Would you look at me?" His voice was deadly calm.

She turned to him slowly. "I'm not ashamed of my life," she told him fiercely. "I'm not ashamed of what I do in the privacy of my own home. If they want to make it public, then fuck them. I'll show them how it's done."

"Fuck them?" He blinked back at her in shock.

Keiley drew in a deep breath, crossed her arms over her chest, and glared back at him.

"That's what I said," she bit out.

"Where is my wife?" he asked then with an air of a man suddenly confronting a stranger in the body of someone he thought he knew.

Her eyes narrowed.

"Fuck them," he repeated. "Keiley, I don't think I've ever heard you say that."

"You don't see me for hours after these meetings," she reminded him. "And after plenty of alcohol."

His nostrils flared as though he suddenly realized the anger of moments past rather than the surprise his wife was dealing him. His gaze went back to the picture he held in his hand, and Keiley couldn't help but stare at it. Whoever had taken it had known how to do it. The perfect angle, the perfect shot. She could see the sweat beading over their three bodies, see the twisted expressions of pleasure, her limbs arranged over Mac's, Jethro behind her, holding onto her, the muscles of his body powerfully defined, his flanks tense, tight as he thrust into her behind as Mac took her below.

She saw it all.

"I'm not ashamed," she whispered, reaching out to touch the curve of Jethro's back before her fingertip ran over the point where Mac's lips touched hers. "But this was private. It was ours—" She blinked back the angry moisture in her eyes before breathing in deeply. "And I want to go dancing."

Jethro watched her, his fist clenched at the side of his leg. He forced the fingers of the other to remain relaxed, laying on her thigh, the silk of the dress between them. He felt her pain, her anger. She wasn't ashamed—she was hurt, she was violated.

He met Mac's eyes over her head and knew neither of them would let this go unpunished. Others would see the picture, there was no doubt, there was no way to stop it, but they would pay for it. And he knew where to start.

"We'll go dancing," Mac told her, his voice low, but Jethro heard the undercurrents of rage, the tightly leashed violence that foretold the hurting someone was going to feel.

He sat back against the door of the truck, watching as Mac lowered his head, his lips touching Keiley's, comforting her, whispering words Jethro couldn't hear, but words he echoed in his heart.

He wanted to hold her. He wanted to kiss her soft lips, feel the passion and the promise, the dedication and the exhilarating warmth he had felt only with her.

"My turn." He pulled her from Mac's arms, ignoring her gasp, ignoring Mac's chuckle.

Hell, he had played into his friend's schemes from the moment they had first met. He wasn't fighting this one any longer.

He pulled her over into his lap, right there, parked in front of God and whoever decided to drive by, and took the kiss he was aching for.

He felt her surprise, the shock, then the rich, heated promise of her lips parting for him, her tongue touching his and her arms twining around his neck.

In his arms. Arms that contracted around her, that held her close to his chest, that followed the vow his heart was making.

He would protect her. He and Mac. Against everything, even the wagging tongues of a county that had no idea the hell he could bring down on them.

"You picked a hell of a place to decide to mark her, Jethro," Mac growled as he watched Jethro consuming Keiley's kiss.

Seeing it, hearing her pleasure, her whispered moans, was making him crazy. His dick was hard enough to pound nails, and every muscle in his body was tight with the need to find release in the soft body twisting against Jethro's chest.

And she wanted to go dancing. God help them both. Because he knew how Keiley danced. How her sensuous body swayed to the music, how she tempted with her eyes and her smile and made grown men whimper like babies in need of their momma.

His hand stroked up her bare leg, her knees, heading for the richness between those slender thighs, when he suddenly jerked to awareness.

He gripped her hips instead, pulled her from Jethro's arms, and set her back in the center of the seat.

"Damn, we're going to get arrested for lewd acts in public," he informed them both.

"It was his fault." Keiley was breathing hard, her hazel eyes glittering with green, her cheeks flushed with need. "I don't want to go dancing after all. I want to go home."

"Take her home, Mac," Jethro snarled. "We'll go dancing tomorrow night if she still wants to."

Mac heard the silent message. She was angry now, hurt, and anything she did in public tonight could haunt her later. And Mac knew that well.

He pushed the truck into gear, pulled back onto the road, and headed home.

Dark was falling, casting the mountains in shadows and the interior of the truck into an intimate oasis of darkness. As Mac drove, his free hand moved along Keiley's thigh, inching higher, beneath her dress, until his fingers brushed another hand searching for the same secrets he was intent upon.

"Hell!"

Keiley's laughter filled his head before it turned to a gasp, the sound assuring him that Jethro had found paradise first.

Desperate, he clamped both hands on the steering wheel and glared at the road ahead.

He couldn't watch, but he could listen. He could feel her leaning against him as Jethro turned her, arranging her legs until one foot rested in the floor and the other on the seat behind his back.

Keiley was arching, her strangled moans destroying him as he lifted his arm, allowing her head to fall against his chest, giving him a clear view down her body.

"Fuck you, Jethro," he bit out.

Jethro's fingers pumped inside her in a long, powerful

stroke that had her crying out. The dress lay around her waist, her panties were pulled aside, and the sight of her juices gleaming on Jethro's fingers as he pulled back nearly had Mac coming in his jeans.

"She's so tight." Jethro's voice was reverent, filled with hunger. "I'm just using two fingers, Mac."

He knew exactly how tight she was, how hot and sweet. How her pussy gripped around his fingers or his cock and squeezed until pleasure became rapture. He knew how wet she got, how the silken heat became slicker, creamier as her arousal was pushed higher.

"Mac," she moaned his name as she shifted against his chest, her arms twining around his neck as he held her against him with one arm and drove with the other.

"Hot, baby?" he groaned.

"Wicked hot," she purred against his neck, her tongue peeking out to lick over his skin like a living flame.

"Oh God!" She tightened in his arms.

"What's he doing, Keiley?" He had to blink the sweat from his eyes to concentrate on the road. "Tell me what he's doing to you, sweetheart."

She jerked, whimpered.

"Tell me, Kei." He was dying. He had to know, needed to know.

"Oh God, his fingers, Mac."

"Are they in your pussy, darlin'? Stroking that softest flesh?"

"Yes. Yes."

"And you're clenching on him? Burning him because you need more?"

"Oh God, Mac, I need more," she whimpered, her breathing jerky against his neck as her hips arched again and a cry slipped past her lips.

"Tell me, Kei," he snarled. "Tell me what he's doing."

"I'm so full," she cried out, her head falling back to his shoulder as she fought to breathe. "He's in me everywhere, Mac. Everywhere."

"Your sweet pussy?"

"Oh God, yes."

"Your tight little ass?" He was dying. He swore he was dying.

"Yes—" Her breathing hitched, a moan slipping free as he heard Jethro bite off a curse, felt the vibration of the next thrust inside her body as he finally realized how close to the farm they were.

Hell, he needed just a few more minutes. He lifted his foot from the gas, easing the speed as the sounds of Jethro's fingers sinking repeatedly into the liquid depths of Keiley's pussy nearly pushed him to the edge.

She was chanting his name. His, Jethro's, begging, demanding. Then a low, drawn-out cry seared his senses as he made the turn onto the farm road and came to a stop.

His arms surrounded her as she shuddered through an orgasm, jerking and writhing against him as Jethro used his fingers to draw the release out longer, to build the pleasure until she was shaking from it.

Mac watched her face, the gleam of perspiration on it, her eyes wide and unseeing, the glow of passion and release that gave her an ethereal, otherworldly appearance.

"Get us to the fucking house," Jethro gritted out as she finally relaxed in his arms. "If I don't fuck her, I'm going to die here."

Mac's chuckle was rusty, strained, as he helped Jethro ease her back into her seat.

"Check the security alarm." He put the truck back in gear. "We'll check the house out first."

The passion was enough to blind a man, but he couldn't forget his priorities. Keiley's safety. Nothing mattered except keeping her safe.

"The house and grounds show no movements," Jethro told him as the house came into view, the outside lights blazing around the farmhouse, stables, and barns.

The grounds showed up clearly, without so much as the first odd shadow. It looked peaceful, serene.

"After today's shooting he would likely choose to lay low." Jethro was still breathing hard, but hell, so was he, Mac thought. And it had nothing to do with the damned stalker.

"Pappy is laying by the front door where we left him."
Jethro nodded to the large animal as it rose, its tail wagging
at the sight of the vehicle pulling in.

"Let's get in," Mac growled. "Before we both come in
our jeans."

CHAPTER TWENTY-THREE

Jethro and Mac escorted Keiley to the bedroom Jethro was using. A thorough check determined that nothing or no one had been in it. They left her there, gun in hand, with strict orders to lock the door behind them, then left the room to check the rest of the house and reset the alarms throughout it.

Nearly an hour later, Mac's knock sounded on the door.

"Unlock the door. We're clear out here."

Keiley laid the pistol on the end table, rose from the chair she was sitting in, and went to unlock the door. She knew what was coming. She knew the time away from her would do little to dim the lust raging through the two men. It would have built; the threat of danger mixing with the hunger would have their bodies hard and ready for her.

As hard for her as she was soft and wet.

She unlocked the door slowly, moving back as it swung open to reveal a temptation so forbidden Keiley wondered if any of them would survive it.

She retreated, a hard thrust of need slamming into her womb, clenching it with enough force that her abdomen rippled, drawing Mac's gaze as both men stepped into the room.

The door slammed closed behind them, the lock snapping into place.

The candles she had lit on the dresser cast flickering

shadows over the two men as, simultaneously, they began undressing.

"Stay still," Jethro ordered as her fingers went to the buttons of her dress. "Unwrapping the present is just as pleasurable as playing with it."

She shuddered at the dark cast of his voice. Her breasts were immediately more sensitive, her nipples hardening and pressing tightly beneath the lace bra and the material of the dress. She could feel the anticipation pounding in her bloodstream now, whipping through her with enough force to steal her breath as both men dropped their shirts to the floor.

She had done this before. She tried to reassure herself that surviving with her sanity intact would be a snap. It would just feel like she was losing her mind.

She touched her tongue to her lips as boots, socks, jeans, and underwear were shed in a matter of minutes, leaving them both naked, furiously aroused, and powerfully dominant.

"Look how pretty." Jethro's croon was a shadowed sound of hunger as he watched her, the fingers of one hand curling around the thick shaft of his cock.

She stepped back again, watching their gazes flare, watching the dominance in their expressions notch higher.

Mac's lips tipped in a knowing smile as her breathing grew harder.

"Come here." Narrowed and intense, his gray eyes looked black in the dim shadows of the room.

"Not on your life. If you want it, take it."

Take it. It was the ultimate dare and she knew it. A challenge neither man would reject. She watched the muscles flex over their bodies as she moved further away from them, smiling back at them with a mixture of temptation and anticipation.

"Mac," Jethro growled as though in warning.

Mac's smile was confident. "She likes to fight it sometimes," he murmured. "Don't you, sweetheart?"

"Maybe she needs to learn the error of her ways, then." Jethro smiled and they moved.

They caught her easily, and she did try to duck around them. There was a chance she could have slid around them if she had maneuvered it just right.

But Mac had played this game with her before, and he was ready for her. And she had forgotten how easily he and Jethro seemed to work together.

Mac's arms wrapped around her from behind, holding her firmly while Jethro began unbuttoning the dress. And he took his time with it.

Keiley shuddered as Mac's teeth scraped over the back of her neck, laying in heated kisses that seared her nerve endings as Jethro laved each inch of newly revealed flesh with his wicked tongue.

Her arms were restrained behind her back, pressing her breasts forward as the material fell away from them. The bra was disposed of with a quick little flick of Jethro's fingers, the cups peeled back and his lips covering one hard, heated tip.

Fire lanced between her thighs, tightened around her clit, and slammed into her vagina as the violent pleasure drew her body tight. He didn't suckle the tip easily, he ate at it. Drew it into his mouth, rasped the sensitized nipple with his tongue, and sucked at it with firm pressure as Mac dragged the dress and bra from her arms.

She stood before Jethro, clad in nothing but black lace panties already damp from the juices spilling between her thighs. She was hot. Achy. Burning for touch, yet no one touch was enough.

The wildness she had always tried to keep trapped inside her was winging free. It was arching her breasts closer as Mac held her wrists in one hand while moving before her. He cupped the other mound, his gaze meeting hers before opening his lips over the neglected nipple.

Shock resounded through her. She couldn't tell which arm was which behind her back, holding her to her feet, keeping her upright as she stared down at the two men tormenting, torturing her stiff nipples.

At once.

Two pairs of lips, two tongues, two hot mouths, sucking and licking, nipping and devouring the peaks. She didn't expect the crashing orgasm that ripped through her womb. Her body bowed, her fingers curling into fists as she felt the ripping explosions of sensation tearing through her with exquisite force.

"Mac!" She screamed his name. "Oh God. Jethro!"

They didn't stop. As the pleasure peaked they drew on the hardened tips further, lashing and laving with their tongues as she tried to writhe, fought to buck against their hold, to get closer. She needed to be closer.

"Easy, sweetheart." Mac's head lifted, his lips running up her neck as Jethro's lips began to lower.

"Not like this," she cried out, struggling against Mac's hold. "I can't stand it like this."

It was too much pleasure. Mac nipped at her neck, Jethro licking down her side.

"You don't have to stand it, Kei," Mac whispered at her ear, nipping it erotically. "We'll hold you up. Just let it have you. Let us have you."

Keiley shook her head desperately, feeling the perspiration gathering on her forehead and along her neck as she tried to breathe. She couldn't breathe. Pleasure was whipping around her, snapping along her nerve endings with fiery heat and violent pleasure.

She lost the strength in her legs when she felt Jethro's teeth nip at her hip bone and his hands pulling the lace panties over her thighs.

"Mac." She could barely whisper his name, could find nothing to hold onto with her wrists still in his grip.

"We have you, darlin'."

Jethro spread her thighs, his hands smoothing down her inner legs as his cheek brushed over the damp curls between them.

"So sweet and hot," Jethro growled. "The juiciest little treat in the world." He blew a soft puff of air over her straining clit, causing her hips to jerk involuntarily as Mac's lips covered hers. A second later, Jethro's tongue eased into the moisture-rich slit of her pussy and began licking erotically.

Sensation filled her world now. Cascading colors exploded behind her closed eyelids as pleasure ruptured through her body.

How many times had they done this with other women? Each touch, each kiss was laid with exacting precision, with a choreography that stole her senses with destructive ease.

Jethro lifted her leg over his shoulder, giving him better access to the juices easing from her body. His groan vibrated against her flesh a second before his tongue plunged inside her.

She could feel him licking, drawing more pleasure, drawing more heat to his devouring lips. And Mac. His kisses were destroying her, flying through her as his tongue pumped into her mouth with the same dominant force that Jethro's tongue pumped into her pussy.

She was being consumed, and the pleasure was killing her.

"We need her on the bed." Mac tore his lips from hers to growl the order to Jethro. "Now, damn it."

Jethro's response was a snarl, but his lips eased from her aching folds, his tongue giving a farewell lick to her clit that had her crying out at the impending orgasm that raced through her.

Her wrists were released, though, and as she was lowered to the bed, her hands found the nearest raging erection.

"Sweet mercy." Jethro's body tightened as her lips covered the throbbing head of his cock.

His body tightened, his hips jerking forward as her lips, tongue, and mouth sucked him in.

He tasted like the night. His cock felt like silk-encased iron, his balls drawn tight beneath it. And Keiley used every trick Mac had taught her to erode his control while Mac's hands eased over her quivering body.

The fingers of one hand gripped the straining shaft, while she calmed his balls in the palm of her the other, her fingers working over the straining flesh of each portion of his body.

She licked beneath the head, then sucked him deep as she worked her tongue along the straining flesh. Blood was pumping, throbbing beneath the skin, making it steel-hard, sensitive.

"She has you." Mac's chuckle was rough. "Once that hot little mouth gets hold of you, you're a goner."

Jethro's hands were in her hair, tightening, tugging.

"Spank her. Let me watch her ass blush."

Keiley moaned. A second later she cried out around the hard flesh filling her mouth as Mac's hand landed on her rear.

A second later, it rose between her thighs, a light little tap to her pussy exploding through her senses. Another to her rear. Back between her thighs. Jethro's hands were tugging at her hair, and Keiley was fighting to keep the pressure on his cock as too many sensations began to invade her body.

She was so wet that the soft slaps to her pussy only heated her further, made her want more. Need more.

"I want her waxed." Jethro was panting. "Soon, Mac. I want that pussy waxed."

"Do you know what that would feel like, Kei?" Mac's voice whispered at her back. "Your pussy bare and soft as silk when I do this." His hand landed on her again, slapping against the damp curls that shielded it.

She would be bare. Nothing to soften the small spark of heat between his hand and her flesh. She moaned at the thought.

"Fuck, stop playing around, Mac," Jethro snarled. "Distract her before I lose it."

The head of his cock jerked, spilling a small amount of semen onto her hungry tongue. Behind her, she felt Mac's fingers spreading her rear, and a second later a kiss so destructive she jerked back.

Jethro's cock slid from her lips as she tried to pull away, trying to reach back, to push him away.

"Come here, sweetheart." Jethro caught her, easing her to the bed as Mac continued to lick along the narrow crease between her rear cheeks.

"Mac!" Her cry was shattered as they laid her out across the bed, on her side. Mac's hand lifted her leg, holding her beneath the knee, opening her to him further, and he was taking full advantage.

"Oh God! Mac. What are you doing?" She heard the shock in her voice when his tongue found the small opening and began to rim it with lightning strokes of his tongue a second before it plunged inside her.

She tried to jerk away. She drove her hips forward, pushing her clit straight into Jethro's waiting lips.

"Suck my dick, Kei." His voice was strained. "Do it now."

Her head shook, her eyes opening, dazed, nearly unfocused as she felt the broad head of his cock touch her lips, press forward.

She opened on another cry as two fingers stroked inside her pussy and drove the last fragments of thought from her mind.

They were fucking her. Tongues, fingers, suckling lips at her clit. They were destroying her. Minutes later she felt thickly lubricated fingers easing into the damp entrance behind. Mac's teeth were scraping over the curves of her rear as her body opened for him, taking the penetration of first one finger, then two.

Jethro was licking, sucking her clit. His fingers were impaling her vagina, sliding deep, curling and stroking until she wondered if she would ever be able to live without both of them. Both of her men touching her. Both of them stroking her.

Her mouth was filled with Jethro's erection, but her senses were so scattered that tormenting him was out of the question. She could barely breathe. Barely cry out her pleasure.

"Fuck! I'm going to come like this." Jethro jerked his cock back, his fingers sliding from her as Mac's slid into her rear, hard and deep.

"No!" She needed Jethro back. Needing his fingers pumping into her. She was so close. Sensation gathering upon sensation and threatening to explode through her.

She was being moved. Lifted. Her legs spread as a hard cock pressed against the opening of her pussy. A second later, it drove deep and hard inside her as hard hands on her hips slammed her down.

"Tight. So frickin tight." Jethro was beneath her. His cock filled her.

Keiley forced her eyes opened as hands, Mac's, Jethro's, she wasn't certain, pressed her against his chest.

"Jethro." She stared up at him, fighting for breath as his hand smoothed her hair back from her face and behind her, Mac worked more of the cool lubrication into her rear.

"We have you, sweetheart," he groaned.

"Jethro."

"Yes, baby."

Behind her, she felt Mac move closer, felt the thick crest of his cock press against the entrance to her rear.

"I need more," she moaned desperately, tightening on the cock spearing her pussy as she felt Mac opening her behind.

She needed that touch of pain. Needed it with a sudden hunger that raged inside her and sent her senses careening.

"Easy, Kei." Mac's voice was hard as she tried to press back, tried to take more than he was giving her.

He was too slow. Too easy.

"Now." The strangled demand was more of a cry. "Now, Mac."

She couldn't wait. The need was tearing her apart, hunger and lust and forbidden pleasure whipping through her like a conflagration racing toward the fiery explosion.

The head of his cock stretched her, burned her. Hard hands held her, controlled her.

"Fuck! She's tight," Jethro groaned beneath her as Mac eased in further.

Panting, Keiley forced herself to still beneath them, waiting. Waiting. Seconds later their hold eased. Behind her, Mac whispered her name as she felt Jethro ease back.

Just enough. His cock retreated just enough to allow her to move.

Before they could stop her, before their restraining hands could hold her still, she bore back, her hips jerking onto the two invading erections with a force that slammed Jethro fully inside her pussy and forced Mac's cock more than half-way inside.

"Oh God!" she screamed out at the sensations. Fire and pleasure rained inside her, exploded, and echoed with a force she didn't think she could survive.

Male voices cursed. Hands gripped her. She used her muscles to tighten on them, to draw Mac deeper, to hold Jethro inside her, and her mind shattered.

"Fuck me!" she cried out, her fingers curling into Jethro's shoulders as she fought their hold. "Now, damn you. Now."

She couldn't have imagined more, better, harder. But they gave it to her. The tightly leashed control they used when taking her together shattered. With a hard jerk of his hips Mac plunged inside her rear, burying full-length, filling her, stretching her, burning her.

Jethro retreated, but as he thrust inside her again, Mac was retreating, repeating, so attuned to her body, to each other's movements, that within seconds the synchronized thrusts kept her filled, kept her burning higher, hotter, racing through her mind and her senses until they exploded with a force that convulsed her entire body.

Never-ending. The orgasm that claimed her seemed to never stop. Powerful, violent spasms ripped through her body, jerking through her muscles and tightening tender tissue on the impalements tormenting her.

Their cries joined hers, and seconds later their thrusts were harder, deeper, the lava-hot spurts of their semen filling her and sparking a second, harder orgasm inside her as two male voices grated their devotion in each ear.

"God, I love you, Kei. Love you." Mac bucked inside her rear as the words tore from his lips.

"Fucking love you. Fucking love you." Jethro's was

rougher, more primal, the newness of giving his emotions voice reflecting in his husky tone.

And between them, Keiley collapsed, sweat-soaked, feeling their hard bodies still rippling with pleasure, still filling her, holding her. Needing her.

"I love you both," she whispered against Jethro's chest. "God help me. I love you both."

CHAPTER TWENTY-FOUR

Jethro held her, his hands cupping her breasts, his finger tweaking her nipples as he watched the folds of her pussy flower open for the slow, measured thrusts of Mac's cock between her thighs. Her clit was swollen and straining as he held her still, her hands gripping his biceps, her nails digging in as she bucked beneath her husband.

Mac's body was tight as he fought to hold back, determined to drive her into another climax before he gave in himself. Jethro could see the determination stamped on his friend's face, see the hot lust and soul-deep devotion in his eyes as he stared down at Keiley.

And he should have felt like an interloper. Even now, he wondered at how easily they were sharing the little vixen. Jealousy wasn't clouding their heads. Nothing but pure sweet pleasure was tearing through him, just watching her, holding her, his gaze moving to her face, staring into her unfocused eyes as Mac's thrusts became harder, deeper, as they shook her body and finally triggered the release awaiting her.

She couldn't scream. She whimpered, arching in his arms as he moved one hand from her breasts and stroked himself to a rapid release as Mac's low groan signaled his own climax.

They collapsed to the bed, damp, overheated, fighting to relearn how to breathe.

"Touch me and you die," Keiley groaned as Jethro shifted

beside her, his arm pressing against hers before he turned to his side to stare at her.

Her arms lay over her head, her eyes were closed, and her delectable body was sprawled out in careless sated abandon. She was so damned pretty it made his back teeth ache. It made his chest tighten in fear as he remembered the picture she had come out of that meeting with.

Because of his and Mac's hungers, because of their weakness, she would be facing a community with certain knowledge of what went on in her sex life. And they would punish her for it. Because they could. Because it made for such titillating gossip. And the thought of her being hurt in such a way was enough to make him want to kill.

"You look so angry," she whispered then, reaching up to touch his cheek, her eyes seeing far more than he would have wanted her to. "Is everything okay?"

"Tired." He forced a smile to his face. "You've worn me out."

She snorted at that, her gaze dropping to the half-hard erection between his thighs.

"That doesn't look tired to me."

"That is a beast of its own," he assured her. "He never gets tired. I'm another story."

"Uh-huh. Try that one on someone who will believe it," she snickered as she stretched languorously.

"It doesn't do that for just anyone," he warned her. "Only very special ladies."

Her eyes rolled in response before drifting closed.

"You're not going to sleep yet, princess," he chuckled, moving from the bed before pulling her into his arms. "Mac, change the bed. I'll head her to the shower."

"I have to find my legs first," Mac mumbled. "She wiped me out."

Jethro was finding his own legs. They were weak from the pleasure she had given them through the night.

"You have ten minutes," Jethro informed him.

"Doesn't take me that long to shower." Keiley yawned. "Five minutes."

To which Mac opened one eye and grunted at the sight of Jethro's aroused body. "Try twenty minutes. Hell, I have time for a nap."

"And I'm hungry," Keiley suddenly complained. "You two keep forgetting to feed me. This is uncalled for. I'm using up a lot of calories here."

Mac rubbed his own stomach. "Hell. I'm starved."

Jethro's stomach rumbled, causing Keiley to snicker back at him. "See," she pointed out. "If you're hungry, just imagine how hungry I am."

Jethro glanced at the clock. Hell, midnight was a good time for a snack.

"I'll make the bed. You two hurry with that shower and we'll scrounge something up in the kitchen."

"Yeah, that soup I was working on earlier would have been good. Too bad someone wouldn't let me finish it."

"Shower." Jethro led her into the bathroom.

"A bath would be better," she murmured. "In my big bathtub. We would all fit."

Her sultry voice had his erection bobbing in agreement.

"Shower." His stomach was growling in demand. "You can bathe tomorrow."

"Make me wait and I'll bathe by myself." She pouted.

The love that suddenly flooded him at her half-teasing, half-seductive look nearly brought him to his knees. He shouldn't love her this much, he told himself as he adjusted her water and pulled her in behind him. He shouldn't love her to the point that his knees weakened and his chest tightened with the ferocity of it.

As he washed her hair, then cleaned her sleek body, he couldn't help but caress her washrag. To worship her here just as she did in that damned bed. He couldn't help but to want to give her anything, everything she could ever want.

And now he knew the hell Mac must have gone through before resigning from the Bureau. He remembered watching his friend's eyes that last day in the club, seeing the regret, the love, and the fears that filled him.

One man could give a woman more pleasure than she

ever conceived. But two, two who knew each other as well as he and Mac did, could give a woman such pleasure that she glowed from the inside out with it.

Keiley glowed. Her eyes were more green than hazel, her body sated and relaxed beneath his hands. There wasn't so much as an inch of her body that hadn't been kissed, stroked, loved.

He rinsed her gently, then stood staring down at her, his hands framing her face.

"I love you," he whispered.

"I love you," she sighed, still not comfortable, he could tell, with loving two men. "But you two are going to drive me insane with it, and I know it."

"No one has ever gone crazy from too much lovin', sweetheart." He grinned down at her.

"No, they went crazy from trying to control all that testosterone," she told him, her gaze assuring him that she was clearly laughing at him.

"Well, then, you have it easy. You'll just let the testosterone control you. No danger that way."

"Uh-huh. We'll just see how that one works out for you. Ask Mac. He'll tell you how easy that one is."

He leaned forward, giving her a rakish smile. "He already told me. I particularly like the story where you chased him through the house with his own baseball bat."

Her face flushed. Jethro remembered Mac's amused chagrin at that one. His jealous demand that she not take a particular local job because the business owner was a known charmer. The argument that lasted three days. The day of the meeting Mac had slipped her keys from her purse and she caught him.

By time she left for her meeting, a less than happy Mac had been nursing his bruised pride. Not because she had hit him, but because he hadn't been certain she wouldn't hit him. She had taken the bat with her and Mac had waited at home. Because, as she had put it, if he followed her, it only proved her didn't trust *her*. And no marriage could survive without that trust.

"Mac overexaggerates sometimes." She cleared her throat, obviously holding back her laughter.

"I think he underexaggerates," he said then. "He said you were as beautiful as a pissed-off fairy. I bet you were a damned sight prettier."

"Have either of you macho men seen a fairy?" she suddenly burst out. "No comparison. They could be ugly. Haggard. They could have warts on private parts of their bodies. You could be insulting me."

He caught her around the waist as she pushed at his shoulders, the water pelting around them, her laughter shining in her face.

"No. I see a fairy every time I see you. Delicate and shining. So innocent you make grown men weep to make you wicked and so sultry you make them howl to possess you. You're pure, Keiley. Never let anyone tell you different."

She paused then, staring back at him with narrowed eyes. "What happened with that picture isn't your and Mac's fault."

"We didn't protect you."

"God save me," she snapped. "Get out of my shower, Jethro. Go help Mac."

"Keiley. I won't let them hurt you like this."

"I said enough!" Her voice rose, firmed. "I made this choice. You and Mac didn't force me into it. You and Mac didn't take those pictures and you and Mac are not to blame. And the next time I have to threaten a man with a bat, I'll use it."

The shower curtain whisked open and Mac stood outside, his brow arched, his naked body relaxed.

"If you two are going to fight, then let me use some of the hot water." He crowded in behind Keiley, pushing her into Jethro's chest before she bit off a curse and, before he could stop her, stepped from the shower. "I've had enough. I want to dress and eat. Then you two need to get things in perspective with this damned fairy crap you keep laying on my head. Any self-respecting fairy would have turned you both into toads by now."

"That's a witch." Mac obviously felt the need to prick her temper, Jethro thought with a wince as he stepped out of the shower stall. "Fairies are so much sweeter."

She stared back at her husband archly. "You live in such a dream world, Mac. You really need to visit reality sometimes."

If the look she shot both of them as they chuckled meant anything, the bat might be coming out sometime soon.

"I need to get dressed." She just shook her head at them, but Jethro saw the joy shining in her eyes.

She was happy. Hell, she was happy when he came to her home, but he could see that that happiness had increased. His had increased. Increased to the point that he was seriously considering taking Mac up on the offer of the farm. The farm next to Mac's was coming up for sale as well. Jethro had enough saved to purchase it and add to what Mac already had.

The horse breeding was the backbone of the property right now, but with some careful management and extra hands, the cattle could become increasingly prosperous. Jethro knew cattle. Mac wasn't the only one who had a little experience on the land.

It would be worth considering, he thought as he helped Keiley dry off. Or rather, caressed the water from her as she batted at his hands and laughingly shooed him away.

"I need my gown and robe," she told him as she moved into the bedroom with nothing but a towel covering her.

"Here. See if this will work." He tossed her one of his shirts from the drawer before pulling a pair of jersey pants out and pulling them over his legs.

The shirt did indeed work. It nearly hung to her knees and make her look smaller, more delicate than ever. Hell, all she needed were the wings.

"It's not my gown," she sighed. "But it will work. One of these days you two are going to have to replace the door in my bedroom. I like my bedroom. I like sleeping in my bed, if you don't mind."

"What's wrong with my bed?"

"It's not mine." She rolled her eyes. "Don't worry, Jethro, I like the middle, as Mac will tell you. You can sleep on the other side."

"There wasn't a question," he informed her. "This room is more defensible."

"This is not my room." A frown snapped between her brows. "Listen, Jethro, there are a few rules cut in stone in this house. Number one, Keiley sleeps in the room she likes." She counted off fingers as she continued. "Number two, Keiley likes her bedroom and her bathroom, and she does not change simply because Jethro now shares it. Do we understand these rules?"

He stared at the delicate fingers. "Are those all of the rules?"

"Of course not. I'll let you know as others crop up though. Mac has adjusted quite well, just as I'm certain you will."

Mac chose that moment to walk out of the bathroom and lay his hand against her rear hard enough to cause her to jump in surprise.

"Rule three is, if Keiley gets out of hand with the rules, she gets her butt spanked," he laughed.

"Since when?" Her eyes narrowed.

"Since I said." He grinned. "And Jethro agreed."

A pout pulled at her lips. "Where's my bat?"

"In your car." His gaze flicked over her as he pulled his jeans on, a smile tugging at his lips. "Want to go after it again?"

A blush stole over her cheeks, and Jethro remembered Mac relating that little tale as well. How she had stalked to her car for the bat during a summer rain shower. She had ended up bent over the hood while he took her from behind.

Anger surged through him at the thought. There would be no taking her outside, on the car, in the hot tub or the pool, or anywhere else until that crazy damned stalker was caught.

"Let's go eat." Jethro anchored his holstered gun in the back of his pants before pulling a t-shirt on and slipping his feet into leather running shoes. "While we're at it, we need to figure out how to catch that bastard fast. I want him gone, Mac."

"No more than I do," Mac sighed, his gaze lingering on Keiley before he moved and pulled her beneath his arm. "No more than I do."

Keiley could feel the tension returning now, and the fear. For a short time she had forgotten about the man determined to destroy their lives.

Dealing with an addition to her heart was hard enough. She had thought it would never be possible to love anyone but Mac, but she was learning better. The adjustment to it was less than comfortable at times. The knowledge that everyone they knew was going to have explicit proof of it was driving her crazy.

With Mac in front of her and Jethro behind her they moved downstairs to the kitchen, and a quick meal of canned soup and sandwiches.

As she ate, Keiley couldn't help the feeling of impending doom that rose inside her. They weren't safe and Mac refused to leave the farm, even for a few days.

She could feel something dark, something smothering gathering in her chest as she cleaned up the dishes and listened to Mac and Jethro talk behind her.

"I want to know where that picture came from." Mac's voice was too cold, too controlled.

Keiley turned from the dishwasher to face the table, seeing the anger that lit his gaze.

"The Playboy always researches his victims well," Jethro reminded him. "He would have pinpointed Delia first thing as a weakness. I'm betting he sent her the picture."

"Now we have to counter the fact that she's likely sent it to everyone she knows," Mac growled.

"What if we hack her computer?" Jethro questioned. "Target her address book and resend the picture with a virus attached. It shuts down the computer after the e-mail downloads and wipes the hard drive."

Mac shook his head. "It's gone too far. We would have to use a worm. One that goes into the address books, sends itself to each address that that particular attachment was sent to, and wipes computers out one by one as it's found. It would take time, a week maybe, but it would take care of the attachment."

"What about the printouts? They can be scanned back in. Or the copies backed up on disc?" Keiley shook her head. "It's not worth the effort or the worry. So they have a picture of us. So what? You two are buff as hell and made me look damned good between you. Why worry about it?"

She picked up her wine and sipped from it as she met their brooding looks.

"Keiley," Jethro finally answered. "It's not a matter of how the picture looks. It's a territorial thing. But even more than that, it's a matter of the insults that could be directed to you. I'd prefer not to kill over this. But I will."

Keiley stared at Mac, hoping for a little backup.

"Don't look at me." He shook his head. "I agree with Jethro. Our home was invaded and our privacy violated. Your privacy violated. I won't let that go."

"This isn't the Middle Ages," she snapped back. "And I don't need either one of you protecting my honor. Would you like to know the sheer number of women who have at some point had some lowlife bastard post pictures of them? And let's not even get into the women who post the pictures themselves. Do you really think the fact that our picture is up there is going to be anything but a three-day wonder?"

"Do you really think I want anyone seeing my bare ass and you sandwiched between me and Mac?" Jethro bit out. "Excuse me here a minute, Keiley, but I can safely say there are no pictures of me buck naked anywhere on the Internet."

Oh boy. This would not be a good time to point out that she knew better. She dropped her head, staring at her bare toes intently rather than at him or Mac. Because it was definitely the first time a picture of her nudity had been displayed anywhere. But these two were another story.

Geeze, one would think with them being in the FBI, they would have checked these things. Duh! Get a clue. It was one of the first things she had checked for the night she had met Mac. Hell, she still had those pictures on one of her backup discs. She had just forgotten about them. Maybe she should have mentioned it to Mac when she started to, years ago. She just *assumed* that with him being in the FBI and that being his bare ass and all, he would have checked it out for himself.

Big mistake there.

"I don't like that look on your face, Kei," Mac suddenly growled.

"What look?" Her gaze jerked to his, eyes wide, and a hell of an attempt at false innocence.

"You found pictures of us?" The abject horror in his gaze would have been amusing under the circumstances.

"Well, in your defense, the pictures are not listed under your names. I promise."

"Names? Pictures?" Jethro snarled. "Not of me."

They were amusing, she had to give them credit. Unfortunately, she might have to wait a while to laugh. She cleared her throat instead.

"Stag party. Chet Waterson. Really, I had to type in a *lot* of key words to find those pictures. I swear."

"Where's Chet now?" Mac asked darkly.

"Texas."

"When this is over, I'm going to kill him."

She could tell by the look on his face that he knew what was in the pictures.

"She was really a cute little blonde, Mac." Keiley gave him a droll look. "I think she was really proud of that picture, too. It was on her Web site for several months before she took it down. But by then it had spread like a virus. You two were very popular for a while."

"Good Lord, she's enjoying this." Jethro was staring at her as though he had no clue she had a sense of humor.

"I thought you would have known, to be honest." She stared back at them in confusion. "You two were pretty wild back then. Didn't it occur to you that *someone* might take pictures? A video? Something?"

Evidently it hadn't.

"Look, I don't like this any more than you do. My bare butt might not be showing, but someone has a picture of me enjoying the hell out of having my bare butt covered. But let's be realistic about this. There's not a damned thing we can do to stop it. That doesn't mean we have to be ashamed of it."

"You are the girl who cringes at the thought of anyone gossiping about us, right?" Mac snapped as he jerked to his feet and went to the refrigerator. She knew exactly what he was after.

Two beers. He handed one to Jethro before twisting the cap of his with a furious movement of his wrist.

"Damaging gossip. Lies. Yes," she amended. "But do you really think we're the only ones playing bedroom games in this county?" She snorted. "Or the only ones who will be living openly in a ménage relationship? You know better, Mac."

His pride was smarting, though, and she knew it.

"That's not the point," he retorted furiously.

"No, the point is that someone stole it and there's no way we can take it back," she guessed. "You can't control it, so you have to fight against it. If you do that, then the gossip will only get worse. We go out, hold our heads up, and show them we don't give a damn, and it will become old news."

"Except to the perverted flakes jacking off to the thought of you being double-fucked by us?" His voice rose angrily.

"Yeah, well, what about the perverted women masturbating to the thought of being between you and Jethro? Just think of all the hot dogs we'll sell at the festival next month."

She swore they paled. Both of them.

"Call Gladsteen in cybercontrol now." Mac turned to Jethro. "Now. Get Delia's e-mail address, it's in my address book. I want it targeted. I want every computer that attachment went to, was forwarded to, or viewed by, annihilated."

"Gladsteen will charge you the moon."

"I'll pay fucking Venus!" Mac snapped. "I don't give a fuck. Do it."

"I'll call her."

"Her?" Keiley frowned. "Gladsteen is a her?"

Jethro ignored her. He moved from the kitchen, his feet pounding up the stairs.

"Gladsteen is a her?" She turned on Mac.

"I'm going to my office." Mac finished his beer. "Come in here and sleep on the couch while I program in some information on that program you made for me. This shit is getting taken care of."

He came to his feet with a surge of energy she wished she could just imitate.

"Who is Gladsteen?" She wasn't letting that go. "You didn't say anything about paying a her whatever was required. And if Venus is a sex trick, I'm going to be pissed."

She trailed after him, aware of Pappy moving in closer, brushing against her legs as they moved into the office. She never even knew that dog was around until he slid past her.

"Venus is not a sex trick," Mac snapped as they moved through the back hall to his office. "It's a figure of speech. Stop worrying. The most she'll ask for is a case of Scotch for her booze-licking husband."

"Oh. Well. That's not so bad then. Right?" She stared up at him as he pushed her onto the couch and knelt before her on the floor.

"It's not bad at all," he sighed, reaching out to touch her cheek, then her lips. "I want you to sleep. Okay?"

"I'd sleep better in our bed," she mourned. "The couch isn't nearly as warm."

"But the couch is in the room with me. I'll know you're safe."

Her lips quirked. "I meant the bed is warmer with you in it. I don't want to sleep without you, Mac."

"Just this once," he whispered, pressing her shoulders down as he positioned the small arm cushion into place beneath her head and pulled the quilted throw from the back.

He tucked the blanket around her, then kissed her lips. Gently. A melding of flesh as they stared into each other's eyes. And like always, for Keiley, it was like coming home. Like being in the midst of warmth and security.

"I'm not ashamed," she assured him again. "The picture doesn't matter."

"It does matter, Kei." His hand tightened on her arm. "I can see it in your face."

"Not enough to let it hurt me." She smiled back at him. "I won't let them hurt us. Don't you do that either, Mac."

Mac brushed his fingers on her eyelids, watching as they closed.

"Go to sleep, little fairy," he whispered, watching the smile that flitted at her lips before she burrowed against the pillow and sighed deeply.

She needed to sleep and he needed to work. Rising to his feet, he moved to his desk and pulled up the program still working on the laptop. The sheer amount of information being uploaded was almost enough to boggle his mind. Thankfully, the second phase of the program would categorize the entries.

Pulling up the entry cell he began typing in the names of his employees, past and present. Something he had only thought of earlier. It would take a lot of work to figure out the perfect position to lay in wait with a gun from the base of the hill across from the house. It would take someone familiar with him and his home though to get a picture like that. Perfect positioning, perhaps a hidden camera.

Just because he had left the Bureau didn't mean he wasn't still a paranoid son of a bitch. Because he was. He had laid out the stables, barns, and landscaping around the house in a very precise manner. It would take someone who knew every angle, and had worked it.

That meant someone he knew, because he didn't allow strangers on his land and he didn't have a schedule that would allow for an easy invasion into his property. Not to mention the alarms on the house and the animals around it.

The position of the pastures and buildings around the house ensured that the animals would be disturbed by anyone moving onto the property. Someone could do it without being detected, but it wouldn't be easy.

The shooting he could explain away. Cameras in the house were another thing.

Finishing, he then turned to his stationary computer, powered it up, and pulled up Google. Half an hour later he sat, his cheek cradled in his hand, staring at several pictures that had been taken years before.

He was bare-assed naked and having a hell of time. Drunk as a loon and grinning for the camera. The other window held a variety of pictures of Jethro in a similar state.

Damn, they had been wild then. Fifteen years had aged them, given them a measure of maturity. Maybe. At least enough to know better than to get into antics as they had then.

A third window was still working, looking for information on Keiley that didn't involve the pictures splashed in newspaper articles regarding her father's embezzlement and her parents' deaths. Her father's death, her mother's suicide.

At eighteen, Keiley had been alone, faced with a mountain of debts she had no hope of paying, and the condemnation of a town that had no one left to punish.

Shutting the computer down, he turned as Jethro stepped quietly into the office, his gaze going immediately to where Keiley lay sleeping on the couch.

"We need to get her to bed," Jethro told him softly.

Mac nodded slowly. "Did you talk to Gladsteen?"

"She's working on it. Said she would let you know the charge later."

Mac winced. He was going to end up paying out the ass for this one and he knew it. The case of Scotch might be a small, very small, portion of it, but there wasn't a chance it would be the entire thing.

He wiped his hand over his face, glanced at the clock, and winced.

"Let's head to bed, then. Keiley doesn't sleep well on the couch."

He caught the slight stiffening of Jethro's expression and stared back at him questioningly. He hadn't expected this to be easy, not for any of them, but he admitted that for the most part, the relationship was working out well considering the circumstances.

Did he feel guilty that he had maneuvered his wife and his best friend in such a way? Sometimes. Enough to draw back? Not in a million years. Keiley was his soul and his life, and her pleasure, her protection were worth everything. The fact that he enjoyed the hell out of watching her pleasure was secondary. Besides, he missed Jethro. They worked well together, understood each other.

And they both loved Keiley.

CHAPTER TWENTY-FIVE

"Everything in moderation," Keiley murmured as she smoothed her hand over the sleeveless vest top she wore and checked the fit of her snug blue jeans and stylish boots.

The jeans were a little tight, hugging her butt and legs perfectly. They weren't as low at the hips as those that she wore around the house, but she was going out. That required a whole different perspective.

"Less is better," she reminded herself as she attached small hoops to her ears. "Don't go overboard. They belong to you. Just remember, you don't have to stake a claim, just show ownership. Simple. Easy. Very aboveboard."

Mac tilted his head as he stood in the doorway, shot Jethro a confused look, then stared back at his wife as she turned, ran her hand over her curvy little ass, and checked the fit of her jeans.

"It's not like you have to get dirty," she murmured.

Mac looked around the room. There was no one else there, and he knew damned good and well she hadn't seen them yet.

"All you have to do is hold your head up. And remember, a ménage is not the same as embezzlement. Ménages are fun. Embezzling is illegal. They can't stone you."

Pep talk. Damn. He had never heard his wife give herself a pep talk before.

"You will be the envy of the county." A smug little smile curved her lips as she faced the mirror again and brushed back her bangs. "Both those hard cocks are all yours. You can show your pride without being wicked."

He bit his lip as Jethro's shoulders shook soundlessly.

Damn, he had lived with her for six months and been married to her for over three years and he had never heard her give herself a pep talk. And he sure as hell hadn't seen the blatant smug smile such as the one she had on her face when she declared herself the proud owner of his and Jethro's cocks.

"When you've finished cheering yourself on, we're ready to go," Mac announced, holding back his laughter as she swung around, a delicate pink blush working from her throat to her hairline.

"Eavesdroppers," she snapped.

"Eavesdroppers hear nothing good of themselves," he pointed out with a grin. "What we heard was infinitely satisfying."

Keiley felt her own laughter bubbling in her throat. Okay, so it had sounded bad of her, but she was determined to do this right. Sometimes that took a few reminders.

Besides, it was hard to get mad at either of them when they looked so damned good. Well-worn jeans hugged powerful legs. Their feet were encased in boots. Mac wore a white short-sleeved shirt and Jethro wore a black t-shirt. Both men had tucked their shirts into their jeans and wide belts cinched their hips. And those pants bulged perfectly. She must have a naughty streak she hadn't recognized until now, because the proof of their very virile bodies sent a surge of pride racing through her.

"Okay. I'm ready." She spritzed a quick spray of Poison over her shoulders and chest before smoothing her hands over her jean-clad hips and watching as Mac's gaze was drawn to her tanned legs and low-heeled Western boots.

His and Jethro's gazes both sparkled with heat and approval. Confidence filled her. She could do this. She had been preparing all day. While Mac and Jethro had removed the other cameras from her bedroom curtains and worked to trace the remote link they had found, she had prepared herself for tonight.

Dinner and dancing at Casey's, the old Western saloon–style club outside of town. She had taken a long, soaking bath filled with bath salts, waxed her brows, spent hours selecting her clothes, and called Maxine for moral support. Maxine, her husband, several of her sisters and their husbands, and half a dozen of the women from the charity committee were all going to be at Casey's as well. Moral support, Maxine had raged. The picture Delia had shown Keiley had arrived in their in-boxes late last night from Delia's e-mail address. It had arrived several more times from friends of Delia's.

Maxine was outraged. Joseph was coldly furious with the Statens and had demanded to speak to Mac and Jethro. What had happened during that conversation she had no idea, but she knew Mac and Jethro had seemed particularly smug after he handed the phone back to Keiley.

She had friends. Keiley had been terrified that the few friends she had made would turn their backs on her. She would have hated that. Would have mourned it. But her friends were jumping in with both feet, giggling on several conference calls and demanding details until Keiley laughingly refused.

Not that it wasn't tinged with a bit of embarrassment. Well, a lot of embarrassment. Maxine, the wretch, had noticed Keiley's birthmark right off, the little strawberry on her hip, and teased her mercilessly. Her sister Fayrene had insisted her husband invite his Army buddy for the summer, which resulted in Fayrene hastily hanging up the phone amid giggles and half-hysterical reminders to her husband that she was on the phone.

Her friends were gathering around her, though. The phone had rang unceasingly throughout the day. Many of the men who had received the picture were calling Mac. They were smart enough to throw their support behind the men with the FBI rather than the witch with the pictures.

Smart of them, Keiley thought.

"Heinagen and Sheffield are watching the house tonight," Mac told her as the truck doors closed behind them and he put the truck in gear. "We caught a transmission from inside the house. We think he's using a remote-activated electronic bug. Those are harder to pick up. It has to actually be activated to be detected. They're working on it while we're out. If they don't find it before we return home, remember, anything you say could be heard."

"What about the truck?" Keiley asked nervously.

"You can hide them in the house because the wires are easier to conceal. I pulled the truck into the garage earlier and went over it top to bottom. There's nothing on it or in it. It's safe. Going through the house would be a hell of a lot harder and damned near impossible to find without the right equipment. Director Williams is having that equipment flown in tomorrow afternoon. It's the quickest we could get it."

Keiley inhaled roughly.

"It will be over soon, Kei," Jethro assured her as he leaned back against the door and watched her with narrowed eyes.

He was doing that a lot, just watching her, as though he were drawing her into himself somehow. It was disconcerting to be probed in such a way. He was quieter than Mac in a lot of ways, still the bad boy, but the wildness she had glimpsed in his gaze when he first came to the farm wasn't there any longer.

"How much of it will be over, Jethro?" she finally asked. "Are you going back to D.C. or staying here?"

Could she handle it if he returned to the Bureau? She had had nightmares while Mac was still an agent. The day he announced his intention to resign, she had cried for hours in relief.

"Mac and I are discussing it," he finally said.

"You are?" She glanced back at Mac, seeing the small curl of his lips at the tone of her voice. "Interesting that you two didn't think to discuss it with me."

She stared back at Jethro coolly. "None of my business?"

"All your business, beautiful. But some things men have to settle between themselves first. Get used to that. Where you're concerned, I have a feeling, we'll have a lot to discuss."

That part, she didn't like. She bit her lip as she considered the two men who were filling every part of her heart and soul and wondered about the whole outnumbered thing.

"Two men against one defenseless woman seems like lousy odds for me." She pursed her lips in disapproval. "I may have to reconsider my own battle plans here."

Jethro looked at her warily. "How so?"

"That," she whispered as she leaned to him and placed a butterfly kiss on his lips. "Is for me to know."

"And for you to worry about, Jethro." Mac suddenly laughed. "Damn, I won't be tortured alone. At least I'll have an ally now."

"You are so wrong, John McCoy," she snorted. "Just so wrong. Give me a month, he'll be all about being on my side," she teased.

At that, pleasure tilted Jethro's lips. "Oh, sweetheart, I'm already all about being on your side. Your back. Your front. Whichever way I can get you. I promise you that most sincerely."

"Perv," she accused him as he pulled her closer, kissing her soundly before smiling back at her with devilish humor.

The drive to Casey's was completed in the same vein, but it didn't stop the nerves from building in her stomach. As Mac pulled the truck into the crowded parking lot, she almost demanded to go back home.

Damned near the whole county seemed to be there. She could safely say she had never seen Casey's so packed.

"Maybe I shouldn't have called Maxine." She swallowed tightly. "I think she's told everyone I would be here."

Her stomach was pitching tightly as fear suddenly began to fill her. The fear of facing condemnation, of hearing the whispers behind her back.

"Too late to turn back now, darlin'." Mac's voice was firm as he opened the door and stepped from the truck. "Come on. Let's go show them how hot you are. Hot enough that it takes two of us hard cocks to keep you satisfied."

Heat blazed through her as shock had her lips trembling with laughter.

"You are so bad," she accused as he lifted her from the truck and Jethro's laughter joined Mac's. "What am I going to do with you?"

"I have suggestions, but this might not be the place for them."

It was a place for hilarity. For over a dozen men and women crowded around Mac, Keiley, and Jethro. They were the friends she and Mac had been drawn to when they first arrived, couples they were comfortable with, whose interests and sense of humor seemed to align with theirs.

Now they were friends who drew around them in support and extended their hand in friendship to Jethro as well. Through dinner and drinks, Keiley watched him. He was quiet but friendly, laughing in genuine amusement at some of the women's antics with their husbands but saying no more than he had to. As though he were watching for enemies amidst friends and categorizing strengths and weaknesses.

As plates were carried away by the waitresses and more drinks arrived, Keiley noticed the subtle tension invading him. His demeanor hadn't changed, but she could feel it, just as she sometimes felt it with Mac.

On the stage across from them the band was gearing up, swinging into a slow, sensual love song. It was couples night, which meant lots of slow songs.

She turned to Jethro slowly, meeting his eyes, and whispered, "Dance with me."

Hooded, his deep blue eyes wary, he watched her for long seconds before pushing his chair back and holding his hand out to her. Talk ceased behind them, every eye at the table turning to them as she took his hand and let him lead her to the dance floor.

Mac sat back in his chair as several of the other couples followed behind Keiley and Jethro, leaving him at the table with Joseph, his wife, Maxine, and her sister and brother-in-law.

"Ladies' room trip," Maxine announced as she grabbed her sister's arm. "Come on, Fayrene."

Fayrene rolled her pretty brown eyes before kissing her husband's cheek quickly and following after Maxine.

"She hasn't shut up since that damned picture hit her e-mail box," Joseph sighed, watching as his petite wife made her way along the side of the room toward the restrooms. "I had to take the phone out of her hand before she called Delia Staten herself."

"Delia's not living peaceable." Chase Sinclair, Fayrene's husband, told him somberly. "I talked to her husband, Robert, today. He's furious, Mac. He wanted to call you himself, but Victoria asked him to wait."

Mac nodded. He hadn't expected Victoria to take his side in this. She had her opinions on things, and her beliefs. She was more likely to toss Keiley from the charity committee than she was not to. If she felt Keiley had disgraced the rules of decency that she lived by, then she would cold-shoulder her until hell froze over. And the same went for Mac. Mac had no doubt it would snow in hell before she extended her hand in friendship again.

She lived by her own rules, she upheld them. She wasn't a cruel woman, but she could be a strict one.

"Robert called the bank today and had Delia's name taken off their account and canceled her bank cards," Joseph muttered.

"I heard computers have crashed left and right across the county as well," Chase commented. "Everyone who forwarded that e-mail that I know of has found themselves with the hefty expense of replacing them. The hard drives were totally ripped."

Mac's lips quirked. Gladsteen had a way about her, he had to admit.

"I have to admit, I was worried when Maxine started screeching like a banshee this morning," Joseph said. "She was torn between laughing in amazement at your and Keiley's daring and crying in rage at what Delia had done. She's worried about the three of you as well."

Mac's gaze flicked to Chase.

"I saw the helicopter land at your farm, Mac, I'm not a

fool. I don't know what your problems are, but I'm betting they're not easy. If you need us"—he nodded to Joseph—"we're here."

"He would be better off with the information," Joseph muttered. "Chase is handy as hell in a fight, Mac."

Mac explained about the stalker quickly to Chase, keeping his voice low, his gaze on the tables around them to make certain nothing was overheard. As he finished, he watched Chase's blue-gray eyes narrow dangerously.

The Ranger was home on medical leave for a gunshot wound to his leg, taken in action. Rumor was he would never return to his unit, but that didn't cancel him out of a fight.

"You have the house covered?" Chase asked when he finished.

"I have help." Mac nodded. "We'll catch him. Right now, I'd prefer to keep you and Joe out of the line of sight. I don't want to give him someone else to target."

"We catch him here, and he'll never target anyone else," Joe suggested softly, the lowered tone of his voice doing nothing to disguise his fury.

Joseph Bright hadn't always been a banker. He had been a cop first, wounded in the line of duty just after his marriage to Maxine. It was then that he allowed his father to convince him to join him at the bank. He was the best damned bank president Mac had ever known.

"If I need you, I won't hesitate to call," Mac assured him. "Right now, I'd rather keep this on the farm, though."

The other two men nodded before their gazes flickered to the dance floor, then back to Mac. It was well known that no other man ever slow-danced with his wife. But there he sat, relaxed, at ease, and on the dance floor Jethro Riggs was wrapped around Keiley like a winter blanket.

"You surprised me," Joseph told him without censure. "He's a lot like you were, though, when you first came home. Wary. Kind of dark. She fixed you."

"And she'll fix him." Mac nodded.

The question Joe didn't want to voice was in his and Chase's eyes, though. They were his best friends, his only true friends from the years before he left town. Two of only a few men who knew the truth of the life he had led before his mother died.

"You know why, Joe," he finally said. "I was never just like everyone else. This is just a part of it."

Joe grinned at that. "Keiley's living every woman's sexual fantasy, you know that, don't you? The rest of us are going to catch hell now."

Mac looked back at him in surprise.

"No kidding," Chase grumped. "Fayrene's already wondering why the hell none of my Army buddies can't visit for the summer. You have those women frothing in fantasy. Man, we should kill you for that alone."

Mac looked out at the dance floor. Jethro was indeed wrapped around Keiley like a winter blanket, dancing slow and easy, his head bent to hers, and laying against hers. Like Mac danced with her. And there was no jealousy, just a sense of comfort.

There would always be someone to protect her, and Jethro would heal. The bleak shadows of his past would go away, and beneath Keiley's influence and her love, he would soften. She had that effect on people. Her love had that effect on men. He didn't expect it to be easy. Jethro had been rejected from hell and back during his childhood. It would take a while. A year. Maybe two. But he would realize he was where he was meant to be.

All three of them. They were exactly where they were meant to be.

CHAPTER TWENTY-SIX

"Come on, sweetheart." Jethro eased Keiley from Mac's hold as he opened the door, careful to keep her body shielded with his as Mac tucked his weapon behind his back and eased from the vehicle.

She was aware that they shielded her from the time she moved from the truck until they entered the house. Keiley fought back her apprehension, easing into the house behind Mac, hating the fact that he had to stand in front of her, that she had to be protected, that she wasn't able to protect herself.

"When this is over, we're going to talk about my own training. You've been neglecting me," she hissed at Mac as they entered the foyer and headed upstairs to Jethro's room, where she knew they would stash her until they had secured the house.

She heard his amused snort and felt Jethro's hand smooth warningly over her rear as they stepped to the landing and headed for Jethro's room.

She really wanted her bedroom back. Her comfortable bed, her familiar surroundings.

Jethro moved into the bedroom, his weapon held confidently in his hand as he swept through the room. He checked the bathroom, the closet, and behind the curtains. Within seconds he was motioning them in and Mac was pulling his backup weapon from the holster at the top of his boot and pressing it into her hand.

"You know the drill," he told her. "Lock the door behind us and don't open it until I give you the okay."

She nodded sharply as worry continued to gather inside her. She tried to draw the confidence she felt radiating from both of them into herself and steel herself to be strong.

When this was over, Mac and Jethro were going to train her to help them. She made that decision as she stared at her husband, then her lover. She would never again hamper their movements if danger followed them.

"We'll be right back." Mac kissed her quickly, his lips taking hers, catching them in a kiss of heated promise and desire before he moved away.

Jethro moved by her then, caught her to him, and pressed his lips to her brow. "Be good," he growled with a sexy warning. "Or you won't get spanked later."

"Hell of an incentive." Her breath hitched shakily. "Hurry. I get lonely very easily."

"Spoiled fairy." His voice was teasing.

"Remember it," she ordered as he pulled away from her.

They moved out of the bedroom, closing the door behind them. Holding the gun in one hand, Keiley locked the door with the other and pressed her face against it with a ragged breath.

Ten to fifteen minutes was all it took, she assured herself. The security device they carried that worked with the motion-sensor alarms had shown no disturbance in the house. No one was here. They were all safe for the night.

Weren't they?

She turned and stared into the room. The small lamp Jethro had turned on spilled a circle of golden light on the edge of the bed, but it left the rest of the room in shadows. Long, sinister shadows had a chill racing down her spine.

She wished she could turn on the brighter overhead light, but Mac had forbidden that several nights before. The brighter lights allowed shadows to reflect against the curtains, and despite their heaviness there was still a chance of becoming a target.

Low light worked best, he told her. There wasn't enough glare to penetrate the heavy curtains or to cast shadows. Just enough light to see by. Not enough to shake the feeling of oppressive danger that surrounded her.

Get a grip, Keiley. She laid the gun on the dresser top beside the door and rubbed at her arms briskly over the wrap she wore. She felt cold. Frightened.

Three minutes. God, they had only been gone three minutes. The clock on the bed stand confirmed it, but it felt like three hours.

She paced the floor at the end of the bed, from the bathroom door to the window on the other side of the room and back again. She rubbed her arms, counted her footsteps, and prayed.

She glanced at the clock two minutes later. Four minutes later.

Shaking her head, she pushed her fingers through her hair and paced to the window again. Where she froze at the sound of a soft shuffle, a sliding sound out of place with the beating of her own heart.

She turned, staring across the room at the shadow that began to lengthen beneath the soft light, then darken and materialize.

Wide-eyed, shocked, she watched as the figure rose from beside the bed, a malevolent smile on his face, his brown eyes glittering with triumphant glee as he straightened from beside the bed.

"No one ever thinks to check beneath the bed properly," Wes Bridges crooned with diabolical smugness. "They'll check everywhere else. They'll bend and look at the floor beneath the bed. But they never look up once they get down."

"Wes? What are you doing?"

"Showing them how incompetent they are," he snickered. "And you're the prize. If they had caught me, you would have lived. But they didn't catch me, Keiley, so I get to kill you. Just letting them go isn't any fun anymore. There have to be stakes in any game, don't you agree?"

"Game? What game?" Terror was shaking through her, stealing her strength as he pulled a wickedly long knife from behind his back.

"Cat and mouse," he sneered. "I could have been an excellent agent. But they wouldn't let me in. They made all the tests harder for me. I was smarter and brighter than all the others and they couldn't accept that, so they had to make it harder. They had to make sure I failed."

"Who?"

"Those bastards at that fucking FBI training center. They didn't realize my genius. Well, I'm showing them now, aren't I?" He smiled with relish. "I've been showing them for years how inept they are. And do you know, Keiley, none of those stupid agents think to look at the underside of a box spring or pay attention to the fact that the bed slats are sometimes just a little out of place?"

"How do you know?" She had to keep him talking just a little longer. Mac and Jethro would be back any minute. Just a few more minutes, she prayed.

"Pappy," he said triumphantly.

"The dog? Mac's dog?"

"My dog," he snapped, a furious frown brewing on his brow. "That's my dog. I trained him. I made his collar. I inset the rivets on it with a remote listening device and miniature camera. I saw everything. I heard everything. And I knew they wouldn't check beneath the bed the right way. They bend down and check the floor," he cackled. "They never check the box springs."

"Mac will know it was you," she whispered. "He'll kill you."

"Mac will never know," he crooned. "I don't leave witnesses. And I'm tired of disguising myself when I make my final move. I'm going to cut you into little pieces, Keiley." He glanced at the clock, then back to her. "I can do a lot of cutting in five minutes. And you will bleed a lot. Then I'll just go out the window and come to work tomorrow like usual. He'll never know. Never ever know."

"He'll know." Terror gripped her throat, making her voice hoarse, ragged. "He'll find you, Wes."

He shook his head. "Poor Keiley. You're just a pretty little pawn, and all pawns must be sacrificed." He lifted the knife higher.

Her gaze flew to the gun. His followed. And they both dove for it at the same time.

Mac and Jethro checked the upstairs first, each room, one by one. Closets, bathrooms, the two spare bedrooms, and the utility closet before moving downstairs.

They made their way from the back of the house to the front, checking the offices first, and working their way to the living room and the front door as they checked each of the motion-activated alarms on the door frames. They didn't find a problem until they checked the alarm on the wide frame between the foyer and the living room.

"It's rigged," Jethro muttered as he ran his fingers over it, dislodging a metal sliver that had kept the alarm activated while allowing it to send a clear signal.

Mac moved through the room, his weapon held ready as he swept the area before moving to the window on the other side of the room.

"How did he get in?" Mac growled.

Jethro looked up from the alarm he was checking against the monitoring device in his hand. Keying in commands, he began to run a diagnostic on all the alarms, tracking any anomalies that wouldn't have shown up otherwise.

Finally, his gaze lifted, horror reflecting in his expression. "The bedroom alarm was deactivated and then reset without triggering the monitor."

"How?"

Jethro didn't have time to answer. Keiley's scream shattered the silence of the house, followed by the sharp explosive retort of a weapon.

"Keiley!" they screamed in unison as they hit the stairs, taking them two and three at a time as they rushed for the bedroom.

Mac reached the door first. Gripping the doorknob, he threw his weight into the panel, bursting into the room an inch ahead of Jethro, where both men came to a resounding, shocking stop.

Keiley's head jerked around, the weapon held in both hands, white as a sheet, her eyes dark and too round in her face, her hands shaking.

Her gaze went back to the man lying on the floor, blood pooling beneath his body, then back to Mac.

The gun dropped from her hand, and before they could catch her she ran for the bathroom, sliding to the floor as Mac caught her at the toilet, where the violence and fear began to heave through her body.

Jethro knelt beside the fallen body, checked the pulse at his neck, and smiled. The smile was one of anticipation and pleasure.

He gripped the outstretched arms, jerked them behind the Playboy's back, and was rewarded by a fractured cry.

"Oh, you're going to live, aren't you, my friend?" he asked the trainer with increasing triumph. "You're going to live and you're going to pay. And pay. And pay."

"Jethro?" Mac called from the bathroom.

"He's alive," Jethro called back as the sound of the front door breaking in caused him to wince. "Heinagen just took out your front door."

Jethro cursed as the sound of Keiley's sobs reached him. He jerked at the trainer's shoulder again, feeling a surge of furious pleasure race through him at the bastard's pain.

A second later Heinagen and Sheffield rushed into the room, weapons drawn, to stare at Jethro in surprise.

"Cuff this bastard and read him his rights." He turned the moaning trainer over to Heinagen as he jerked restraints from the back pocket of his jeans. "This is our Playboy, gentlemen. Meet Wes Bridges, alias whatever the hell we can find on him."

Bridges moaned again as Heinagen restrained him and Sheffield made the call for law enforcement backup on his radio.

"How did you catch him?" Heinagen was breathing roughly. "How the hell did he get in?"

Jethro had to chuckle as he glanced toward the bathroom. The hell if he knew what happened, but the next time Keiley demanded to stay in a hotel, he had a feeling he and Mac both might be listening to her.

"Get him out of here, we'll give you a report later," he breathed out roughly. "Call the director and let him know we have our stalker. I want the D.C. bureau to handle this one. Keep him out of the hands of the locals, if you don't mind."

"We have to inform them, Jethro," Heinagen reminded him firmly.

"So inform them, but get the director on the line and tell him to get jurisdiction on this one. I want him in D.C." Jethro's fists clenched as he gritted his teeth against the need to pound the life from the bleeding body at his feet. "Mac and I have this case. He goes home where we can interrogate him. Now get him the hell out of here."

He turned and stalked to the bathroom, slamming the door before he slid to the floor behind Keiley, where she was safely wrapped in Mac's arms. He touched her hair, her neck, then let his hands grip her waist below Mac's arms as he leaned into her, pressing his lips against her neck and whispering a prayer of thanksgiving.

She was sobbing raggedly, her hands biting into Mac's shoulders, but as he touched her, one hand moved, gripped one of his hands, and pulled it around her, between her body and Mac's, gripping it between her breasts.

"We have you, sweetheart," Mac murmured, his own cheeks damp from the feeling of helplessness that swept through him.

That same feeling swamped Jethro. They had left her alone. They had let that bastard get to her. How the hell had he gotten to her?

"How?" He whispered against her hair. "How did he get in?"

"He was under the fucking bed," Mac snapped. "Under the goddamned bed, Jethro, where he had somehow managed to wedge himself into the box springs."

The horror of that miscalculation swept through Jethro. They had checked under the bed. He remembered bending down, looking for a body, and seeing nothing. Because the body hadn't been on the floor, but somehow had been above the floor?

Because of their mistake, she could have been dead. It could have been her lifeless body lying on the floor of the bedroom rather than Bridges' wounded body.

"He said—he said no one checks the box springs," Keiley hiccuped then. "He said that all the women, he laid under their beds like that and no one checked. No one checks under the box springs."

Not when the rooms were monitored and supposedly secured. Jethro knew he himself had rarely checked beneath a bed because it was so damned obvious. Too obvious. And that arrogance had nearly cost Keiley her life.

"Pappy has a listening device on his collar," she whispered then. "That's how he knew everything. When to strike, when we were gone. He was using Pappy. He always used Pappy."

The dog. Mac blinked furiously against the dampness in his eyes as he realized how easily Bridges had managed to maneuver all of them.

"Let's get her downstairs and get some whiskey in her before she goes into shock. Before the sheriff gets here." Jethro moved back, staring at Mac with the remnants of the horror still racing through his system reflecting in his friend's eyes.

"You take her downstairs." Mac lifted her to her feet and gave her to Jethro.

"Mac. No." Her hands reached out for him, her voice shaking. "You'll do something you'll regret. I know it."

"Go with Jethro." He leaned forward, whispered a kiss over her trembling lips, and then stepped away. "I have to find out who he is, Kei. Go on. I promise. I won't kill him."

Wes would wish he were dead, though, of that Mac would make certain.

"Mac," she whispered again, her voice filled with fear. "If you do something violent, then I'm going to hurt you. I mean it. I really will use that baseball bat on you if you get put in jail. I swear it."

A smile touched his lips. She kept him centered. As he stared at her, he found the control to push back the rage.

"I won't do anything to risk our lives, Keiley. I swear it. Never again will I risk your life or your happiness. Never."

Her wide hazel eyes held his as Jethro wrapped his arm around her and led her from the bathroom.

The bastard had hid under the fucking bed. Mac wiped his hand over his face and breathed out roughly. Right there beneath their noses, all he had to do was bend down and look, and he hadn't.

He stepped into the bedroom, staring at the bloodstained carpet, then at that bed. Like all the beds in the house, the frame itself was higher than most. He stared beneath it, tilted his head, and wondered how the hell he hadn't seen anything.

The first thing he had done was look around the edges of the bed. He hadn't bent down and checked beneath it because only a child could have hidden there without being seen.

He knelt down, lay on the floor, and stared beneath it.

And there was why he hadn't seen anything, why Jethro hadn't. Why no one would have seen anything unless they lay on their backs and looked.

At some point the box spring itself had been carved out and reinforced. Just enough to allow someone to wedge inside it and, with enough leg and arm strength, hold himself out of sight for the amount of time it would take to check a room.

He lifted up, braced his hands on his knees, and stared at the bloodstained carpet. This was why the Playboy had been able to get so close to his victims. Because he had somehow learned how to reinforce the inner springs after cutting part of them out and make himself a secure hiding place when he needed it.

Son of a bitch. He pushed his fingers through his hair and

breathed out tiredly. That was it. Every bed in the fucking house would be tossed out and they would sleep on the floor if they had to. This would never happen again. Never would he let Keiley be at risk in such a way again.

Moving to his feet, he clenched and unclenched his fists as he heard the sirens in the distance and shook his head. At least he knew the sheriff. The same man who had once been a boy and kept his mouth shut about the horror Mac had lived with as a child.

Tobias Blackwood knew how to keep his mouth shut. And he would keep his mouth shut this time. Because Mac intended to do a little interrogating now.

breath softly before. Then she straightened, a look in her eyes that
folded into his soul. . . . Trust. Blind, trusting love. It rocked his
world as he stared back at her, felt it wash around him, felt . . .

She smiled then. A soft, gentle smile that eased something nerve-
rackingly fierce that had always lingered inside him. Something he
had feared, he realized, something he hadn't tamed but that now,
with her beside him, he didn't have to fear. He could trust her. Trust
her not to draw away from him, trust her to be his mate.

CHAPTER TWENTY-SEVEN

*Keiley's gaze flew to the gun, and Wes's followed. She saw
the realization on his face the minute she jumped for it. She
was closer. She had a chance. Oh, God, all she needed was
a chance.*

*The phrase "everything moved in slow motion" and the
cliché that one's life flashed before one's eyes at such moments had always seemed a little far-fetched to her. But not
now.*

*Now she saw Mac and Jethro, their expressions creased
in desire and wonder as they made love to her. She saw her
own emotions, felt them overwhelming her, filling her, giving her a strength she hadn't known she could find. Because
her knees were shaking and her heart racing so fast, it
should have weakened her as she jumped for the gun.*

*The safety was on. She remembered that as her hand fell
on it and she felt Wes's breath on her neck. Her thumb fell
into position, flipped it as she brought it up.*

*The knife glittered above her head as she heard her own
screams and the sound and the feel of the weapon discharg-
ing, throwing her hand up even as she stumbled to throw herself out of the trainer's way.*

*And she watched him fall. Slowly. Shock rounded his
eyes, parted his thin lips. It was a curse that croaked from
his lips as the knife fell to the floor milliseconds before his
body did.*

And then she saw the blood—

"Keiley! Wake up, Wake up now!"

Jethro and Mac were yelling at her as hard hands shook her shoulders, bringing her from nightmare to reality with a jerk.

She stared up at Jethro, fighting to breathe, seeing the emotions that washed over his face the moment he realized she was awake. The emotions displayed there were heartbreaking. Fear. Remorse. Love. He loved her, just as fiercely, just as possessively as Mac loved her.

"God, you're going to give me a heart attack at this rate." He jerked her into his arms, his powerful, naked body shuddering once as his hold tightened on her briefly.

"I'm okay." She was shaking, shuddering in the aftermath of the nightmare that had come two days after the attack.

The day before had been filled with questions, from the FBI, the local sheriff, and the reporters who had caught the story.

She didn't think the house was ever going to empty of people. She had finally collapsed in exhaustion at midnight while Jethro and Mac were still compiling information on Wes Bridges, alias so many different variations of the name that she had lost count.

"Is she okay?" Mac stood in the doorway, already showered and dressed, his gaze concerned as he moved to the bed where Jethro held her.

"You could ask me, you know." She pushed back from Jethro, dragging her hand shakily through her hair as she swallowed back the remnants of fear.

"Are you okay, Kei?" He sat down beside her, reaching out to brush a tear from her cheek as Jethro collapsed back against his pillow.

"Stupid nightmare." She shook her head. "I'm fine."

He watched her carefully for long moments before slowly nodding. "If you two want to get a shower, I'll fix breakfast. We need to head to D.C. later this afternoon to give our depositions and finish up some red tape."

"Great," she muttered as she looked over at Jethro. "Why is he still in the bed? I thought he got up with the chickens with you."

Mac glanced over at Jethro with a smile. "He was up later last night."

She looked at Jethro suspiciously. "Why?"

A frown etched over Jethro's brow as his eyes opened. "I had things to do."

Keiley glanced back at Mac, barely catching the concern in his eyes before they became shuttered.

"Get a shower. I'll put breakfast on while you two have your coffee." He rose from the bed before leaning forward and kissing Keiley's lips gently. "I'll see you downstairs."

Evidently someone had decided that she got to deal with Jethro's early-morning grouchiness.

She turned and stared back at him silently.

He was staring at the ceiling, avoiding her gaze, his muscular body tense, as though prepared for battle.

"Are you coming home when we're finished in D.C.?" she finally asked, terrified of the answer.

His gaze sliced back to her before moving away again.

"Should I?" he finally sighed, his thick black lashes shielding his eyes.

"What does that mean?"

She pulled the sheet over her breasts and stared back at him in apprehension.

His lips tightened, his jaw flexing as though he were holding back what he wanted to say, what he wanted to feel.

"So, you're just going to walk away?"

"That's what a third does, Keiley. They leave."

"You aren't a third," she said painfully. "You know you're not a third. You're a part of us. You made yourself a part of me, let me think you would stay, and now you think you can just walk out and everything will be fine?"

"It will be. You have Mac—"

"You fucking coward." She didn't raise her voice. It wasn't an accusation. It was a statement.

His gaze snapped back to her, the blue of his eyes glittering in anger.

"What the hell did you say?"

"I called you a coward, Jethro," she repeated ruthlessly.

"You're too scared to stay here and be a part of me. This has nothing to do with who my husband is or feeling like a third. It has to do with your fears."

"Bullshit."

"Bull yes!" Flinging the sheet away from her body, she blinked back her tears and jumped from the bed. "Fine. Run away. Go play the badass agent and remember what you can't ever have again if you walk out on me. Because I'll be damned if I'll give you another chance at my heart."

"Mac likes ménages, Keiley." He caught her at the bathroom door, dragging her around to face him as he pressed her against the wall. "There'll be another third, and when he's gone another—"

Her hand swung out, connecting soundly with his cheek as he stared back at her in surprise.

"Shut up!" she yelled furiously, tears filling her eyes. "Mac doesn't just like ménages, you asshole. Do you think he would ever share me with just anyone? Do you think I would let him?"

"Sharing isn't love."

"Neither is cowardice," she snapped. "You're terrified to make that commitment, aren't you, Jethro? That's why you've always let Mac find the woman and you've stayed on the sidelines. That way you don't have the responsibility."

"You don't know what you're talking about," he snarled.

"The boy who was rejected, thrown out, and shoved through a cold unfeeling system," she whispered. "You were orphaned and so wild, so full of adventure that you were shuffled from one uncaring foster parent to the next, weren't you, Jethro."

He stared back at her bleakly.

"You would care, and then they would turn you away. Until you stopped caring. Until you started walking away first."

"That has nothing to do with this."

"It has everything to do with it." Her lips trembled as a tear slipped past her control. "You're punishing me and Mac because of the past. You love me. And in that incomprehen-

sible male bonding mystery, you love Mac. We're your family. We're what you always wanted and couldn't quite seem
to grasp. You told me that. So you're going to walk away.
You're going to reject us before we can reject you. God,
Jethro, don't you know Mac better than that by now? Don't
you know me better than that?"

Something inside her was breaking apart. She stared into
his eyes, so filled with shadows and old pains, and ached for
the boy without a home, the man without love.

"I love you." She tightened her lips and forced back
the tears. "In time, I'll love you with the same strength I
love Mac. I'll love you to the point that I'll shatter if you
leave me. So if you're going to go, maybe it's better that you
go now. You can only break my heart now. Later, you could
destroy my soul, and Mac's. And I'd rather regret than to be
left hurting like that."

His nostrils flared as his jaw tightened to the breaking
point.

"And when you're tired of sharing your bed with two
men rather than one? When you find out I'm harder than
Mac? That I'm not some fucking knight in shining armor
who never gives you a grouchy word or a hard time?"

"You think Mac is perfect?" she bit out incredulously.
"Do you think he's joking about the baseball bat? Or about
sleeping on the couch? Do you think we never fight, Jethro?
That you and I will never fight? That's a part of love. Just
because you disagree doesn't mean you don't love. Or that
you don't hurt." She reached out and touched his cheek with
shaking fingers, then his lips. "You both have your prick
sides, it's a part of who you are. And I can be a bitch, but that
doesn't mean we can't love."

His hand caught hers, pressing her palm to his roughened
cheek, turning his lips into it as he seared the flesh with his
kiss.

"You terrify me," he grated out. "You always have."

"Me?" She stared back at him in surprise. "How do I terrify you, Jethro?"

"Because I'm used to rejection," he said harshly. "But if

you turned away, I don't know how I'd survive it, Keiley. You're like a light where there was no light before. If I get used to it, then going back to the dark—" He swallowed tightly.

"Would hurt," she said softly. "And hurting sucks, doesn't it, Jethro?"

"Hurting makes me crazy, Kei," he snarled, his arm sliding around her back and jerking her to him. "Do you understand me? Decide later that it's not love and I'll be worse than that fucking stalker you had on your ass."

She shook her head as a tear slipped free. "Don't leave us, Jethro. My back gets cold at night. I need it warmed, too. And my heart wouldn't be full without you now, don't you know that?"

He drew in a hard, ragged breath, his gaze turning fierce, dominant.

"I can't breathe without smelling you, without wanting you. Three fucking years I waited, Keiley, and in one week you've chained my soul to you. In three years, I wouldn't be able to let you go."

"Then don't let me go." She pressed closer, dragging her hardened nipples over his chest, feeling the heat and controlled power of his arousal as his cock brushed against her belly.

Her hands slid into his hair, tangled around the strands, and pulled him forehead.

"Love me, Jethro," she whispered against his lips. "Just love me."

One arm locked hard around her hips, lifting her against him as his hand gripped her thigh, guiding her leg around his waist. This wasn't the smooth, practiced lover she had come to know. As his lips bore down on hers, his erection nudged between her thighs, found her slick and wet, and drove home.

Sensation exploded through her. The sudden burning pleasure clawed a scream from her throat and sent her pulse racing with an overload of pleasure. As his cock buried in her to the hilt, his tongue plundered her mouth, her lips, tangled with hers and licked at the sudden passion that blazed from her.

Colors burst behind her closed eyes as he began to thrust. Pushing her against the wall, his hands clamped on the cheeks of her rear and he began driving inside her. Deep, desperate lunges that drove the breath from her lungs and reality from her head.

She held on tight and let the pleasure have her. She let Jethro have her. The hard thrust of his cock inside her, his lips ravishing hers before moving to her neck, to the rounded tops of her breasts.

His breathing was rough, ragged, matching hers as she tightened on him, feeling the pleasure washing over her, through her.

"I love the feel of you," he snarled as he buried his lips in the side of her neck. "The smell of you. Sweet taste."

"Don't stop," she pleaded, her arms tightening around his shoulders as his hips moved harder, driving his erection deeper. "Oh God, don't stop, Jethro. Never."

"Never." He nipped her neck, drove inside her harder, faster, stretching her, burning her until the conflagration of sensations began to ripple in ever-widening circles, tightening her womb, her clit, driving into her soul until she screamed out with the fiery explosions that ripped through her.

A harsh male growl left his lips as two powerful strokes sent Jethro into his own release, his semen pumping furiously into her, branding her, marking her as his as well and sealing her to him.

When it was over, she lay limply against his chest, just trying to catch her breath as her eyes opened.

And there, framed in the doorway, was Mac, his gray eyes glittering in hunger as he winked back at her with wicked lust and heated love.

"Better shower," he told them both huskily. "I heard Victoria and Robert are on their way here. You know how the old girl hates to be kept waiting."

Jethro let her go slowly, his lips pressing to hers as his

eyes opened, the blue glittering with love and laughter rather than the dark shadows and pain.

"I think we need more land," he said then. "If Mac and I work hard enough, then we might not wear you out."

"You're staying?" she cried out, staring back at him as the tight knot of pain in her chest began to unravel.

"I think I better." He shook his head in mock sadness. "Mac spoils you worse than a Christmas puppy. Someone has to have control."

"Give me another week, you'll spoil me, too." She wrapped her arms around his neck, though her eyes met Mac's again and she saw the warmth there, the approval. Hell, she saw joy.

"I love you both," she whispered, her voice rough as Jethro eased back and Mac stepped into the circle.

One arm around his neck, the other around Jethro's, their arms surrounding her, their heat filling her.

She was selfish. She didn't want a third, she wanted a whole. And it was here, in her arms. Two men and a future filled with promises.

Victoria Staten entered the foyer in front of her son Robert, her expression drawn, her eyes dark with sadness as Keiley stood at the entrance to the living room and watched Mac step back to let them in.

Robert was a few years older than Mac. He was shorter, distinguished rather than rough around the edges, controlled and methodical. He ran the family businesses now, a mix of enterprises from computer hardware to cotton production. His shoulders were broad, his dark hair cut close, his sea-green eyes shuttered as he and Mac shook hands before Mac introduced him to Jethro.

"Can we talk?" Robert pushed his hands into the pockets of his slacks as he stared back at Jethro and Mac.

"Come in, Robert. Victoria." Keiley stepped forward as she extended her hand to the living room. "I'll fix some coffee."

"No, dear," Victoria said firmly. "This is something you need to hear as well."

Keiley glanced to Robert. He nodded abruptly.

"Come on in," Mac said then.

Jethro moved ahead of them, standing by the couch and indicating the two chairs that faced it across a low coffee table. Once Victoria had sat down, Jethro moved to one end of the couch as Keiley took her seat beside him, with Mac on her other side.

The move wasn't lost on Victoria. She watched them with a closed expression, but her eyes took in the nuances of the seating arrangements.

"I want to apologize for Delia's behavior, Mac," Robert stated as he stared back at them. "I know she received the picture from Wes Bridges. The sheriff found the e-mail on his laptop. She's been a nuisance, and I take the blame for that."

"Why?" Keiley asked him, seeing his surprise. "Why take the blame for her?"

"Because I knew she was rabid where Mac was concerned and I married her anyway," he stated coolly. "She won't bother you any longer."

"What makes you so certain?" Mac's voice was dangerously low.

Keiley knew his anger toward Delia, but she also knew his fear that Robert's anger could have manifested itself in physical harm toward her. No matter how angry he was, he wouldn't have condoned Robert striking her.

"Delia's staying with her sister in Pennsylvania until our divorce is final," Robert stated then. "I doubt she'll be back. I know the condemnation against her was strong. She didn't have many friends left the way it was."

"And I would like to extend my apologies as well," Victoria sighed. "I should have kept closer tabs on her. I had hoped Robert's warnings that he would divorce her would stay her hand. And I'm sorry for that."

Keiley glanced away as Victoria caught her eye.

"We don't blame you or Robert, Victoria," Mac said then. "But I won't have this backlashing on Keiley from your end."

"In what manner?" Victoria suddenly straightened imperiously. "Young man, since when did you get big enough for your breeches that you could dictate to me?"

Keiley turned her head as Jethro snickered. Mac did have the good grace to flush at her rebuke, but he wasn't to be outdone that easily.

"When my wife's position in this community is placed at risk because of your daughter-in-law's actions," he stated coolly. "Delia demanded her resignation from the charity committee, and your board members were present when she did so. I want your assurance that her position there will be upheld and that your support toward her is still in place."

Keiley winced. She expected Victoria to calmly tear a strip off his head for even suggesting she would back Keiley now. Instead, her lips twitched.

"It's going to be interesting watching the two of you serve hot dogs this summer," Victoria drawled instead. "My support remains constant as long as you and Jethro both are in attendance at that booth. If your wife can face the public with the grace and pride I heard she showed at Casey's, then you can do the same at the festival. Are we agreed?"

"I have work—" Jethro sounded almost panicked.

"Young man, are we understood?" Victoria demanded, her voice frosting over. "If you are going to be a part of this small family, and if I am going to back such a relationship, then I shall, of course, demand my own satisfaction. That satisfaction being watching all the droves of curious women spending good money to buy hot dogs from the two bad boys of our fair county. This is not negotiable."

Jethro sent Mac a furious look. A demand to intercede.

Mac held his hands up in surrender. "You don't fight her, man. She's tougher than you are."

Robert leaned back in his chair and chuckled at the display, his gaze meeting Keiley's with an edge of admiration.

"Congratulations, Keiley," he said. "I can safely say you are the only woman I know of to have survived such scandal intact and with such a promise from Mother."

"Shut up, Robert." Victoria's gaze jerked to him in warning.

Robert's lips twitched. "We should all be so brave."

Keiley's eyes widened as he then rose to his feet and nodded to Jethro and Mac as they straightened as well.

"Thank you for allowing me to take care of Delia before you retaliated. I'm aware of the problems you could have caused had you wanted to."

"Robert, I told you, John McCoy has a cool head." Victoria rose as well, her tone reproving as she spoke to her son. "You should heed my council more often."

He sighed. His look said this argument was a common one.

"Good day, Keiley." He nodded in her direction before extending his hand to Mac once again. "And again, thank you for the cool head."

"Thank you for sending her to Pennsylvania. I might not have kept that cool head otherwise." Mac grimaced.

"That I assumed." Robert nodded. "We'll leave you now. I'm aware you have a trip planned later. If you ever need anything." He left the sentence hanging, his meaning clear.

"He knows who to ask," Victoria informed him, her tone offended. "Really, Robert. John has always known he could come to me."

"Yes, Mother." His lips quirked with a faint tolerance that bespoke his affection for his mother.

"Victoria." Mac stepped forward, his hands raising to clasp her shoulders as he bent and kissed her cheek gently. "Thank you."

Victoria blinked then, her expression softening, then firming once again to its normal, imperious lines.

"You heathen," she muttered fondly then. "I always knew you had a wild streak. You didn't fool me."

"No, ma' am, I didn't." He smiled. "And you'd better buy a hot dog off me this summer, or I'll send all the old men to you. Imagine the lines at your booth if I send out the message you're selling kisses."

"That threat will not always work." She shook her finger at him reprovingly. "Now be good. All of you. These shenanigans of yours are too hard on my composure. Not to mention my phone." She sighed expressively. "The phone was still ringing when I left this morning. You and that young friend of yours are going to be very popular for a while. The young ladies are scandalized and curious. It does not bode well for keeping them in line, I'll have you know."

"No, ma' am," he agreed, hiding his smile now.

"Come see me soon." Victoria reach up and patted his cheek in such a motherly gesture that it brought tears to Keiley's eyes. "I've missed our chats, you know."

"Soon," Mac promised as she drew away from him, following her son to the doorway as she looked back affectionately.

"Very soon," she reminded him. "All of you. Very soon."

As the door closed behind them, Keiley sighed in satisfaction. As Mac and Jethro returned to the doorway, she smiled in sensual anticipation. Both men were loosening their belts with the same anticipation with which she was toeing off her sandals and pushing her capris from her hips.

In seconds, they were naked. Within minutes they were sweat-dampened, and not long after Keiley was between the two men she loved with all her soul.

She screamed with pleasure as she felt Jethro press firmly into her rear, tightening her pussy on Mac's furiously throbbing erection as her lips ate at him. Her tongue licked over his, her teeth nipped at his lips and were nipped in turn.

Behind her, Jethro's lips attacked her neck and shoulders, kissing, licking, nipping in turn. Together they were devouring her body as her body devoured them in turn.

"Mac," she moaned in rising pleasure as they began to move, thrusting, invading, penetrating her body and her soul.

Her back arched as she stared down at her husband, seeing the love gleaming in the gray depths, and the peace settling inside him.

"I love you," she whimpered, delirious with the pleasure now. "I love you both. I love you so much."

"God, Keiley." Mac's hands were tight on her hips as he held them still, his hips jerking harder, driving deeper inside her. "You're my soul."

"My life," Jethro groaned, his hands gripping her shoulders, pressing her to Mac's chest as the pleasure/pain of his possession mixed with the burning ecstasy of Mac's and created an inferno that swept her higher than ever, threw her into the star-studded expanse of an orgasm that left her shuddering, and an emotional kaleidoscope of joy that left her dazed.

This was the dream she thought she would never have. A forbidden pleasure she never expected to be able to hold forever. But she was holding it. Or they were holding her, filling her with their release, their harsh voices filled with love as they whispered their love.

Forbidden pleasure. And all hers. Forever.

**Turn the page for a sneak peek at Jordan and Tehya's
smoldering story:**

LIVE WIRE

(ELITE OPS)

Coming March 2011

from St. Martin's Paperbacks

Tehya had lived too long in the shadows, had spent too many years hiding and worrying.

Accelerating out of the parking lot and pulling onto the street, she tried to tell herself those years were just catching up on her. She didn't know how to relax and live rather than fight and run.

The drive back to her small house was quick, the lack of traffic on the streets assuring her she wasn't followed. But her neck was still aching, her senses still fine-tuned and restless.

Maybe it was time to leave, she thought. Hell, this was the longest she had ever lived anywhere other than the suite at the Elite Ops base. She had lived there for six years. For a while, she had had something resembling a family. She hadn't realized how thin that resemblance had really been, though.

Once the team had broken up, there had been no contact. Everyone had gone their own way, and despite the fact that she still had the secure satellite phone and the secure number she had been given, there hadn't been one call. They had forgotten her.

Mocking amusement flitted through her mind. Had she really expected anything more? She was the daughter of the man who had ordered the torture of one of their own. Who had aided in the kidnapping of a young woman who had later become the wife of one of their own. Who had murdered the parents of one of their own.

There were days she had been amazed they had even allowed her to live. Of course, killing her own father might have helped in the allowing her to keep breathing area.

They had protected her. They had given her a secure life for six years. But, she had to admit, she hadn't expected them to desert her once it was over.

As she pulled into the small driveway of her home, the garage door slid open, allowing her to drive smoothly inside. As the doors closed behind her, the security display in the car once again flashed the words SYSTEM CLEAR before she turned off the ignition and set the parking brake.

There hadn't been so much as a Girl Scout selling cookies at her door. Her neighbors didn't visit often, but they did wave when they saw her. Sometimes, when she was cutting grass or pruning her flowers, they would stop to chat. Once, a nice young couple at the end of the lane had invited her to a party they had thrown. Tehya hadn't joined the party; instead, she had watched from a hidden, shadowed corner, both amused and envious at the innocent hilarity that had often erupted.

The block she lived on was just peaceful. It was quiet. It was serene.

So what the hell had her senses on high alert?

Sliding from the car, she closed the door softly before moving to the door that led into the kitchen through a connecting door.

The security wired into the house had dim lighting flipping on throughout her home. She hated coming into a dark house. She hated coming into an empty house.

Maybe it was time to get a cat. Or better yet, one of those little toy dogs she had always wanted.

Locking the door, she reset the security before turning and staring around the open kitchen, dining, and living areas of the neat little rancher she had bought.

It had taken a while to decide what she wanted, where she wanted to live. The minute she had seen this little house with its nice little enclosed patio, she had fallen in love with it.

Breathing out heavily, Tehya moved across the ceramic tile of the kitchen floor, to the gleaming hardwood of the open living room and dining room. She had scattered bright rugs in warm colors across the area.

The warm autumn colors of the couch, sofa, and recliners went perfectly with the earth tones of the pillows and light throws draped over them.

Tonight, she didn't stop to watch television or grab another beer. She didn't stop at the computer to check her e-mail. A quick glance at the telephone showed no messages or calls.

God, what a pitiful life she was living. In six months she didn't have a friend or a lover, and every instinct she had was screaming at her to run.

Stepping into the bedroom, she began unbuttoning the white silk sleeveless blouse she had worn with the leather pants. Her mind was on a shower and ignoring the hard, almost panicked throb of her heart.

She should have heeded the warning.

As she moved into the bedroom, the lights suddenly went out, throwing her into darkness as the door slammed closed behind her.

She was ducking and rolling as hard fingers glanced off her shoulder. Kicking out in the direction the attack was coming from, she was rewarded with a solid thump, but not a fallen body.

Rolling across the room she came to a crouch, straining to see through the pitch blackness of the room to catch a shadow of movement, the gleam of a weapon.

Cold determination replaced panic. There was no fear, she had stopped feeling fear years ago, long before she had joined the Elite Ops, even before she had put a bullet in her brother's and father's chests.

She was at a disadvantage, though, and she knew it. She was wearing white, and whoever was in the room with her was obviously dressed in black.

She could barely glimpse a shadow if it moved. She was certain whoever it was could clearly see the white of her blouse as she crouched there, panting.

She inched closer to the nightstand and the lamp atop it.

Her fingers reached out, less than inches from the light when she saw a shadow moving swiftly toward her.

A hard kick against the thick carpet and she launched herself away from the coming attack, almost making it. Hard fingers gripped her ankle as she twisted and kicked out, breaking the hold and rolling to the side before a hard, heavy male weight suddenly came over her.

Her fingers curled into claws and moved for his face, only to have her wrists caught and jerked over her head as muscular thighs trapped her legs.

"You're wearing white, baby. Didn't I teach you better than that?"

She froze. For a second, Tehya felt her heart stop just before it began to pound with a hard rush of adrenaline. The cold hard determination to survive became something more. It became brilliantly hot, sensitizing her flesh, rushing through her and burning away the chill that had wrapped around her for the past six months.

Jordan was here.

His fingers tightened on her wrist as she suddenly bucked against him, the urge to fight against an attack suddenly morphing into something she didn't understand.

"Get off me!" she hissed, uncertain if it was fury or lust suddenly raging through her. "What the hell are you doing?"

His lips cut the furious words off, covering hers, slanting across them and taking advantage of her parted lips with strength, a power that had her stilling beneath him.

Her eyes flared open, then drifted closed. Sensation began to race through her body, surging through her bloodstream with a punch of heat so brilliant it felt blinding.

Suddenly, she was starved for the taste and the feel of him. Dying to take back the months she had been so alone, drifting, uncertain what to do or where to go, because she had nothing or no one to hold on to.

As his hands loosened from her wrists, one hand cupped her face as his tongue pressed inside, licking at hers as a groan vibrated against her lips.

Tehya arched against him, her legs parting as his hips lifted, moving to lift against his thighs as he settled between them, the hard ridge of his cock riding against her sensitive pussy, pressing the seam of the leather pants against her clit and stroking it sensually.

Heat wrapped around her, a wonderful, building warmth that bloomed through her belly and rushed to wrap around her swollen clit.

The instantaneous switch from survival to arousal tore through her. She was thrown headlong into an inferno of sensation that threatened—no, it didn't threaten, it did over-whelm her. Completely.

His hair was thick and rich beneath her fingers as she clenched them in the heavy strands. His body was hard and demanding above her, his cock a hard, thick wedge beneath his pants as he ground his hips between her thighs.

The illicit strokes of his shaft over the sensitive bud of her clit sent hunger tearing through her. Her lips parted, her tongue stroked against his, her fingers tightened in his hair to hold him to her. She was desperate to embed each sensa-tion into her memory, into each cell of her body for the day when it would be gone again.

Jordan wouldn't stay, even she knew that. For whatever reason though, he was here now and that was all that mat-tered.

Don't miss the Bound Hearts novel from
New York Times bestselling author Lora Leigh

SINFUL PLEASURE
ISBN: 978-0-312-54187-3

Coming in July 2011

…and the other red-hot novels in this series

GUILTY PLEASURE
ISBN: 978-0-312-54186-6

ONLY PLEASURE
ISBN: 978-0-312-36873-9

WICKED PLEASURE
ISBN: 978-0-312-36872-2

FORBIDDEN PLEASURE
ISBN: 978-0-312-36871-5

AVAILABLE FROM ST. MARTIN'S GRIFFIN